Megan Clawson was born and [...] In 2018, she moved to Lond[...] at King's College London. The daughter of [...] Megan lived inside the Tower of London with her dad and little dog, Ethel, for many years The experience of living inside the real-life palace and fortress and falling for her own royal guard still inspires much of her writing. Working as an English tutor and TV and film extra alongside her writing, she is always at her happiest when living a life that feels like fiction. *Falling Hard for the Royal Guard* was her debut novel, published in 2023.

By the same author:

Falling Hard for the Royal Guard

Love at First Knight

MEGAN CLAWSON

avon.

Published by AVON
A division of HarperCollins*Publishers*
1 London Bridge Street
London SE1 9GF

www.harpercollins.co.uk

HarperCollins*Publishers*
Macken House, 39/40 Mayor Street Upper
Dublin 1
D01 C9W8

A Paperback Original 2024

24 25 26 27 28 LBC 7 6 5 4 3

First published in Great Britain by HarperCollins*Publishers* 2024

A catalogue copy of this book is available from the British Library.

ISBN: 978-0-00-864734-6

Typeset in Birka by Palimpsest Book Production Limited, Falkirk, Stirlingshire

Printed and bound in the United States

CV 03.01.2024 0806

*For the people who have had to hide behind a
mask for so long,
they no longer know what's real, and what's pretend.*

Chapter 1

'Lady Alenthaea, finish him!' Mum's voice bellows across the battlefield. The tip of my sword brushes the exposed throat of my twin. Heaving with every panting breath, the breastplate of his armour is dappled with the same blood that now dries in a crust around his nostril. Weaponless fingers claw at the mashed earth at my feet. Eyes identical to my own search my face for any weakness, any hint of mercy. He won't find any. He will pay for what he's done.

'E-end it!' Dad joins the battle cries. There's a tremolo in his words. They're weak in his foolish emotion. Removing my gaze from my wounded prey, I take just a second to look back at my father as he clutches the collar of his tunic, his tall shoulders rounded and hunched.

'Oh, for Odin's sake, Simon.' Mum reminds him where he is by leaving an imprint of her crooked staff in his stomach, straightening him back up to his giant height. He sips his mug of tea nervously, his eyes flickering back and forth – evidently torn between supporting his kids in their fight, or retreating back into the Village Hall, unable to watch on any longer.

Sam takes his moment to strike from under me. Slamming his heavy gauntlet against my own, Sam knocks my sword from my grip and in a single swipe, relieves my legs of the weight of my body and lets gravity do the rest of the work in ploughing me into the loam.

Unable to fight against the weight of my armour, I am bound to the earth, just waiting for his return attack. I don't wait long. He looms over me like the Grim Reaper, not bothering to pin me down. I feel like I am sinking into the ground, retreating into my grave as his dirty face shifts further and further away. He is the God of Death, descended from the clouds to hand me my fate. I can't see him tearing off his armour but it clatters in a heap behind my head and he returns, his boots knocking my shoulders as he brings his sword back into play.

'You fought hard, sweet sister, but hesitation was always your folly.' Lifting the hilt above his head, unrestrained by his steel, he brings the blade down to my trachea. 'Goodnight.'

Scattered applause echoes under the porch of the Village Hall and snaps me out of my strangled coughing and spluttering.

'That was bloody brilliant, Daisy.' Sam stands over me again, offering me a hand up. With a groan I am finally back on my feet, looking down at the Daisy-shaped dent in the grass. One of my elf ears has been left behind and sticks up like a latex headstone.

'Samwise. Language.' Mum, too staff-happy, gives him a soft clobber over the head with the gnarled stick as she reaches us. 'But you are correct in your statement. Good work, kids.' She kisses the both of us on our dirty foreheads, or rather attempts to; it is her false fangs that leave a damp patch.

As the adrenaline of the fight finally settles, I turn to my brother, my debrief ready to be laid out. 'Next week we should really work more on our hand-to-hand – it needs to be perfect for the Battle of Helm's Geek, Sam, you need to stop being afraid of going for the face. Just whack—'

'Oh, I do hate to see you two fighting.' Dad cuts me off. His eyes are wide with concern, and we all roll ours.

'It's not real, Dad,' I assure him. 'Just how Mum isn't actually an ugly goblin on steroids.' We look her up and down: her transformation is quite comical when you think about it. By weekday, a successful accountant, never seen with a wrinkle in her pant suit; by weekend, one of Tolkien's orcs. She was up at four this morning, and her face has been metamorphosed with the help of a hell of a lot of silicone. Beauty the last thing on her mind, her own hair is hidden and replaced by a few wild and greasy strands. The iris in one eye is blacked out with a contact lens, and her jaw protrudes in an underbite, with weighty fangs bursting from her mouth in a dribbling mess. Even at barely five foot one, she is the most terrifying and imposing creature on the field. She is a work of art, in an ugly, malevolent sort of way.

She actually met my dad looking like that too, at the

Battle of Gibraltar Point. His first character wasn't the terrified squire that he is now – before he had kids, he was the coolest paladin anyone had ever seen. At six foot six, his holy knight loomed over everyone else and stormed through evil with the skill of ten men. But he was corrupted by my mother, the beastly orc that he just couldn't bring himself to cut down in his mission of piety. So, he hung up his crusader's cape and became her squire, married her in real life, right here in this old cabbage field – in full livery.

Right now, he is fussing at Samwise – and yes, he was named after the Hobbit, and I his Hobbit sister. We never stood a chance of being anything other than massive nerds, so it was lucky that we practically came out of the womb challenging one another to a duel. Our younger sister wasn't quite as successful in her fate.

'This is real though.' Dad licks a handkerchief that he pulls from his pocket and tends to Sam's bloody nose, much to my adult brother's dismay.

He is right though. It is real blood. I may have gotten just a little too overexcited with my elbows as the battle began, forgetting that my rubber armour is not only much harder than my flesh, but also leaves a stinging slap every time it is unleashed on bare skin. I feel a wince of guilt as I watch Dad dab at Sam's nose, but he *did* break my finger a few weeks back with a pretty savage strike of his sword, so I don't feel too bad.

Live Action Role Play, LARPing for short, may just be 'playing pretend', but it isn't child's play. Though my sword is unable to divorce a man's head from his shoulders in one fell swoop, it could break a few noses, and maybe a couple of ribs too. When the Battle of Helm's Geek comes around every August, it is nothing short of a bloodbath. We spend all year perfecting our weapons and costumes. Hours are spent wrapping the carbon-fibre skeleton of my sword first in foam, then latex, then paint and varnish. It needs to be perfectly weighted, accurate in its measurement. None of this cardboard and duct-tape bullshit. *Never* underestimate how seriously a nerd will take the opportunity to accurately live out their fantasies.

Once my twenty-three-year-old brother has ceased having his face wiped by his dad, finished off with a ruffle of his hair, we make our way back towards the rest of the group. I will admit, they're not much to look at right now, toeing the line between period-accurate medieval reenactor and a 'would be offered twenty pence if they stood outside of Tesco for too long' kind of thing. But this, right here in the damp and musty Village Hall, is The Friskney Fellowship – the most esteemed group of LARPers this side of the Humber (probably).

The Fellowship is made up of twelve members: us four, obviously, plus my younger sister, Marigold (much to her own embarrassment at seventeen); Richard, our elderly neighbour, a wizard who casts most of his spells from the comfort of a chair and speaks almost entirely in insults; Hazel and Terry, a middle-aged couple who I am certain use this as a freaky sex thing and frequently take it in turns playing either a helpless noble, or the overtly horny lower-class rogue who is constantly saving the other; Callum, our eighteen-year-old bard, who plays the guitar, the lute, and sometimes a bugle, and is the only reason that Marigold still joins us here on a Sunday afternoon; and the last three are the O'Neills: Violet, Bernard, and their daughter Flora, the most perfectly put together family of healers that really bring out the orcish rage in Mum.

Richard is in his familiar place, hunched asleep in his chair, his packed lunch ransacked in front of him. The remnants of a children's party cover the lino around his chair in colourful confetti and I can almost see where he has attempted to kick it away before sinking into the spot he hasn't moved from. Callum sits in the corner, playing a soft song on his guitar. A doe-eyed Marigold watches him from the table opposite. Taking the space beside him is out of the question unless she wants to explain why her face is the same colour as her scarlet hooded cape – the only piece of costume that she will agree to wear.

Sam's face flushes the exact same colour when Flora O'Neill comes over to congratulate him on his win. I have to nudge his chain mail before he can formulate a thank you. Training to be a nurse at university, Flora mostly joins us as a first aider, but she suits the fantasy – her elegant fae-like face is framed with soft honey hair that escapes in wisps from her ponytail. Her white dress is littered with embroidered flowers and is so bright and graceful that it makes me wonder whether she really does have powers and has charmed it with a spell that keeps it so clean. Looking down at my own costume caked in filth, I debate asking her if she can charm mine too. There is a soft perfection to her. If the petal of a peony could walk and talk, its name would be Flora

O'Neill and Samwise Hastings is completely and utterly in love with her.

Despite the fact she is here every Sunday, Flawless Flora is still just slightly too normal to look at him and see something other than a geek who gets a little carried away and is in constant need of bandaging. Nor does it help that if ever Samwise finds the gall to say more than two words to her, somewhere in the middle of the sentence he begins to speak in Klingon and she definitely isn't enough of a nerd to understand that and is certainly too real-worldy to realise that he's flirting.

'Nice one, Twinnies.' Terry, today dressed for the role of horny rogue, claps us heavily on the shoulders, breaking Sam's awkward gaze that is fixed on Flora as she floats back across the room to her parents.

Terry and Hazel got side-tracked fifteen minutes in and started snogging on the battlefield. I took that as my opportunity to turn them into a PDA kebab and skewered them with my broadsword – it had taken them an additional twelve minutes to notice.

'Cheers, Terry.' Sam answers for us both, though he is still distracted watching the healers pack their flasks of tea back into their picnic basket. I give Terry a tight half-smile and try to mask my sigh of relief as he finally removes his hands from our shoulders. Twisting strands of my hair between my fingers, I make an attempt to rub the dried mud from the back of my head.

'You need to show me how to do that.' Hazel stares at the intricate plaits I have knotted over the top of my head in a crown of dark copper. The rest of it coils at the back

– or did before my brother treated me to a mudbath – just long enough to prevent the back of my neck being exposed to enemies, but short enough that not just any clumsy beast could grab it in battle. Practical.

'And that thing with the spear, you know the spinny thing—' She mimics my signature move, pretending to twirl a partisan above her head before shoving the invisible weapon through the gut of her husband. Terry plays along, and crumples to his knees, his breath strangled and wheezing in his faux pain.

Terry clambers to his feet and kisses his giggling wife on her forehead. I'm never quite sure what to do with myself when I'm around them. It seems that anywhere I look, it's like I've stumbled in on a private moment and I can't figure out where to put my eyes. So, I agree quickly. When they do decide to unstitch themselves from one another, Terry and Hazel are the kindest, most loyal friends, so spending time to teach them a few new skills wouldn't be too much of a hardship.

'Same time next week, yeah?' Terry points at Mum, inviting her response. She nods and the pair collect their weapons – of course their pièce de résistance is a whip that they definitely owned before they took up this hobby – and leave to a chorus of see yas, cheerios, and a grunt from Richard who has clearly been woken by the chatter. Another grunt signals that he too is ready to leave, meaning the session has ended and we must take him home.

Our house is the kind that would give a builder an aneurysm if my mum ever allowed one past the threshold. I'm not sure a spirit level was ever part of her tool box when she fixed the place up. Every surface of our little white cottage is so wonky that if you ever set one up on the sideboard, the bubble would pop from vertigo. She likes it that way though. She says that because the rest of Lincolnshire is so flat, so straight, so samey, it's okay to have things a little skew-whiff sometimes, even if that means you have to Blu-Tack the tat to the mantelpiece so it doesn't slide off. Thinking about it as I look at him now, even the dog is a bit askew – he's missing half of his teeth on the right side so his great tongue lolls out of the edge of his jowls and Sam always dips it in the dregs of his cup of tea just so it doesn't dry out. He used to be called Sméagol, but he's more of a Gollum these days.

Wooden stairs creak under my weight as I climb them. If I were ever the type to enjoy sneaking around, it would be impossible in this house. Every step is like pressing the key of a dilapidated piano and the tune of your movements ring out to the whole house. Abandoning my plan of sticking my pyjamas on ready for dinner, I find myself pressed into the cushion on the upstairs windowsill looking out on the view that stretches for miles. Only fields and farmhouses make up the landscape, uninterrupted by hills or valleys. The trees are sparse and isolated. A few of them stand in the distance, scattered across farmland, never in reaching distance of their own species. It's a landscape of loneliness. At night you can see the dim illuminations of the Boston Stump over in the town; the last few lights accompany it until midnight, when all of the street lamps are killed and we're all plunged into a forced darkness. A midnight adventure is highly discouraged.

This is where Lady Alenthaea's escapades would begin though, if this house was an elven palace and the fields a kingdom of magic. Lady A is my LARPing alter ego but our relationship goes far beyond the battlefield. She is me, if I was everything that I'm not. She's a beautiful elven noble – confident, loved by her people. She knows exactly what she wants and she gets it. Her life was peaceful, perfect, her lands ruled by her mother's matriarchy, and for her entire life Alenthaea was raised to be her seamless successor.

That was until tragedy struck. Her mother was ambushed by orcs on her way to pay a royal visit to the druid kingdom and never returned. Knowing it was her destiny, Alenthaea rose up in the face of her grief and strode to the throne room to fulfil her duties – only to find her younger sister already crowned and Alenthaea's twin brother at her side. Usurped by her own blood, Alenthaea is chased from the palace when her attempt to rally her own supporters goes horribly wrong and she realises she has been betrayed. She walks the land alone, with just her sword, and her skill, until she can return home and reclaim her crown. But first, she must avenge her mother. What are orcs and monsters to the fury and grief of a betrayed woman?

When Daisy gets in the way, Lady A takes over – but instead of fighting mythical creatures for me, she usually just tells the old lady in the garden centre café that she gave me the wrong coffee, or phones the dentist to book an appointment.

'Daisy?' Mum's voice brings me round from my daydream. My whole family are staring at me from their set places at the dining table. Clearly on autopilot, too busy with my imaginings to take notice of the world around me, I had moved from my window to dinner – hardly realising that I wasn't in my own elven kingdom. None of my family bear a look of surprise at my mindlessness though. Marigold only rolls her eyes, and I notice for the first time that my fist is clutching the handle of my butter knife – its tip forcibly jammed into my placemat.

'Get a bit carried away with the plans of revenge up there, did ya?' Sam pokes me in the temple with a smile. Blushing, I free my cutlery from the table and resume eating the long-forgotten, and now cold, Sunday roast in front of me.

'Actually, just one second. Excuse me.' Thoughts of Alenthaea's story swirl around in my head and I clutch on to the thoughts so they don't leave my mind. Too overcome with ideas for her next adventures, my knife and fork clatter back onto the plate as I stand up in a rush. 'Need to write something down. So I don't forget.' Mum, used to my antics, dismisses me with a flick of her head and a soft chuckle that the rest of them share.

Chapter 2

'I can't die like that.' A whingeing voice interrupts my daily dusting. 'Please let me roll again.'

'Don't think I didn't see you reroll your saving throw when you landed on a two last time, Willow,' Dad replies to one of his regular patrons with a teasing eyebrow raised. 'Anyway, you should be getting back to school. Your dinner hour will be finished soon enough.' They both stand up from the table scattered with dice and mini figures and my dad forces a handshake out of the grumbling schoolgirl.

Dad owns a little hobby shop in town. It used to be some boutique run by an eccentric old woman before she died and the place still has a ghostly smell of wet dog and cigarettes. But the rent is cheap and that's good when Dad can't bring himself to charge anyone full price for anything.

The shop's clientele is small to say the least. A few parents pop in every now and again looking for supplies for school projects, not realising that rather than poster paint and cardboard, they'd instead be met with thousands of tiny models of sci-fi beasts and my dad's look of marvel at a new human passing the threshold (and disturbing his own tabletop wars).

The rest are the regulars: people who drink energy drinks for the taste, people who have Discord accounts, members of the Fellowship, and students reminiscent of Sam and I at school, looking for a safe nerd haven. During lunchtimes and after school hours, it essentially turns into a youth club for the kids who would have been bullied out of the youth club. He spends hours with them, teaching them how to paint miniature models, playing tabletop games, listening to them talk about the things that others would roll their eyes at. The shop may come out in the red every single quarter, but as long as those children have a safe space to be themselves then, to Dad, the shop is a success.

Willow collects her school bag with a huff. The other players follow her lead, except they're considerably less aggressive with packing away their character sheets and notebooks. Though not accepting her defeat with very much grace, Willow still thanks Dad on the way out, and he sends her and the other students off with a smile before settling down behind the counter to paint a few of his own models.

Armed with a feather duster, I go about the room, tickling each of Dad's tiny decorations, from dragon eggs and potions, to stacks of books on 'how to slay a kraken'. The dust seems to magically appear in thick blankets as though the shop is enchanted to look like you've stepped into an ancient emporium. Part of me wonders if Dad spends his evenings reapplying it, perhaps to suit the atmosphere, or maybe to make sure that I always have something to do, some purpose here.

Instead of wallpaper, the walls are draped in thick tapestries, some dark paisley patterns, and others, maps of lost and made-up lands with holes burnt in by Mum and her blowtorch even after it had cost three months' rent to get them. I sweep the duster over the swords that are hung on one of the curtained walls crossed behind a shield ornamented with the family coat of arms that Dad designed for us one day when business was even slower than usual. Of course, Mum and Marigold are represented by their respective flower namesakes that weave across the whole crest. I trace them with my fingers. Sam and I as the twins take form in a two-headed dragon. Sam's side offers a wide-fanged smile, and mine holds a delicate Daisy between its sharpened claws. Dad wasn't too sure how to represent himself so he popped a twenty-sided dice in the corner and called it a day.

'Dais.' Dad interrupts me as I neaten up the same shelves that haven't been touched since I did the same thing just days ago. 'Have you spoken to your sister recently?'

When I look over to him, his glasses are perched on the end of his nose as he takes his paintbrush to the wings of his tiny 3D-printed dragon. This is the kind of conversation that is going to make us both uncomfortable as Dad refuses to cease his work and make eye contact as he awaits my response.

'I haven't,' I reply, a little embarrassed. Being best friends with your sister was something I thought should be instantaneous, like your souls are bound together in some sort of natural sisterly affection, but it hasn't been like that with mine, certainly not in the last few years anyway.

Marigold is our white sheep in a family of black sheep. She fits in when none of us have ever. I envy her. And she is embarrassed of me.

'She's applying to unis.' Another strike of jealousy pangs through me, and I scorn my selfishness.

'I thought she would.' Moving so my back is now facing him, I busy my twitching fingers with arranging the shelf of paint pots.

I never made it to uni. In fact, I never made it out of this county for anything other than a weekend festival, and that's only when accompanied by my whole family anyway. And the only person who stopped me was me. Me and my stupid brain that sends the wrong stupid signals to my body and is only content and not screaming bloody murder at me once I walk through the threshold of the cottage I have lived in my entire life.

'You could try again, you know.' My silence makes him falter. 'If you'd like to. I overheard you and your brother talking a while back, about how you wanted more, that you regret not going when you had the chance . . .' He trails off, aware of how he's digging a hole.

'You do know that if I got a degree, you'd have to pay me more.' Composing myself, I turn back to him with a smile, deflecting his surprise emotional attack.

Finally looking up from his model, Dad doesn't quite make eye contact but he forfeits his attempt at seriousness. 'I'd just outsource the help – maybe one of the lads from

Griffin Academy would work for free if I offered them all of the new special-edition models before their mates.'

'Hmm, that may be true, but it has taken me twenty-three years to perfect how you like your cups of tea. Would one of the Griffin boys be able to get the one and a quarter teaspoons of sugar dead on?'

He knits his brows together as though seriously debating it in his head. 'No, no, you're right. Touché.' He visibly shudders and returns to his painting.

Watching him for a moment, I think about how long I have stood in this shop. Rearranging the shelves that never deplete their stock. Memories surface of all of the times I have had to duck behind a bus shelter or into a shop I don't want to go into just to avoid crossing paths with someone I went to school with as they flaunt their bloated pregnant bellies, or exaggerate every action with their left hand so your eye really cannot avoid the rock on the ring finger. It almost hurts more when I don't see them, knowing that they left our tiny town and discovered a whole new world beyond the number fifty-seven bus route. I panicked at eighteen and forgot that this giant space rock that we pay taxes to live on still turns every twenty-four hours, and our orbit around the sun never ceases because someone is too scared to just *live*. And now my baby sister, six years my junior, has caught me up.

Before I can meditate on the subject any longer, the bell on the door steals our attention. Instead of a standard ding-dong sound, like every other shop, Dad decided he would record his own jingle of sorts so his voice booms around the shop in a comically deep voice, alerting us to a new entrant:

'*Welcome, weary traveller, to the Hastings' Emporium of Orcs and Crosses, the greatest kept secret of the realm. May you enter at your own peril . . .*'

'I still think it's a bit—'

'*Not really, we're all friendly here. No one bites, except the pixie out the back and the seventh book on the sixth shelf . . .*'

'. . . long-winded, Dad?' Sam follows the voice through the door and he has to raise his own to be heard above the God-like speech booming around the room. 'And a tad loud?' He grimaces as the message ends with slight feedback through the mic that was used to record it.

'I like it.' Dad shrugs nonchalantly, unfazed and still with his nose close to his dragon, which is finally taking form.

My twin stands before me and his countenance instantly changes. His face tightens. His cheery expression is pulled taut and replaced with grave seriousness as he bows his head low and begins slowly, 'Sister, I come to you on this neutral and holy ground . . .' a grin stretches across his lips, and his patchy moustache that he's been attempting to grow smiles with him '. . . to show you something tremendous.'

Sam whips out his phone from his pocket and shows me a photo advertisement with the words 'Knight School' in bold lettering.

'One of the guys from that LARP forum I'm on sent it through.'

'That's for kids though, isn't it?' I ask, my eyes scanning the rest of the page as it advertises lessons to '*transform your 6–13-year-olds into brave knights inside the walls of*

His Majesty's Royal Palace and Fortress, the Tower of London. Learn how to use a sword, how to joust and, most of all, learn what it is to be noble and chivalrous'. 'How cool would it be if they had an adult one? That finally might be a class that you'd pay attention in.' I laugh at my brother and he shakes his head with a knowing smile.

'Yes, but look at this!' Sam swipes across his phone and returns it to my view and I read the words: *Now hiring knights errant searching for their latest adventure to pass on their wisdom to the next generations. (Temporary ten-week position, Tuesday to Saturday, full-time, £10 an hour, must have full DBS check, costume included.)*

Sam blinks at me expectantly. He has come straight from work and his suit is slightly wrinkled at his knees from where he has been sat at his desk all day.

'Now I don't think my work are going to cope for that long without me there to tell them to "switch it off and on again" when their computers "break" so I'm sadly out of contention – but what do you think?'

'Me?' I'm not sure why this takes me by so much surprise. Why else would he have shown me? Well, I guess I just presumed he was showing me something I might find interesting, like the line-up for some music festival in Japan where I'd just say 'that's awesome' and neither of us would actually consider the possibility of going there.

'Well, I suppose I just presumed that Lady Alenthaea is more than qualified for that job, no? I bet plain old Daisy Hastings wouldn't be too bad either.'

'By myself?' Does he even know me at all? He's only been with me almost every waking minute for the past twenty-three years; surely he'd know that whims and adventures begin and end in the pages of a notebook for me?

'As much as I'd love to quit my job to spend a summer being paid to be a knight, I need the wage that this soulless job affords if I'm ever going to stand a chance of getting that flat.' My stomach throbs with the cadence of his sentence. I had thought that when Sam mentioned his plan of moving across town into his own place, talking about getting a second bedroom just for his PC, it was simply another of his impulses. No more fact or plan in it than the time he said he was going to establish a pirate renaissance and sail the high seas looking for all of the treasure lost by pirates in the centuries before. Barely giving it a second thought, I had hoped that if I didn't stoke the fire, it would just fizzle out, but now it's me who stands here, feeling as though I'm being burnt.

I had always expected Marigold to grow up and move on. Every time she sits down to dinner she looks as if she'd rather be anywhere else. But I had never entertained the idea of Sam leaving too. When I watched the whole world pass on by without me, I never once imagined that my family, my only happiness, would one day follow them too.

'That wouldn't be for a while yet anyway . . .' Sam, noticing my pained expression, backtracks. 'I just thought it would be great to see you doing something like this, sharing your talent with people outside of the Fellowship.' He treads carefully, scanning my face with a sad smile.

'But . . . but it's in London.' I shake my head furiously,

trying to push down the selfish feelings of betrayal that had climbed through me again and try to concentrate on the real reason he's here, though I can hardly focus on anything but the way my heart beats loudly in my ears.

Dad has put down his model for the first time all day and shares the same expectant look as my brother. 'Show me that, Sam.' My twin does as he's told and hands his phone to our dad. He scrolls through, nodding – a smile pulls at his mouth and he pushes the phone across the desk towards me. 'Daisy, it's made for you.'

'You're both being stupid. It's in London.' My chest grows tighter. The usually unimposing sound of water running through the pipes grows louder. The sound of my own pacing feet pounds in my head. The sound of my trousers as my legs brush together only swells to a disturbing crescendo. As much as I know that their tone is no different than I have heard every day for the last two decades, their voices and the one in my own head only seem to grow louder, to multiply until I am filled with the compulsion to flee.

'I'm failing to see the issue here. You'd be *getting paid* to do what we spend our whole lives doing. All you'd have to do is teach it to kids and that definitely isn't a far cry from trying to get Rich to get involved on a Sunday when you have to drag him away from his sandwiches.'

'Samwise. When was the last time you saw me leave Lincolnshire? When was the last time you saw me do anything with my days aside from spending it with one of you?' I don't mean to shout at him, but the world has grown so loud the only way my voice seems to break through is if I raise it over the top of everything else.

'Dais, I just thoug—' I cut him off and continue.

'You *didn't* think, Sam.' I push the phone back towards Dad and walk calmly off into the back room.

Finally, out of the heat of their gazes, I am free to pace the stockroom, or pace as much as you can in a room that's barely four square metres, piled high with boxes, and half-filled by a tea urn the size of a small child. Covering my ears and closing my eyes, I try to drown out all of the noise, but it doesn't help when the crashing inside my head is an atom bomb of thoughts that come so quickly I have no time to process any of them.

Screwing my eyes shut even tighter, I press my ears with even heavier palms, wishing, begging for silence. Thoughts, feelings, white noise, bounce around in my skull and all I want to do is break it open and throw my brain away. With a heaving chest, I dig my nails painfully into my scalp, searching for any kind of escape.

I know he means well. He always means well. But all of this is just a reminder that I haven't ever moved on, that I have spent almost every day in the comfort of this shop, with the comfort of my family, too afraid to step out into deeper water. Sam and Marigold are floating away, leaving me on the shore, unable to keep my head above the surface long enough to catch up to them.

'Hey, hey, it's okay. Look at me, Daisy, look at me.' Sam has joined me in the stockroom and holds me gently by the elbows. Just the sight of his face, so like my own, yet so calm with that goofy smile always lingering on his lips, instantly lowers the volume by at least half. But it is when he places my hands on his chest, letting me feel the way it rises and falls with deep breaths, that my equilibrium is restored. 'You okay?' he asks after a short while. Nodding, I pull myself out of his grip.

'Thanks,' I mumble, a little embarrassed. He just watches me for a moment, not saying a thing, but I know what he is searching for in my face.

'Marigold is going to uni,' I answer his wordless enquiry to the source of my pain. He knows that just some stupid ad wouldn't set me off like this.

Sam's brow softens and he looks at me with sympathetic eyes. 'I know.'

'What's wrong with me?'

'You mean aside from all of the daydreaming at the table that causes you to start eating like a cow?' He quickly stops his impression when I narrow my eyes at him.

'I'm only joking. There's nothing wrong with you, Daisy – no interesting character is built from doing everything perfectly first time and at the exact time that the world prescribes for the entire population. Do you really think if Lady A had become queen when she was supposed to, she would be as strong, as powerful as she is now?'

I lay my head against his shoulder; he knows not to wrap his arms around me when I'm like this and instead rests his own head on top of mine. 'Just forget about all of that stuff back there. I shouldn't have sprung it on you like that,' Sam mutters with another reassuring smile.

'You promise never to mention me moving halfway across the country again?'

'I promise.' There's a sincerity in his face that is so deeply hardwired into him that he would be hard pushed to ever break a promise. I trust him more than I'd ever trust myself.

'I wish you could come everywhere with me.'

'Erm, no thanks, you stink out the bathroom well enough when I have to use it after you. No way I'm coming in with you.'

'You're so gross.' I headbutt him in the shoulder and stand up straight. His usual smile takes up most of his face and I give him a small one back.

'Come on, the lads on the forum were telling us about this new dagger move where you like—' he squirms about holding his invisible knife and knocks one of the boxes from the shelf '—and I need someone to try it out on.'

'And definitely no more mention of London?' I throw him a warning finger and he crosses his heart with his own. Satisfied, I follow him out of the stockroom and think of all of the ways I'm going to carve him up with his own dagger.

Chapter 3

In a startling turn of events, it is my ringtone that wakes me up in the morning, rather than the usual foghorn of Sam's singing in the shower. Too sleepy to think about ignoring it and assuming that it's more than likely just Dad asking me to bring his packed lunch to work, I answer it with a grumbled 'hello'.

'Good morning, can I speak to Daisy Hastings please?' Realising that the deep voice is not one of the four I am accustomed to, I sit bolt upright in my bed and stammer into the receiver.

'Er . . . erm, yes, speaking.'

'Perfect, hi Daisy, sorry to call you so early but my name is Westley Graham, the Knight School coordinator (and reigning Somerset jousting champion) from the Tower of London. I read through your CV last night and had to call you as quickly as possible to offer you the job.'

CV? Job? My mind goes blank. I can only breathe into the receiver.

'The deadline had passed a couple of days ago but we actually had one of our regulars drop out yesterday so your application was a welcome relief. Looking here at your experience, I would say that you are the perfect candidate. Usually we would need an interview, just an HR formality thing, but I'm not sure we have the time to waste – the preparation for the school begins next week, with us opening our bell tents to the students just a week after that. It's quite unconventional, but we will put you on a four-week trial period instead just to see for ourselves what your skills are, put them into practice, and make sure that you're the right fit – the trial means we could ask you to leave at the end of that period, just in case for some reason it doesn't work out. How does the 10th of July sound for you to come down? A week today? I've got your email address. I can send all the info over to you soonest.' The faceless speaker doesn't give me time to think and I can only blurt out some semblance of an agreement before the phone is hung up.

Taking a few seconds for what just happened to sink in, I fly out of bed and straight down the stairs, not without smacking my head on the low landing ceiling first. Tearing into the kitchen I find my brother, not yet departed for work, leaning over the kitchen sink washing his plate. Grabbing him by the collar I use my strength to turn him around to face me.

'What have you done?! What have you bloody done? I told you I didn't want it! I bloody told you!' I yell.

Sam's expression is one of wide-eyed confusion and a childlike fear.

'Whoa, whoa, whoa.' He takes my hands from his collar and places them back at my sides. 'Daisy, what on earth are you going on about?'

'You promised me! You swore that you'd not so much as mention it again and yet all along you were planning your greatest betrayal yet!? Is it because you're all leaving me – is that it? Get little old nervous Daisy out of the way first so you don't feel so bad for leaving her all by herself?'

Having heard the commotion, Mum and Dad rush into the kitchen, the former demanding what all of the fuss is about.

'He's signed me up for that damned Knight School thing he was going on about. And now they've offered me a job in London.'

'A job? Oh, that's brilliant, darling!' my mother replies, clearly not reading my expression.

'Are you even listening? I said it's in London,' I snap, and my regret is instantaneous as her face drops. 'Sorry, I didn't mean . . .' I take a step back from Sam and take a few deep breaths to steady myself.

'Dais, I didn't sign you up for anything. I promised you, and I'd never break a promise. You know that.' Sam is sincere and my guilt only rises at my outburst.

'It was me,' Dad says timidly from the corner. All I can do is stare at him, open-mouthed, and it seems everyone else is in the same position. 'That was a role made for you, Daisy. I see you every day staring out of that upstairs window, and I know you know there's more to life than my wee shop. Uni might not have been for you, but this isn't even three months, and those few weeks could be the start of everything.'

26

'But I'm happy here.' Is this a real kiss from Judas? The one person you thought you could depend on no matter what the circumstance, the only being who would put you before himself without a second breath, being the one to deceive us all?

I hardly know how to feel. Sam is an easier target for anger. Berating him is like berating myself, as much as it disgusts me to admit it. But with Dad, he's the kind of man who tiptoes across our landing for fear of disturbing the nesting robins in the thatch. The only decisions he ever makes are ones to the benefit of everyone else. We are his peace, just as he is mine. Why is he so willing to send me away, at a time where all of his baby birds are flying the nest, when everyone knows that he would cling to us forever if he could?

'I know. And we are so, so happy having you here. Don't think I'm trying to get rid of you; I just thought you'd regret it if you never went for it – just because it's a few miles away.'

'A few hundred, Dad.'

'What's a couple of hundred miles when you have trains and cars, eh? It's not like you'd have to walk to Mordor and back just to get home.'

'I could come down to see you at weekends too,' Sam chips in cautiously, afraid of spoiling the calm air of contemplation that surrounds us all.

'And me. You know I'm down every now and again for those awful corporate meetings.' Mum follows suit.

'Would you at least think about it?' Dad has always had that kind of face that could make you do anything – not in the stern, scary way. But you almost pity him. There's a kind of purity in his angelite eyes, as if he has never had one bad thought in his life.

I nod. All three other bodies in the room release a heavy breath.

'Oh shit, I'm late for work. Got to go.' Sam gathers his things from around the kitchen and rushes out the door – although not without first pushing me by the face and setting me off balance with his impish giggle. 'See ya!' he shouts and without waiting for any reply, the front door slams with a jingle of the wind chimes outside.

'Bye, darling.'

'Have a nice day, son,' Mum and Dad shout after him, despite knowing it's in vain.

'That's my cue too.' Mum kisses both me and Dad on the cheek and the wind chimes once again sing with her exit.

The scored and marked wooden table separates me from Dad. Heaps of fabric cut-offs surround the sewing machine, and one of Marigold's red capes hangs above the old fireplace, now embroidered with a chain of flowers along its hem.

'I am so proud of you, Daisy. No matter what you do. Remember that. Okay?'

Another of the creases of his face smooths over once a smile follows my nod and he too departs the kitchen.

Turning to face the garden, my eyes follow a bumblebee as it hops from the rosemary, to the dahlias, and then nestles itself into the breast of a foxglove. The tiny thing looks so contented, skipping across the whole garden, tasting every petal on offer. No distance is too far for a creature so small. It knows what it wants, and revels in the joy of achieving it. When that tiny bee returns to its hive, drunk on pollen, the thrill of life, of family, of destiny, must electrify them. Perhaps that's why they buzz – they're just humming with life.

Hiking myself back up to my bedroom, I pull out my laptop from the drawer and open up my emails. Right there at the very top is an email from one 'SirWestley. Grahamton@knightschool.co.uk'.

I want to delete it, not even look at it, forget my promises of thinking about it and just tell everyone that they changed their minds and don't want me anymore. Thinking about how I felt almost six years ago the day before I was meant to start at uni makes me feel sick all over again. My breathing becomes more laboured as I remember Mum's silence after she gave up following an hour of sitting in the car, packed to the roof with all of my things waiting for our new adventure, only to find me locked in the wardrobe in Sam's room as if I was at least half the age I actually was. The world was too loud, just like it is right now.

But what stopped me? The thought that everyone I meet will be the same as they were at school? That I would be completely and utterly alone? That I would fail and return only to have let everyone down? The fear that the adventure could never live up to the one I had formulated in my head so everything would only ever be a disappointment? All of the above? All of the above.

Lady Alenthaea would never be so afraid of something

so unthreatening as an email. It's not like it could stab or poison her. Well, actually, she would probably be a little perturbed if a magic box that could communicate messages from across the kingdom in seconds, without the need for specially trained ravens, appeared on her writing desk, but that's beside the point. What would Alenthaea do if she received a message that could alter the course of her life, mess up everything that she had contented herself with, all that was comfortable? Lady Alenthaea, the great elven noble, prepared to charge into a horde of orcs alone just to reap her revenge, would not be caught dead feeling anxious at the sight of a mealy piece of virtual parchment. She'd open the bloody thing, and burn the contents if it displeased her.

Rubbing my face with calloused palms, I wish I could just rub it all away, erase every thought in my brain that makes me afraid of supermarkets, of passing an acquaintance in the street, of life itself. But Alenthaea would spit in my face at my cowardice. So, with a jolt of her fire coursing through me, I open the email, a little disappointed it didn't quite achieve the same satisfaction as snapping a wax seal and ripping open a letter, but I can't dwell on that now as it flashes in huge golden letters:

Dear Sir Daisy,

The Tower of London cordially invites you to attend an 'Introduction to Knight School' on the 10th of July the year of our Lord 2024. Bring yourself, your sabatons (comfortable shoes – preferably trainers), and your thirst for battle.

Packed lunch will be provided – please let us know if you have any dietary requirements – sadly we cannot accommodate 'the blood of my enemies' due to the supply shortages incurred following Brexit.

Hours will be discussed in detail on the day, but be expected to work full-time Tuesday–Saturday for an hourly rate of ten British pounds and the promise of eternal glory.

Any further questions, contact Westley on this address (carrier pigeon or raven preferred – but an email will suffice).

Your loyal servant,
Sir Westley Graham

Distracted from my ruminations, I can't help but smile at the excess of it all. As much as it pains me to admit it, I think Dad could be right. This job sounds scarily perfect. Reading the email over and over, I try to find something wrong, some other small print, some clue that it's some elaborate prank. There's nothing, no fault, no way to sabotage myself.

My heartbeat tapping out some irregular jazz improv is the only thing that is still me, as Alenthaea, fired up from the adrenaline of opening the email, takes the reins completely. Tasked with showing off her swordsmanship to a crowd, to a champion, she would waste no time in planning the routine to perform. So, my head swirls with ideas; my fingers twitch as my mind plays out each swing of my sword. Before my thoughts can scramble to something else, I have joined that bumblebee in the garden, covered in Lady Alenthaea's armour and sweating with the strain of a fight with no one.

I could never do it. I could never move to London and leave everything I know just to start again with strangers for a few weeks. I would rather hide in my brother's wardrobe and rot with the rafters of this house. But I don't like me; I don't want to be me. I want to be the woman whose muscles burn with the pleasure of exertion, who longs for a challenge, who yearns for adventure. I want to be Lady Alenthaea, the warrior who doesn't run from the unknown, but runs straight into it, sword raised, so sure of herself that she doesn't even stop to draw her shield. Daisy Hastings is a coward. Lady A is who I truly wish to be.

Only when I am completely exhausted do I stop. The sky bruises in bursts of pink and purple and the sun has begun to drag itself away for another night. Looking back at the cottage, I notice the faces of my parents watching me from the window. Mum leans her head against her husband's chest as he circles his arm around her in a snaking embrace. When they see me noticing them, they break apart to offer a muted round of applause. Lifting my sword up in a deft salute, I feel full.

'I'm going to do it!' I shout, sending a huddle of pigeons fleeing the nearby apple tree. My words surprise myself most of all. They leave my lips before they had even made a pit stop in my brain.

Mum and Dad squint at the glass and turn to each other with the same look of confusion. The former mouths 'what' and points to her ear.

'Ah. Double glazing,' I mutter and Dad pushes open the window.

'What did you say, love? We didn't quite catch that.'

'I said, I'm going to do it. The job.' The energy isn't quite the same when I'm having to repeat myself but the feeling is still there.

They both rush from the kitchen with open arms.

'A-a-a-a.' I warn them off with a gloved hand and they share a look of rejection. Taking their moment of pause to toss aside my sword, relieve my waist band from the dagger, and my sock from its *sgian-dubh*, I encourage them both in for a rare embrace, and with the warmth of their arms around me, for the first time I truly believe this could all be possible.

Chapter 4

'Are you sure you have everything?' Dad is frantic in the doorway as Sam and I prepare to clamber into his car, Mum following closely behind. 'You did remember Sniffles, didn't you? You won't be able to sleep if you don't have Sniffles!' He refers to my childhood teddy bear, a stuffed doll that used to have a nose and cheeks so rosy that she looked as if she had a terrible cold and wore an expression as if she was about to sneeze at any given moment. Now all of her colours have faded and she sits at the very bottom of my suitcase.

'First thing I packed,' I assure him and his eyes flit about the place manically, as if searching for another worry to harness.

Today is the 8th of July. In the last five days, I have hidden in Sam's wardrobe six times, drafted an email of resignation twice, and packed up most of my bedroom into Mum's Toyota. We managed to find a last-minute flat-share in Swiss Cottage at the kind of price that makes me nervous to see the state of it.

Mum suggested that we leave Dad behind to take care of the dog and Marigold – and I silently thank her, knowing the real reason he isn't coming is that his anxiety is infectious. That, and every time Alenthaea's confidence leaves me, I can't swallow down the bitterness that has been left to stew in my gut from his betrayal. As soon as I stop to think, as soon as my Daisy realisation hits, it's Dad who's flagged up as the cause of all of this anxiety, all of the gut-wrenching pain, all of the conflict that keeps me up at night. My source of peace becomes the scapegoat for my greatest fears so I'm sure it's best not to have him by my side as I venture into the lion's den.

'Today's the day, is it?' Richard's voice calls from the end of the driveway. He leans heavily on his walking stick. His mouth hangs open as he tries to diminish the appearance of his exertion.

'It is indeed, Rich. You walk down the field to say bye did ya?' Sam's shoes crunch against the gravel as he walks over to meet our neighbour and place both an affectionate and supporting arm around his shoulders. 'Fancy a seat?' He guides the older man back towards one of the chairs on the front lawn. Richard's face would imply that he's disgusted at this treatment, but he willingly obliges and plonks himself down.

'Long drive ahead for you there, Iris. You going down the A1 by any chance?'

'A1 (M) and then down the M 11,' Mum answers, provoking a grunt from her interlocutor.

'And you have enough change for the tolls and the like?'

'Why, are you offering, Rich?' Sam interjects.

'You can pay for anything with one of these little magic boxes now,' Mum interrupts Richard's scowl at my brother and shows off her slightly battered iPhone.

'Silly things. They're listening on them you know.' Richard doesn't specify exactly who 'they' are – I don't think even he himself knows – and Sam and I share an amused glance.

'That's all right. All they'll know is what we're having for tea next Tuesday and that Simon needs to remember to take his pants out of the tumble dryer. No secrets in this household I'm afraid.' After twenty-five years as his neighbour, Mum knows exactly how to deal with Richard and his antics and once again she reduces him to incoherent grumblings.

'Tea!' Dad suddenly cries. 'None of you have a flask of tea!' He flies back into the house with a dramatic flail and everyone else rolls their eyes.

'He's flapping even more than you.' Sam approaches and speaks in a low voice, his elbow poking softly into my side.

'I just know how to do it quietly.' We can see Dad through the windows – he runs around the kitchen frenziedly. We lose sight of him for a moment, only to see him in the next window along freaking out in the living room.

'I think you'll surprise yourself, you know.'

'I hope so.' The bottom of my stomach twinges. If Mum doesn't get in the car quick, I may have to spend the rest of the week in the cupboard under the stairs.

Lady Alenthaea would be brave. She would know that

this is something she has to do, that this is the beginning of forever. Lady Alenthaea wouldn't hide, counting the shoes on the shoe rack, regretting her actions in real time. Lady Alenthaea would get her arse in that car and go to bloody London and make it her own.

'Thanks for stopping by, Richard. I'll be sending over the scripts for the Fellowship and you had better listen to your new leader whilst I'm gone – I'm not having you asleep in the woods during the Battle of Helm's Geek like last year.'

'A wizard's only master is his magic,' he interrupts his attempts to engage Mum in some inflammatory political debate to respond in all seriousness.

'And the magic commands you to be a lazy arse, does it?' To everyone's surprise except my own, Richard doesn't get offended; instead, he shifts on his chair to face me, a phantom smile appearing on his stubbled lip.

'It does indeed, my lady. It also commands me to inform you of the prophecy: "Don't trust a southerner, or anyone who pronounces *bath* as *barf*. And always remind them that you can outdrink them in your sleep."'

'Noted. Cheers,' I say, knocking my finger against my temple.

Before he can begin another of his grumbles, I take the flask of tea from Dad, kiss him on his damp cheek, and hop in the car.

'You two coming or not?' I roll down my window to speak to my fellow passengers who still stand outside of the car unable to stop themselves from staring. At the sound of my voice, they snap out of their surprised trance and scramble to the car as quickly as they can. Before I know it, we are pulling out of the drive and it doesn't escape my notice when the loud clicking signifies Mum has locked the car – probably in the hopes that I won't try a tuck-and-roll manoeuvre halfway down the motorway.

Dad has called three times before we finally pull up to the place that I am to call home for the next couple of months. To say it is the antithesis to my actual home doesn't even cover it. The single square metre of grass outside of the building hosts a dead tree that has been cable-tied to a metal pole. The grass itself is more like hay and is ornamented with a series of cigarette butts. Instead of birdsong, the constant rumbling of cars from the road soundtracks the view. Although, it is quite fitting: the building is only a few storeys high but has a certain dystopian look about it. Brutalist concrete crumbles around the flaking windowpanes, and instead of hanging baskets, weeds spring from the cracks up and down the building. Only adding to the ambience, the door swings open and someone exits, dragging their feet across the pavement, jean hems picking up the dirt, and looking suitably apocalyptic.

'Well, this looks like the beginning of a dream if ever I saw one,' Sam remarks as he hauls the largest suitcase from the boot. I can't bring myself to respond at all, much less match his humour or ability to find something to smile about – sarcastic or not.

Things have been a little awkward between us since all of this came about. It would be a lie to say I haven't harboured just a little resentment towards him too, for storming into the shop a week ago and putting this stupid, stupid idea into Dad's head. But if it is to happen, if I am about to change everything I have known for this, I wouldn't want anyone else beside me. Though I feel in a constant state of vertigo and am unsure if I'm going to make it past the threshold without vomiting, his presence – always jolly, always calm – is at least enough to stop me from hot-wiring Mum's car and joyriding the whole way home.

'Oh hush, Sam. I do apologise that we cannot afford a castle and all its grandeur but I'm sure it will be much better on the inside – you know how these things are.'

Sadly, Mum's optimism is grossly misplaced and as we enter the reception, greeted by its overwhelming smell of weed and absentminded receptionist, I can almost see her chewing on her words.

'You were saying . . .' my brother teases and quickly shuts up when Mum's stare is unleashed.

After a while of getting the receptionist to understand our requests, with the keys firmly in my hand, along with several bags of my belongings, we three haul ourselves into the lift, just narrowly avoiding dragging the wheels of my suitcase through a cold pile of sick.

Riding up to the third floor with the niggling worry that the rickety lift may not even make it that far, none of us say a word. When the doors slide open, I speak for the first time since we arrived.

'Why don't we just go—' Before I can even finish my sentence, two resounding 'noes' echo against the bare walls and my twin pulls me by the arm and into the path of my new home.

They give me the honour of unlocking the door. It takes a little shove against the rusted hinges before it swings open. Instead of revealing some sort of secret room, hidden and closed off from the dull building around it, filled instead with magic and inspiration, it is overwhelmingly grey. I never knew that a place could be simultaneously cramped and barren, yet here we are. There's a coldness that greets us, both in the draught and its lack of conviviality. The ceilings are low and the rooms squat, and filled with a vast emptiness.

'Hello?' a voice calls from the void. It is high-pitched, but not shrill, and I notice Sam straighten with the warmth that fills the room following the call. 'A-ha! You must be Daisy! I thought I heard someone come in, though I did worry for a moment that it was a ghost – they're not too uncommon around these parts.'

The voice reveals itself in an explosion of colour in the shape of a woman. She looks as though she has been cut out of a scene of a rather psychedelic children's TV show and dropped into an episode of *World's Toughest Prisons*. The room brightens with her in it and I can't tell if it's the reflection from her pink and purple swirled flares or the wide smile that she hasn't once dropped in what must be an incredibly exhausting greeting.

'Yep, hi. I'm Daisy.' I awkwardly wave at my new housemate after a prompting poke in the ribs from my mother.

'Oh, aren't you lovely. I'm Elizabeth, but no one ever

calls me that, except my granny. Everyone just calls me Bobble.' She takes a few of the bags out of my hands with her long fingers. Each one is stacked with at least three rings, all of differing colours and materials.

'Bobble?' I can't help but enquire, struggling to see how the nickname derives from the original.

'A friend of mine at school once decided that I reminded him of a bobble hat, and thus it has been impossible to shake ever since. But I rather like it.'

I respond with an understanding nod and wordless 'ah' and she seems satisfied. In fact, if at all possible, her smile widens again to reveal even more of her shiny teeth. One of her canines, I notice, is bedazzled with a tiny gem.

'Nice to meet you, *Bobble*. I'm Samwise, but everyone just calls me Sam. This is our Mum, Iris.' It surprises me that Sam has actually made it to the end of his sentence and is still speaking in English, as his face has practically melted into a gooey mush of awe just at the sight of her. Rolling my eyes, I pull him discreetly by the arm before he has the opportunity to creep out my new housemate before we even get past the hallway.

'It is so lovely to have you all here. I've been excited about this all week!' She claps her hands together, dropping my bags for a moment, and then picks them up in a hurry. 'Let me show you to your room and I shall get you all a cup of tea.' She scuttles off back down the hallway and we follow her.

'Seems nice,' Mum mutters and I nod in agreement.

'Now I know it is very plain in here, but I brought you Steven.' My flatmate points to an out-of-control spider plant on the windowsill. 'I thought he might brighten the place up a bit before you got all of your stuff unpacked.'

I thank her and she seems pleased enough with my reply. 'Right, teas. I have lemon, mint, avocado, honeybush, bamboo, turmeric, green, jasmine—' She reels them off on her fingers, and we all three share an overwhelmed look. Tea is just tea in our house – milk, one sugar (and a quarter for dad) – in a novelty mug.

'—and I know it is a little strange but I do have a liquorice tea for anyone with a more adventurous palette.'

'I'll just have a water please, darling,' Mum requests.

'Just three waters please,' I add, speaking for my twin too, who looks as if his head is ready to explode in a tea overdose. We have indeed been incredibly sheltered.

'Is anyone else exhausted?' I enquire to the room.

Mum sits down on the bare mattress of my bed and Sam nods. Despite the sheer energy of her, I have to admit that my new roommate is a welcome distraction from the constant turmoil that plays in my head. How can one think of anything else when one is blinded by dyed faux furs and friendly smiles? I think I like her.

When Bobble returns, she wastes no time in helping us unpack. Her blonde hair, dyed with streaks of purple, bounces around her face as she hops between boxes, carefully placing my things around the room in her own artistic style. Mum and Sam engage her in conversation for most of the afternoon. I enjoy listening to them and learning about my flatmate without the heavy burden of asking the right questions being on my shoulders. Bobble tells us that she is a fashion student at Central Saint

Martins, although she's now in her fifth year of study, as opposed to the usual three after being forced to retake two years. The idea of failure doesn't seem to plague her though. She seems almost happy to have spent even longer with a course that she evidently loves – I find myself questioning whether her flunking was entirely unintentional.

When she asks about us – who we are, what we all do – her eyes fill with a sparkling awe. She sits down on my bed, one of my ornamental knives in her hand, and asks as many questions as she can fit in with room enough to let one of us reply.

'Wow.' She breathes, stroking the chain mail shirt I have just unpacked. 'You guys are just so cool.'

'I don't think anyone has ever said that before.' I find myself with enough confidence to laugh and I'm encouraged when she actually smiles at my contribution.

'Well, you are – just look at all this stuff!' She picks up one of my Alenthaea crowns and places it on her own head. Usually, a stranger touching my things fills me with the desire to snatch it back and hide it away, but there's a real appreciation in Bobble that is refreshing. She is genuine and I leave her to it as she swishes around the open boxes.

'It's getting on a bit now. We should think about heading home, darling.' My confidence crashes as Mum gets to her feet, checking her watch. I had been so caught up in the prospect of a new friend, being here with Mum and Sam, talking about all of the things I love most, that I had forgotten that they weren't to stay and, for the first time since a school trip in year ten, I was to go to sleep in a room under the wrong roof.

'Oh . . . Oh, yes, of course.'

'I think we can rest assured that you're in safe hands here.' Sam grins warmly at Bobble but it falters when he catches my expression.

My mouth moves in an attempt to say something but nothing comes out. Reality has hit like the attacking fist of a giant. This wasn't just some weird little day out. What on earth am I doing?

'Dais?' Sam shuffles closer towards me as I blankly stare at the wall behind him. In my peripheral vision I notice Mum gesture to Bobble and they both leave me and my twin alone in the room.

'What am I doing, Sam? I can't do it.'

'How do you know you can't do it, if you don't even know what you're doing?' He steals my full attention again and quirks one of his eyebrows mischievously.

'Can't you stay, just tonight . . . on the sofa?'

He places a hand delicately on my shoulder and his face softens again into seriousness. 'You know that I would if I could, but I have work in the morning and you have a day to figure out the Tube before you start work.' My face lights with an idea and before I can share it with him, he stops me. 'And before you say . . . that's one thing I cannot help you with. I am scared of very few things but trains in tunnels only just big enough is definitely one of them.'

'And hamsters . . .' I mimic his playful smile as he widens his eyes, furiously shaking his head.

'No, no, nope. Not *all* hamsters, just that one Marigold used to have – you know with those red eyes. I'm sure that thing was sent by the devil to punish me for putting

44

chewing gum in Mari's hair that one time.' He visibly shudders at the thought of the tiny fur ball that left him with a scar between his finger and thumb when we were fifteen.

I wish we could do this together. That we could get a flat together, work together, be those badass twins teaching everyone how to swing a sword and fire a crossbow.

'If you need anything at all, Daisy, you only have to call. You know that, right?'

I nod wordlessly.

'But please just give it a good go, for me? If you hate it after two weeks I will get in my car and drive down here to fetch you back myself, but I would never tell you to do something if I didn't truly believe that it is for you.'

Outstretching my arm, I wait for his to clasp it. He wraps his hand around the top of my forearm and I do the same to his in an embrace we have done since we were kids. Neither of us were the hugging kind, the restrictive embrace almost guaranteed to trigger the fight-or-flight response every time – so we instead opted for this odd handshake. Each closing our eyes, we silently tell the other whatever we wish, and rely on twin telepathy for the rest.

I promise you. I speak only in my mind. *I won't let you down. I promise.*

Chapter 5

Instead of using the day to figure out the Tubes like my brother had suggested, I spent the entire day in bed. And now I stand next to the ticket machines in Swiss Cottage station, feeling much like how I'd imagine Merlin to feel if he was handed an iPhone with Instagram opened and told to post a video.

I have to get to the Tower of London by 10 a.m., and for once I pat myself on the back for leaving three hours to make the five-ish miles. Stood stiff in the station like a lost child, my eyes track the sole member of staff who files past like a passing ship and I can't raise the courage to ask for help. Everything moves around me in a blur as commuters begin their journeys, children begrudgingly make their way to school, and tourists commence their holidays. But still, I stay, stuck, just watching them by the ticket machine, watching the hands of the station clock tick on.

After a while of observing, I bite the bullet. Noting that most people opted for pressing their bank card against the barrier, I dig around in my bag for my purse and find it tucked under a cotton tunic and a chain mail coif. Allowing the next stream of people to go in front of me, for fear of causing a queue, I take a deep breath and do it. As if by magic, the barriers swing open and I audibly breathe a sigh of relief.

Okay, now I just need to get on the right train. After only one missed stop and far too long stood in the soggy armpits of other commuters, I finally get out of the station at Tower Hill, with an overwhelming feeling that I have already done a full day's work.

My legs wobble their way out of the station and that's when I see it – the Tower of London. Don't get me wrong, I have seen it so many times in photos, films, books and this week I've done little else aside from research it to an obsessive degree, but there is something about seeing it in person. With my eyes fixed on its imposing white brick, my body moves towards it almost without a thought. I am not quite sure how I make it over the road without being hit by a rogue food delivery driver on his moped but all of my limbs are intact as I clutch the railings.

A surge of energy ripples its way through me and I can't help but do a little happy but involuntary twitch to release it. Bricks and mortar are stacked before me in a palimpsest history. It has a ruggedness to it – the outer wall is scarred with crossed arrow slits and I picture each one filled with the alert eyes of archers – the strings of their bows pulled tense, loaded and ready to attack any that attempt the deadly trip across the moat. Rounded towers rise above them, like the commander on the high ground, looking down over his army. Other buildings, with varying darkness of brick, mosaic the empty spaces until it is only the clear sky and a fluttering union flag that looks down on the fortress.

Thinking about what I'm there to do, I feel compelled to leap this fence and land straight into the moat. The landing would potentially be a little messy, however. Drained of its water, it's now a field of wildflowers only broken by a camp of rounded blue-striped bell tents. Wooden tables are lined with swords and shields and a platoon of people mill around them, occasionally laying out another weapon with the collection and stoking a smoking fire in the centre. A wooden trebuchet towers above all of them and if it weren't for one of the party wearing a pair of chunky headphones over their ears, you could tell me that I have fallen back in time to the thirteenth century and I would believe you.

'First time seeing it?' A voice interrupts my excited trembling and I scorn it in my head but politely turn to face the source. The stranger is smiling as he takes up the space at the railing next to me. His warm bronze skin is carved with a pair of deep dimples and framed by long dark stubble across his lip and jaw. At first glance he looks barely older than me, but as I study him further, the lines that spring from his eyes and the way he holds himself with such an air of self-assurance, it's clear that he's no twenty-something at the beginning of figuring it out. Very well put together, this is a man of maturity, intelligence.

With my facial expressions always giving away my feelings more bluntly than if I just straight up insulted him, he has clearly noticed my confusion at being approached by a stranger and clarifies, 'The Tower, I mean. Have you been here before?'

I notice a North American twang to his pronunciation – the exact region eludes me but that would explain his openness. 'No, I haven't – it's my first time. I've read about it,' I reply.

'Beautiful, isn't it?'

'I'm not sure.' His smile falters as though I have disrespected him directly and I continue, 'Saying it is "beautiful" implies a sort of perfection to it, but its beauty comes from its imperfection – perhaps "sublime" is more fitting.' I speak more to the Tower itself but my uninvited guest hums what I assume is an agreement.

'Have you come to see it on holiday?'

'No, I work here.' The stranger's eyes widen for a moment. They're bright, beautiful, like the sun glowing across the smooth surface of a horse chestnut. Then his dimples deepen with a renewed smile. Something in me warms at the sight.

'No way! Me too! First day?'

I nod.

'Which department?'

I point to what I can only assume is the Knight School in the moat. 'I believe it's there.'

'Knight School? Awesome! My name's Ellis, archivist, nice to meet you!' He sticks out his hand for me to shake and as much as I don't wish to offend him, especially with his intense friendliness, I can't bring myself to shake it and I shiver at the thought. Touching strangers has never been my favourite pastime and my first thought when a hand is extended to me is why are we, as a culture, so obsessed with swapping hand sweat with people we don't know? Don't even get me started on a French kiss. Racking my brains for an alternative, I put on my best and widest smile.

'Daisy. Lovely to meet you, Ellis.' He clears his throat awkwardly, looking at his outstretched hand for a moment before pulling it quickly away and busying it by clutching the straps of his rucksack. Guilt pangs in my stomach and I try my best to reclaim face. 'Do you know Westley? Westley Graham? I am meant to meet him but have no idea what he looks like.'

Ellis seems satisfied at being asked for help and not completely rejected in his attempts at friendliness and he waves me to follow him. 'Sure, I'll show you. He's not too hard to spot.' We walk together along the moat path and I don't take my eyes off of the Tower.

'Lion Tower,' I read out loud as we reach the end of the moat and a series of ruined bricks border a pride of wire-sculpted lions. Stopping in my tracks, I tilt my head to look at them. Two females look poised to attack next to a more placid maned male. Their eye sockets give way to a black void and there's something haunting about them.

'There used to be a menagerie here,' Ellis says, taking my moment of intrigue as an invitation to display his acute knowledge of the place, 'Kings and queens from across the world would bring exotic animals as a gift for the monarchy and, with the high walls, the Tower became the most suitable place to keep them – well as suitable as it is to keep a polar bear in central London. . .'

'Hmm,' I muse, entertained by his stories and curious for more.

He uses that as an invitation to continue, 'If you couldn't guess, this is where they kept the lions. You know, they actually found two lions' skulls in the moat in the Twenties – Barbary lions too, so, er, extinct now. The museum researchers believe one was from around the fifteenth century, and the other the thirteenth!' He laughs to himself, as though still captivated by the same information he has clearly studied extensively. He could be talking to himself and I don't think he would mind. 'That means that potentially even up to Edward V, we had lions here! How fascinating is that?'

I look to him and smile. It is indeed fascinating. 'I wouldn't want to be this close to them though.' The wiry replacements are in leaping distance and I shudder at the thought of the poor medieval servant tasked with feeding them.

'Yeah, took them a while (and a lot of missing limbs) to decide it was a bad idea. Ah, there he is!' Ellis points to a group at the gates. A mass of hair pokes out from the top of the circle. 'I'd better get going. Nice to meet you, Daisy!'

'Yeah, you too,' I say softly but he's already rushed off and through the gates.

Walking over to the group, I realise that I am one of the last to join, though it's still ten minutes before ten and my timings were definitely perfect. Kicking myself, I make a mental note to be twenty minutes early tomorrow.

Managing to find a spot behind two of the shorter women in the group, I peer over their heads and see my new boss for the first time.

Westley looks exactly like his email would imply. A lean man in his forties, his fair and greying hair explodes from his freckled head in a bristly mass, yet his goatee is perfectly sleek and pointed at his Adam's apple.

'Ah, a new face has graced us. What be your name, young one?' He points to me with the tip of his dagger that lies skilfully in his palm. The rest of the group follow his gaze and all eyes are on me. Losing all of the confidence I had gained in my short conversation with Ellis, the stranger from before, I blush.

'Daisy,' I say quietly and Westley squints in my direction.

'Sorry my lady, you will have to speak up, for I have forgotten to pack my ear trumpet today and the oldé lugs are struggling.' A West-Country twang ornaments his words as he feigns the intonation of a jolly nobleman in some sort of early 2000s costume drama, and there's something about him that feels homely. The comfort of Westley himself doesn't quite translate to the other members of the group, and I only manage to choke out my words slightly louder than before.

'Daisy . . . Hastings,' I croak.

'Indeed, Ms Hastings, you are most welcome. Welcome.' He claps his hands together and his dewy cheeks glow red. 'Right, let us proceed. Follow me, young sirs and madams – into the castle we shall go.' Clapping again, he turns and walks past the security guards and we follow him under the archway of the first Tower. Staring up into the sloping wall, I notice its murder holes are still intact, still ready to have tar and excrement poured through them to stop trespassers in their tracks. The rusted points of a portcullis also peek out from above, tucked away to welcome visitors, and I picture the ancient ropes holding it up snapping under its weight and trapping us all in.

Having followed our leader not too far into the fortress, we divert down into the moat and congregate in a circle around him as he replaces his dagger with one of the claymores on the table. A murmur travels around the circle as the new colleagues begin to get to know one another. I remain in my silent world, patiently waiting for Westley to begin speaking again.

'Good morning, good sirs, and welcome to His Majesty's Royal Palace and Fortress, the Tower of London. You each are here at the special request of the king himself, as we are tasked with finding and training the next generation of gallant knights.' He stops himself for a moment and drops the accent to add in a hushed tone, 'Just to clarify, I don't speak for the actual king; it's just a summer holiday club, not linked to the royals, but I thought that would sound a bit cooler.' He is almost certainly not Scottish but his slim and freckled legs are exposed in a kilt of the Black Watch tartan and he lunges deeply as he paces in front of the group, his sword resting on his shoulder as he goes – clearly showing off the range of movement he is afforded when not constricted by any more fabric than necessary.

My smile is broad and unrestrained for the first time in a while and I itch for him to continue. One of the other knights beside me turns to his friend to snigger and I find myself placing a mental hex upon him and his rudeness.

Resuming his original theatrics, Westley recommences, 'Your main responsibilities will include demonstrating your skills in combat that you will then teach our students. Not only that but you shall be conducting lessons in chivalry, noble history, and all of the things that it takes to be a knight. We will be transforming lost young people into strong and confident chevaliers. Now, does anyone wish to volunteer their skills first, to show us exactly what you can do?'

Without a second thought, Alenthaea breaks through my anxiety and my hand flies up. It is the only one. 'Sir Daisy, oh yes, our experienced swordsman – I have been most excited to see you handle a blade.' Blushing, I falter for a moment as the pressure begins to mount.

Others in the party look between one another sceptically. The knight I cursed only moments before, for mocking Westley, repeats his snigger and the rage of Lady Alenthaea burns deeply in me, ready to prove them wrong. I have never felt more grateful to have spent the best part of my life hitting my brother with swords. The only thing more comfortable to me than this is breathing. Even then, I'd say that with the amount of hyperventilating that often overcomes me, perhaps swinging a blade around is more relaxing. If I only have a month to prove myself as a worthy knight, and a worthy employee, this is the one thing that I know I can do, and do well, the one thing that my nerves can't take away from me. With a weapon in hand is the only time I truly trust myself, so, leaving the self-doubt to Daisy, Alenthaea consumes me.

Westley tosses me a sword with his left hand, and I catch it adroitly by the handle and raise it to meet the attacking blade in his right. With the weapon much lighter than those I am used to it's far easier to look more impressive than my lack of exertion would imply. But Westley is evidently skilled with his blade. When I aim a few provoking jabs in his direction, he steps it up with a series of swipes that I have to deflect as he forces me to the edge of the circle. After dodging a couple more blows, I duck beneath his sword and reclaim the open space behind him. Now it's my turn to have him pinned. He fends off my attack but our swords clash in muted clangs and, with an invigorated series of blows, I manage to relieve his hand from the grip and he is forced to raise his hands in surrender.

A single clap echoes in the moat, and soon the rest of the circle breaks into applause at our display.

'Good work, kid.' Westley breathlessly claps me on the shoulder and smiles through his panting. A few of my colleagues follow suit and offer their compliments and I blush with my eyes fixed on the ground. Why is Sam always bloody right?

'Right, you lot, who wants to follow that?' Westley, having caught his breath, points his sword at the rest of the team threateningly, and now he doesn't have a shortage of volunteers.

Most of the day is spent getting to grips with the weapons. I fight and defeat three of my colleagues and manage to earn their respect in the process. I wish that this was how all acquaintances were formed. It's far easier to just bash them around with a sword for a bit than go through the torture of the small-talk script to try and convince them that I'm interesting enough to chat with.

'How did you even learn to do that?' one of my colleagues pants at my feet. Before I had put her there on her arse, I learnt her name was Erin and this was her second year at the Knight School.

'I've had far too much time on my hands,' I confess and offer my arm to help her up. Her eyes flick between my outstretched hand and the breathless grin on my face before clambering to her feet by herself with a grunt. Trying not to think too much of it, reminding myself of the way I too refused to swap hand sweat with a stranger this morning, I brush down my trousers and maintain my smile.

If I am to be here for the summer, I should at least try to make some friends. My prejudices that had stopped me from being so approachable until now have somewhat subsided upon meeting my housemate and realising that not every one of my peers are terrifying and praying for my downfall at every moment. Perhaps there are more Bobbles out there too. Alenthaea may be a lone wolf, distrusting of strangers, but even she makes friends during her voyages. All of those deuteragonists add to the plot, help her get to the places she needs to reach. Perhaps Erin could be like my wise wizard who accompanies me through the goblin kingdom or the faerie queen who offers her advice on how best to cross the sickening seas?

'You make a good opponent,' I say, in my best attempt at a compliment.

Erin turns away without a word and heads over to the weapons table. I have to jog a little to catch up with her and together we return ours to the pile. Before I can come up with another offering of friendship, she retreats into the group and finally cracks a smile amongst the others.

Not allowing myself to feel the sting of rejection yet, I set myself to the instructions from Westley to return the camp to its tidy state ready to resume in the morning. I don't mind the tedious cleaning – I'm allowing myself to feel good about today, that, and the adrenaline of so many sword fights still courses through me like an electrical thrill.

'Daisy!' I turn to the sound of my name and find Ellis, the excessively friendly archivist from this morning, waving to me from the path across the moat that must have once upon a time replaced a drawbridge. I offer a stiff and awkward wave back and he rushes on down to meet me.

'How was your first day?' My hair has escaped my ponytail and most of it clings to my face as I sweat with the day's exercise.

I'm still excited and buzzing to tell anyone about it, and all of the words that I was hoping to release in a debrief with my new colleagues flow out of me as we walk together towards the station.

'Amazing,' Ellis manages to squeeze into my onslaught of conversation. The change from my unintentionally cold conversation from this morning must have surprised him.

'I could show you around the place sometime if you like. We have a whole armoury of weapons and such, if that's your kind of thing?'

Surprising myself, I agree to his offer and we part to separate sides of the platform and as soon as I return to my usual state of silence, when Alenthaea in the form of adrenaline finally dissolves from my bloodstream, I am just about ready to fall asleep on my feet – the effort of conversation far more draining than a full day of sword fighting.

When I finally crawl into bed, I allow a single, tentative tremor of excitement to flow through me at the thought of waking to do it all again tomorrow.

Chapter 6

The next few days follow in a similar fashion. Well, except the fact that I have been first to arrive each day, after I had sussed out the exact time to leave that meant I'd come into contact with as few people as possible on the Tube. And every evening I stay later to help Westley do all of the tidying that he had asked his workers to do, but being too shy to make any demands, ends up doing himself.

Though home calls to me in every heartbeat, I can't be seen to fail here. If this is going to be my new adventure, it cannot be anything but perfect. With only four weeks to show everyone who I am and what I am capable of, I will give everything I have to prove that I am not a failure. That, and after day one I realised that if I keep busy enough, my brain doesn't quite have the chance to keep up with my growing feelings that I have been dropped into the mouth of a sea monster with only a pair of armbands to try and keep me afloat. So, with every minute focused on being the perfect employee, by the time I get home, I have just enough energy to text the family group chat to let them know that I'm still alive and flop into bed to space out and daydream about elves, knights and monsters.

Tonight, Bobble stands in my doorway hand-stitching a faux peacock feather onto a furry bucket hat. 'Have you actually done or seen anything except for work this week?' Her bleached eyebrows furrow with gentle concern as she perceives me in bed with my notebook, the exact same place she has found me every day since I moved in.

'Does the pigeon lady in the park on the way to the station count?'

Bobble shakes her head.

'Not even if she's feeding them a different birthday cake each day?'

A look of confusion and then concern passes over her face – she has one of those expressive faces, the kind where you can see each one of her thoughts on her features. Usually, the fear of an awkward silence or the pressure of carrying a conversation and finding the right things to say cripples me into silence – but with Bobble, she has enough conversation for the both of us. A moment of silence to allow for a breath is scarce and there's a comfort in that. Not once has she joked about my inability to get my words out quick enough to keep the rally going, or mocked my shyness. She doesn't force me to try and be more extroverted; she looks content in knowing me as me.

'What kind of birthday cake?' Her confusion turns to intrigue and she invites herself into my room and plonks herself down on the bed next to me. 'Victoria sponge? Lemon? Chocolate?'

'I can't say that I asked her for a slice, Bobble.' I laugh. 'But I'm pretty sure I saw one of those Colin the Caterpillar cakes the other day. The one this morning had these huge lollipops sticking out the top.'

She hums. 'Good taste.' She knots off her sewing and cuts through the thread with her teeth. After fluffing the feather, she sticks the needle halfway into the bun in hair. The leftover thread hangs from it like a piece of purple bunting. I might have to buy her a pincushion for her birthday . . . 'How come you haven't explored the city? I could suggest a few places if you weren't sure where to go.'

I can't help but assume that anywhere Bobble suggests would be far too loud in both noise and colour for me, but I appreciate the suggestion. 'I just get so tired.' Perhaps it's the kind slope of her brow, or the way she watches me closely as I speak, as though she is listening to every breath, but I am compelled to carry on, to open up. 'It's like those few hours at work, along with the commute, just exhaust me. It's not even hard, not busy or anything, but just being in the company of that many people for that length of time without being able to escape to calm down or relax for a while gets intense – so when I get home I just shut down, I guess. I think my social battery is considerably smaller than most people's. Every single conversation I have to plan out and practise in my head, and ask myself all of the right questions to make sure I've said the right thing, so it's like my mind has run a marathon before my lips even move.'

Bobble is quiet for a moment, and my blood pressure begins to spike. Why did I tell her that? Why would she ever want to know the strange logic of my brain that doesn't even make sense to me?

'We could go for a walk at the weekend if you'd like? You wouldn't have to talk to me. I can talk enough for the both of us,' Bobble says as if she could hear my own thoughts and she smiles warmly. A wave of calm washes over me. She giggles to herself before saying gently, 'Silent Sunday.'

There's a strange kind of sadness, yet elation, at someone not responding in the way you've always assumed they would. When you've stayed quiet so long, playing over and over all the ways a person can reject you, or make you feel stupid for even opening your mouth, for someone to then just . . . not. I can't help but feel that my brain is sabotaging any prospect of happiness, or even just of calm.

'I'd like that.'

When I reach the moat the next morning the mood from the preceding few days has changed, considerably. When Westley greets us as usual, he drops his theatrics and they are instead replaced with an almost grave formality. Flanked by two other men, he seems to have the fear of a politician standing up to all of the media to confess his controversies, and the two beside him are his advisers, making sure he says exactly the right thing. One of the men looks as if he should be a gangster in a Guy Ritchie film, played by Jason Statham. His bald head gives way to a sour expression on his deeply lined face, though looking barely in his forties, he gives the impression of having lived a few lives already. His eyes rake across all of us with intense suspicion, as if one wrong move would see him rugby-tackle someone to the ground and beat them with a truncheon.

The other is a different kind of intimidating. Considerably younger – I'd say he is only in his mid-twenties – but he towers over the two he stands next to. His dark hair matches his dark eyes and springs from his scalp in a smooth flourish of obsidian that breaks in a wave of strands at the front that, despite his efforts to smooth them back with his wide palms, still fall over his face and tickle at his thick brows. When the stranger finally manages to tame them, a twinge of disappointment hits me, and I find myself waiting for those little rogue strands to return again.

Unlike his friend, his gaze never lands on a single one of us; instead, his eyes either burn holes into the leather of his shoes, or look off into the sky with a clear expression of annoyance. That doesn't stop everyone else studying him like a lost Michelangelo displayed for the public for the first time, though. With features that look so deliberately carved to construct a vision of masculine beauty, so ordered, so perfect and uniform, even I find myself fascinated to be faced with such a stranger.

Once we have all assembled, Westley clears his throat and begins to speak in a shaking voice: 'I would like you all to welcome Mr Theodore Fairfax to the school.' He gestures to the man beside him who dwarfs him in both height and build. 'As he is joining us last minute and it is but a couple of days before our students join us, I was hoping one of you would be willing to, er, mentor him, just get him up to date with the schedule and the like.'

A few hands, mostly those belonging to the women of the group, go up, but Westley's eyes fall to me. 'I was actually hoping that you'd be happy to, Daisy, just as I believe you are the least in need of practice yourself.' You'd have thought I work with a parliament of owls with the speed at which every one of their heads spins on their necks to stare at me like the last mouse at the buffet. Mr Theodore Fairfax himself looks up from death-staring the grass for a moment to fix his penetrating gaze on my face, and my breath catches. Under its scrutiny, I begin to pity the earth for having to put up with such a stinging glare for so long. How neither myself nor the grass have burst into flames under the heat of it perplexes me. When he finally decides he is bored of my reddening features, I desperately fight to reclaim the breaths he had unwittingly deprived me of.

Westley's face looks pleading and I think about it for a moment. The thought of having to spend so much of my time talking to a man who looks increasingly like he wishes to be anywhere but here appeals little to me, especially when I am still smoking from the fire of his glare. But with each second that ticks past without an affirmative answer, Westley fidgets in his boots, so, for him, for the sake of seeing this job through to the end, I nod. He releases an audible breath and seems to regain a little of himself.

Clapping his hands together, our mentor delegates his tasks for the day and we get to work. Mr Theodore Fairfax makes no attempt to come to me, so, with a huff, I walk across the moat to him. Never choosing to be the first to speak in an initial meeting if I can help it, I stand in front of him expectantly. For a moment, I attempt to hold his gaze. His eyes are so dark I can see myself warped and reflected in them, but after only a second I look away and clear my throat. Before I can formulate a sentence, he speaks.

'I won't be needing your help.' His voice is gruff and I am taken aback for a moment at his coarseness.

Standing up straighter, I look over his face – perfectly shaven, though with a shadow of dark hair lying across his cheeks ready to break through. He has a powerful nose, and the classic alabaster brow of a man who thinks highly of himself and is handsome enough to hoodwink foolish others into believing the same.

My stomach churns at the confrontation. Sweat begins to spring on my forehead but my body chooses neither fight nor flight. This anxiety only excites the stubbornness of Alenthaea as her power prickles in my chest and I stand my ground. 'Well, have you done this before?'

'No,' he says, staring intensely at my face as I look anywhere but his eyes.

'Ever used a sword?'

'No.'

'Then you're going to need my help.' I cross my arms over my chest as he scoffs, a sarcastic smile breaking through his lips.

'It's hardly difficult is it, Petal, playing around with toys?'

I falter for just a moment, ready to give in to Daisy, but Lady A refuses to let it go. My heartbeat is so erratic that

I can feel the way my blood throbs in my veins, all the way down my legs.

'My *name* is Daisy.'

He smirks, and I redden.

'Why don't you show me? If it's so easy, *Teddy*.' I grab one of the rapiers from the table and toss it to him in hopes of catching him off guard – he snags it deftly and I inwardly curse. The bald man approaches us, but Theodore raises his free hand and the man retreats back to his corner like an obedient dog. He does look a little like a hairless pug come to think of it.

'I would if I had an opponent.' I raise my own blade to his. 'You?' Theodore doesn't attempt to hide the amusement on his face.

'You scared that I'll show you up?' He leans on his front leg and presents his sword as if we are about to start fencing. Chuckling at his blind – and unfounded – confidence, I raise my sword, preparing for a battle not quite as pretty as the those of the Eton fencing club. 'Lesson one . . .'

Before I can bring the steel down onto his smug face, Westley slides himself between us. 'Whoa, whoa, whoa, what are you doing?' A bead of sweat rolls down his flushed forehead and past his nervously twitching eyes.

'I was just showing him what we do. He doesn't know how to use a sword.' I shrug, my sword still raised.

Theodore huffs a contradiction as Westley leans closer to me, speaking quietly from the side of his mouth. 'Not. This. One.' He looks back at my opponent with an uncomfortably wide smile and addresses him with quivering politeness: 'Don't worry, sir, Daisy here just got a bit carried away. She won't *actually* be fighting you.' He turns back to me, eyes wide, eyebrows drawn tight. 'She's just going to show you how to hold it, and then give you some technical terms. Aren't you, Daisy?'

Now I am suitably confused. He had no issues with me fighting all of the rest of his workers for this whole week, why does he care so much now? I nod anyway, as much as I was looking forward to wiping the smug look off his face, if I want a perfect record, that means following orders.

'Daisy?' he says again, his eyes burning into the hand that clutches my sword.

'Oh . . . yeah,' I say, placing it back onto the table. 'Sorry.' Theodore smirks again at me once Westley runs off to stop Robin, one of the Knight School staff who's a bit more of a liability than the rest, from attempting to sharpen one of the plastic battle-axes.

'Sorry to disappoint, Petal. Looks like you'll just have to try and beat me up another day.' The wink that follows disarms me completely. Without the comfort of an actual sword in my hand, Alenthaea's confidence dissipates and I am back to anxious old Daisy blushing at my feet.

'Come on,' I mutter without looking at him, and we duck down into the closest tent to us. Inside is essentially one giant Persian rug. Conflicting patterns adorn both the floor and the walls of the tent, with bushels of grass peeking between them. The tent is wide and round and there's just enough room for me to stand comfortably, but Theodore stands behind me with his neck bent at an awkward angle – I can't help but feel a little satisfied at his discomfort.

Three long tables occupy the space. We approach the first one and just like the smaller tables outside, this one is lined with one of each sword in Westley's collection – made from actual metal and far too heavy for most adults, let alone children, these are the swords used for display.

Before I have the chance to challenge him to another duel, his little friend punches his way through the doors and stands just feet away, looking ready to pounce on me. As I pick up the first weapon, he steps forward and pulls it from my hand before I can even name it.

'Excuse me?' As soon as I see his face, contorted like the arse of an angry baboon, I wish I hadn't spoken at all.

'Morton,' Theodore begins in a bored tone, 'let the girl play with her toys. If she somehow manages to stab me with a blunted sheet of aluminium then you are welcome to snatch them like a spoiled child. Otherwise, she is harmless.' Finishing off with an eyeroll, Morton takes a silent step back and offers his master a nod. How much money must this arrogant creature have for men to be so obedient? The thought repulses me. Is this what rich people are doing for community service now? Why else would someone with a damned bodyguard be here, awaiting my lesson on fake weapons?

Theodore Fairfax gestures for me to continue with an impatient hand. With a jolt, that sprig of hair falls again over his face. Swallowing down the impulse to reach out and touch it, I remind myself why I'm here, trapped in a room with two insufferable men, in a city that will never feel like home.

Walking slowly down the length of the table I point to each one and tell my mentee their names: 'Longsword, claymore, sabre, spatha, dirk, rapier, great sword.' Theodore resumes his unimpressed expression, but I continue my mumbled lesson. 'Longsword, a sword wielded with two hands, late medieval. Claymore, the Scottish version. Sabre, backsword, curved blade, mostly used on horseback, mostly associated with the Napoleonic wars. Spatha, Roman, double-edged longsword. Dirk, Scottish long dagger. Rapier—'

'The one you just wanted to kill me with?' Theodore interrupts, clearly paying more attention than I gave him credit for before.

'M-hmm,' I agree, and renew my onslaught of facts. 'Rapier, two-edged blade, thrusting sword, sharp, mostly designed for stabbing. Great sword, essentially just a later version of the longsword. Any questions?'

'Yes, why on earth would anyone this side of the Industrial Revolution bother to learn all of this?'

My face burns and I move on to the next table, giving my ungrateful student an equally boring lesson on the types of shields in front of us.

'The first lessons next week are going to be weapons, and designing the crest of your own shield, so it would be good to remember these.'

'You'll be there won't you?'

I nod.

'Then couldn't you just do it?'

'Well, yes, but—'

'Good. I've already forgotten.' He turns and strides out of the tent and I have to suppress the urge to just scream after him.

69

'Who does he bloody think he is?' I mutter to myself, pacing out after him, my fists balled at my sides.

'Oi!' I shout after him, Alenthaea in my blood again. 'Where do you think you're going?' The rest of the camp turn at the sound of my voice, many of them having not heard me utter more than three words in as many days. I can't afford to listen to the alarm bells blaring in my mind at my outburst so I stand firm, arms folded, staring him down.

Theodore turns to me, breaking off his conversation with the bulldog. His dark eyes are blazing. 'Excuse me?' he spits.

'You heard me. I've been told to teach you in preparation for next week, and that is exactly what I'm going to do, whether you like it or not.' With the first week of my probation almost over already and with every one of my steps thus far accurately calculated to make sure it goes as smoothly as possible, there is no way I'm going to let one silver-spoon-hoarding goblin ruin everything with his arrogance. Alenthaea wouldn't let someone else's pride get in the way of her ambition. The leg-trembling adrenaline of confrontation blends with my neurotic fear of failure until my chest heaves with the refusal to back down.

He steps closer to me so his toes knock into my own and I have to crane my neck to look up into his searing expression. With every one of my senses filled with him, my heart rate struggles to keep up with itself as it drums out a messy syncopated beat.

'You will learn very quickly, *Petal*, that I will not be doing a single thing that you, or anyone else in this establishment, tells me to do. It is ridiculous that this is even a job, and even more laughable that you take playing make-believe so seriously that you would have the gall to address me in such a manner.' His words are a stinging slap across my face but I refuse to falter.

'Then why are you here, *Teddy*? If you think you're so much better than everyone else?' His eye twitches again at the nickname and it is my turn to smirk at him.

He leans his face close to me, but I hold firm. Theodore takes a breath as if about to say something but at the last second decides against it. Sucking in another breath, he straightens up, clears his throat and strides back across the moat. He doesn't look back, nor does he stop as Westley jogs after him – in fact, he walks straight out of the Tower, leaving his little friend to follow after him.

My heart sinks as I watch Westley calling after him. Judging from the expression on my boss's face, I can't help but feel like I've done something horribly, horribly wrong.

Chapter 7

'D aisy!' Ellis's voice startles me out of my reverie on my lunch break. He strides across the grass and sits himself next to me in the shade of the Tower wall. I had purposely chosen a space away from the clusters of picnickers so I could make the most of the silent solitude and escape their frequent questions and awkward stares, presumably relating to Theodore, but Ellis – with his cheery disposition – hasn't noticed my slight irritation at being interrupted.

I smile at him as he sits down, and I take another bite of my sandwich in hopes that it might mask some of my revealing facial expressions. 'How's it going?' he asks and pulls out his own lunch box.

The new introduction of a question has made the whole, massive bite of a sandwich thing an absolutely terrible idea . . . I can either chew at an uncomfortable pace and wear my jaw out, or simply reply with the threat of showering him in soggy breadcrumbs. Trying the first option, I curse myself for going for the baguette, and curse the supermarket even more for selling one with the toughness of a strip of leather. Moving for the second, I cover my mouth and mumble a "Sall right".

'I've heard you left a bit of an impression with our royal visitor.' The chewy baguette lodges itself in my throat and I choke on the surprise of his words. Ellis springs to his feet and lands several blows on my back. Once he is satisfied that I am not going to die at the hands of an egg and cress baguette, he returns to the spot beside me and I am almost certain he can feel the heat from my cheeks from there.

'You good?' he asks once I've swallowed a little of my water and I nod.

'W-what did you say before?' I ask, the most attentive I have been to him in the short time of knowing him.

'What? Oh, yeah, I just heard that you'd called out Theodore Fairfax in front of everyone. I'm surprised we've not been told to prepare the scaffold for your treason.' He chuckles to himself, proud of his own joke.

'I mean what *exactly* did you say before?' I press, my mind swimming.

Ellis, confused, answers my question slowly, 'You left an impression on our royal visitor?'

'Royal? You mean that he's just another boarding school boy with an "I'm a king" kind of superiority complex, right?' My heart pounds in my chest and I fill up with regret until it bubbles at my throat. I feel sick. 'Right?' I press Ellis for an answer.

'You didn't know?'

I shake my head erratically.

'He's a working royal. He's the king's nephew. The princess royal's son. Viscount Fairfax.'

No. Oh no, oh no, oh no.

Ellis's mouth moves but I hear nothing. My skull throbs with a surplus of thoughts that I can't organise into anything that makes any sense apart from a collection of words that my mother would tut at me for using.

When his accent finally cuts through the cacophony of my inner turmoil, it does little to soothe me. 'They tried not to make a big deal out of it, but he's had his face in the papers quite often lately so it didn't take everyone long to recognise him. I'm surprised you didn't.'

I'm not. Perhaps if I had paid more attention to the world that I live in rather than the one that only exists in my head and the Village Hall playing field, I might not have messed up as *royally* as I have. Now Westley's reaction makes complete and utter sense. What have I done? In trying my hardest to prove that I am capable, that I am a paragon of employability, I have managed to fail on the biggest, most catastrophic scale yet. I'd have more chance of keeping my job if all I had done was punch my boss in the face. The first week hasn't even reached its conclusion and already I have proven myself to be a disappointment.

'I have heard that he's a bit of a jerk. I'm surprised they've let him out in public after the last few weeks.' Ellis keeps on with his chattering, oblivious to the way I am crumbling before him.

'A real arsehole,' I mutter. The guilt of offending a royal doesn't quite repress my desire to insult him further behind his back. I blame Lady Alenthaea.

'I heard they had him taken back to St James's Palace in a cop car last week and the king met him there directly to confront him. A bit of a party animal by the sounds of things.'

Ellis is interrupted by a few gasps that domino across the moat. Several pairs of eyes flick to us and I colour with the unexpected attention.

Ellis leans closer to me and whispers, 'Is that him?' The sky is sinking to burrow me further into the earth that swallows me in a crushing embrace, so the feeling of his breath brushing my cheek jump-starts the overwhelming feeling of needing to flee, of clawing my way out of the world that is crashing in around me. Too afraid of offending him, and looking like a madwoman for sprinting away and bulldozing anything in my path, I try and breathe to hold on for as long as possible.

In hopes that it will provide some distraction, I follow his eyeline but what I see does little to steady me. Theodore strides his haughty strides into the camp again. Nodding to Ellis, I can't deny the slight relief I feel at knowing that I haven't made him leave for good. Westley toddles behind him, his smile bordering on a grimace and his whole face flushed red. The viscount passes close to us and his attention, which was firmly on the path before him, only diverts to stare me down. Holding my breath, my composure fractures even further under the intensity of his gaze. Busying my eyes on my lunch again, the heat of his stare continues to burn hot on me until he ducks down into the tent again and out of view of everyone.

Finally releasing my breath, I watch the entrance of the tent expectantly – like a traitorous soldier waiting to be called before the king in all of his furs, to be handed his sentence. Ellis talks but I don't hear him. What are they doing in there? Why hasn't anyone said anything to me? Will he get me fired on the spot?

My thoughts are interrupted by Erin and a few of the other Knight School girls physically placing themselves between me and the tent.

'You *have* to tell us what happened in that tent earlier!' one of them who I haven't yet spoken to exclaims.

'What's he like?' another interrupts.

'What did he say to you?' Erin's tone is snappy, impatient, her blue eyes wide and expectant.

All of their voices mix together in an onslaught of curiosity. A low-flying jet rumbles overhead. Schoolchildren laugh on Tower Hill. Voices grow louder, then louder still until I have to cover my ears. It's too much. I never should have come. I never should have tried. I should have stayed in my little house in my little village, in control of my boring little world.

Not looking back at Ellis, Erin, or any of the other girls, I run and keep on running until I slip into a roped-off doorway. Not even light follows through the doors behind me as I find myself in a cool stone archway. Closed in at either side by wooden doors carved with at least half a millennium's worth of graffiti, I run my fingers along their scored surfaces; but tracing the names of vandals long dead and buried fails to distract me.

I am entirely alone but I feel clammy hands raking over my body, prying fingertips prodding and poking, pulling me apart at the seams. I'm too hot. My clothes cling to my body, another suffocating layer I am desperate to tear away. I want it to stop. Why won't it stop? Why did I have to try? They all expected me to fail, I expected me to fail, but why did it have to be so quickly? I am even more pathetic than I thought.

Placing my palms against the cold stone of the sally port to steady myself, I breathe deep and heaving breaths. The warm smile of my brother comes to mind in a haze, the ghost of my father's soft kisses to my forehead ground me, the phantom echoes of my mother's calming words reach me, until finally the noise is quiet and I can think again.

'Look at this one.' Bobble points to an article on her laptop with the headline, *Royally Screwed: Has the viscount finally destroyed the British monarchy?* 'Ouch. Looks like he isn't liked much by anyone.'

After getting home a lot more dishevelled than usual, Bobble made me a concoction of one of her exotic teas and sat with me until I could tell her everything. Since then, she has been lying with me in bed, researching everything she can about The Viscount Fairfax.

I have another article open on my laptop. This one reads: *Vicious Viscount Lashes Out at Reporters During Another Messy Night Out in Soho.* Bobble is right, every one of these articles mentions something about his excessive partying, his run-ins with paparazzi, and the shame he brings to the royal family. It's intense. It seems that every single thing he has done since the moment of his conception is free for me to peruse at my leisure, with none of them encouraging me to make a favourable judgement of him.

'I feel sorry for him.' Bobble sighs. 'He seems sad.' She turns her screen to me and it's filled by a slightly blurred photo of Teddy on one of his famed nights out. His eyes are bloodshot, glassy. His dark hair is dishevelled and his white shirt is stained with red wine.

'I think he's just drunk, Bobble,' I reply, although I know what she's talking about. There isn't a jolliness to his drunkenness, no tipsy joy. 'You wouldn't feel sorry for him if you met him,' I tell her, suppressing any empathy I have for him by reminding myself of his conceit.

'I'm sure I'd be a little grumpy too when I had a bunch of sweaty paparazzi photographing my every move and I couldn't pick my nose without it making the front page.' She's right. With the sheer concentration of articles on offer, I'm genuinely surprised that there isn't at least one where he has snapped and things have ended with a physical fight. 'Surely, you'd have been fired straight away if that's what he really wanted?' Bobble continues.

The Viscount Fairfax didn't emerge from the tent once I had rejoined the camp. Westley was still grateful for me staying late as usual to help him tidy, only having told me to 'try and be a little gentler with Mr Fairfax'. Those words alone renewed all of my desires to show him just how 'gentle' Lady A can be, but I swallowed my pride and agreed.

'I wonder what he's even doing there,' I say, mostly to myself. The Tower is a royal palace, yes, but not a residence that they actually use, or even seem to visit very often by the way everyone has fawned over this royal guest. And why would he be coming here to work? All the man has to do for work is shake a few hands and smile for a few cameras – it seems it's the only place that he hasn't been stalked by paparazzi so it can't be some sort of media stunt to reclaim his reputation.

His black eyes stare at me from my laptop and I narrow my own at him, though it's only a photo. He has already proven that he doesn't care for the job and I refuse to let him ruin my chances. But it's so difficult to control my emotions. It's like anything that happens that I didn't plan deluges me in feeling that just builds and builds until the banks of my façade break and I can no longer hold my tongue. The smallest thing in that moment feels like the end of the world.

For the first time all week, I am dreading going back to work.

Just as the thought of jacking it in before I'm forced out begins to cross my mind, a name flashes up on my phone that brings with it a wave of joy.

'Blood of my blood, sharer of my mother's womb, pain in my backeth of sides . . .' I answer the call.

'Sister, born of my mother and father, and massivest of morons, how are you doing? Surviving?' The voice of my twin acts as some kind of anxiety suppressant; just one word from him seems to make the tension melt away. Though he is hundreds of miles away, I feel at home again.

'Just about. How are you managing to survive without me?' I ask.

'Honestly no idea.' Sam sighs dramatically. 'I tried to tell Rob from work about how I was spending the weekend LARPing. When I elaborated on the whole elf thing he thought I meant that I was spending a nice sunny July weekend working in Santa's grotto in the garden centre. It is *hell* out here.'

'That's it, I'm coming home. However will you live when surrounded by such fools?' My brother laughs and my heart swells at the sound. I have missed him – I've missed them all.

'You're definitely not doing that. Anyways, what's this I hear about you insulting a prince?'

'He's not a prince,' I quickly reply, before mumbling, 'he's a viscount.'

'Prince, viscount, rich boy, posh boy – it's all the same tosh.'

'And anyway, where did you even hear that?' I pause for a moment before a horrible thought washes over me. 'Oh God, it hasn't made it into the papers, has it?' From our research it's clear nothing that Theodore Fairfax touches goes unreported. What if I am the next bout of gossip for their double-page spreads?

'You may have a rat in your camp.' Sam chuckles.

'Huh?'

'Or a Bobble in your flat . . . ?' I glare at my housemate as she attempts to tiptoe out of my room and she gives me a guilty smile.

'Hmm, I'm not sure what's worse: the fact that you're texting my housemate, or that she's ratting me out.' Bobble mouths a 'sorry' but I assure her with a smile and a laugh that I'm not actually angry. If anything, it's quite helpful that someone else is letting my family know I am still alive as keeping in contact via the phone has never been my strong suit.

'So? This isn't your next script for the Fellowship is it, because I'm not sure we'll be able to find anyone willing to play a prince who is under the age of forty-five . . .'

'Not a prince! And sadly, it's real. I am awaiting my order to present myself in the town square to be shamed and then executed on Tower Hill like a traitor.' I recount the day to my brother, just as I had done with Bobble an hour before and after listening in silence for half an hour, he sighs.

'Sounds like a real prick.'

'Yup.'

'I don't think you said anything *that* bad though. And how were you meant to know? If someone expects you to behave in a certain way, they should tell you. I don't get all of this unspoken politeness stuff. What happened to the rules of the round table? Straightforward, no fuss, written down in black and white.'

I murmur my agreement.

'They don't like to make it easy for us, do they?'

'Life would be boring if it was easy. Anyways, I don't think you should treat this guy any differently than anyone else. If he's not there as a royal, why change who you are just to satisfy his ego and treat him like one? Hey, maybe you should give him a bit more Alenthaea; it might knock him down a peg or two.'

Chapter 8

The hot fiery feeling of Mount Doom sits heavy in my stomach as I approach the entrance this morning. Still the first to arrive, I find Westley in one of the tents, glasses perched on the very end of his nose as he flicks through a series of papers.

'Oh . . .' I startle him with my entrance. 'Morning, Daisy.' At first, I assume he is alone, until a second voice follows from behind me.

'Good morning.' Theodore's low timbre stirs the sickness again and all I can do is give him a tight smile. He leans back on his chair, his white shirt open at the collar, and one of his legs crossed leisurely over the other. Flashing a set of perfect teeth, he offers me a suspiciously wide grin and my stomach throbs at the sight of it.

Just as my brow begins to furrow and my hands fidget erratically with the hem of my shirt, Westley speaks again, forcing me to shift my attention back to him. 'I'm glad you're here actually, Daisy. I thought it would be beneficial to have a wee chat about yesterday.' His eyes flick nervously to the figure behind me, and my blood pressure spikes with each passing second. This is it. After working for five whole days, he's going to send me home. Banish me, tell me never to return again. 'I understand that Lord Fairfax and yourself did not exactly get off on the right foot yesterday.'

Looking at the man in question, I notice that the grin has yet to subside, and Alenthaea breaks through my crumbling exterior as I am compelled to roll my eyes. 'Well luckily he has assured me that he is still happy to be mentored by you,' Westley continues. He looks again to Teddy, his relief not quite cutting through the fear of scrutiny. Finally, the crushing boot of failure lets up just enough for me to be able to take a full breath for the first time since I laid eyes on Theodore Fairfax.

'Isn't he kind,' I mumble, my own relief not quite overtaking the dread of spending even longer in the company of a man so arrogant. With the immediate danger past, my trembling gut begins to think of what this truly means. Being in the company of this man for barely an hour yesterday saw me unravel a week's worth of work, of confidence. How am I meant to last for the next three weeks weighed down by *him*? How am I meant to hold my tongue when Pretty Boy's Cheshire cat grin mocks me from the corner, temping me to duel? How am I meant to get through the rest of my probation doing everything right when I am burdened with the progress of a man who would rather besmirch my character and insult my job than fulfil one tiny task?

Now, no matter how much I try, no matter if everything I touch turns to gold, my future rests on His Lordship. My fate is in his smooth, uncalloused, unworked hands, and I hate him for it.

'What?' Westley's voice brings me back into the room.

'That's exceedingly kind of him,' I rephrase.

'Yes, it is indeed. Thank you again, Mr . . . Sir . . .' Westley trails off with a blush.

'Thank you, my lord.' I address Teddy directly, and it's clear that he hasn't been as blind to my sarcasm as Westley has.

'You're welcome, Petal.' He winks. Like a shot of acid, that wink bubbles through me, stinging its way through my every fibre.

'Now, Daisy, I was hoping that you could show His Royal . . . my royal . . .'

'You can just call me Theodore, by the way,' the viscount cuts in with a bored tone as Westley once again fumbles his title.

'Thank you, Lord . . . Theodore.' He blushes again. 'Yes, as I was saying, I was thinking that you could perhaps show *Theodore*—' he says the name as if it's a diamond balancing on the tip of his tongue '—the costumes, perhaps size him up for one of his own? How does that sound?'

Absolutely horrendous is how it sounds. 'Perfect.' I make another attempt to smile.

'Perfect.' Teddy mimics my tone, but this is enough to satisfy Westley.

As soon as I am convinced that he has nothing else to say, I rush outside and attempt to claim some of the fresh air; the proximity to *him* in the tent, the tension of the meeting, my anxiety of losing my job, has made my chest tight and I crave a deep, unlaboured breath.

The moment is interrupted and the feelings flood on back as soon as Theodore steps out behind me. His bulldog bodyguard, Morton, seemingly appears from thin air as he too emerges and I shudder at the thought that he must have been lurking in the shadows, entirely undetected, the whole time.

'My lord?' Teddy raises an eyebrow, a smirk on his lips.

'Don't get used to it,' I mumble, though I told myself to bite my tongue to avoid more trouble, it seems being in his immediacy brings out every single bit of Lady A in me and her vivacity is impossible to silence.

Teddy follows me across to the next tent. This one is filled with row on row of clothing rails, stacked so tightly that cotton tunics and foam armour stick out in several places. Walking along the collection, I pull out a few items, though none of them with their bright colours seem to suit.

'Save your energy, Petal. We are only in here to appease that idiot out there. I'm not wearing any of this. I would rather not become a walking pyrotechnic with all of that cheap nylon.' I ignore him, trying not to rise to his words, knowing my reaction will only lead to a return of that stupid smirk.

Lifting up a khaki-coloured tunic, I don't even suggest it out loud before Theodore snaps, 'Absolutely not.' His rapid rejection catches me off guard and he must notice the expression on my face as he continues, much calmer this time, 'I can hear the headlines already. If I so much as look at that colour, they'd particularly delight in acting as if I'd just spat at a veteran in the street. *Royal family mocks the British Army. Fairfax the Fascist.* Take your pick.' A flash of anger shadows his face for a moment as he avoids my eye to run his fingers over the rack of belts.

'Surely not? It's just a costume.' Taking a closer look at the tunic, it would be a reach to twist something so clearly designed for Halloween or cheap parties into any sort of political agenda.

Teddy scoffs, 'You'd think. But they feed their families with every lie they spread, and they sure love making a meal of me.' Watching him as he avoids my eye, I notice for the first time how tired he seems. His eyes are heavy as they flick over the tables of outfits nervously. He really isn't joking this time – he is actually afraid.

'So, none of it is true?' I ask softly. His gaze hits me with such force I choke under the strength of it.

'I am here to save face, not be interviewed.' His words are clipped, staccato, and they are a stinging contrast to his vulnerable confession. My sympathy dries up.

'Fine, put this on.' I pull the hanger that I had been examining from the rack. 'The Black Knight. This should suit your disposition nicely.' I hold up the costume to his body and he pushes it from him. 'Looks a nice fit too.'

'Didn't you hear me? I am not wearing a costume.' His eyes grow dark as he flits them between the costume and the tent door, before settling on my face.

'Oh yes, I heard you, I just chose not to listen as listening to you would only flatter you, and I'm not here to do that.

I have been given a job to do, and you taking yourself too seriously shall not get in the way of that.'

He raises a dark eyebrow again.

'Changing rooms are just there.' I gesture to the curtain on the other side of the tent and thrust the hanger and its contents into his hands.

I'm unsure if it's the shock of simply being told what to do by a nobody like me, but he actually does it. The tent falls silent as I wait for him to re-emerge. Morton, the fierce guard, stares me down from across a rack of costumes, his emotionless eyes tracking me like a phantom haunting a living foe. 'What are you looking at? Fancy me or something?' Alenthaea bites and I am almost certain I hear him growl in return.

Thankfully, though with a face like thunder, Teddy re-emerges from behind the curtain minutes later, clad in knee-high boots and a black tunic to his knees embroidered with a red dragon on his breast. Crossing his pleather-gloved arms over his chest, he peers at me from under his low brow and I can't help but smile.

'Very nice, Teddy. Suits you.' He rolls his eyes and a little laugh escapes me. 'Now . . .' I scan up and down the tables. 'I just think it needs a, yes, this one . . . a helmet.' I grasp at the most eccentric helmet on the pile. Ram horns twist and frame the face, only enough of it open to expose the wearer's eyes and chin.

'That's where I'm drawing the line. They'd have a field day.' He grumbles the last part so quietly I'm unsure if he meant for me to hear it at all. Resting his full attention on the door of the tent, a nervous twitch on his features, he doesn't even look at me as he pushes the helmet away. With his bluntness reminding me that he isn't actually fun or a good sport, the little glimmer of playfulness, which had seeped its way into my mien, dies out like the beginning embers of a fire that hadn't quite had enough attention to really alight.

'Fine.' I replace the ram-horned helmet with a basic traditional helmet and toss it to him carelessly. Teddy looks between myself and the helmet for a moment, debating what he's going to do with it, and sets it down on the table and leaves the tent again. Releasing a rather dramatic sigh in hopes he would be able to hear it, I follow him out.

The rest of the school have begun to arrive and had clearly been milling around the camp before Teddy made his grand entrance in full regalia and stopped them all dead in their tracks. They stare at the both of us, forgetting all about their tasks at hand. Grunting, Teddy turns on his heel and seems to hide himself with his arms as though his colleagues are not a gaggle of students working a summer job, but a great beastly horde of paparazzi armed and ready to summon a sheet of lightning with their cameras. Pushing past me, he finds refuge in the tent again before, just seconds later, re-emerging clad once again in his smart shirt and trousers.

With that short moment of civility nowhere to be seen, he strides past with the confidence of a king and tosses the costume over my head. In just the few minutes of being on his body, the fabric smells faintly of him – like bergamot and black pepper. Flustered, I rip it from my head as though it could transmit some disease if left too long and I notice a few faces attempting to hide their giggles.

'Did you really have to do that?' I confront him again, though mindful of not attracting too much attention to myself.

'You look a little shocked . . .' His eyes flicker from my face to my hair with a coy smile. My paranoid hands fly up and smooth down what I can only assume is an explosion of static strands standing on end.

Placing an accusatory finger on his chest, I prepare to unleash Alenthaea's uncensored, very much non-PG observations of the viscount. 'You are . . .' I catch eyes with Westley; his face is flushed, his brows furrowed in concern '. . . just great.' Giving him a softer more playful poke than I was intending, I finish my remarks through gritted teeth and pull myself away before it's too late. *Three weeks, Daisy. Three weeks to prove yourself,* I repeat to myself like a mantra to soothe my frustration.

Retreating across the moat, I grasp a few of the worksheets from a nearby desk and swan off to find Ellis's office under the pretence of using his photocopier.

After a few wrong turns and having to convince security that I was not in fact trying to steal the Crown Jewels, I find it. Spying Ellis through the window of the door, I see him chewing on the end of his pen, and peering through a pair of thick-rimmed glasses at a dusty-looking book. For the first time all week, I notice he doesn't have a smile on his face, and he instead wears an expression of intense absorption in his work. His prominent dimples are ironed out into a tense jaw, his forehead lined softly in concentration, and he rubs a palm across his stubbled chin. Whatever it is he is working on engrosses every fibre of him. Not only are his brain and eyes evidently working a million miles per hour, but his whole body seems to be reading along too. Every inch of him is expressive, immersed, and it's fascinating to watch.

While I'm debating whether or not I should bother disturbing him, he notices me and the familiar grin melts onto his face once again. He waves an excited hand to encourage me in and I oblige.

'Well, this is a nice surprise.' His thick accent cuts through the room as I enter. Now I am here, my mind goes blank and I have no idea what I set out to do in coming. It seemed like the only option to get a bit of respite from Teddy, but now the embers of Alenthaea have died and I am back to plain Daisy who forgets how to speak when faced with a real-life interlocutor.

'What have you got here?' He wheels his chair across the office, slips the sheets out of my hand and flicks through them with interest. '"Design your own family crest", "Write a riddle", "Design a mythical monster."' He reads from the pages with an amused smile.

'What were you reading?' I suddenly blurt out, taking myself by surprise. Ellis looks back at his desk and the dusty book still open to its page.

'Oh, that. We're looking for a missing Yeoman Warder.' Pulling up a spare chair, I sit next to him as he pulls out a file of papers. 'When the Duke of Wellington took control of the Tower, he reformed the Beefeaters and made the rule of them being ex-servicemen, in hopes that they would perform better in the job. Before then you could buy and sell your Yeoman Wardership and I guess you could say they did as little as possible.' He flicks through his papers and shows me a photograph of a board of names. 'They started this list that's in the Byward Tower with the Duke of Wellington and from then on, they recorded each new Beefeater by number. We are up to number 430 but there are fewer names on this list than there are numbers and we have no idea who is missing and why. So, it's my job to find out.'

Looking closer at the sheet, my eyes scan the names and numbers. It begins at 1826 and ends with this year. It would take hours of study to notice that all wasn't as it should be. The names are almost as uniformed as the men and women patrolling outside, and it fascinates me that someone, or many people, have taken such time to research a mystery like this.

'How interesting.' I give him a smile, picturing Alenthaea storming through the realm, tasked with finding a rogue Beefeater, struck from the records as perhaps he has some information to get her back home. She finds him in the dark corner of a tavern, his long beard soaked with the foam of his ale and her real task is getting him to speak. Hardened by the world, it is only the point of her concealed dagger, poking into his thigh under the table, that finally convinces him. 'But what if you never find out?'

'There are many things in history that we can never know for certain; we make educated guesses based on the evidence but the exact stories are lost to time. That is the thrill of it, finding all of the pieces of the puzzle just to get one scrap of information closer to knowing the truth. And who knows, there could be new evidence revealed next week, or in another century. Or it could just be some silly mistake that will send people like me mad trying to figure it out and all of the ghosts will be laughing at us.'

'I think that the mystery is perhaps more exciting – it can be anything you want that way. Well, I suppose not in the records you're curating, but in your head. Imagining all of the possibilities is surely the best bit? Trying to get into the minds of people who lived lifetimes ago. Fascinating.'

Ellis chuckles softly and my hands twitch gently at my sides. My eyes flicker to the clock and I realise I have been gone too long. My excuse will be wearing thin so after asking for use of Ellis's photocopier, I return to the camp, a few hundred sheets of paper heavier and having promised to accompany him to the Tube station this evening.

'Where have you been?' a low voice whispers behind me as I attempt to rejoin the group, unnoticed. They have all gathered around Westley for him to give another demonstration on how to joust on a hobby horse. Turning slowly, trying not to reveal that he startled me, I find Teddy leaning down close to me, his breath warm on my neck.

I don't answer him and turn my attention back to the group again.

'When you all return on Tuesday, we shall be opening our school gates for the first time this year. We have not had long to prepare but I have every faith that you all shall give our students the chivalrous education they deserve and watch them leave here as even better young people than when they came.' Trying to listen closely to Westley,

I find myself distracted by Teddy pacing behind me, evidently not listening to a word.

Refusing to let him and his rudeness irritate me further, I turn back to our speaker again.

'As you all know, 'tis not just swords and costumes that we care about here, so I just need to go through this safety pack with you all this afternoon to make sure that accidents are kept to a minimum.' A slight groan travels through the audience and the others begin to take a seat on some of the nearby benches to await the lecture. Moving with the crowd, I divert into one of the tents to retrieve my notebook from my bag and take a seat again towards the back to take notes.

Teddy, having taken a seat on one of the benches close to mine, talks unreservedly to another knight – Alice – about life in the palace. She's a student at one of the nearby universities and has volunteered to be here as part of some history placement – she doesn't seem too interested in her grade at the moment, however, as she gives the viscount her full attention, blinking her wide doe-eyes slowly as she giggles a little too hard at everything he says. Rolling my eyes, I supress the urge to gag. Their voices aren't loud enough to interrupt Westley, but they're close enough to me to pull my attention in their direction until my latest sentences read: *No child should be allowed in any of the tents without you really have a butler and everything? Ugh, I'd love a butler. Did he . . .*

Shooting another agitated glance towards him, I scribble out the mistake a little too harshly. Teddy meets my eyes and as I narrow mine, he winks one of his.

Chapter 9

'So, I walked into the interview with my portfolio in tow, thinking that I had applied to a job in theatre, fixing show costumes and the like, and I suppose it was in a way. They handed me the job there and then, got me to work straight away and it wasn't until I was in a huge van being driven through the Eurotunnel that I thought it was all slightly peculiar. Turns out I'd accidentally joined the circus. Spent all of last summer travelling through the south of France. It was actually quite fun.' Bobble finishes her story with a shrug as though it is just another mundane conversation.

With the first week of work complete, and the last two days being tortured by Theodore Fairfax, Bobble insisted that I actually leave the flat for my day off and have our inaugural Silent Sunday. Whilst walking at least two laps of Regent's Park, Bobble has told me all about her life at university, the various kooky dresses her grandmother would wear to go to the corner shop, and several stories from her gap year that usually end up with her naked or drunkenly stealing just about anything she can find on the street. Now, we are finally resting our legs on a bench at the summit of Primrose Hill. Bobble's mouth shows no sign of tiring, however, and she continues her tales of chaos.

She's lived so many lives already, and we couldn't be more different. Bobble is free – free from herself, from doubt and anxiety. She takes the world exactly as it is and seems to fear none of it. Hearing her talk is like listening to a fairy tale before bed. It is a life I neither want nor have, but it fascinates me, calms me, fills a little gap of excitement. Looking out over the view, I notice that a thick wedge of green separates us from the peaks and troughs of the metropolis in the distance. Couples lounge on the grass, curious dogs rush over to sniff at our legs, and the city looks just small enough, just far enough away, to not feel so terrifying for the first time.

'Is there anything you haven't done, Bob?' I ask, half joking, half actually genuinely curious.

She looks off into the distance for a moment, her first moment of quiet in the hours we've spent together and my first proper contribution to the conversation. 'Well . . . I've never had a birthday party.' Her innocent eyes are wide and full but not sad in the wake of such a sorrowful confession.

'Never? Not as a child?' My mind doesn't need much convincing to draw up the fond memories of hiring out the Village Hall year after year. I'd watch Sam and his friends skid across the lino in just their socks and eat enough Party Rings that every jump on the bouncy castle felt like I was seconds from seeing a regurgitated explosion of pink and white. We'd play game after game. My favourite was always the one that involved shoving as much chocolate in your face as you could, wearing a full winter get-up and using only a knife and fork, which sounds rather odd now I think about it.

'I was always at boarding school for my birthday. My parents have always been busy people so birthdays weren't much of a priority in our household. They used to take me skiing at Christmas instead. Well, they would ski with the partners; I had this lovely au pair, Elise, who would have snowball fights with me at the bottom of the mountain.' Bobble stands up with a grin that doesn't quite reach her eyes as it usually does. 'Well, we had better get back. I'm sure I've positively exhausted you with all my blabbering.'

My feelings are physical by the time she finishes speaking. She'd already told me today that she's an only child from London, and her parents – clearly with money to spare – put her up in her own flat when she started uni so she would have 'enough room for all of her work'. Although, from what I can gather, it doesn't seem like they were exactly struggling for space. But picturing a child so eccentric, so full of life, alone for birthdays, for holidays, deprived of the relationships that have been my greatest treasure, makes my chest ache.

My family have always been the one thing that got me up every morning and made me live every day. They gave me a place to belong, a safe haven, when the world felt too square for my round peg. I almost want to suggest some sort of wife swap, send Bobble home to Mum and Dad, let them fuss over her, cook her dinners, throw her a children's party complete with sheet cake and party bags. Bobble is a free bird, that much is clear, but even the most untethered spirits sometimes need a hug from their mum, or for their dad to tell them he's proud.

'Absolutely not. Far from it.' And I mean it. Her smile grows again and the panic that I have ruined an otherwise perfect afternoon subsides a little. 'Thank you, Bobble.'

'What are you thanking me for?' She chuckles as we begin our walk back.

'For your kindness. You have known me not even two weeks and yet you just . . . get it. It probably won't come as a shock to you that I don't usually have this much luck when it comes to finding friends and I have no idea how to articulate this in a way that will make any sense, but I'm just glad that it was your spare room that we found.' I attempt to cover up my awkwardness with a laugh, and she bumps me affectionately with her shoulder as we walk side by side. The silence between us for the rest of the journey is like Mum's embrace – soothing.

'Ah, sister of mine, what an ugly sight on such a beautiful twilight,' Sam teases as his grin fills most of my screen.

'Cheers, brother. Always a pleasure.' I make a rather obscene gesture before relaxing back into my bed, resting my blistered feet after getting just a little too carried away with Silent Sunday. 'How is everyone?'

My brother's smile takes up most of the screen. A dusting of red facial hair dapples his chin and cheeks in un-uniform patches. Calling him is bittersweet. Seeing his face, hearing his voice fills me up with affection for him, but the affection only makes me realise how much I miss him, all of them. The lost frequencies of his voice that float through the tinny speakers is no replacement for the comforting timbre of his laugh, or the smell of Mum's perfume that she hasn't changed since I was five years old, or the calming pressure of Dad's palm as he scruffs it across my hair.

'All good here. The robins hatched! Dad has been playing Mum – well until their actual mum comes back– and he says she gives him a look that makes him feel like he's being pushed out of his kids' lives . . . I never thought I'd have to remind my dad that a bunch of baby birds aren't actually his children.' I chuckle and imagine the scene. Dad got the sensitivity of the whole household. He's always the first to cry at the 9 p.m. films – the title credits only have to appear on a Pixar animation and it sets him off.

'What's life like in the big city? Have you met any celebrities yet? When's the next Comic Con? I'll have to come down and we can go!' It is the face of Theodore Fairfax that springs to mind: his smirk, his disarming wink, that stupid bit of raven hair that he tries desperately to keep under control – his alluring little imperfection. I debate whether I should tell my brother about the way the viscount shrunk at the thought of the press, how, for just a moment, he was something other than his self-righteous self. Should I tell him that the royal draws Alenthaea out of me, like a moth to a flame? Or that even the thought of him now fizzles feeling in my gut and all I desire is to get him on the battlefield and hand him his arrogant arse on a silver platter? Thankfully, the interruption of Mum's voice saves me.

'Is that your sister?' I hear her in the background.

'Daisy's here? Where?' Dad quickly follows.

'Not here, of course, she's on the phone with Sam.' Suddenly both of their faces appear in the frame. Mum squashes her face against Sam's and Dad's appears in front of them both, upside down as he leans over the phone.

'Hey, darling! We miss you!' Dad grins into the camera. An ache spreads across my chest; all I want to do is reach through the screen to hold them all.

'Simon, shift out the way so we can all see.' Mum softly pats the side of his head and he takes the space next to Sam who is now pinched between them.

'Yes, do all just come and get in my bed with me. Not odd at all.' Sam rolls his eyes and I can't help but chuckle. My bed feels too big.

'How's it going? You need to tell us everything! Any attractive eligible bachelors?' Mum leans in closer and my cheeks must be glowing through the screen. My mind flickers for a moment to Ellis and my blush deepens. Thoughts of Teddy try to squeeze back into my mind, attempting to mock me now even from within my own head – I strike them down.

'Absolutely not,' I insist, much to their disappointment. Thankfully it seems as though Sam hasn't let it slip about my new rival, and the fact he is the nation's most eligible bachelor, and it will stay that way. I don't want them getting any ideas.

'Oh, there must be one! Any new friends? How's Bobble?'

Dad looks around the phone as if he will somehow be able to see a full 360-degree view of my bedroom to spot my housemate. Sam clears his throat, his expression identical to mine only moments ago.

As if she was listening to me from outside the door, Bobble lets herself in and mouths 'You on the phone?' I nod. 'With Sam?' Once I nod again, she hops into my bed and waves into my iPhone.

'Bobble!' Mum and Dad say in unison. Dad, having never met or spoken to my housemate, must have heard so much about her from the other two that he too has accepted her as another member of the family. Is it possible to adopt another child, when said child is now in their twenties?

Last week, I hadn't made a new friend since the Dutch exchange student who came to my school in year seven. Now I have spent an entire day with a girl I've known for barely five minutes, and she's tucked into my bed chatting to my family like my sister – well, like *a* sister. Marigold would never lower herself to socialise with me outside of the requirements of someone living under the same roof. Most surprising of all, I'm not irritated by any of it. I'm not silently hoping she will leave, or exhausted at the sight of her; I am quite content. I have a friend.

The extroverted blonde babbles away into the speaker. Myself and my twin stay mute but for vastly different reasons – I'm glad of someone else relieving me of the pressure of a conversation. He, no doubt, is simply mesmerised by the way her lips move.

'Is that Daisy on the phone?' Richard's voice quietly sounds through the speaker.

'Oh hello, Richard.' The three in Sam's bed share a look of confusion.

'Door was unlocked. You should really keep it bolted; you never know who could just wander in.' Mum rolls her eyes and Sam struggles to hide his amusement.

Richard, our grouchy neighbour, hobbles into frame and pats my dad on the shoulder to make room for him to sit down. Sam is swallowed up in his bedclothes and the fleece jackets of my parents. Although, I'm pretty sure with both of his parents and our seventy-year-old neighbour in his bed, he would happily sink into the covers and never return.

'Hello, young lady,' Richard shouts at the phone. 'You decided you're too good for us yet?'

'Hello, Richard,' I reply, coolly.

'Who's that next to her?' He turns away from the screen, not quite understanding the fact that I can still hear him. 'Five minutes in the city and she's a . . .' I am almost certain that he mouths the word 'lesbian' before Mum introduces him to Bobble who, for the first time, isn't sure what to say.

'Where's Marigold?' I ask. She is the only person within a two-mile radius of my childhood home who isn't squished into the navy sheets of my twin brother's bed.

'She's a busy, busy bee, these days. Off with some more friends, I think. Getting ready together for university. They've been up to Edinburgh this weekend just to get a feel for the city. I think that's the one she's been leaning towards.' Envy scales my chest and lodges itself in my throat. I finally work up the courage to travel three hours from home, and here's my little sister travelling double the distance by herself, just for a fun weekend – she really must think me pathetic for kicking up such a fuss.

After saying 'goodbye' at least three times before remaining on the phone for another half an hour to hear about all of the injuries and ailments of the whole village, I finally hang up the phone, exhausted – in the best possible way.

Chapter 10

Today is the day.

Dressing this morning with purpose, I twisted my plaited hair into a bun, poked a few fake daisies into the braids, and even painted around my eyes with a dark liner to really play up to my desired mysteriousness. After kindly suggesting that 'it sort of looks like Batman if he took off the mask', Bobble fixed it for me over breakfast, so now I look slightly less three musketeers, and a bit more badass biker chick. Although I'm now also covered in glitter so every time I blink, I see tiny grains reflecting in my lashes and I feel almost like a cartoon character that's been hit over the head a little too hard.

The Tube carriage is heaving by the time it stops before me. Men in suits use their briefcases to push me aside and cram themselves into the mass. Not worrying who they touch, or whose space they invade, they push and push until the coat-tails of their blazers are out of the teeth of the doors. With no other choice, I have to wait for the next one, and then the next one, and the next. My hands tremble harder every time a train rumbles through the tunnel and the tidal wave of commuters getting off clashes with the tsunami of bodies bustling in the station – leaving me trapped in the middle, fighting to stay afloat. The fear of the people, the noise, the thought of their crushing touch, the heat, combined with the ever-ticking clock, drowns me.

Lady Alenthaea would never allow herself to be swallowed up in such a sea of selfishness. Any man who would so much as take a breath in her space wouldn't have time to even see the hilt of her sword as it crushed the bridge of his nose. But I can hardly go assaulting businessmen on the London Underground now, can I?

I cannot be late. I cannot fail. Had this all been for me, had I only needed to get the Tube to run a personal errand, or do something for myself, I would have run back up the escalator and hidden under my duvet the moment I noticed that you couldn't see the platform for all of the bodies. But the thing is with whatever *this* is, as soon as it comes to letting someone else down, bringing disappointment to another, there comes this unfounded stubbornness, a renewed sense of duty that forces you to tighten your corset and just deal with it – and if that means vomiting into a Tube platform bin, then so be it.

That's exactly what I do. With that, the sea parts. Instead of pushing past, everyone gives me, and my steaming bin of sick, a wide berth and I am able to gather just enough breath to push myself onto the next train and keep my eyes shut tightly until my stop is announced.

By the time I reach the Tower, the taste in my mouth is acrid, my hands are black from rubbing my eyes, and there is a whole fanfare to greet me. Literally. A few of the Knight School staff had been training for a while in the art of making a noise with a bugle and as I pass them, they straighten their backs, and play their flourish to announce my entrance to everyone.

Unsure whether or not to be offended at the fact they have all just assumed that my smudged makeup is intentional, I pass through without question. Even Teddy says nothing, no teasing comment, no mocking look – he only watches me blankly as I rush to compose myself in the closest tent. Moments later, the fanfare draws me back into the crowd as the opening of the school is announced.

A lanky young man with a bright blue bonnet and giant feather poking out of the top races across the moat with a roll of parchment. He unravels it as a line of children begin to waddle through the raised instruments, swaying from side to side as if their backpacks weigh just as much as they do. Some of the tiny faces are filled with awe, but a young boy towards the middle of the pack bursts into tears, and attempts to race back the way he came, shouting for his mother. The town crier with the scroll clears his throat and begins to call a series of names as each child passes him.

'Abdallah Arun Esquire, Nia Adebayo Esquire, Lily Davies Esquire.' Lily does a little squeal of excitement as her name is called and she leaps towards the crier and wraps her tiny arms around his legs. He breaks character only for a moment to giggle and then clears his throat to continue his list in all seriousness.

When he reaches 'Tristan Huntsford Esquire' a boy of around ten steps forward. His dark hair is slickly Brylcreemed back and he's already clad in a suit of plastic armour that rattles with each of his small steps. Standing before the man who had called his name and towers over him, at least double his size, Tristan folds his arms (or folds them as far as he can over the bulky breastplate) and confronts the town crier with raised eyebrows.

'I am Sir Tristan Huntsford, Knight of the Realm, *sorn protecteror* of princesses, and slayer of big scary dragons.' The boy seems at least six feet larger than he is, and, his childish pronunciations aside, speaks with a confidence of someone three times his age. My eyes wander across the group, looking for one face in particular, to see if he too has drawn the same comparison between himself and the plucky new knight. But it seems that Teddy Fairfax has decided not to grace us with his presence.

'Ah, not yet, good sir. Those who enter my school are equals and only when you have completed my lessons and proven yourself shall you bear your title as proudly as you do now.' Westley strokes his stomach as he walks over to the muster of children whose attentions are pulled in vastly different directions. One child even faces in the complete opposite direction to everyone else, just staring at an empty wall of the Tower.

'My mum says I'm a knight,' says Tristan stubbornly.

'And indeed, you shall be.' Westley places a hand on his shoulder plate and encourages him to join the rest of the pack.

'Welcome, Children of the Realm. You join us here today

at His Majesty's Royal Palace and Fortress, the Tower of London. Before you—' he gestures to us behind him '—are the finest knights in our kingdom . . .' It is only now that I notice everyone else is in costume aside from me and as Westley continues his introduction, I slip through the group and into the costume tent.

'Sneaking off again already?' Teddy's voice greets me as he sits on one of the tables, scrolling through his phone. For a moment, I forget why I've even entered – the single thought that bounces around in my brain like a computer gone into hibernation mode is the fact that this tent really doesn't have much air in it.

'I need to get changed, and so do you.' As usual, he is wearing a shirt and pair of trousers so fine that even as he lounges on the table, he exudes an air of wealth and power. Not waiting for his response, I grab my costume from the rack and slip behind the changing curtain. 'Your little pet isn't hanging around in any dark corners peeping now, is he?' I suddenly think aloud as I slide my shirt over my head, and quickly cover myself with the fabric in a panic.

'Don't flatter yourself,' Theodore replies. 'I had asked him for five minutes alone to prepare myself for what is to come, but alas, here you are.'

Not bothering to ask him to elaborate, or even reply at all, I resume dressing. Still a little nervy of finding the viscount's great beast of a bodyguard lurking in the shadows again, I dress how I used to for school swimming lessons – shimmying about under a towel (or in this case an old curtain I found) and flitting my eyes about erratically just to make sure no one is looking.

'How come Little Miss Perfect was late this morning?' I can almost hear the teasing smile on his face as his voice floats into the changing room.

'How come Lord "No One Tells Me What to Do" is still here, being told what to do?' I reply after I hear the sound of a hanger being pulled from the rail and the zip of his trousers descending.

Teddy doesn't respond right away. Only a frustrated grunt is emitted from his side and I can imagine that's due to him struggling to get his tunic over his overly enlarged head.

'I won't be for much longer,' is the response that follows yet another grunt and a sigh.

'I bloody hope so,' I mutter to myself, as I add the finishing touches to my costume.

'Heard that.'

'Good.' Throwing back the curtain, I find Theodore looking a little more dishevelled than when I left him. Refusing the Black Knight costume I had picked out for him last time, he has attempted to put himself into half a suit of plate armour. Heavy metal pauldrons hang lopsided from his shoulders and his breastplate is unevenly fastened at his sides.

'Let me guess, you have someone dress you in your palace too?' I walk over to him and shuffle around the heavy metal until it is suitably straight and looks a little less like he had fallen head first into a pile of slain knights at the foot of a dragon.

'You'll be surprised to know that we don't swan about in suits of armour and joust in the courtyards anymore, so forgive me for not being an expert.'

I pull the buckles at his waist a little tighter than I should and he lets out another deep grunt, but attempts to pass it off as a cough.

'There.' I knock on the chest plate once I'm satisfied with my work and leave him to rejoin the school, this time suitably dressed and ready for anything.

Well, perhaps not everything.

Blinking through the bright sunshine, it's the sound of screeching that greets me before I can fully perceive the scene I have just walked into. When the floating specks have cleared from my vision, I am met with what I can only describe as a scene from *Lord of the Flies* that the editor swiftly deleted. Westley's feet, relieved of his shoes and sporting only a pair of bright blue stockings, peek out from a circle of tiny bodies as they skip around him. The rest of my colleagues are spread out across the moat, chasing other students as they flee in possession of various weapons. Thankfully, the table that has been ransacked is only a selection of plastic swords and shields but it seems in just five minutes, we have a major coup on our hands.

It wouldn't take a genius to guess the ringleader. Clearly Sir Tristan didn't take too kindly to having his title disrespected by the master, and he now stands on a chair in the centre of camp with his sword raised above his head in triumph.

'For the love of Odin,' I mumble to myself. I had hoped to have as little interaction with the children as possible, aside from teaching them how to safely hit their sibling with a plastic sword, obviously. But it looks like it is up to me to intervene before the entire Tower is occupied for the first time in its millennium . . . by a bunch of nine-year-olds.

As I steal away into the tent to retrieve my bag once again, Teddy opens his mouth to say something, more than likely something annoying, but I grasp the thing I need and flee before he has the chance. Being in such proximity to him draws Alenthaea out of me as if she *is* me. The sight of him makes my heart race with the adrenaline of her preparing for our battles in what she knows will be a long war. Right now, I'm grateful of her confidence as I redirect it from him, to the mayhem of the camp.

Clasped tightly in my hand is a horn, moulded to look like an ivory tusk; the smooth pearly plastic curves upwards and is hollowed in the middle. Wildflowers are painted in muted pastels along the whole of the outside and a lilac ribbon is fastened to each end so it can be slung over my shoulder in battle. Pursing my lips over the thinner end, I blow hard into the horn and a deep call is propelled from the other end.

Silence falls across the moat as each set of eyes is cast onto me. Faces begin to peer over the Tower walls to discover the source of the noise. Perhaps dinner ladies should invest in one of these instead of a school bell or whistle . . . Westley takes the moment of calm to peer out from behind several pairs of Spider-Man trainers and blinding Lelli Kelly shoes; his basset hound eyes have only increased in their wideness and look of fear.

Faltering with the attention, I freeze for a moment, unsure of what to do next, but as a few voices begin to resume their noise it is Alenthaea who returns to finish the job.

Grasping the only remaining sword on the table, I point to a patch of the grass that is scattered with cushions and my voice seems to come from somewhere else within me: 'ALL PROSPECTIVE KNIGHTS MUST FOLLOW THE ORDERS OF THEIR COMMANDERS. ANY SQUIRE CAUGHT MISBEHAVING WILL BE SENT WITH NOTHING BUT A SHIELD TO FACE THE GREAT RED DRAGON . . . er . . . MOLAX. WHEN I SOUND MY HORN AGAIN, YOU MUST PRESENT YOURSELF ON THE CUSHIONS BEFORE ME TO HAVE YOUR NEXT QUEST BESTOWED ON THEE.'

Giving the horn another forceful blow, the children, and the staff, scramble across the field and sit before me with their legs crossed, arms folded, and guilty expressions plastered on their faces.

Sam was right: this lot really are no different to the Fellowship. Threaten them with a dragon and they will do as you please.

Chapter 11

With all of the tiny knights assembled, Westley takes centre stage. Ever the thespian, he paces the patch of grass at the front as though soliloquising to his captive audience.

'Knight, o'knight, what maketh thou a knight?' Each child seems to tilt their head in unison, trying to figure him out. 'Is thou a knight because of thy family? Or the coins of gold in thine purse? Nay, a knight is only a knight when thou hath more honour than coin, more valour than titles, more principle than pride, and more love for the people than thyself.' Westley looks over the sea of confused faces and realises for the first time that he is speaking to a bunch of primary schoolchildren, not the Somerset Jousting Association. I, however, am thoroughly enthralled. Managing to squeeze myself between two little boys who had more interest in plucking the grass, all of my daydreams feel as though they are becoming a reality.

Feeling more of a child than all of the people here who

were born after the last Harry Potter film was released – a thought that both disgusts and terrifies me – I watch open-mouthed, my fingers twitching for my sword. The more he speaks, the more I'm reminded of all of the bedtime stories that would keep us awake for hours as Mum and Dad created whole fantasy worlds every night to transport us into the land of sleep. They'd re-enact sword fights at the ends of our beds, have weddings, perform magic. With every word, I feel more at home than I have since I left.

'The Code of Chivalry is the lore that knights have abided by for millennia. Before thy hands are burdened with weapons, thou must first prove thyself a worthy knight, and prove thyself a disciplined soul.'

As if to test me, the universe sends me my antagonist. Theodore Fairfax finally emerges from his tent, running a hand through his dark hair. Onyx eyes scan the scene before him, uninspired. He is perhaps the one who needs the lesson the most, learning to be chivalrous, disciplined, to have more 'love for the people than thyself'.

More content to play the villain, he spots me and, with a smirk gracing his face, he walks around the crowd towards me. Rolling my eyes, I attempt to focus back on Westley as he begins to list the commandments. I'm hoping that Teddy has actually spotted a friend as insufferable as he is and diverted his course.

'Perhaps one of the most important of the codes is to "protect the honour of fellow knights." Each person sat or stood on this ancient ground right now is an equal. When you are in trouble, when a day comes where you need the aid of a friend, your valiant comrades will be there, but only if you first have been there for them in a time of need.'

I feel Teddy's presence before I see him, his dark shadow falling over me in a chilly covering devoid of sunlight. Even from the featureless outline, I can just tell he has that stupid smirk stitched into his face, awaiting my discomfort, praying for my annoyance.

Not allowing him the satisfaction, I focus my attention on Westley, barely. Clearly he's disappointed at his inability to intimidate me, and I hear the fabric of his costume, the grinding of his armour as his shadow retreats, but his presence remains. Kneeling behind me, Teddy leans forward until his face aligns with my own as our eyes fix on Westley. His thick hair tickles my ears, sending a jolt of ice down my spine, and I have to grip to my pride to prevent leaping away from his closeness.

'A noble knight must never refuse a challenge, and once a venture has been accepted, thou must persevere until the end. A good knight never gives up in the face of adversity.'

'Do you get your horn out often?' Teddy whispers lowly. 'Or just for special occasions?' Like fire to brimstone, his challenge lights Alenthaea and she burns in me. Straightening my back, I press my shoulders against his chest with the intent of confrontation – refusing to concede to his clear test of will.

Gritting my teeth, I clutch at my composure. 'Why? Would you like a private performance?'

He chuckles, his breath hot on my neck. 'No, I'm just wondering what else you've got hiding in that bag, Queen Susan. Perhaps a bow and arrow, or even Aslan himself?'

'Hilarious,' I quip, trying to focus on the lesson again. No one else seems to notice Teddy's proximity to me, but no one else can hear how my heartbeat rattles around my skeleton. He taps the boy next to me on the shoulder and points for him to move. Obediently, the child follows his command and opens the space beside me, which Teddy fills before I can catch my breath to protest. He is so close now that his wide shoulders reach out and press against mine, paralyzing me under the spell of his touch.

'What are we learning?' he bends his face to mine to ask.

'If you listen, you might just find out.'

'A noble knight must never tell a lie. Thou must endeavour to tell the truth, no matter the cost,' Westley continues.

'If that is so, then if you're a noble knight, you must tell me what you're thinking right now,' Teddy presses again.

'I am thinking that I would like my personal space back, preferably with you back in your little royal tent over there.'

'Come on, Petal, I'm just trying to be friendly.'

'Didn't you hear? Noble knights aren't meant to lie.'

'I never claimed to be noble.'

Struggling for a comeback, I search for the words as I stare at him. His eyes stay locked ahead, though I know he isn't listening to a word Westley says.

Satisfied that he has succeeded in intimidating me, he stands to leave.

Alenthaea has few codes of her own: 'survive at any cost' pretty much blurs any lines of morality and makes most other codes redundant. But I have broken one of the most important: 'never be distracted by a man'.

I finally tune back in to Westley and refocus on my task. 'The final of our codes today is "never turn thy back on thine enemy".' Naturally, I scan the moat for my own rival, awaiting another surprise attack. But I see him stood at the very back beside Morton. Stony features freeze his face – no cheeky smile, no teasing wink in sight. They are both stood in silence, as though they are two strangers beside one another waiting for a bus. Seeing him now, from this distance, I note that he has the same cold look that he has in the newspapers – as though one word to him would make him lash out. I wonder if Morton has given him any news, a new headline perhaps? I suppose he was right to fear being caught here by the press. It's probably a good thing he didn't wear the Black Knight costume – they'd have relished in that one. Monty Python puns galore I could almost guarantee.

I let out a slight giggle at the thought and Teddy's dark stare catches mine for a moment. The intimacy of our gazes shocks me like a bolt of current and my attention leaps back to Westley again. My heart pounds in my throat.

'Though for our twenty-first-century knights, we shall take this to mean "befriend thine enemy". Usually 'tis our enemy who needs our help most. Be a friend to those who push thee away.'

'Where are you sneaking off to?' If my eyes roll any more, I'm sure they will get stuck. Teddy has to jog to catch up with me just as I reach the Bell Tower.

Still not quite a fan of spending my lunch half hour making small talk with the people I work with, I had planned to find some peace inside the Tower. Today with the added racket of several children, said peace is needed more than ever.

'Who are you meant to be, my bodyguard?' I retort. Teddy brushes my shoulders with his own as he squeezes close to me to keep up through the crowds. His own bodyguard stalks a few paces back, though is cautious not to follow closely enough to hear our conversation.

'Just checking that you're not trying to leave me with all of the work.'

'Please,' I scoff, 'you wouldn't know the meaning of the word "work" if it was handed to you on one of your silver platters.'

'Come on, it's a full-time job being this handsome.' We stop dead outside Traitors' Gate and I stare at him for a moment. He holds his cheek in his palm, flashing a boyish grin, and wafting his long lashes like a prize pony. I can't control the spluttering laugh that bursts from me.

'This is what us taxpayers are paying for is it?' Still holding his pose, he attempts a nod. 'I want my money back.' Dropping his hand back to his side, he resumes his rigid posture, eyes narrowed.

'I'm sure that somewhere that would be considered treason,' he jokes, unable to control the slight smile behind his faux seriousness.

'Well, we're in the right place for that.' I point to Traitors' Gate behind me. A portrait of Lady Jane Grey as she is blindly thrust towards the execution block is printed onto a sign overlooking the murky water gate below – a melancholy reminder of the innocents who had passed through this very gate just centuries before, never to leave again.

'Oh my gosh. That's the king's nephew,' a voice half whispers from behind us. 'You know the one – always in the papers, likes a party. Pretty sure he was sleeping with that singer you like. What was her name?' Teddy's face hardens. With his jaw tense you can see him grinding his teeth. Keeping his eyes on me, any hint of amusement is gone, and instead a terrifying callousness spreads over his features. With shadows falling over his high cheekbones, his dark eyes only grow darker as they swim with fury – now he looks like his tyrant ancestors, powerful, ruthless. He looks like a king.

'Come on.' Pulling him by the wrist, I manoeuvre us through the crowd that has begun to form. If I weren't slightly unnerved by his silence, and his unfeeling expression, I think I'd pity him.

Passing under the archway of the Bloody Tower, we come face to face with the White Tower herself. Not able to pause and soak in its beauty, we push on until we reach the Chapel of St Peter ad Vincula. The Beefeater who guards the entrance stirs from his chair at the sight of two knights rushing into his holy ward – a scene reminiscent of the assassination of Thomas Becket. The Beefeater clearly decides against exerting himself too far and instead of assessing any threat of a copycat attempt at a twelfth-century murder, he sinks back down and reopens his newspaper.

Despite its diminutive size, the chapel is bright and airy. I'm not quite sure what I had expected, but I certainly didn't expect a place built over the bones of disgraced headless queens, traitors, and those lost to history, to feel so . . . charming. At the very least, I had anticipated a few Gothic arches, definitely a handful of cobwebs, and maybe even the glowing ectoplasm of a disgruntled ghost lighting up the shadowy corners. Alas I am disappointed.

Instead of pews, uniformed wooden chairs face towards the altar. Teddy and I walk wordlessly between them. Not a single syllable has been uttered by him since our interruption, but he doesn't protest against my company. Though both of our bodies remain tense and unyielding, he seems to trust me and follows each of my steps closely.

Silence is my friend. No noise, no expectation of conversation, is where my erratic mind can rest. But Teddy seems to stew. Though his black eyes see nothing before him, his jaw flickers with pressure, his whole face splintering into a picture of pain.

'Do you like gory stories?' I utter into the tranquillity of the chapel, which only murmurs with low tones of whispered speech. Teddy looks at me for a moment, as though he hears my voice from within a dream, but he gives no reply. 'That crest right there . . .' I point to the floor next to the altar '. . . is the gravestone for James Scott, the Duke of Monmouth.'

I have been doing a little research in my downtime, in hopes that I could feel a bit more up to speed when Ellis tells me stories of the Tower. Well, 'a little' is a tad of an understatement. I can never just do anything by halves when it comes to research, and the last two nights I have been awake until the early hours scrolling in the infinite pools of Google. Having now admitted that, I realise how embarrassing it is.

'He was terribly popular, an illegitimate son of the very popular King Charles II – you know . . . the *Horrible Histories* one?'

Teddy watches me with contempt again.

'No, okay. Makes sense for that to not be fit for palace viewing. Anyway, Charles died without a legitimate heir and his Catholic brother took the throne. Scott staged a rebellion that ultimately failed and ended up with him taking up lodgings in this very fortress and prison. There's a great deal more to that story but that's not the interesting part.'

Teddy doesn't look interested in any of it. He barely raises his eyeline from the patterned stones before us. In all honesty, I have no idea why I am attempting, though not in the most successful way, to raise his spirits. I suppose I know what it is to be judged, how unfairly in this case I couldn't comprehend, but royalty or not, no one deserves to have their story written without them.

'It's his execution that went down in history. Though condemned as a traitor, he was still tremendously popular insofar as all of the axemen in the city refused to be the one to relieve him of his head. So, the task was given to Jack Ketch, part-time hangman, part-time butcher, full-time drunk. It went just about as well as expected. The protestant hero was hacked to pieces but even after five blows, his head still wasn't severed. As a beheading is only legal once the head is off, the butcher had to get out his knife to finish the job. They only realised after the fact that Scott, as the son of royalty, was required to have his portrait painted, so they had to sew him back together again to sit for the artist.'

Getting a little too excited by the gore, and even more enthusiastic at getting to use my new-found knowledge, I grin up at him, awaiting his reply.

Seconds pass. My face melts to a reddened mess; Teddy's only stiffens. 'Why are you telling me this?' He seems to grow with each tightly pronounced word, until he towers over me with his scorn.

It's only now that I realise that I wasn't relying on Alenthaea as my crutch. I had waded out too deep by myself, allowed my confidence to grow, and it's his tone that reminded me that I don't know how to swim. 'I-I just thought . . .' is all I can muster before he speaks again in a voice as hard and cold as a steel blade as it plunges straight into the warmth of a fired belly.

'You thought I needed pity?' Venom drips from him, his words, his manner – like a man possessed by one of the conceited spirits that inhabit these walls.

'Pity? No, no – it's just a story. I—' Not bothering to hear the rest of what I have to say, he leaves me at the altar like a bride scorned.

Chapter 12

'If there be one thing in battle more important than your ability to run away, it is your ability to defend yourself. Now can anyone tell me what is the most imperative thing that a good knight must never be without?' An array of hands shoot up at Westley's question. An excited little girl, Lily, flaps hers so manically I am sure she is about to take off.

Teddy didn't return yesterday, after his little outburst that elevated him from 'arrogant prick' to 'genuine arsehole' he took himself away to do whatever a royal does on a Tuesday afternoon. He was on the front cover of a newspaper someone had left on the seat beside me on the Tube into work this morning. '*Fairfax Favours the Blonde?*' was the headline that hung above the photo of the viscount with his arms wrapped around the waist of the eponymous blonde – his familiar look of loathing still etched into his features as he stared down the lens of the offending camera.

Thankfully, with him gone, the afternoon continued

without much of a hitch; except the sick feeling that grew in me after his departure from the chapel hasn't quite left me yet. I know he's here now, and every face that passes makes me jump – none so far have been him. Today's lesson pushes on without him – for the distraction, I'm grateful.

'Yes, you, young mistress.' Thankfully Westley chooses Lily to answer before she pulls a muscle. She has to catch her breath before she can answer.

'A pony,' she says, still panting with the excitement.

'Now one's noble steed – a horse – is an integral part of one's knighthood, you are correct, but there is something even more important. Any other ideas?'

'It's *obviously* a sword.' Tristan doesn't bother to raise his hand and answers in a bored tone.

'Ah, it is not a sword. A knight must first learn how to defend before they attack. There is no point knowing how to wield a sword if your opponent swings theirs first and you have no idea how to fend them off. And all good knights must also learn to raise their hands if they wish to speak to the assembly.' Westley shoots a glance at Tristan and shows another side of him that I have yet to see – the side with a backbone. The tiny knight huffs and crosses his arms over his chest – I can imagine the plans for another coup are already forming.

'The most important thing a knight can carry is their shield.' Westley continues, 'Never underestimate the power of a shield. When you're on a battlefield and a flock of arrows are fired from the high ground and are descending on you like a plague of pain, it is your shield, not your sword, that can help you. When you have fallen, what is the use of flapping your sword around, not able to reach the enemy looming over you? 'Tis your shield that will be of most use. Therefore, today, we shall be designing and making our own. On each of our shields we shall make a family crest, using pictures of things that represent your family most. You will be able to ride into battle with the constant reminder of why your bravery must triumph.' Each of us takes a stack of sheets, printed with the blank outline of a shield, and hands them to each of the children as they move over to the picnic tables.

Teddy Fairfax finally emerges from his royal tent and has almost joined the group. He looks a little worse for wear today. With a pair of sunglasses covering his eyes, he hardly looks up from his phone. Attempting to squeeze his long legs under the picnic table, he soon gives up and instead straddles the bench, his wide back facing the student next to him. It's a doe-eyed boy, slightly younger than the rest of the group, who has the misfortune to be partnered with him for this task. Barley is his name if I remember correctly, and he looks as if just the piece of paper in front of him is enough to scare him. With wispy blond hair and enough freckles to cover his whole face, he is an archetype of childhood innocence. He looks fit to burst into tears with each glance he shoots in Teddy's direction.

'Daisy. Can you do me a massive favour?' Westley pops up behind me and speaks in a hushed tone, distracting my stake-out of the viscount.

'Yes, anything, of course,' I say a little too energetically – the people-pleaser in me excited to prove myself.

'Please can you stay with Mr, er, Vis— Lord Fairfax during our lessons? I think he may need some encouragement to be involved and since your little disagreement you seem to have grown close.'

Close? Westley really is a glass-half-full kind of guy. Either that or he's just terrible at reading the room. Likely both.

Curse my fear of disappointing. 'Er, yeah, sure.' I can only hope that the viscount hurries up with his plans to leave, or in some miracle, he has a total personality transplant and discovers an ability to work hard so I don't even have to utter two words in his direction. It's just until I pass my probation, just until I've proven myself – no matter how much I keep reminding myself, I still can't let myself relax.

Westley claps me on the back with a wide smile. 'Knew I could count on you!' And he skips off to continue his class.

Throwing my legs over the tiny bench, I take a seat opposite *him* and attempt to busy myself by watching the little girl next to me drawing what I can only assume to be an elephant, or perhaps a donkey, on her template.

'Just can't keep away, can you?' Teddy leans forward so his folded arms press against my own. His usual mischievous tone has returned, as if yesterday never happened at all.

'Don't flatter yourself.' I use his own words against him. 'I've been ordered to keep you in line. A babysitter, if you will.' Alenthaea takes over.

'Is that right?'

'Yes. Somebody needs to keep you in check.'

'Don't worry, Petal, people have been trying for years.'

He leans across the table and whispers so close to me that no one else could hear even if they tried, 'If you're one of those girls looking for a broken man to fix, you're welcome to try, but you'd only be wasting your time.' He straightens up with a smirk and turns his back on Barley again to resume whatever is so interesting on his iPhone. Flustered, Alenthaea betrays me for a moment and I sit frozen, looking at his side profile. The colour of his eyes is so vivid that despite the distance he's placed between us, it feels as if he is so close that I would only have to twitch for my lips to stumble onto his. Shaking my head, I try to throw out the thoughts that are making my cheeks burn. Reminding myself of my promise to Westley, I compose myself as much as I can.

'You have to help him you know.' I gesture to the young boy and his eyes widen even more than I thought was possible. Teddy glances at him and places a hand on his shoulder, swallowing his whole clavicle in his palm.

'You're just fine, aren't you, young man? You don't need my help, do you?'

Barley shakes his head frantically, then nods, then attempts a kind of nod-shake.

Not wanting to encourage any more interactions that may result in a crying child at my table, I allow Teddy to continue in the same fashion, hoping Westley will just assume he's working if he isn't off somewhere else. And it is quite nice to not have to listen to the sound of his voice too. Though, the less he speaks, the more I find myself watching his lips, awaiting their next movement.

Trying not to worry too much about whatever trouble

he will be causing us both, I attempt to focus on my own student, Fatima. By the time she has filled in her shield, the elephant–donkey hybrid has actually turned into some sort of trunked cat, a strawberry occupies another corner, a pink and orange flower in another, and a castle finishes it off. Although the wooden table is now speckled with a rainbow of felt-tip pen, it's not too bad.

Once Fatima skips off to hang up her masterpiece on a board, I hear the small voice of Barley tremble out a sentence for the first time. 'Is th-this okay, t-teacher?'

Teddy doesn't even look at the boy, only replies monotonously, 'Just go and put it with the others.'

Barley doesn't need telling twice, he slides off of the bench and hangs his work with the rest.

'You really should try and make more of an effort, you know,' I say sharply.

'Petal, I could list off right now at least one hundred things more important than this that would actually be worth expelling my effort upon.'

'Well why aren't you doing those?'

'Because I am here.'

'Why are you here?'

Before he can answer I am distracted by a loud gasp coming from the noticeboard. The children have all gathered around, their inquisitive eyes staring at the work of their peers. Westley stands before it, his face a picture of horror. Rushing over to the scene of the crime, I know straight away what the problem is, and all I can do is gawp.

In the very centre of the wall of shields is one whose centrepiece is rather pink, rather detailed, and incredibly phallic. Snatching it down, Westley demands the name of the artist, only for sweet, innocent Barley to raise his hand. My boss falters for a moment, us all perhaps sharing the same idea of the culprit most likely being the unruly knight Tristan.

'Come, over here, child.' The three of us walk back over to the table we have just left and Westley places down the picture in front of Teddy. He glances over it, does a double take, and chokes through a snigger before composing himself again. 'Now what is this that you have drawn here?'

'A snake.' Barley squeaks out and myself and the interrogator breathe a sigh of relief. 'My mummy has one in her bedroom that she says only she is allowed to play with. It even moves and makes a noise!'

The silence is deafening.

Even Teddy is at a loss for words. Barley's eyes like saucers flick between the three of us, waiting nervously for any kind of reply.

After a few more moments of silence, Westley clears his throat. 'I think we will have to show this picture to Mummy tonight. You go back and join your group – there's a good lad.' Barley, as obedient as ever, leaves us and busies himself plucking some of the daisies from the grass.

My cheeks burn hot. Unable to tell if my embarrassment stems from the obscene picture that seems to glow from the page before us, or the disappointed gaze of my superior, my eyes find a patch on the grass. I watch the bead of sweat that has tickled a damp caress down my face as it drops into the blades and disappears in the exact same way that I wish I could.

'I cannot believe that this has been allowed to happen. Did no one think to ask him what he was doing? Was no one watching him?' Stealing a glance at Westley, I see his full attention and his words are aimed at me. My own burning complexion is mirrored on his. He too struggles to maintain any sort of eye contact. 'I expected better of you, Daisy. Had someone else seen that, we both would have been gone. God forbid any of the other kids tell their parents.'

My throat feels tight. I genuinely think I could have taken a punch to the gut better – it already feels as though I have.

My internal self-flagellation is infiltrated as Westley speaks again. 'I am afraid this will have to be your first official warning, Daisy. Company policy states that after three warnings, I will have to terminate your employment at the end of your four-week probation so please do keep that in mind.' How can I explain that keeping this job has been the only thing on my mind, the thing that has been keeping me up at night, when I stand before him now, disgraced?

'Oh, and you both shall stay behind tonight to launder the uniforms ready for tomorrow.' Westley finishes with a sigh. His voice sounds so far away yet so loud he could be screaming in my ear.

'Oh, I don't think that will be necessary. It is entirely my fault.' The only thing preventing the meltdown that is usually imminent post disappointment is Teddy Fairfax. His voice takes me by surprise, his words even more so.

Well, they are truthful; I just hadn't anticipated *him* actually owning up to it.

'I asked Daisy to supervise this table, sir. I am afraid it is protocol.' Westley, unable to continue his jolly façade, wears his disappointment on his face and walks off to resume his classes without another word.

He's right, though. He had given me a job and I failed – all out of spite.

'Daisy, I—' Teddy starts but I walk numbly back to the group.

I can't say a word for the rest of the afternoon. My mind swims with his words '*I expected better of you*'. It's worse than your parents telling you that they're 'not mad, just disappointed'.

My only achievement in the last five years is getting this job, and it wasn't even me who applied for it. Yet here I am, just days into it, and I have almost lost it several times already. I never wanted to come. I never wanted to leave home. If I hadn't come, I wouldn't be fending off another panic attack in a new city over failing at a job I didn't even want. I am so used to being the failure, to being the one going nowhere, and I feel the fool for ever hoping I could show anyone anything different.

By the time the afternoon ends, I haven't said another word. Silently observing the children, I still make sure we have no repeats of the 'snake' incident but Alenthaea has well and truly disappeared into the ether. My voice is corked, and I am in complete danger of an emotion overload if I try and shift it to talk.

Teddy has retreated back into the costume tent and I

can't bring myself to hunt for him, the persistent throbbing in the base of my stomach wouldn't allow me anyway. As I'm unable to look Westley in the eye either, the day is lonely. It's like everything I had feared.

Chapter 13

'All you need to do is take this trolley down to the laundry room on Mint Street and stick it all on the wash and dry cycle. Then just hang it up on the rail when you bring it back here. Really simple. May take a little while, but you should be able to manage.' Westley hands me a jumbo pack of detergent tablets and taps the side of the laundry trolley.

Still unable to squeeze out a word, I nod. Satisfied, Westley picks up his messenger bag and salutes us before turning and leaving me alone with Teddy once more. He hasn't attempted to speak to me again. Still barely looking up from his phone, he talks in clipped, vexed phrases to Morton. The bodyguard pretends as though he had just arrived to collect Teddy, like all of the other parents coming for their children, but I've noticed him lurking all day in the archways of the Middle Tower and in the quiet corners of the moat — observing his ward from a distance.

Not waiting for him to get me in any more trouble, I

plonk the detergent into the basket and make an attempt to push it across the grass. Twenty-five knights' costumes are considerably heavier than I had anticipated. Judging by the state of the wheels, I wouldn't be surprised if this trolley was left over from when this place was a Victorian garrison and used by maids to ferry hundreds of red coats to the wash houses. The rust is thick across the spokes and the tyres are worn almost to nothing and thus turn at a pace similar to the speed you'd get pushing it through tar.

To many I wouldn't look particularly fit, but under the softness of my thighs, the pouch at the bottom of my belly, and arms that are a dress size larger than the rest of my torso, are a whole load of muscles that I have only cultivated from swinging around a sword since I was about five years old. Not one person in my family has ever stepped foot in a gym; in fact I think we'd all rather take on an army of barbarians with only a ladle than ask the gym bro on reception for a membership, but the only reason we are not all boasting abs is because my dad is far too good at cooking, and far too liberal with the garlic oil. It turns out fighting your family is a brilliant form of exercise.

For a moment, I am Alenthaea, and after losing my horses to the murderous terrain of Mount Oldrid, I push my cart up the rest of the summit. I could have given up, allowed it to splinter off of the rocky face as it tumbles back below the clouds. But I promised the mountain elf tribe that I would bring them supplies, magical healing potions, weapons, all in exchange for information on the whereabouts of the orc tribe, and their allyship for when I reclaim my throne. I refuse to let them down.

The stuck wheels cut through the grass as I grow more and more damp with each exerting push. My hands slide from the handles but after a swift wipe across my trouser leg, I manage to reach the concrete ramp out of the moat. Stealing a moment for breath, Teddy finally catches me up. Managing to insert himself between me and the cart, he pushes it up the incline with ease and stops at the top with a smug look.

'Nice of you to help once I had done the hard bit,' I mutter, still catching my breath from the low ground.

'Don't lie to yourself, Petal – you were never getting it up there by yourself. You're sweating on me from here.'

I toy with the idea of climbing the ramp to push the cart back down, just to prove him wrong. Sadly, my slight touch of asthma defuses my pettiness.

'Whatever.' With a faintly wheezy huff, I scurry ahead of him. If he wants to play gallant knight, then, oh look, I am just too weak and feeble a maiden to help him.

Trundling along the path, the trolley spits out a screeching racket of metal grinding against concrete but it abruptly stops just as I reach out to grasp the handle of the door. Checking that the viscount hasn't run off to polish his tiara, I turn back around to see him struggling to manoeuvre the cart over the cobbles. I watch him for a moment. His perfectly groomed hair has flopped into his eyeline during the brawl and with a frustrated huff, he rolls up the sleeves on his pristine shirt and unbuttons the top two buttons – I assume in an attempt to extinguish some of the redness that has crept over his face. The look suits him. His skin glistens with the exertion, there's colour in his face – he actually seems rather human, as opposed to the heartless, spineless, posh twat that he's seemed so far.

Taking in the spectacle for just a few seconds longer, I catch a glimpse of myself in the windows of Mint Street, a wide smile taking up my face in a disgusting moment of weakness. Reminding myself of who he is, who I am, I resume my irritated seriousness, and venture to help him – though only once he admits he needs me . . .

'Bloody hell, you're sweating on me from here,' I gloat.

Teddy looks at me through his lashes, his eyes darkened with the irritation. Refusing to give up, instead of replying, he shoves the trolley again, grunting with the effort.

'Jesus, careful you don't wrinkle those expensive trousers.'

Another black look is shot in my direction.

'You can just admit you need help, you know. I'm sure you're used to getting plenty of help from Mummy and Daddy.'

With that, he takes an arm either side of the basket and lifts the entire thing over the first row of cobbles and throws it down with an echoing bang. Without a word from either of us, he pushes the cart to the entrance of the laundry room, wipes his brow with his handkerchief, composes his posture, and leaves the Tower without so much as a second glance in my direction.

Stuck for a moment, my feet rooted in the cobbles, the high walls of the Bell Tower on my right seem to rise and block the sun's warmth from reaching me. What just happened? *You took it too far*, the niggling voice in the back of my head accuses. I can only agree. It is so unlike me to be so . . . nasty – or so I thought. I have been so caught up in this job, his insolence, in my attempts to not be a disappointment, that that is exactly what I've become.

But it's his fault that we're both in trouble, I remind myself, selfishly. And now he's left me to do all of this work alone. My skull feels tight, as though I can feel my own brain in my head. What am I meant to do? What is the right thing to do? I should keep away from him, that much is obvious, but how can I if I have to work alongside him every day and nanny him to make sure he's actually working?

Knowing my only option now is to complete the task at hand – so I at least have some way to make it up to Westley – I haul a few of the costumes into the industrial-sized washing machine, follow all of the instructions, and sit and watch as it spins and spins. I think of nothing and everything all at once and I wish I could stick my brain in there on a boil wash to weed out all of the stains that are cluttering up my thoughts. Hopefully the detergent would be strong enough to erase the blemish of a certain viscount.

'Daisy? What are you still doing here?' Ellis's voice finds me just as I emerge two hours later, my arms laden with as many tiny uniforms as I can carry.

'Laundry duty,' I say with an exhausted breath.

'Here, let me get that.' Before I can protest, Ellis grabs the heap of nylon out of my arms and his dimpled smile is just visible over the bundle.

'Thank you.' Though I am so exhausted that a conversation would usually be far from desirable, today I am relieved to see him.

'Now why has the knight become the squire?' Having collected the rest of the costumes, we walk back down Water Lane, under the portcullis of the Byward Tower and back across the moat with arms full of brightly coloured fabric.

Recounting the story, in full seriousness, Ellis tries to stifle a laugh but fails.

'It's not funny, it's a disaster!' Though a smile creeps back onto my face at the sight of him gradually cracking up.

'You have to admit, it is a bit funny,' he says between laughs and I find myself chuckling along with him until we're both in hysterics in the middle of the moat. The setting sun touches his face and his complexion glows a warm gold and illuminates his eyes like a flame though honey.

'Okay, okay—' I stop for a deep breath. 'Maybe a little.' Staring at the heap of costumes that we have just created on the floor of the tent, I sigh. This will take me another hour at least.

'I am going to assume that your task wasn't to create a textile mountain in the middle of a tent?' Ellis teases and I shake my head with exasperation, picking up the first of many to place onto a free hanger. The grinning American follows my lead.

'No, no, you really don't have to do that. You should get home too!' The guilt of dragging him into my punishment creeps up and manifests as a red glow on my face.

'I share my apartment with three guys – honestly I would rather spend my evening hanging up laundry with you than having to look at and smell whatever they have left on the counter this week.'

I laugh quietly and offer him my thanks, though making a mental note to not accept an invitation to Ellis's flat – not that I was ever expecting one, of course. That blush returns again.

'What had you in your office until this time anyway?'

'The Byward Angel,' he says with a delighted grin, clearly more than happy to spend his evenings, as well as his whole day, engrossed in his work.

'I knew this place had ghosts, but angels as well?'

'I'm pretty sure there's actually a ghost in my office. If ever I lose things and take a tour of the Tower to find it, by the time I get back it is always right there on my desk as if someone had placed it there for me.'

'Are you sure you're not just in need of some new glasses?' We laugh and I find my shoulders lowering, my jaw unclenching.

'You know, that might just be it.' He picks up another costume with a grin and I, too, resume the task at hand.

'So, what is this Byward Angel?' Genuinely interested in hearing his stories, I watch him intently as the pile diminishes quickly. Bending down to reach the next one, my limbs seem to move in slow motion, subconsciously drawing out the action for as long as possible.

'It's a fourteenth-century Catholic painting of St Michael they uncovered in the Byward Tower – one of the finest examples I've ever seen, so well preserved— Are you okay? Have you hurt your back?' Ellis interrupts himself as I reach down into the pile again whilst still trying to keep my eyes on him. Realising how stupid I must look, I snap back up to my full height, ironing out my posture, and avoiding his gaze as though to be caught in it would turn me to stone. That, and it would only worsen the heat that radiates from my face – perhaps it would be better if he were a Gorgon; that way at least my cheeks wouldn't be glowing like the beacons of Gondor.

'Sorry, all fine, just a niggle,' I lie, rubbing my lower back like I've seen my grandmother do after a rather strenuous stretch to reach her cup of tea. 'And that, the Angel I mean, is just sitting right over there and people just like us have seen it for seven whole centuries?' Walking out of the tent, I stare off at the Byward Tower. The sun has retreated behind it and the white stone of the gate Tower begins to glow in the moonlight.

'It was actually covered up for many centuries, most likely because of the Catholic idolatry. Once England switched over to the Protestant faith, it would have, or should have, been torn down, but someone must have taken great pains to make sure this one survived.' I can only muster a soft 'wow' before he speaks again.

'I'm going to have to shoot off now, but I could show it to you one day, if you'd like?'

Nodding, I allow my gaze to fall on his face once again. He too seems to glow in the shine of the moon, his dark eyes filled with a sparkle as they reflect the lunar surface. Though my brain is telling me I should be excited, be warmed by his kindness, by the objective beauty that radiates from him, the feeling doesn't quite follow.

But I never can trust my feelings, especially not after

the last couple of weeks with the way my body and my mind have responded to a man so clearly put on this earth to infuriate me. So instead, I push on with the eagerness I *should* feel.

'Soon?'

'Soon.'

Chapter 14

'You so have a date!' Bobble squeals. When I entered her bedroom, she was slouched over her sewing machine in the corner, wrestling with a sheet of fabric that looks as if she had just skinned the Honey Monster. Now, once the recount of my day has reached its climax, she jumps up and down in the middle of the room, the dress she handmade by sewing together six ballet tutus bouncing with her.

Blushing again, I staunchly deny it. 'He's only being nice because I was interested in the painting. Definitely not a date. I think. Well, I have no idea. He's older, far more intelligent, actually seems like he has his life together. There's no way I would be his type . . .' We are both silent for moment and a quiet rush of pride flows through me at the thought that there could be even the tiniest possibility a man like him would look at me twice. 'How would you know if it's a date? He didn't say it was or anything.'

'Daisy, men don't have to converse with your father to

let him know that he is courting you anymore, you know. This is how it starts, hanging out . . . alone. I wouldn't be surprised if he's already planning to top it off with a kiss.' She wiggles her eyebrows suggestively.

'Oh God – gosh no.' My face throbs in embarrassment from the thought. 'Surely if he wanted to do that, it wouldn't be an old religious painting he takes me to see? I can't imagine it will be particularly *sexy*.' I cringe at my own words. 'Nope, not a date. Definitely not a date,' I mumble.

'Daisy, Daisy, Daisy. You sweet, innocent soul,' Bobble says with a soft smile. I try and grapple with her meaning and fail. 'Come on, you must have written romantic storylines for Lady A? Hasn't she got some history with a sexy elf or something? Had to give him up after one night of passion for the greater good of her empire?'

'She's very . . . focused on her mission. No distractions.' This feels almost as embarrassing as when Mum tried to explain sex to me in the context of how the Minotaur was created – fewer birds and bees, more messed-up Greek myths of punished wives and white sacrificial bulls. I'm not thinking about that in any more detail right now.

'Well maybe she needs to live a little too, let go and enjoy the journey. Even a character hellbent on power and revenge needs a sweet little redeeming romance, even if it becomes their weakness.' Bobble clutches her hands to her chest, a gooey expression on her face.

'Ever thought of writing, Bobble?' I ask as she melts further and further into the narrative she is currently dreaming in her head.

Snapping out of it quickly, she gives me a firm look.

'Don't change the subject. You're going on a date with the hot American history geek. You'll really enjoy it. If you don't, I'll eat my hat.' The hat closest to her on the desk is a felt beret shaped to look like a frog with a tongue piercing.

'I'd pay to watch you eating that one.' I point to the punk-rock amphibian and she clutches it protectively to her breast.

After a moment of pre-mourning, she continues, 'I once went on a date with a girl from Georgia. I was hoping for cute Southern cowgirl, you know with that twangy accent . . . Anyway, turns out she was from the country Georgia, not the American state.' She sighs dramatically. 'I never thought I'd ever regret wearing my adorable pink cowboy boots on a date, but there's a first for everything.'

'I'm assuming you didn't get a second date?' I say through a snigger.

'I think it was when I asked if they actually say "yeehaw" or if it was just a thing in the movies that did it. She unmatched me whilst she went to the toilet.' She shakes her head with a laugh.

'I'm not sure I should be taking any advice from you in that case.'

'You're probably right, but I'm afraid I'm your best hope.'

I plonk myself in the futuristic-looking egg chair in the corner of her room – it is much lower down and much more reclined than I anticipated and as I flop into it the whole thing spins erratically. After a few giggles at the sight of my long limbs flailing to make contact with solid ground, Bobble reaches out to stop it.

'I can't stop thinking about Teddy.' I'm unsure if it's the motion sickness but I blab the words to her without even knowing what I'm saying. Thoughts of him, what I said to him, the look on his face, keep replaying over and over in my head. My brain can't seem to figure out if I should settle on guilt, or anger. 'About him getting us both in trouble, and leaving me with the punishment, I mean,' I say, trying to worm my way out from under Bobble's playful smirk.

'He's really got in your head too, huh?'

'Too? What? No. He's just being a pain in my arse. He's going to ruin everything.' Westley's words as he handed me my first strike still sear in my chest. I have made the first step and boarded the train that's only destination is failure. It's Theodore Fairfax who has cut the brakes and sent me hurtling down the track with no way to stop.

'It sounds like his family are a bit of a sore spot for him,' she muses, seriously this time. 'Really what you said wasn't *that* bad, but even tickling a stab wound would still hurt, right?' She looks at me, empathy swirling around her irises.

'You think I should apologise?' I can't return her gaze. I'm in my own head, playing out how that would go – no doubt any apology from me would be met with some more of his insufferable sarcasm. And why should I? What he's done far outweighs any offhand comment I've made – how was I meant to know that something like that would hurt him?

'Well, that's up to you. I can't tell you what to do; I don't have to put up with the guy on the daily. I only have to listen to you talk about him, *constantly*.' She rolls her eyes but the motion quickly turns into a wink.

'I never talk about him. I've known him for barely two weeks.' Sitting up straight in this weird sci-fi furniture without sending myself into orbit again is much harder than I expected. I'm still half stuck and battling against the unnatural positions it pulls me into as I feebly attempt to defend myself.

'*Teddy wouldn't wear his costume. Ugh Teddy said this. Teddy did that today. Can you believe Teddy* . . . Need I go on?' She smiles a sinister smile as she ceases her annoyingly accurate impression of my evening rants.

'No.' Shame seeps through my skin in patches of red that climb my neck and drown my face. 'Okay, maybe I do talk about him. But only because he drives me mad!' Sighing, I stoop back into the chair. 'He's getting in the way.'

'Maybe it's him you need to bone, get all that tension out.' I hate how excited she looks at this suggestion.

'I'm not even going to dignify that with a response.'

'Come on! That's the perfect story! A night of lust with the royal enemy, the one you're supposed to be taking down. All that frustration comes out in one . . .'

'Nope, nope, no.' I cut her off just as she stands up to act out what I can only imagine to be a rather powerful thrust into the air. 'I'd rather fight him to the death.'

'Hmmm,' is all she can say as she slowly returns to her seat, her eyes still clearly plotting all of my sexual escapades that will *definitely* not be happening. 'He just sounds like one massive tease to me. Maybe you should just play him at his own game. Boil his piss, just like he boils yours.'

'Really lovely image there, Bob. You really should be writing all of this down – bestseller quality.' She throws one of her latest hat creations at me. With a smile, I place it on my head. It's made from the Honey Monster fur that she's been grappling with all this time, and it tickles my ears.

'Seriously though.' My housemate's face is uncharacteristically unsmiling. How is it only now that I am wearing a hat that reminds me far too much of a yeti's pubic hair that she decides to take on this new tone? I suppose that pretty much sums her up. 'I think he's misunderstood. Maybe you should go easy on him? I doubt he meant to get you in trouble.'

'It's hard to misunderstand when someone is an arrogant arsehole,' I mumble.

'Daisy.' She gives me a stern look. 'Give him a chance; he might surprise you.' I haven't told her about the chapel, about the way people spoke of him as if he wasn't human, as if they knew him and his innermost thoughts. Nor did I tell her about the way he harshly rejected my attempts to distract him, and rejected my sympathy. Teddy doesn't need a chance; I gave him one already. Teddy is the kind of man who lives in his own world, distanced from everyone, above everyone – no amount of empathy will bring him down to earth. It's a challenge he needs.

But Bobble gives me another strict look following my prolonged silence, my face no doubt giving away my vengeful plans. 'Fine, fine, I'll give him a chance,' I concede as her petite features grow more intimidating.

With my words, she removes her seriousness like a mask and smiles widely again. 'Hey, what did knights think about fur?' she says as though the conversation just seconds ago never took place. 'How would you feel about a fluffy helmet? Oooh or fluffy chain mail?' Bobble excitedly thinks up different ways to make me a whole new outfit using only her beloved highly flammable synthetics. The Haberdashery Tyrant only allows me to escape once I agree to let her take a couple of my measurements. Soon I am able to drink in the silence and stillness of my own space.

Just because I have agreed to give him a chance, doesn't mean Alenthaea has to. Almost afraid of being caught, I draw out my notebook from my desk drawer, keeping a suspicious eye on my door. Sitting down to open it, I flick through to a blank page and set to work scrawling *The scourge of the Black Knight* across the top.

Until the early hours, I sit furiously scribbling on the page as Alenthaea, the rightful elven queen, must take on the Black Knight, a rogue of the human royal family, as he declares war on her kingdom and threatens all she has built.

Concealed beneath the shade of the great forest, Lady Alenthaea saw her foe in the flesh for the first time. The man she had crossed continents for, the man whose death she had fantasised about for months was finally in striking distance of her broadsword. The Black Knight was leaning against the trunk of the ancient oak, tracing his fingers over the druid runes scarred into its bark, his back to his predator.

That same thick black hair that sprang wildly from his crown, unrestrained, free, she had run through her fingers so many times in her mind. Alenthaea's hands were throbbing with the desire to finally clutch the soft strands in her fist, to draw back his head, and expose his naked throat to the wind. The thought excited her. Twitches of pleasure glowed through her like a will-o'-the-wisp as she stalked closer to him faster than ever. The elven heir could have used one of the spells she had picked up from the blood mages of Raven's Peak, kill him with one click, so fast that the only sign that anything was amiss would be the rustle of the leaves. But she desired to be close to him, to hear him groan from within the depths of himself as she laid her hands on his skin.

She drew her sword from its scabbard as quietly as a breath, reached out ready to strike, but the Black Knight was not as ignorant as she had assumed. He had felt her presence the moment she had stepped on the same soil. She had lived in him all these months as he had lived in her. In a climax of feeling, of anticipation, his sword clashed against hers. Through their crossed weapons, he leant forward, pressing himself against her, as she pressed into him.

'What took you so long?' The blades that framed his face reflected the smile of her enemy. Alenthaea knew she should attack. If she had manoeuvred her steel only slightly, she'd have had his head in her hands, emptied his deep black eyes of their life. But something stopped her. These were hallowed grounds, impregnated with *magic, though what she felt in that moment was no elven-made enchantment. With her blade clattering to her feet, she grabbed her nemesis by his neck, and fiercely pressed her lips—*

Slamming shut my notebook, I stare at it on my desk, my heart pounding as though attacked by a wild beast that had just leapt from its pages. I should throw it out of the window, or set fire to it. Too terrified by my own mind, by the work of my own hand, I crawl into bed fully clothed, praying to all that is good that my dreams don't stray too far from my senses as well.

Chapter 15

'Jousting!' Westley announces with a clap of his hands to the gathering before him. Two thoroughbred horses flank him from either side. One takes quite a shine to the feather in his hat and Westley has to push the beast away to prevent her from taking it for a snack. 'One of a knight's favourite pastimes, a chance to prove thyself to an audience and perhaps win the favour of a fair maiden or master.'

As usual, the children don't seem to take much notice of Westley. Instead, they stare at the horses, some faces filled with awe, others intense fear. It's a brown mare that nibbles at Westley's feather. White patches litter her wide back, and green and blue ribbons are plaited into her mane. The other is sleek and black, stood so stoically that if it weren't for the occasional slow blink of its eight-ball eyes I'd have believed that it wasn't real at all.

The morning was spent marking out the jousting field that runs up and down the moat. Ribbon-tied flowers trace the boundaries and foam lances are lined up against the brick of the Tower walls. Teddy has yet to arrive. Days have passed, yet the throb of guilt that has sat in the pit of my stomach since the day of our laundry punishment convinces me that his absence is in some way my fault. Another strange feeling has lingered since I closed my notebook and refused to look at it since, but I can't quite make sense of it. I don't wish to. Just the thought of it now has me sitting here blushing like a grandmother on Wattpad.

'Did you know that Henry VIII was a keen jouster himself? You may all be familiar with his portrait, of the portly, grumpy king . . .' Westley pops out his belly and dons a scowl that is scored with lines from too many years of smiling. A few giggles pass over the children. 'But before then, he was one of England's finest sportsmen. He was a keen footballer, back when footballs were made out of the bladder of a pig!' Westley exclaims as they watch him with disgusted awe, 'And when it came to jousting, the tall and athletic young Henry was a force to be reckoned with. But I'm not sure many would fancy their chances against royalty, I can't imagine that many were jumping at the chance to injure the king. The same king who went on to behead two of his wives!'

Westley has fully claimed their attention. Apparently, children seem to learn more when it is pig's organs and beheadings on the curriculum. I seem to have a lot more in common with pre-teens than I initially thought . . .

'It was eventually jousting that led to his downfall, and his path into becoming the giant tyrant we know today. Thrown from his horse during a tournament, the beast

– wearing full armour – fell on him too, damaging his legs. His legs would never be the same again. It was the end of his sporting career, the beginning of the pain that fuelled his anger that ended up leading to the end of many of his closest friends.' A wave of fearful looks pass over the children. Perhaps he has taken it a little too far, particularly when we are all currently in the path of two rather large horses.

'But fear not . . .' Westley disappears into a tent and emerges with his hands clutching the wooden poles of four hobby horses. 'Today will not be the making of any more tyrannical kings or queens. Today, you may challenge one another on the jousting field, but instead of trying to inflict life-changing injuries, we will be trying to inflict as much laughter and joy into your lives as possible.'

'Well, there's all of the fun gone then.' Teddy's voice makes me jump as he sneaks up from behind me.

'Do you always have to weirdly approach me from behind?' Like usual, I don't turn to face him. I have to wait until the heat has settled from my face before he sees that he has succeeded in surprising me, as I'm sure is his aim. I'm glad that he can't hear my heartbeat as loudly as I can. That always takes a little while longer to steady itself.

Teddy grins as though nothing has been amiss. As though I didn't anger him, as though he didn't storm off, as if I haven't been wondering where he has been for the last few days. He just resumes duties as normal. 'Never turn thy back on thine enemy. I like to test you.' Sadly, for me, that means he's back to his ever-annoying self.

'I haven't noticed.' Rolling my eyes, I attempt to cover

up my surprise – less about the fact he referred to himself as my enemy, more about the fact he had remembered the codes.

'Perhaps I should try harder then.' He stands beside me now. Opting for only half of his costume today, his bright white dress shirt glows under the metal armoured pauldrons that hang over his shoulders. It's a weighty bit of kit, one of the only pieces not made of painted leather or plastic, but he carries the weight with ease. The sleeves of his shirt strain around his biceps and display every contour of his figure to be enjoyed, or envied, by half of the class who now watch us closely rather than watching Westley's demonstration of how one rides a hobby horse.

'You were hoping that you'd have the chance to knock me from a six-foot horse, were you?' I revert the conversation back to his earlier disappointment.

'Not at all,' he replies, though I'm not quite convinced. 'I was looking forward to seeing your attempt at trying to beat me.'

'*Trying* to beat you?' I scoff. 'You really think you'd stand a chance?'

'There's no competition.' Fighting talk. Either this idiot has managed to figure out my pressure points in just the couple of weeks he has known me, or he was simply sent by some bad karma to torment me. It's working. I am barely Daisy around him; Alenthaea rages in full force with just a whiff of him, with just the idea of him.

'Why? Because just like Henry VIII, if I so much as unsettled a single hair on your perfectly groomed head then I'd have your little friend over there make me disappear?' I twitch my head in the direction of the middle-aged companion who follows Teddy like a bad smell as he stands just a few metres behind us.

'Morton? He's more likely to make me disappear, or at least hide from him,' he mutters. 'A little intense, isn't he?'

'Just a tad.' With a flick of his wrist, Teddy dismisses his shadow – well dismisses him by an extra three metres as his emotionless eyes still track us like prey from the other side of the class. 'He watch you sleep as well, does he?'

'Only on weekdays.' The ghost of a real smile crosses his face. What is he up to? What is his evil plan? Force me to let my guard down so he can get me sacked when I least expect it? Why is he being so . . . normal? After his dramatic exit from our laundry punishment, I at least expected some coldness. Perhaps he is challenging me? Should I challenge him first? What would Alenthaea do? I hardly know anymore.

Westley wraps up his demonstration and interrupts my scheming as he offers Teddy a kind of bow, kind of curtsey before speaking. 'I have a team leader meeting over in the Waterloo Block. It should only be half an hour, but you know how these things are. Anyways, can I rely on the both of you to supervise the joust whilst I'm gone? The others are busy preparing for the Battle of Bosworth re-enactment this afternoon.' He nervously passes his eyes over Teddy.

'Of course, you can rely on me. Always,' I rush out as though pledging my life to him. He still trusts me. Not all is lost. Westley has hardly spoken to me since the 'snake' incident. He almost got excited after my history of armour lesson, but not quite enough to imply that he had regained any respect for me. This is my chance to not only cling to my job, but actually do it well.

'Good. Thank you, Daisy. Don't let me down.'

'I would rather pour the venom of a basilisk into my eyes than let you down,' I shout after him as he begins his retreat out of the moat.

'The venom of a basilisk?' Teddy turns to me slowly, that Machiavellian smirk mocking me once again.

'Shut up,' is the only reply I can muster before I take my place at the front of the class. Rallying as much of Alenthaea as possible, I imagine I'm preparing my troops to charge on the motherland and reclaim the crown. 'You each must now decide on what is to be your noble mount and your lance. Choose wisely.' Clambering to their feet, children rush in all directions acquiring the tools they need.

'I want that one!' a shrill voice screams across the field.

'Well, you can't, it's mine,' another responds, provoking the former to let out a piercing squeal. Two students stand locked in a stalemate, both chubby hands clutching the same hobby horse.

'Hey, hey, hey.' I try and intervene, bringing another identical horse as a peace offering. 'Why don't you take this one, Janey? It's exactly the same.' I offer the screaming child the replacement. She looks me up and down with a disgusted expression as though I had offered her a Garibaldi rather than a chocolate chip cookie.

'I want that one,' she huffs.

'It's mine.'

Janey stares at her assailant with such fire, I'm genuinely beginning to worry that she may resort to using her fists to win her furry friend.

'They are literally the same,' I say, unable to entertain their childish awkwardness. 'Janey, just take this one or you're not going to have time to pick out your lance. Or would you prefer to joust without a weapon?' This seems to convince her and she accepts, although not without first baring her teeth at me and gnashing them like a feral dog. I don't quite recall 'be prepared to have your throat ripped out by a nine-year-old who still has half of her baby teeth' being on the job description but here we are.

Teddy lurks, chuckling to himself at the scene he has just witnessed.

'I really don't think I'm cut out for working with children,' I groan, making him chuckle harder.

'I can't help but agree.'

I shoot him a look similar to one recently worn by Janey, but seeing his dark eyes screwed up into a tight smile softens me just slightly.

'I'm still better at it than you.' I don't know what compels me to *tease* him after the last time, but it feels oddly natural. The smile grows.

'Are you sure about that?' He raises an eyebrow. I nod, straightening my back with my challenge.

'Considering you think, foolishly, that you could beat me in a joust, and now this . . . I reckon you should put your money where your mouth is.'

'Are you challenging me to a joust, Petal?' Teddy leans

closer to me, his eyes flickering over my face as he gives me a better look at his amused expression.

'I don't know. Am I?' Alenthaea inside me is thoroughly entertained. My body vibrates with adrenaline, my heart hammers hard in my chest with the risk, the excitement.

'I think you just might be.' Teddy is so close now that each time he draws a breath, his chest presses against mine. He holds me captive in his gaze, his cocky smile lingering on his lips until I can hear nothing but my own heartbeat.

For a moment, I wonder if I have fallen through the pages of my notebook, or if the Black Knight has escaped to haunt me in the flesh as well as in ink. One thing I know for certain is that my body is too awake, too alive for any of this to be a dream.

I open my mouth to speak, but my words make no sound. Black eyes break their hold on me for a moment to flick to my mouth. Those deep pools of shadow hide all behind them, but everything they look upon tumbles into their depths, hoping to find the starlight in the dark night of his stare. For a moment, I am sure I see a glimmer. As quick as it came, he retreats, distancing himself from me. Choking on the thickness of the air, I can't watch as he stalks away.

Instead, I return my attention, or as much of it as I can focus, to my class who have organised themselves on the grass, impatiently awaiting their chance to whack each other with a polearm. Unable to suppress a grin, I address them with a renewed enthusiasm. 'Let me hear a cheer if you're excited to get jousting!' I pump my fist in the air, expecting to be met with as much passion as I saw as they collected their weapons but my fervour deflates when I'm met with an underwhelming cheer – it's more of a mumble come to think of it. Coughing, I give up on my morale-raising tactics and instead go straight for the task at hand; they clearly just want to get on with it.

'Now who wishes to be the first brave knight to take on this challenge? Sir Alfie perhaps? Or Sir Ryan?' No volunteers. 'Come on, who's feeling brave?' Half of them don't even look at me. My mask of confidence slips. No one tells you just how terrifying judgemental children can be. Now, as I try and stumble my way back into control, the true, unmasked Daisy returns.

'How about we show them how it's done?' In true Teddy fashion, I hear him before I see him. Not giving him cause to think he's better than me, again, I ignore him and the thundering in my chest. Rubbing my sweating palms back and forth across my tunic, I rock on my heels, searching for a way to reclaim my composure.

'Er . . . erm . . . Fatima. Can you – um – come up here?' I pick the first child that my gaze lands on.

The relief of being able to produce words again is short-lived, however. Her attention isn't on me. Nor is anyone's attention. With open mouths, each child stares behind me – it is that moment in the movie where the group has just fled a monster and the loveably stupid side character begins some sort of silly dance unawares of the beast right behind them. Turning slowly, I prepare to feel the breath of a dragon, or the slobber of an ogre.

It is far, far worse.

I see his legs before anything else. Six legs. Four: bony,

sleek, black, hooved. Two: thighs parted, three feet above the ground.

'What in Odin's name are you doing?' I try to keep my voice low but it is almost impossible when Teddy now sits abreast the largest of the two horses like the Duke of Wellington in Glasgow city centre. Oh, how I wish I had a traffic cone to throw at him right now.

'Jousting,' he states, as if it is the most normal thing in the world to be overseeing an army of primary schoolchildren on horseback, in the middle of a bloody moat.

'Are you out of your mind?' Sweat pools in my costume. I'm going to lose my job. What if he tramples a child? Could I go to prison? Oh God, I wouldn't last in prison. I know my way around a stainless-steel sword, not a shiv! 'Get down. Teddy. You could kill someone. Children, get back. In the tent, go!' None of them move.

'Keep your chain mail on. I know my way around a horse.' His calmness makes me want to close the gap between us, grasp him gently, softly, by the shoulders, lean in, and then plant him straight into the earth. Even the horse stands stoically, under his spell.

'We had one job to do. One job! And it certainly didn't include mounting an actual real-life horse. Are you hellbent on ruining everything? Get down.' The beat of my heart spreads up my throat, as though the pounding flesh is lodged in my trachea. I choke on it, and on my breath when I can manage to squeeze one in.

Unbothered by my imperatives, Teddy nudges the horse with his boot and expertly guides it in the opposite direction of the crowd. Once clear of anyone, he kicks

159

the mare into a gallop and they both disappear into the wildflowers.

Chasing after him, my lungs burn before I even reach the first corner and Teddy is long gone. I'd stand no chance charging him down on foot. I know what Alenthaea would do in this situation, but she's reckless. I can't afford to be reckless; I can't afford another mindless mistake by getting myself involved with him. But if I don't stop him, if I don't take control, who knows how far he will go?

'Stay there, all of you.' Running back to the camp, I address the children as my hands obey Alenthaea's irrational ideas and I reach for the reins of the second horse, untying it from the post that they had both been safely attached to only moments ago. 'Pretend you have infiltrated the dragon's lair. If you move, he will see you and you will be dust!'

Of course, I couldn't have been raised without knowing how to ride a horse. What elven noble doesn't know how to ride a horse? It would be stupid to not learn. That, and our old neighbour Mrs Lacey had horses that would escape into our garden and eat the fat balls we had left out for the birds and by way of an apology she would let me, Sam, and Marigold ride them on a Thursday afternoon. I, however, was always the worst.

It takes me five attempts to swing my leg over and by the time I am seated high on the back of the horse, I am out of breath and the immediate dizziness is a nauseating reminder that heights are, in fact, not my friend. The semi-hyperventilating isn't helping either.

It's the knowledge that I have to stop him before Westley

returns that spurs me on. I need to catch up to him before he ruins everything. The horse has other ideas. The stubborn thing is unresponsive to my tug of the reins. Pulling and pulling – nothing.

In a last-ditch attempt, I copy Teddy and just softly knock its stifle with my foot. The mare bucks into action with such speed that I wrap my hands into the reins, holding on for dear life, eyes clamped firmly shut, brain only thinking of all of the things I should have done with my life before my early death at the hooves of a feral horse. Thankfully it had taken off in the direction of its fellow, but instead of following the path, it storms straight through the bushes and meadow. Thorns rip through my clothes and then claw at the skin on my ankles.

Prying my eyes open, I see Teddy watching me from the other end of the moat. Thankfully now around the corner, we are both out of sight of anyone else. Well, anyone inside the Tower – tourists gather on the wall outside, forming quite the audience. If I could get this thing to stop, we would be having a stand-off right now, but the stupid beast zigzags across the flowers – exactly the opposite outcome I was hoping for.

'Teddy! Just bring the bloody horse back!' I scream down the moat. My voice echoes in the valley between the walls.

The viscount finally listens to me. Galloping towards me, moving with purpose. Towards me. At me. Of course, my wild horse has decided that this is the exact moment it would stop its uncontrollable springing through the plants. Instinctively, I plunge myself into darkness, squeezing my eyes shut and burying my head in the ornamented mane. I think of home. When the impact doesn't come, one sneaking eye takes a glance to see what on earth has happened, and make sure that I haven't just been instantly transported to the afterlife.

Teddy's laugher reverberates between the walls. Trotting calmly, he circles me. All of the oxygen feels as though it has been sucked from the atmosphere. My heart beats erratically, but everything swirling around in my head couldn't be slower. *Don't have a meltdown. Don't have a meltdown.* Not in front of him.

'I guess that makes me the hero? Have we found Sir Daisy's weakness, finally?' he taunts in his merry way.

Kicking the horse back into action, all I want to do is get as far away from him as possible. I should never have chased him. Why did I rise to the bait? Invited to return to her unruliness, my horse resumes her sporadic leaps across the moat.

Before my horse continues on her path of destruction, she's stopped by something else. 'Whoa, whoa,' Teddy's voice soothes. He is beside me now. His wide hand grasps the reins close to him and his leg pushes against my own, squashed between the two horses. 'She's got a bit of fire in her this one.' He strokes her mane and she pushes herself further into him. 'Are you okay?'

I don't answer him. Tapping my fingers in a regular rhythm across my palm, I attempt to regulate myself, to regain control of yet another thing that I had lost. My other hand scratches down my thigh, and staring straight ahead, I just want to block it all out. Disappear into

Alenthaea, where I can be strong, protect myself, be powerful.

'Here, can you put your leg across over this side?' Teddy taps his saddle. He makes an attempt to gently place a hand on my arm, but before his fingertips can even leave a print, I flinch away. The tapping gets quicker. So does the scratching. 'Daisy? If you can manage to slide yourself over this way, we can head back. Before Westley gets back.'

Westley. My job. My responsibilities. I comply. Shifting my leg over the other horse, I haul the rest of my body across so I now sit on the saddle behind him. Teddy chats tenderly to the two horses, and they both walk back the way we came.

'Be careful, I have a few straining buttons over here.' I realise for the first time that my hands grip tightly at Teddy's shirt. The smooth cotton is tense under my fearful grip. Letting go, I am grateful that he is facing away from me, but I know he can feel the damp patch my sweating palms have left behind. Dipping into a bit of uneven ground, the horse jolts and I find myself wrapping my arms around his waist again, pressing myself into him, knowing that in this momentary truce, he will keep me safe.

For a moment, I'm glad of his presence. I will hate myself, and him again, as soon as my feet are back on solid ground.

Chapter 16

We can hear it before we see it. Carnage.

In our absence, the children, a law unto themselves, decided to continue their own joust – without horses, without rules, and are mostly just whacking each other with foam lances. My colleagues, who had clearly emerged when they heard a ruckus, have been dragged into it also. With every attempt to disarm the rebelling knights, they are slapped with the supposedly 'child-proof' weapon.

Bringing the horses to a halt, Teddy hops down with ease to tie the two back where they had been before the turmoil that followed in the last half an hour. Attempting my own dismount, I try and shift one of my legs over to slide down, but my foot catches in the stirrup and I hang against the horse, too ashamed, too stubborn, to call for help.

Teddy watches me for a moment, clinging to the saddle, that all too familiar smirk kissing at his lips. 'Need a hand?' Smug prick.

Little does he know I'd rather hang here until I am reduced to a dusty skeleton than ask for him to do anything for me. 'I'm just allowing you a ten-second head start to hide, before I get down, steal Lily Davies' lance, and commit high treason.' I smile as sweetly as is possible when all of one's blood decides to shift entirely from one end of one's body to the other.

Teddy only raises his eyebrows, amused, and turns away to leave me to hang in peace. With him finally out of the way, I can shift my attention to the way my leg fizzes with pins and needles and how one of the children has now chosen me as a target and is hitting me repeatedly over the head with a foamy sword.

Just as the feeling begins to disappear in my lower body, and I surrender to the idea that this is how I will die, pressure circles my whole body before my trapped foot is unhooked. Teddy holds me in his arms, freeing me from my own personal hell, by subjecting me to another. Pressed into his chest, I have no choice but to succumb to him, to allow him to intrude on every one of my senses. Despite the fact he is carrying a human who's almost six foot and built to go with it, he doesn't seem to strain. He is firm and unflinching beneath me and I can feel every curve of his body pressed against me. Dryness spreads down my throat and I desperately swallow to regain some movement that would allow me to close my gaping mouth. I have never been this close to anyone before.

Almost in spite of myself, I can't look away from his face. We are so close now, I can see every crease, every perfect detail. For the first time, I notice that he wears a little makeup under his eyes. Some of it has rubbed away to reveal a dark, tired streak. Seeing myself reflected in his Stygian eyes, I notice they too seem to hang heavy with exhaustion. The impulse to touch his face rattles through me, to caress him, to tell him he's okay.

Another whack over the head snaps me back into sound mind and I leap out of his arms. With my legs still numb and tingling – from the horse, of course – I stumble and have to steady myself against the mare after a series of wobbling steps. Once I have thanked the child who had whacked some sense back into me, I quiver away, doing everything I can to stay on my legs.

'You're welcome!' Teddy laughs from behind me, but I am too busy catching my breath to face him again.

Returning to the battlefield, I plan my assault. A group of children have Erin pinned against the Tower's outer wall; another group run in circles engaged in a civil war amongst themselves, chased by and in turn chasing two more teachers: Robin and George. The more conscientious of the bunch cower in one of the tents; their round, flushed faces peeking from behind one of the flaps every now and again. I'm not sure that even Alenthaea can help me now.

Looking around for backup, I realise I am quite alone. The shouts of children melt with the low rumbling of overhead air traffic and it all swirls into the mix of sirens blaring in my mind at the knowledge of Westley's impending return until it turns into a raging cacophony, loud enough to blow your head off.

Only to make matters worse, it's this exact moment that Teddy decides to saunter over, smile in tow.

'What do you want now?' I snap. My frustration, my fear, all flood from me and pile onto the man before me.

'I wanted my orders . . . to help?'

I eye him suspiciously. So now he acts all sweet and innocent, as if all of this isn't because of him?

'Haven't you done enough damage? I am going to lose everything I have worked for, my one chance to feel like my life isn't a disappointment, that I can be something. Why? Because some guy who has been handed everything that he could ever want in life is bored and treats everything like it's a game? I don't need your help; I need you to leave me alone.' It barrels out of me before I can stop it and I wince at the sound of myself, my cruelty.

Teddy's smile is wiped clean as his face hardens to shield him from my wrath. In the middle of no man's land, we stare at each other, at war with our gazes as the chaos plays out around us. The guilt is already rising in me. It battles against the overload of anxiety until they join as allies to take me down in full.

Before I lose all of my resolve, I cross back to the task at hand. The children. Running almost aimlessly, I demand their obedience, beg for them to stop – but none of it works. Unable to even look in Teddy's direction, let alone accept his offer to help, I scurry around the moat chasing my tail just like the rest of my colleagues, my throat burning with the threat of tears. How have I been defeated . . . by children?

Just as my vision begins to blur with frustration and despair, they stop. Just like my feral horse, as though bewitched, they stop all of their torments, drop their weapons and march off in the same direction. Stupefied at the scene before me, wondering if some zombifying switch has been flicked that has summoned all of these children back to their alien master, all I can do is watch them. Tracking their movements, I notice they are beginning to form a congregation at the entrance of the tent.

Teddy stands surrounded. I can't see, at first, what magic he has unleashed onto them, but they peck around him like hungry pigeons, barely a word passing between anyone. And then I see it. The thing that has tamed an army of feral children, what has silenced a battalion of mischief – one single tin of biscuits.

By the time each miniature fiend has been fed, they return to their human form and sit at Teddy's feet, chattering quietly. I want to be annoyed with him, curse his smugness, but my heart rate is finally settling. With one strike on my probation already, if Westley had arrived a moment earlier, I would have stood no chance of retaining my job. If he had taken one look at Teddy and I on those horses, or Erin pinned down with toy weapons, he'd have put me on the first train home. I have come so close to losing it all, and somehow, it's the person who started the fire who gets to take the credit for putting it out.

Westley crosses the moat just a few moments later, his cheery disposition firmly fixed in place, a sight that finally allows me to release a breath. Teddy has retreated back into the tent. A few of the other teachers have now taken his place at the front of the class to attempt to teach them even just a little about the original lesson in jousting.

To an outsider's eyes, all is well.

'What a model class! Superb work, Daisy. Now I am feeling sorry indeed that I had to miss such an exciting morning.' Westley claps me on the shoulder and I choke on my own saliva – at least I think it was my own spit and not the big horse-sized wedge of guilt lodged in my throat. Unable to reply, I am glad when Westley doesn't wait for my response and goes over to one of the tables to lay down his messenger bag.

Just as I start to believe that I've gotten through this mayhem unscathed, the universe delivers me my karma. One of the Beefeaters, the wardens of the Tower of London, journeys into our camp. His uniform is perfectly pressed. The king's cypher, stitched across his wide chest, stretches down over his rounded belly, and a tall Tudor bonnet is fixed to his head, held on by his perfect upright posture – practised from years in the British military. This is a rare sight in itself, but the sight of a child, Tristan to be more precise, slung over his shoulder, still wielding a foam sword, is one none of us could have even imagined.

'I assume this one belongs to you, Wes? Found him trying his luck against one of the ravens. Lucky I got him when I did, or he'd have been turned to birdseed.' The Beefeater drops Tristan onto his feet. The little lord, overcome with shame, lashes out at the burly man whose calloused palm now engulfs the child's skull, forcing each assaulting swing to miss – only riling Tristan more.

Westley doesn't move to relieve the Beefeater of his assailant – he has it well under control – but when I look over at him, he is staring back at me. With his cheeriness abandoned, he releases a chest-rattling sigh before shaking his head. My boss may as well string me up on the battlements and fill me with arrows – the shame of his disappointment would still outweigh the pain.

'You're just lucky no one was seriously injured, or we'd be having a very different conversation right now. I should just sack you both on the spot right now, but Daisy, I offered you three chances, and Lord Fairfax, I made a promise to your parents to keep you here and see you improved and I am a man of my word.' Westley's words are peppered with a contempt that I had never thought would be possible for him to produce.

Teddy and I stand before him like a pair of naughty schoolchildren, having confessed our earlier crimes. Teddy keeps his eyes fixed on me; I feel them burning across my neck and face. I can't tear my own eyes from my shoes. How have I failed so terribly? I have one week left of my probation but they may as well just send me home now, disgraced. Hopelessness spreads through me like a sinkhole, dragging all I am into its void until I stand here an empty shell. Who am I? Who am I meant to be for the next sixty years of my life, if I can't even succeed for four short weeks?

'Our guests today have made quite the mess.' Westley points to the various patches of horse dung scattered across the moat. 'I want this place spick and span when I return in the morning. That includes replanting the flowers that you both selfishly tramped. Any questions?' Neither of us respond. I've already grovelled. Teddy, of course, was unfazed. He owned up to it all, just as he had done before, as though being caught was his intention all along.

With one last gut-punch of a sigh, Westley leaves us alone again. Not waiting for Teddy, or anything he has to say, I grasp one of the shovels, throw it into a wheelbarrow and set off to work. My body aches from the battle with my horse, my lower back burns with each bend, but I don't mind – I deserve this pain. Working frantically, I shovel the shit so fast my forehead springs with sweat, my chest heaves, and I find myself crying. Full choking sobs.

Teddy's hand, grasping the handle of the shovel, urges me to halt.

'Daisy?' His voice is soft as he scans over my face again, judging my tears, inwardly laughing at my weakness, I am sure of it. I wrestle him for the shovel, but he barely moves against my tugging. His one hand clutches it, unrelenting to my frustrations. With one final growl, I concede. The rogue royal resumes the task; with unwavering seriousness and rolled-up sleeves, he finishes the job as I sink further and further into the grass.

Dropping his tool into the wheelbarrow, Teddy takes the seat beside me. After a pause, he sighs.

'Why does this mean so much to you?' Teddy speaks, though barely audibly.

'Why do you care?' We still don't look at each other.

'I'm sorry.' He mumbles the words as if he's tasting them for the first time.

'No, you're not,' I snap at him, thrusting my fingers into the soft earth in frustration.

'Okay, I'm not. You happy? You want me to play the bad

guy in your little fantasy? Fine. You're just like the rest of them.' The last bit comes out in a murmur and he lies down in the grass beside me.

I whirl around to face him, 'But you are the bad guy.' I can't help but insist. 'You make my life here insufferable. You want to know why this means so much to me? When I finished school, I didn't leave the house for two years. The world terrified me, and the more it terrified me, the more I grew ashamed until the only place I found comfort was my home. The last three years have been better. I can make it to the next town over from my village, I perform my stupid little fantasy in front of crowds, I help out in my dad's shop. To do that, I had to make up a whole new person in my head, be someone else, just so I could be something, anything but me. But I contributed nothing to my family, to anyone. I was a burden. Imagine a twenty-something still needing to go everywhere with her parents because the idea of taking a bus alone was enough to make you physically ill. Every single day I drag myself out of my bed and force myself to live in a world that doesn't make sense to me, in a body that fights me at every turn. This was my first chance to prove myself, to prove that I am not just some failure who's going to be confined to the walls of my parents' house forever. And I did it! I moved to London for Christ's sake! But you. You! It is because of you that I am on my final warning and I am one more of your fuck-ups away from going right back to where I started and the reminder that I have achieved nothing.'

I lie down beside him, exhausted from my rant, from my candour. I've never admitted all of that out loud to anyone. After a long pause, I can feel Teddy roll onto his side to face me.

'I never meant to get you involved—'

'So, I'm just your collateral damage?' I scoff, propping myself up on my elbows to get a good look at his face. Teddy does the same, eyes ablaze just a breath away from me.

'Will you not just let me speak?' he fires, frustration burning through him. 'Your way out of your rut is to succeed here; mine is to fail.' Hot breath fans my face as he leans ever closer. I can't form the words to interrupt him.

'If I can prove to everyone that I am a lost cause, that I have nothing of worth for my family to leech from me, I will be written out of my family history, banished if you will. I'll be sent to live out my days as far from the British press as possible.'

My furrowed brows give me away. Teddy must have seen the cogs of my brain working incredibly slowly to understand his meaning. Surely to avoid expulsion from the institution, he should be on his best behaviour?

Teddy can see that I'm struggling to keep up. 'Being sent away and disowned is as close to freedom as I'll ever get, Daisy,' he says, and everything falls into place.

This whole childish scheme is an elaborate attempt at being renounced by one of the world's most powerful families?

I'm being brought down in a royal plot.

'Am I interrupting something?' In the tension, neither of us have noticed the arrival of Ellis. He stands over us with his hands tucked into his pockets. The sight of him makes me spring from Teddy as though caught in a position far more precarious than in actuality. Teddy only flops onto his back once again, not attempting to acknowledge Ellis's existence.

'No, no, not at all. We had actually just finished.' I wring my hands and pointedly ignore Teddy. Standing beside Ellis, I notice for the first time that he's wearing dusty overalls. 'New uniform?' I raise an eyebrow, pointing at the soiled trousers.

'Ah yes, getting my hands dirty for once. One of the Beefeater's houses was falling down and when they went in to do some work, they found a Tudor forge under it.' He glows with excitement. 'Had to get right in there and have a look for myself. You found yourself in trouble again?' Ellis looks over to Teddy as he speaks. The viscount still doesn't move to introduce himself.

'Looks that way.'

'I had promised you a date.'

I choke on his words as they rip all of the air from within me. Bobble was actually right. Me, a date? A snort is barely audible over my coughing but I am almost certain it came from the direction of the viscount, who grows again to his standing height before skulking into one of the nearby tents. The colour of my cheeks could fight off the looming night-time for a while to come, so I am grateful for the removal of his judgemental gaze.

'Doesn't have to be a date . . . if you don't want to . . .' Ellis interrupts my rumination, his brows sloped with worry at my prolonged silence.

A date is just a date, right? No expectations? 'I could do a . . . date.' Only the trampled grass fills my eyeline.

'Perfect. Shall we . . .' He outstretches his arm in the direction of the exit. I take the lead, not looking back. I know he is long gone, disappeared out of view like a shadow at midnight, but Teddy follows me. Something in his face, the vulnerability in his tired eyes, that moment of weakness between us both, haunts my subconscious, rattles around my chest cavity.

I can't bring myself to return Ellis's dimpled smiles.

Chapter 17

Ellis puts a slender finger to his lips, encouraging me to silence. He hasn't got anything to worry about. I haven't been able to make a sound since we left the camp – my tongue still tied by the four letters that make up the word 'date', my mind left somewhere in the grass of the moat.

'Technically we aren't allowed in here this late, so that just means we need to be extra quiet,' Ellis whispers as we ascend the thin staircase. 'Just upstairs is an apartment that none other than the deputy governor of the whole Tower lives in, and directly below us is the chief Yeoman Warder's office, and the watch room – that's guarded by Beefeaters twenty-four hours a day. So should be a walk in the park, not getting caught, right?'

As I watch him climb the stairs, I realise that it's his intention to have this date, right here, right now, with both of us still wearing the evidence of a hard day's work on our clothes and under our fingernails. With the added danger of being caught, panic floods me almost entirely – but there is no time to change my mind.

If the objective of a date is to get your partner's heart racing by any means possible, then Ellis is succeeding. I'm not sure he bargained for how much my fight-or-flight response rules my life, however. Does he think from all of my recent punishments that I'm one of those thrill-seekers who enjoys breaking all of the rules? If he does, he couldn't be more wrong. My mind runs away with thoughts of armed guards, Beefeaters with their polearms surrounding us, ready to escort us to their holding cells for getting too close to their sacred artworks.

Noticing that my feet have fastened themselves to the bottom of the step, and refused to move any further, Ellis cracks a smile from the stop of the flight. 'Don't worry, I'm not gonna get you in any trouble. They can hardly get me out of this place, so they're used to me hanging around.' Slightly calmed by the sincerity in his smile, I tentatively make my way up the stairs.

Pushing open a scarred wooden door, the eerie creak that greets us only matches the scene before me. The room is empty. Bare wooden floorboards match the naked stone walls and neither part holds any heat. A shiver runs like a frozen stream through my body and down each of my limbs until I have to cover up a twitch. I'm not sure if it is the cool draught that flows out of the door, or the overbearing sense that someone has died in here and their spirit lingers on that leaves the hairs on my arms standing on end – either way, it's almost thrilling. I picture Alenthaea on a heist into an ancient crypt – avoiding enchanted booby-traps to reach an artefact infused with the magic that will aid her in her fight for her throne and family. Avoiding the cracks in the floorboards so as not to trigger any swinging battle-axes, I follow Ellis inside.

The back wall is the only part of the room with anything aside from its raw materials. The crumbling outline of a stone fireplace is the centrepiece, but the walls beside it boast the main feature. Fading paint, the colour of oxidised copper, is broken up by dark patches of art lost to time. The Byward Angel watches over the slanting fireplace, washed out from its original splendour; it still stuns in its distressed state. Moving closer to it, I no longer give thought to the fantasy of booby-traps and magical artefacts. This is real, this is magnificent. Leaving Ellis behind, I marvel at it. Pinkish wings fan out from its crowned head, tight copper curls frame the angelic pale face, a face that seems to breathe the divine across the room.

'St Michael the Archangel.' Ellis speaks softly as I try my hardest not to breathe too close to it, for fear of damaging it further. 'Those, in his hand, were golden scales, said to weigh the souls of the dead.' Tracking away from his face, I notice his faded hands. They must be worn from the number of souls he has had to weigh just past the gate he sits over; heavy souls of women wronged, the empty souls of traitors and plotters past.

He hasn't done it alone. Three more faces and a litany of birds accompany him, though it's only he that shines. 'That one on the far left . . .' I follow Ellis's direction to the half-faced man in the corner '. . . is St John the Baptist. He holds a lamb. He was the patron saint of King Richard

II, so they believe this whole thing was painted towards the end of his reign in the fourteenth century.'

Unable to find the words, I am lost in the history, in a painting hundreds of years older than the very accent my date speaks with.

'That's the remains of a Tudor rose there too, in the middle of the fireplace.' Just two petals survive but there they are, at the very top of the breast, hundreds of years younger than those beside it.

Ellis spends another half an hour half-whispering its stories to me as I scan over each minute detail. No fantasy, no promises of magic or mythical beasts can ever compare to the feeling of realising you live in a world filled with things far beyond any comprehension.

As the cold night sets in and a chill befalls the room, it becomes easier to imagine headless spirits emerging from shadowy corners. We depart, with the promise of finishing the night with a drink in a local pub.

'How did you end up in this job?' My voice finally returns once we're back into the open night. I know I haven't asked much about him; I realise I hardly know anything about him at all.

'I majored in history in the states. The US has an interesting past but I was just so fascinated by much earlier history. At first it was the Tudors, and then I just got lost in it until I found myself right back at medieval Europe and I knew that I had to visit all of these places I'd read about. Came here on a year abroad, and you have yet to be rid of me.' He chuckles. 'The Tower was of course the main attraction, literally the epicentre of British history for the last millennium, so I applied for every job I could find for this place and . . . yeah.' He shrugs dismissively. I want to ask him more as we pass under the room we have spent the evening in, but a soft light in the moat catches my attention before I can release it. Moving to the railings, I squint for a better look.

He's still there.

Teddy is crouched over a flower bed, shrouded in torch light. A trowel in hand, he digs at the earth before filling the horse-crushed gap with fresh blooms. The sight of him there, knee-deep in topsoil, is a searing dagger of guilt in my gut. He had sat there and opened up to me, admitted his faults, listen to me speak of mine, only for me to walk away at the first offer of a date. Not only that, but I have neglected my half of the punishment. I had been clinging to the moral high ground all this time, not realising that I really am no better than him.

'*Your way out of your rut is to succeed here; mine is to fail.*' Why would he even stay? Why would he finish the job if that goes against his whole reasoning in the first place?

'You coming?' Ellis calls from the Middle Tower. A security guard stands beside him fiddling impatiently with a ring of keys.

My eyes flick between him and the dim lights of the moat. Am I really considering leaving my first ever date to help the man who caused all of this trouble to begin with? The same man who is one step away from getting me fired, all because of some selfish feud he has going with his family. The royal family.

It was my punishment too. I chose to ride after him thinking I could be a heroine. I have neglected all of my responsibilities thus far in an effort to come out on top with whatever rivalry is between us.

'I just need to finish something . . . I completely forgot . . . wait for me, literally five minutes, tops.'

'I'll, er, just wait for you back inside then.' Ellis's smile droops as I speak but before his expression can make me change my mind, I rush towards the camp. The further I push on into the moat, the thicker the blanket of darkness grows. Teddy's torchlight is extinguished and I have to rely on the light of the city that spills over walls to find my way to one of the tents.

'Oh bugger. Oh bollocks. Shit.' The sight of Teddy's toned naked torso slaps me in the face. Spinning back around fast enough to give myself whiplash, I am just grateful that his hands were occupied with the initial stages of unfastening the belt to his muddy trousers and I have not accidentally peeped on a royal. 'I am so sorry, I didn't . . . Oh God, I didn't—' I cut myself off by leaving before I see anything else that a *Daily Mail* journalist would pay seven figures for.

'What do you want?' Teddy's voice is monotone, unfazed by my entrance.

Still with my back to him, I try and keep my mind on the task at hand. 'I just come – camed, came, to say thanks, and sorry.'

'I can't hear you,' he grumbles and I shuffle backwards until I'm back on the offending side of the tent.

Swallowing, hard, I begin again. 'I'm here to apologise.'

'Turn around,' he commands. I do as he says. The mucky trousers have been refastened; the shirt remains off. 'Now, what is so important that you had to rush in here and watch me dress for?'

'I didn't know that you'd be, that you were . . .' I choke on my own saliva. He has a tattoo on his chest. A pointed dagger cut across his left peck until its tip skims his heart, ready to pierce, inches away from the end. 'I'm sorry. I shouldn't have left. With everything going on, I forgot the flowers.'

'How was your date?' He gives me an amused look. My face flushes darker.

'Thank you, for staying and finishing it off.'

'For finishing off your date? Anytime, Petal.'

'For finishing the flowers.' I know he knows what I mean. His smirk gives it away. Having plucked a fresh pair of trousers from a suit bag, he begins to unbuckle his belt again. Taking that as my cue to leave, I hasten from the tent, grateful that the city night cloaks my burning face from view.

Trying to erase the image from my mind, his chest, his tattoo, his belt buckle . . .

'Pull yourself together.' I lightly slap my cheeks, desperate to recoup some of my composure. I refuse to end my date with Ellis while my mind is deluged with the bare chest of another – considerably more annoying – man. I groan internally. Bobble is going to love this.

Making it out of the moat without melting from the heat of my cheeks, I mask my face with a smile and prepare to resume my date. As I reach the main gate, the security guard, who has mastered the art of being able to intimidate you into silence without so much as uttering a word, hops down from his guard box – pausing his game of Candy Crush, to free me from the literal prison. Ellis doesn't accompany him, nor does he occupy any space along the Tower wharf. Remembering his promise to wait for me inside, I take a step back towards the Byward Tower but the grunting of the security guard stops me from going any further.

'Tower's closed.'

'I-I work here, I'm just going to get my friend. The one who was here before.' The guard only stares, and each second of his unimpressed gaze makes my skin feel like it's shrivelling in on itself like some sort of anxiety prune.

'Tower's closed,' is all he says, as though that is the limit of his script.

'You've just seen me leave. Can I not even leave a message? He'll think I've ditched him.' If a kraken could clamber out of the Thames right now and swallow me whole, I'd really appreciate it.

'Nah.' The wordsmith finishes his speech with a flourish. Should I stand here and wait for him? Alenthaea would march straight past the guards and find him herself. But as I watch him, almost snarling like a dog as he watches me, I think I'll wait, just explain everything once Ellis comes to leave himself.

Would he actually come out and find me? What if he's already gone, never waited to begin with? Surely, he wouldn't do that? He's kind, too kind, I'm sure he will understand. But what if he doesn't? What if he gets angry?

Twenty minutes pass. With no sign of Ellis, I panic that if I wait here any longer, it will be Teddy who finds me here first, tattoo covered by his jacket, a knowing smirk on his lips, taunting me for being left here alone. The thought, the vivid images of him, spiral until I'm not sure how much longer my legs can hold me up. I retreat to the Tube with the gnawing feeling that I haven't made a single good decision today.

I autopilot through the next few days. Despite knowing how desperate she would be to hear every detail I haven't told Bobble about my date, or Teddy's confession, or his nakedness. Too embarrassed to relive any moment in my own head, I can't bring myself to recap the events to someone who wouldn't have even thought about making any of the same mistakes.

Ellis hasn't called my name across the moat in days. I have attempted to call, to even find him at his office to apologise profusely, but all of my calls ring to his voicemail, and it seems he has quite taken to actually leaving on time. Even Teddy has gone silent, not so much as a teasing insult or aggravating jibe has been thrown in my direction.

My longing for the Friskney Fellowship burns in me. I realise belatedly that I've barely thought of them these past few days whilst my mind has been running away from all I've known to chase after Teddy, to keep any form of order in my life. But right now, all I want is to swing a sword at Sam for two hours and moan at Richard for eating his piccalilli sandwiches in the middle of battle. Instead, I tap my pen at an empty page as I grasp at my imagination for a story for Lady A, for a new battle, more excitement – nothing comes.

The buzzing of the doorbell stirs me from my notebook. I don't bother to answer; it will only be another of Bobble's course friends asking to use her sewing machine to finish off a faux snakeskin shawl or something. She reminds me of Marigold, always surrounded by friends, disquieted at the thought of spending any time alone. Though my sister would never be caught dead around our village wearing anything but the exact same outfit as her friends, something uninspiring, something that wouldn't draw too much attention. There's a whole wardrobe of clothes in Bobble's room that she will only wear around the house: embroidered corsets she has hand-sewn, a bonnet designed to look like a toadstool, tiaras of woven wire twisted with gems and beads. Perhaps in the freedom of a city, she wouldn't have to feel so embarrassed at being different.

A soft knock at the door pulls me out of my head before I tumble into the bottomless pit of bad memories.

'Come in.' The door clicks open and it's Dad's head that peeks out from behind it.

Springing from my desk, I am stood before him before he can even say a word. The sight of his face, his scarred chin from the time he hit himself in the face whilst trying spin a shield in his hand, the smile that hangs above it, makes me want to cry. Dad is the only person in the world who can make a day brighter simply by existing close by. I didn't realise how much I needed him until he was stood right in front of me.

'Lady Alenthaea, I come with an important message

from the Queen of the Orcs . . .' He steps into the room, and bows low. His burgundy tunic is belted in the middle with a link of chain. Leather boots finish at his knees and give way to a pair of brown pantaloons.

'Then you must tell me at once.' Snapping into character without a second thought, I can't help but allow a smile to creep across Alenthaea's serious demeanour.

'She sends word that you must remember to eat enough fruit and vegetables, and also the threat that if you do not send word to her via raven every day then she must insist on sending an army of her finest orcs to remind you.'

'Then she has my word, I shall do my very best.'

'One final thing . . .'

'Go on, young squire . . .'

'She says you must give your father a hug strong enough that she may see the imprint of your arms around his waist when he returns to her.' We both crack. 'Come here, kiddo.' I lean into his side and wrap my arms tightly around his waist, as commanded.

'I am so glad you're here.' This time I can be Daisy when I speak.

'The shop has been quiet without you so I thought I'd shut it up for a day or two and hop on a train to surprise you. I was thinking you could show me a few sights, maybe?' He grins expectantly. When I give him a nod, he claps his hands together with childish glee and plops his rucksack onto my bed.

'How is everyone at the shop?'

'Missing you.' Dad takes a seat at my desk and flicks through my scruffy notebook. 'Willow is still her usual cheeky, cheating self. The Griffin Academy boys have just started a new campaign, so lots of excitement on that one, keeping them busy.'

I can't quite shift my attention from the doorway, wondering, hoping that he has brought someone else along with him. Only a draught from the hallway follows in and I have to get up to close the door before the coldness overcomes me.

'And at home?' For some reason I am nervous to ask. Perhaps it's the gnawing feeling that they are better off without me coming out to play again. The belief that all of their lives can just continue as if nothing is amiss, that I contribute nothing to their day-to-day is something that has littered my thoughts even before I left. They are everything to me so, selfishly, the idea that they can survive just fine without me is perhaps my greatest fear.

'They're sad they couldn't come with. Mum and Sam are busy at work these days, late nights, not much time for family dinners. Mari is same as always, her own little independent self – a proper teenager now, finds everything I do embarrassing.' He chuckles but his smile hesitates. My heart sinks. I had known Sam and Mum would be working, but Marigold . . . she will have finished school, she's starting her long summer, and yet she probably never even thought to come.

'The shop feels massive now you aren't there to paint alongside me.' Dad draws me out of my disappointment for a moment, only to remind me of what I miss most.

We spent most of our days on the shop floor sat side by side painting miniature figurines. A word wouldn't be passed between us for hours on end but it was nice to have his presence there. Every now and again he'd ask for my 'young eyes' to check over a particularly tiny bit, but aside from that, we barely acknowledged one another. Being alone together is when I feel most whole.

'Come on then, let's have a look if your painting has suffered without me.' I try and redirect the conversation before we both end up on the train back home, never to leave again. Dad willingly retrieves his phone and slides through photo after photo of his latest sci-fi creations. Every now and again I'll make a teasing remark about the state of his dry brushing, but his spirits only lift.

This is exactly what I needed.

Chapter 18

Seeing Dad, still in costume, framed by the graffitied, high-rise, bustling backdrop of the city feels bizarre. He does not belong in the same dimension as the little silver bullets of nitrous oxide that litter the gutters along with emptied balloons. It's like walking in on the queen listening to drum and bass music, or finding out that the king owns a pink Nintendo DS Lite. It's all possible, yet something I absolutely cannot wrap my head around.

He's a boyish man, my dad. There's a kind of childish wonder that permanently glows across his face, but now as we cross through Trafalgar Square, his eyes make up half of his face, his open mouth the rest. Scanning all of the way up Nelson's Column, he hasn't quite got used to the volume of people around him as he stumbles his way through a group of Spanish tourists in the middle of a guided tour. After a polite apology, he catches up to me before breaking out in a chuckle, one I copy.

There are too many bodies around me. Strangers' arms

keep brushing against mine; I still need to wash my hands from our trip on the Tube. I'm sweating in the heat of the summer that only grows with each passing person, and if I were alone, I would have given up. Yet the sight of my dad, his country bumpkin innocence drowning in the thrill of a new place, gives me strength. For him, I am living in my head, thinking *what would Lady Alenthaea do?* If Lady A got to spend one more day with her mother, not even the heavens or the darkest of magic could get in her way – a few too many tourists and street vendors trying to sell her umbrellas with no rain in sight wouldn't ruffle her in the slightest. The squiggles of bacteria I picture crawling across my hands aren't such a big deal when I see how Dad smiles. I want to smile like that.

'You've never been to London before?' I know he hasn't in my lifetime. My first time was the day I moved so we certainly never came as a family. But I had always just assumed with how much Mum came down for work, and how well she integrated into the city as if she was one of those women who wears trainers on the Tube with her suit and has her Louboutins in her bag, that he would have joined her at least once in the twenty-five years he's been with her.

'I once went to a medieval festival in Guildford when I was about your age, does that count?' He's completely earnest and I feel compelled to hug him again. 'What was that for?' he adds with a laugh once I release him.

'I'm glad you're here.'

'Me too. Now, can you take a picture of me so it looks like I'm holding one of those lions so I can send it to your mum?' After half a camera roll full and at least half a dozen different positions, he has the perfect photo and we stroll down the mall in a comfortable silence.

Perfectly uniformed trees mark out our path, and Union flags line the road like a guard of honour in a display of patriotic perfection that you could expect with it being the king's driveway. In the distance, the greenery and flutters of red, white, and blue give way to the wedding cake of stacked white stone, topped with a winged bride of gold: the Queen Victoria Memorial. The great queen herself, immortalised like the aftermath of the gorgon's gaze, stares back at us from her throne of angelic stone as though she guards Buckingham Palace behind her.

In every other face I see my sister. Women, friends, sisters, mothers, grin at one another over the hydrangeas of St James's Park. It's a different kind of joy finding someone to share the complexities of womanhood with, to have someone who understands what it is to exist in this form in this world. I've always had Sam, I know, but a life without sisterhood is lonely. It's only now I have Bobble, I realise just how much I've missed out on.

'Dad,' I say after a moment, interrupting his open-mouthed staring at everyone and everything as we wander. He hums in acknowledgement, still distracted. 'Do you think Marigold would want to come to stay with me? Or visit?'

I'm not sure what answer I'm really expecting from him, but he stops in the middle of the path and smooths my hair with a gentle hand. 'I don't see why not. Why don't you call her?' An obvious solution, yet one I can't quite bring myself to fulfil. Resuming our journey, I continue walking until we reach Buckingham Palace.

I had hoped that by moving away, going to the big city, Marigold would actually find me interesting, that she wouldn't be embarrassed to have a sister five years older with no life experience to share with her. Big sisters are meant to make the mistakes, have the shitty boyfriends, have embarrassing moments across the world, so she can teach her baby sister not to make the same errors. She's supposed to look up to me, but what do I have to share with her? I thought London would be the solution, but I have made mistake after mistake, and in all honesty, I think she'd be better off without any terrible bit of sisterly advice I could conjure. What would I even show her if she came? The bin on the Tube platform I vomited in because I am afraid of almost every aspect of society?

'I've wanted to apologise,' Dad tells me softly, breaking me out of my thoughts. His expression is so different to the last few hours that I grow anxious again.

'Apologise?'

'Yes. I pushed you, and I worry that I pushed you too hard. To come here, I mean.' He looks around as a bar on wheels, pedalled and manoeuvred by its patrons, turns the corner. We both chuckle in disbelief. 'See what I mean? I know you're used to the weird and wonderful with us but I think I underestimated how much of this place is just a different world.'

'I think if you never pushed me, you'd never have been rid of me.' I try and chuckle through the lump in my throat.

'I'm so proud of you – you know that.' Contrails of planes cross in the sky like someone has tried to fill the clear summer skies with cloud again. I can't look at Dad; I couldn't hold it together.

Home has always been safe, home is easy. If things get too hard, too overwhelming, in those walls, I have everything I could ever need. My home is filled with love and the absence of it in every other aspect of the world means that being in that tiny cottage in the middle of nowhere is the richest I could ever be. The world hasn't always shown me love, and to think about leaving something so secure, something so sure, to not know if you'll ever find it again is like being born in a treasure chest only to leave it all behind to brave the high seas to find even half of what you had.

'But Dad, I don't know what I'm doing,' I suddenly rush out. 'I can't help but feel like every decision I make is the wrong one. I keep doing everything wrong.'

'That's how you know you're on the right path.'

Chapter 19

With Dad safely on a train back to his quiet countryside comfort the following day, reality returns.

'Today, we shall all be keeping our feet, and bottoms, firmly on the ground.' Westley's eyes flash to mine and I take a particular interest in the flowers neighbouring my feet. He still hasn't *quite* got over the events of last week, it seems. 'Pens may be your only sword today.'

Alice, one of the voluntary members of the school, leans in close to speak to me with a coy smile. 'I'm afraid you won't find him today. He's got far better things to be doing.'

'Who?' I reply with a bored tone, but I already know who she's talking about. She has clearly misconstrued my attempt to avoid Westley's disapproving gaze as me looking for a certain royal. As he's the resident thorn in my side, I noticed his absence almost immediately. My blood pressure, for one, has yet to spike to an unhealthy level.

'Oh, you know.' She fakes a laugh and her fingertips brush my arm. More bluntly than I intend, I snatch it away from her reach. Her eyes scan me for a moment, her false smile breaking for a second before returning even wider than before. 'Here, haven't you seen this?'

Handing me her phone, Alice watches my face as I read the page open on her screen. '*Belle of his Balls: Viscount gets cosy with supermodel Belle Immington*' is today's scummy headline, partnered with a photo of the Viscount Fairfax alongside a woman so uncomfortably beautiful, it's difficult to tell if she isn't just some AI creation. His wide palm clings to her waist, in a more than familiar embrace as he holds her close. Teddy's back is to the camera but it is undeniably him, from the golden shine of his signet ring on his pinkie finger, to the wide-suited back complete with a shock of tousled black hair. Miss Immington can't hide her pleasure at his intimacy, her gorgeous face glows with a Hollywood smile, her fine blonde hair is clipped elegantly at the back of her head, which gives you a full view of the satisfied elation that seeps from her pores – in a glittering kind of way, not the uncontrollably sweaty way. I'm glad he's found someone who can tolerate being so far into his personal space – he's doing well for himself.

'Looks like he's all loved up.' Alice interrupts my analysis of the photograph, her eyes scrutinising my expression, as though waiting for something. Rereading the headline, I think about Teddy for a moment, about that day at Traitors' Gate, the gossip, how his character crumbled, only to return in the form of cruelty. It has been obvious at every turn that the paparazzi have ruined his life, so why does this photo feel so posed, so deliberate? Perhaps he doesn't mind showing the right girl off to the world?

After a second of indulgence in the speculation, I feel guilty for having the thought, for even looking at such a headline, and encroaching on his intimacy. It's none of my business, no matter the way my stomach turns at the sight.

'You know reading these tabloids rots your brain?' is the response that cannonballs out of me before I can stop it. She's harmless, barely older than Marigold. She is naïve in this whole situation, likely just excited to gossip about her idea of a fairy-tale prince. It's my uncontrollable pity for my enemy that compels me to defend him. As big of an arsehole as he may be, he deserves to be that arsehole without the world and its mother judging him.

'Not jealous are you, Dais?' Not entertaining her childish games, I leave her with her smug expression and hand out the day's worksheets, numbing every single thought that tries to worm its way into my brain.

This is probably all part of his plan. Why bother sabotaging the school, when he can just not turn up, have his racy weekends with supermodels? Teddy's winning on all accounts that way – there's no better way for a royal to prove he's a bum than a public affair with a big face from the media. Before he knows it, he and his girlfriend will be on the next flight to the furthest island in the Commonwealth, never to be heard of again until his messy divorce with said supermodel when she does some tell-all bit on Saturday night TV to earn her millions.

I wonder what they talk about. What does he actually have to say when his entire purpose in the conversation isn't to irritate beyond belief? Musing on many of these thoughts for the entirety of the morning, the hours tick by with little excitement aside from the entire life I have constructed for my devilish co-worker. Really, I am no better than Alice or the filth who write those articles, but it kills me to admit that the days grow long and boring without the drama of him. And I realise that in hating him, he has become my only friend here.

Taking a seat with a collection of quiet students, I observe each of the adult faces surrounding me. I find myself watching Erin. Just like my sister, she has this effortlessness about her, this coolness I could never emulate. Here we are, doing the same job, in the same city, same set of skills, but I still can't seem to find any common ground with her.

She catches my eye and I realise I've been staring like a creep, though really I'm looking at nothing but a repeat of all of the things in my head playing over and over like a film designed only to make me cringe. Noticing me, however, Erin gets up and makes her way over to stand beside me.

'Ignore Alice,' she says unprovoked. 'She comes across as a bit of a cow, but she's harmless.'

A little unsure of what to say, I quietly thank her. Confused at her sudden friendliness when until now she has been reluctant to associate herself with me, I keep on guard, afraid of any ulterior motives.

It's obvious that I have been so caught up in my rivalry with the royal, that he is the only one I know. Even then, I don't truly know him at all – I know how to push his buttons and only he knows how to push mine. I have taken such little notice of everyone else around me, I realise I have made no attempt to integrate myself, judging each of them superficially, as I feared they would to me.

'Erin,' I begin shakily. 'Would you like me to show you how to use a polearm sometime? You know, a partisan, or spear? Maybe?' I explicitly extend my invitation for friendship in the only way I can think how.

She looks confused for a moment, then her face can't settle between whether to take it positively or negatively. 'No worries if not,' I hastily add.

'I learnt last year. I think I can manage, thanks,' she snips, before walking back to her friends. Rubbing my face with my hands, I rack my brains for how I managed to get it so wrong again. I feel like a fool.

Trying to brush it off and hide my shame, I try and immerse myself in work. Though, as usual, my mind ends up back on the topic of *him*. How is it easier to make yourself a nemesis than a friend? And a royal one at that.

A familiar face catches my eye as he wanders through the West Gate and over the moat into the Tower. Like a slap in the face, I realise that just like Alenthaea, I have spent too long chasing my enemies, only to neglect the goodness that had been there all along. Ellis.

My leg bounces under the wooden table impatiently, the compulsive motion transferring its kinetic energy to the bench itself, making the entire thing wobble. One of the more serious scholars looks up from her crayons with a scowl as her page trembles with the table.

'Sorry,' I mutter, and attempt to control my impatient

limbs. When Westley finally dismisses everyone for lunch, I am the first to jump up, pushing my way through the crowd that all stand at half my height, and out of the moat and in search of the archivist.

As has been the same story for the last few days, his office lies empty. Today, I refuse to give up without being able to say what I need to. Continuing along the corridor, I peek into the windows of every office on the floor. My creeping goes unnoticed by most who never break their blank stares at their screens, though it is clear that some in the shadowy corners of the Waterloo Block never anticipate being disturbed. One particularly close couple that have decided to spend their dinner hour with a mouthful of anything but their packed lunch chase me off with a collection of expletives and very, very red faces.

My stubbornness only grows, along with my new-found knowledge of sexual positions. Taking my burning face to the next floor, the sound of voices draws me to the door at the very end of the hall. Just like a child peeking into the window of a sweet shop, I spy through the glass. It's a violent shock of red that draws my attention first. The bright scarlet tunics of the King's Guard soldiers are dotted up and down the room, some worn, others hung from thick hangers on the doorframes of neighbouring rooms. The guards, unaware of any onlookers, mill about the room, their deep voices reverberating against the wooden door I lean against and can't seem to pull myself from.

In the dead centre of the room, one of them stands shirtless, polishing his bugle. No, that is not a euphemism.

The long instrument is carefully rubbed down and the master of the cloth checks his work by watching his own likeness reflected back to him in the silver. Another guard sits in the corner of the room, leaning over a pair of shining boots, tormented by his comrade who stands behind him with a spray bottle, dappling the freshly polished patent leather with water droplets. I have to stifle a laugh as the tortured party looks about the room for the source of the leak, only getting more distressed when he finds no explanation for how it is raining on his boots, on a fine July afternoon, under the cover of a stone building.

'Daisy?' Caught, I jump at the sound of my name, knocking my head against the door. Of course, this summons the attention of each guardsman as they each discard their activities to watch me with confusion. Now the same colour as their uniforms, all I can do is lift a stiff hand to wave, the mother of all fake smiles fogging up the glass with the beginnings of hyperventilation. The boot polisher raises a confused hand in return but I turn to flee before I embarrass myself further.

Of course, it would be Ellis who caught me in my moment of curiosity, and he stands at the end of the corridor, a single dark eyebrow raised.

'Not what it looks like.' The words leap from my mouth and somehow his eyebrow takes on an even higher point of his face.

'Are you sure? Because it looks to me like you've been peeping on the King's Guard.' There's a slight smile on his lips but the embarrassment lands like a sickness in my stomach.

'No, n-o.' I choke on the word. 'I've been looking for you.'

'You thought I'd switched careers and nationalities to become a soldier in the British Army overnight?'

I really, really could use a bit of Lady A right now, but she's disappeared on me. The carpet is worn under our feet, compacted from the heavy boots that patrol this corridor through the days and nights.

Ellis rocks back and forth on his heels. 'Well now you've found me. Mission complete?'

'I wanted to apologise. It was all one big mistake.'

'I know, you weren't comfortable. I know that; I see that. I shouldn't have forced you—'

'No, no, you didn't force me. At all. I mean, it was a mistake because the security refused to let me back in. I tried to wait but I just panicked. I had every intention to continue our date, I really did.'

Ellis looks at me for a moment, though I can tell it is the voice in his head that steals most of his concentration. His face creases, then softens, then creases again as he argues with himself wordlessly. Suddenly his mien shifts. He looks at me with such an intense expression of confusion that I am almost certain I have just sprouted a whole new head. Just checking to make sure, my fingers tremble as they pass over my hair and down my face – all *seems* to be in order. I turn my head from him, unable to bear such a gaze any longer.

That's when I see it. The thing that has got him so terribly confused. Two faces have appeared at the window behind me; a blond and a brunette guard squash their cheeks together as they battle for the best view of Ellis and I.

'Come this way, we can talk without an audience.' Ellis eyes the guards behind me. Under the fire of such direct address, they disappear beneath the window, and just the sound of what can only be described as giggling flows through the gap under the door and gives away their presence now.

Following Ellis back along the hallway, he leads me through a passage tucked away beside a thick golden-framed portrait. It seems to be hiding in plain sight, but I hadn't noticed it on my way past. Unlike the rest of the building, there are no windowed office doors. They're all hard wood, the sort that look like they're hiding whole worlds behind them. I can't help but stick out my hand and run my fingertips along the mahogany as I pass, its smooth surface pacifying the tremors that escape through each compass point of my body.

When we reach about halfway down Ellis opens one of the heavy doors with a creak, holding it open for me to pass through first. The room is an explosion of literature. Pages and pages of loose parchment lie stacked all across the room, heavy leather-bound books are piled to precarious heights, with some leaning so waywardly that I worry that the soft bang of the closing door is enough to send them sprawling onto the carpet – I'm assuming there is a carpet somewhere beneath, but as of right now we have to walk across a stepping stone trail of wooden boxes to reach what is presumably Ellis's desk, which is equally drowned in paperwork.

Preoccupied by the revelation of such a room, my anxiety eases and I get the confidence to speak. 'I am going to presume that the fire safety officer doesn't know this room exists?' One spark in a tinderbox room such as this would see the whole place go up like Guy Fawkes on a bonfire.

Ellis chuckles as he moves some sheets to make room for us to sit down. 'Not many people know this place exists. I wouldn't want them to. I know exactly where each resource is, so anyone coming in here to move anything about would be a travesty . . .' He softly takes the notebook from my hand that I had curiously plucked from a pile after the handwritten words '*The Tower of London vs the Luftwaffe*' on the cover intrigued me too much to ignore. Muttering my apology, I take a seat in one of the newly cleared leather chairs.

'So, this is where you've been hiding the last few days?' My voice is quiet as it breaks through the silence that had settled over us.

'Something like that . . .' he breathes. He's on the other side of the wide desk, and I shrink into my chair. From his pedestal of books, Ellis takes on the form of a professor as he rests. I watch him there, framed by intelligence, his bronze skin glowing against the faded yellow pages surrounding us; power seeps from him. He is the king and commander of this cluttered chamber.

'I've been looking for you.' Every word resists exposure. They cling like climbers to a rock as they make their way across my tongue, but I force them to fall from my lips. They need to be said.

'I may have heard from one or two people that there had been someone asking for me.'

'You were avoiding me?' It's a question but it comes out more as a declarative – I already know the answer. Despite expecting it fully, when he nods, my heart seems to slide from my chest and land like a stone in my stomach.

'I'm sorry,' is all I can manage this time.

'You like *him* don't you?' Ellis's words cut across the space between us, though there is no malice behind them. A soft sad smile follows.

'You mean Ted—Theodore Fairfax?' I repress the urge to laugh in his face. He nods again. 'That's what you think this is about?' Another nod. This time, I don't hold back the laughter. It bubbles through me uncontrollably until the rickety chair wobbles under my shifting weight. 'Absolutely not.' I'm breathless when I finally recover enough to speak again. Ellis's face has finally cracked into his familiar grin, but it is when I see his famous dimples pop out that relief finally settles in. As I explain the whole story, the whole confusion – well, leaving out the whole naked-torso, chest-tattoo thing – Ellis relaxes against his chair, and I think I just might be forgiven.

One thing is for certain, I absolutely, irrevocably, completely do not, and could not, like His Lordship, Teddy Fairfax.

Chapter 20

The rain drums against the canvas of the tent, and I stand, hypnotised by the rhythm, lost in its pulse. From within, the pounding could be the sound of hundreds of boots as they march into battle just a mile or two from the camp, kept in step by the drums, their unison unwavering at the foreboding sense that they may never return again. Left, right, left, right, the pace is measured, yet urgent, as they push on, growing closer, louder, louder . . .

The tent flap is thrust open and, so caught up in ideas of murderous armies, I catch my heart, lungs, liver, and both kidneys in my mouth, as my body prepares to be pillaged by my imagination. Perhaps even worse than an army, it's Teddy Fairfax who crosses the threshold. His usually neat ebony hair hangs over his eyes and ears, sopping. One fat droplet falls from one of the strands and catches on his neck, rolling over the curve of his Adam's apple before escaping into his collar. His white shirt is translucent in the deluge, and as he rips his soaked blazer from his back, the dark outline of his tattoo clings to the material.

Coughing, I inform him of my presence before he angrily rips another item of clothing from his body. He's made a few appearances at the Knight School since the news broke of his new relationship. But Teddy has simply carried on as though I don't exist and every time his gaze flits over me an unfamiliar sensation of emptiness hollows me out. Like a tree fallen in a forest, in a way I can't quite comprehend, it feels that if Teddy Fairfax doesn't notice me, am I really here at all?

When he finally looks up to see me, he sighs, running a hand through his dripping hair. His eyes are black, storming with the thunder. I call on Alenthaea, I need her confidence, I need her hardness to pave over whatever turmoil rages right now in my gut.

'Didn't have anyone to hold your brolly for you this morning?' I try and dispel some of the tension that floated in here along with him only moments ago. He only stares back at me, blankly. 'I thought we'd seen the last of you,' I say, remembering the news article, the supermodel, his defiance.

'I didn't have you down as the kind of person to read the tabloids.'.

I flush. He's devoid of his usual teasing grin, and it's clear that he doesn't wish to engage with me as he has done for the past few weeks. That familiar tiredness is etched into his face but today he doesn't seem as buoyant, as though it has all finally started to sink in. The reality of his life is far beyond this little game we have played. I suppose his deluged appearance doesn't help, but he really does look like a boy drowned, a boy who is no longer trying to keep his head above water.

Picking up my bag, I excuse myself, unable to put my finger on exactly why I feel so disappointed to not be insulted by him in some way.

'Change of plan, good sirs.' Just as I reach the exit of the tent, Westley's bright face emerges, his jolly spirits not dampened by the precipitation that rolls into the moulded lines of his forehead. Upon noticing Teddy, Westley clears his throat and quickly adds an 'Er, majesty?' Teddy doesn't look at him, only moves off to rifle through the costume rack to find a dry set of clothes. 'Today we're going dancing.' Westley giggles with glee at the revelation. 'I was saving it for a ball of sorts at the end of the school, but since the weather is not on our side, we shall head on up to the New Armouries and get our dancing shoes on. Now, we want no chain mail or grass-stained trousers today, glad rags only.' Most likely excited to tell the others of his great plan, Westley skips off, leaving perhaps his least excited subjects to despair on the idea.

'I hope you dance better than you can ride a horse.' The deep timbre of Teddy's voice sounds fully for the first time. Though he's still not entirely himself, I can't help but smile as a glimmer of a challenge appears. Perhaps dancing wouldn't be so bad if there were stakes involved.

No, I'm on my last warning, I remind myself. I can't do this again, get so carried away proving my point to him that I end up banished from London only to return home as a failure.

'Honestly, I'd suggest that whichever person has the misfortune of being partnered with me needs to put on a pair of steel-toe-capped boots,' I concede.

'I shall keep far away then,' he murmurs.

'Probably for the best.' Only the patter of the rain sounds now. It's softer, less rushed, like a melancholy sort of crying.

Joining Teddy at the rack, I scour the row of outfits wordlessly. He's still wearing the clothes that he entered in, and my arm grows damp each time we brush shoulders. Teddy doesn't acknowledge this closeness, or even me, until he plucks a hanger from the mass of fabrics. A long black dress flows from it and he runs a damp hand down the material.

'Black is certainly your colour. Not quite sure you've got the hips for that one though,' I joke.

Teddy huffs, unamused.

'It's for you, Daisy.' He shoves it towards me, his gaze refusing to meet my own. My name on his lips will never not sound foreign. So proper, so perfectly pronounced, as if everyone who had used it up to now had gotten it wrong. I can't argue so I take it from him as he busies himself by looking off into the depths of the tent, grateful that he pays no mind to how every drop of my blood rushes to the surface of my skin.

What is his game? Why is he suddenly concerning himself with how I dress? Has he had a complete personality transplant since I spoke to him last? Oh God, the royals haven't resorted to some sort of torture therapy, have they? That could explain the tired mellowness?

Holding the dress very still in my hands, I almost worry

if I move too quickly it will explode and this whole thing is just some elaborate plan to embarrass me.

'It's a dress – it's not going to bite,' the viscount adds as he notices me looking the sleek material up and down, my face evidently giving away my perplexity.

Catching myself wondering again what Lady A would do faced with such a situation, I think for a moment how she would throw it back in his face, make all of her own decisions. By accepting the dress, she would be showing her weakness. But today, with my probation so close to being over, with my grip slipping on everything up until this point, I don't even know if I should listen to her anymore.

'Er, thanks.' Unsure of everything else, I retreat into the changing room to do as I'm told. Safely behind the curtain, I allow my face to release all of the expressions it had managed to hold back: first confusion, disgust, then the next wave of feeling surges. I'm abashed, amazed, and worst of all I feel just ever so slightly . . . titillated.

No. Absolutely not. *Get it together.* Slapping my cheeks lightly, the quick drop back into reality sends another flurry of disgust rolling over me.

'Surely you know how to put on a dress?' Teddy's voice makes me flinch as it flows through the curtain. My stillness must have given away my hesitation. Just a single strip of fabric separates us. I can hear each of his soft breaths; he must be able to hear my fraught ones in turn.

'Of course I do,' I snap as I drag my tunic over my head quickly.

'Good, because I wasn't going to come and help you.' With each word, his voice grows more and more familiar, like the Teddy I'm used to. Now I remember why I dislike him so much.

'If you so much as put an eyelash through this curtain, I will strap you to one of the targets and use you for archery practice.' Alenthaea leaps out momentarily with the excitement of such a threat.

Dressing quickly so as to avoid giving him the opportunity to call my bluff, I throw the dress over myself, cinch it at the waist with the laces of the corset, and allow the long skirt to pour down my body, collecting in each curve as it goes. Aside from a few touches to its texture, I take little notice of what it looks like. There are no mirrors, and I have never particularly enjoyed the sight of my broad shoulders and squidgy arms in such delicate dresses, much preferring the way they fill out a pair of pauldrons, so I try not to think of my appearance as I collect my discarded clothes from the floor.

'I think you'd have much more than a third strike to worry about then, Petal.'

'And, of course, it would be all of your fault again, Your High-and-mighty-ness.' I step from the changing room. He too, has changed from his sopping shirt and trousers and now boasts a black and white doublet, embroidered by the knots and patterns of the medieval fashions. A thick leather belt is tied at his waist and off it hangs the scabbard emptied of its sword. His black breeches end at his ankles and give way to a pair of distressed brown boots. Teddy's damp hair, now drying under the shelter of the tent, curls slightly at the ends as it's freed from the constraints of his usual prison of perfection.

'Well don't you look positively royal,' are the words I splutter out, after scanning each inch of his decorated form.

'Are you trying to suggest that I don't every day?' Prince Charming's evil twin raises an eyebrow, opening his arms so I can get a better glimpse of his figure.

'You wouldn't be here if you did.' It comes out of me quicker than I can catch it. I've done it again, taken it too far and pressed my clumsy palms into his gaping wound. 'Sorry, I shouldn't—'

'Touché.' He surprises me with a grin. Okay, what on earth has happened to the Teddy Fairfax I know? His eyes shift from my face for the first time, observing his work. Crossing my arms across my corseted middle, the long billowing sleeves cover me with ease, and I am rescued from the inspection of his gaze.

'Come on then, tell me I'm ugly or something. I can tell you're dying to insult me.' I roll my eyes as I try and defuse some of the heat from his scrutiny.

'Why would I ever tell you that you're ugly?' Seriousness overtakes his usually impish face, and I am frozen in it. 'You look fu— fine . . . You actually seem almost agreeable without all of the weapons and armour.' Teddy turns and releases me from his examination.

'Yeah, well, don't get used to it.' My mouth is dry as I speak, and I wrestle with my impulse to run out and tilt my face to the pouring rain. Instead, I take a moment to study him, without the fear of being equally perceived.

Teddy's posture is perhaps the most regal thing about him. No matter what, his shoulders remain high and strong, his back never curves, he never seems to hold himself in a position that could be considered comfy for long. I wouldn't be surprised if he'd had metal poles surgically drilled into his spine to prevent any sloppiness. I picture him as a child, solemnity forced upon a cheeky little boy as he's forced to walk up and down the rooms of grand houses, carrying volumes and volumes of heavy books on his head. Still as rigid as ever, he stands perusing a row of decorative swords, deciding which to wear.

He helped me with something I know little of, so perhaps this is my chance to return the favour. 'The sabre is probably your best option. The curve of the blade will keep it out of the way a little more whilst dancing.' Teddy reaches for a rapier with a hesitant hand. Taking a deep breath, I use my own hand to guide his to the correct hilt, and to my surprise, he allows it. My touch isn't repulsed. Adding his weapon to his hip, he says nothing.

Far too tempted by the table of goods before me, I select my own. A delicate dagger to suit such an elegant dress should do nicely. Wrapping a darkly stained belt around my waist, I fasten the slight blade to it and flee the tent before I choke to death on the thickening air.

The attack of the rain is instant. Fat droplets slide down my face, and I am grateful for the way it cools my burning cheeks, though not quite as grateful for the way it dribbles down the front of my dress and dampens the whole way down to my navel. As quick as it soaks me, it stops.

Teddy stands beside me, a wide umbrella clutched in his

soft hand, sheltering both of us. 'Is this your way of protesting against me being nice to you?' He stares ahead as he speaks, though it's clear he means the almost ruining of the dress.

'I, I forgot . . . that it was raining.' Together, we walk back across the grass. I have to hold the folds of my long skirt to prevent it from dragging across the liquifying ground.

'You only had to take off the armour, you know, not your brain as well.'

'I was starting to think you'd left the real Teddy locked up in one of your palaces, but there he is.' I had hoped that the smile I aim in his direction, as we walk side by side, would go unnoticed, but he's already looking at me, a similar grin mirrored on his mouth.

A flash of lightning breaks the connection and I release a gasping breath – unsure if it was triggered by the shock of electricity in the sky, or the shock through my body. Looking up to find its source, I babble to try and cover up just how much Teddy has got under my skin. 'Lightning fascinates me. I always think a thunderstorm is rather romantic. Thunder and lightning are like forbidden lovers. You think of them as a pair but they always miss each other; they are so close but could never be together,' I murmur, unsure of really where I'm going with such a thought.

'I'm afraid that was no lightning.' Teddy grumbles emotionlessly, lowering the umbrella to cover more of us. I look at him, confused for a moment, until the blinding light flashes again, not from the heavens, but from the hands of three little men stood hanging over the walls of the moat.

'Arseholes,' I growl through gritted teeth. Facing them now, I feel empowered, ready to fight back, fight for hi— fight against them taking pictures of me without my permission. The rain drips down my face again as Teddy continues walking, head down. 'I'll fuc—' Well and truly on my way to confront them, Teddy, finally noticing my absence, grasps me by the arm and pulls me close to him under the umbrella again.

'They aren't worth it.' He still clings to me, his body heat warming the cool trails of rain that had drawn lines of goose bumps into the neck of my dress. Teddy presses me further into his chest with such desperation he must be terrified that at any moment I will run away to show the filth the sharp end of my dagger and make every global headline. But his face isn't as cold and hard as I've seen it whenever their kind are mentioned, or as cold as it was only moment ago. He watches me closely, hardly blinking, with a glow about him, a slight smile gracing his lips.

With red cheeks, I escape from his hold and fix my eyes to the pavement underfoot. As I pick up my pace, the rain finds the back of my neck and I shiver as its beads slide down my spine. Teddy's stride matches mine once again and we complete the rest of the journey in silence.

'A knight is best known for their performance in battle, but to be a truly successful knight, you must also win the admiration and friendship of your fellow courtiers. And what better way to impress the lords and ladies, than with a dance!' Westley's voice echoes around the high ceilings. In an attic over the top of the Tower's café, the sparse furniture has been moved to the borders of the room and the gathering of knights, all dressed in their medieval Sunday best, wear varying expressions at Westley's excited speech.

'Dancing's for girls.' Of course, it's Tristan the Great (Pain in the Arse) that speaks up. Before Westley, or anyone else, has the chance to correct him, it is Teddy, Tristan himself in a much larger font, who steps up for the job.

He bends down to the boy's height, and they stand face to face. 'Listen here, Tristan,' Teddy orders, and he obliges; in fact, the whole room takes heed. 'You wish to be a knight, yes?'

The boy nods cautiously.

'Do you think brave knights concern themselves with policing who can and cannot move their bodies to music? No, brave knights are more occupied with slaying dragons and helping the people who need them. Right now, young sir, your comments are helping no one.'

Tristan flushes a deep shade of red, still nothing to say.

'Now, you interrupted Sir Westley with a very confidently incorrect statement. Can you please apologise?'

Tristan nods hesitantly. 'S-sorry.'

'Thank you, Tristan.' Westley's shock is evident in his voice and manner, and a similar look is shared between all of the teachers of the school. What on earth has happened to the uninterested viscount, the man who has done more to make the students misbehave as opposed to teaching them anything?

'Now, what we would have normally danced in the times of knights and nobles is a dance called a carole, which involves us all holding hands and dancing in a circle,' Westley continues from the front of the room. 'But as I do not have my band with me today, and without the proper music, it may as well not be danced. We will just have to settle for a more Regency style. So, find yourself a partner and line up down the hall. Tristan, you shall have the privilege of being my partner.'

The naughty knight hangs his head in shame as he follows his instruction and meets Westley at the very front.

Teddy is a particularly sought-after partner. Several of the teachers, men and women alike, watch him closely, in hopes of being his choice. Alice approaches demurely, looking at him through her long lashes. Uninterested in watching a scene akin to a Sunday afternoon cattle market with everyone making their bids for the viscount's hand, I make myself scarce; perhaps there will be a lonely student in need of a partner and I will get one by proxy.

Westley begins his demonstration with an unimpressed Tristan in tow. After offering my hand to a lonely looking student, and being bitterly spurned with a look reminiscent of my primary school discos days, I retreat to the back of the hall and do what I do best: reorganise things that have no business being reorganised.

A presence draws up beside me. With my back to the crowd, I don't see them approach, nor do I see their face, but I have become rather familiar with this creeping silhouette and the way it towers above me, how it always stands just close enough for my shoulders to skim its bicep.

'Where's your partner?' the silhouette asks. You can hear the smile in its voice.

'I think knowledge of my superior dancing skills has spread and no one dares to take on the challenge of keeping up with me,' I joke and Teddy chuckles beside me. 'How about you? You were fighting them off last time I checked.'

'You're checking on me now are you, Petal?'

I poke him in the hip with my elbow, and he meets my eye with a wide grin.

'I am a loyal man, as much as people such as yourself and the press would like to think otherwise. I dressed myself to suit a lady, and she is the only lady I shall dance with.' Scanning the room, I look for the dress that matches the black and white breast of his doublet. As I watch, I discover several pairs of eyes already observing us.

'Oh, you are bloody joking.' I finally twig. It's me. The picking out of the dress, the sudden character transplant, it all makes sense. He's going to make me his partner, then in some way humiliate me in front of everyone. 'It's me, isn't it?'

He nods his agreement – that cursed smirk plastered on his face, the amusement glowing in his eye.

'And I have no choice in the matter?'

'Afraid not, Petal.' Teddy offers me his hand. Without taking it, I only look at it, hoping in some way that my non-existent telekinesis can get it as far from me as possible.

'Sir Daisy, Sir Theodore, care to join us?' Westley's voice encourages each of the remaining eyes to land on us, and I have no choice but to take his wide palm in my dampening one and allow him to escort me to the dance floor. Into battle we go.

Chapter 21

Melee combat has always been my strongest suit. Getting in and amongst the action, fighting a man so close you can feel his breath on your cheek as you deliver each blow. The only time I can look a man in the eye is to watch his life drain from him – it's only polite. A melee is just a dance, and dancing is just a melee.

Except the only actual brawls I've taken part in, and the only man's life I have ever drained, has been controlled, scripted, acted. Now there is no script; there is only Teddy Fairfax, and who on earth knows what his next move will be?

I need Lady A. I need to be everything she is. How am I meant to do this as *me*?

'The dagger in my pocket may be plastic, but if you don't move your hand, we will see how easily it can take your eye out.'

Teddy's hand that he had perched on my hip is quickly snapped away and he busies it by brushing down his already spotless breeches, mumbling an apology.

'Now, this dance requires us to pair up in a row, and our starting position is just like this.' Westley angles himself and Tristan so they are facing one another, their opposing forearms touching in the centre. 'Our first steps are nice and easy, just a spin clockwise.' The pair demonstrate, their arms still barely touching in the middle. 'Then anti-clockwise.' Westley displays each of the simple steps before bowing to his partner, and encouraging the rest of the congregation to do the same.

It's me who makes the first move, and I offer out my forearm like the polished silver of a sword, displaying my weapon for my opponent to see. Teddy consents to the challenge. His arm meets my own in the middle. The clashing of competitive weapons comes in the form of a soft pressure caressing my limb. Like the pointed apexes of a blade, the tips of his fingers ghost over mine, not quite touching long enough for him to transfer me some of his warmth, but just enough for the tickle of his touch to spread down my tips and electrify the length of me. Teddy's face leans closer. The stubble of his chin shadows along the sharp edge of his jaw; his dark eyes refuse to concede even the time it would take to blink. We are locked in a duel.

'En garde,' I whisper. My face is so close to his, I have no choice but to hold fast and square up to his gaze.

'Oh, is this how we're playing now, Petal?' The corners of his smirk just infiltrate my tunnelled vision.

With each step, his stare doesn't waver; nor does mine. The room spins slowly around us, but his face is still, unmoving, the only point of focus in my vision. The music is long forgotten. We only move to the melody of our own bodies and the harmony that hums between us. There is no leader in this pair; we are so in tune that each advance feels as though it has been played for me. Each step towards him is an attack, yet he receives it with grace. He cherishes it as each strike lands softly against him and he returns it tenderly. Begging for a battle, for him to raise to me, to fight against me as he has done for weeks, I step again, fervently this time. The metaphorical blow barely lands, and as smoothly as each time before, he twists my passion into the dance, and carries us off away down the hall. My dress catches at his ankles as we spin. The cool draught cuts under the skirts and infects my legs with goose bumps.

Why won't he fight back?

'What's your game?' I murmur into the shortening distance between us.

'My game?' His face doesn't flinch at the confrontation. We move exactly as before. My eyes still won't divert from him.

'Well, I know that for weeks you have tried to sabotage everything, in hopes of your banishment. But now the dress, this dance, you're actually being . . . tolerable. So, what is your game? Get me to put up with you? To what? Or is this one of those stories where you get the girl who's never been kissed to fall in love with you, so you can fuel your ego and break her heart?'

Abandoning the arm's distance, he snakes a hand around my waist in a counter attack. The contact knocks me off balance for a moment and it is his strong ensnaring arm that catches me. He has assumed control. Our pace quickens as we float across the room. It's still only his face in full view, everything, everyone else, unseen and forgotten.

'Why, are you in danger of falling in love with me?' He seems closer than ever, as though he has stepped inside me and my heart is working overtime to sustain us both.

'I have gone this long in my life avoiding such danger; you being uncharacteristically kind to me for a single day isn't going to change that.'

Teddy draws away in the dance and crosses the hall, though he still watches me, as though to take his eyes off me would send me bolting. Perhaps he's right.

'You've never been kissed?' His body returns to me, radiating its heat until a bead of sweat trickles its way down the curve of my spine. I shouldn't have allowed that detail to slip free. I have handed him another weapon with which he can humiliate me. The twenty-three-year-old virgin. Teddy bows his head so our lips are aligned. Every one of my pores feels him.

'Go, on then; laugh at me.' Gritting my teeth, I await his reproach. But it never comes. Teddy's dark eyes flicker from mine, to the curve of my lips. I need to run.

Growing restless in his grip, my body burning as each pulse beat passes, I attempt a renewed attack. We're not dancing, we're fighting – I remind myself. His palm presses harder to the small of my back, and the feeling of him jolts down my body, until I lose all control of myself.

'I thank you for the challenge.' He breathes across my face.

'I detest you,' are the words that claw their way out from behind my teeth.

'I know.'

I am so flustered as the song reaches its climax that my clumsy feet land one final, accidental blow to his boot and just like that, I am released. A rush of cold air fills the space he was in just seconds ago, but now winces a step from me.

'You weren't lying about that steel-toe-capped thing, were you?' he splutters as the final cadence sings from the speakers. Before he can return to his full height, before he has the chance to reach out and imprison me again, I hurry away.

I have allowed Alenthaea to take over. This isn't me. The closeness, the eye contact, the *touching*. In adopting her confidence, I have forgotten my true character. When I am with him, I have no idea where Daisy ends and Alenthaea begins.

Free of the oppressive eyes of my colleagues, of him, I make it out into the courtyard of the Tower. With my chest heaving, I pause for a moment to take in the view. The White Tower stands before me in all her glory. Against the backdrop of stormy London, she glows against the clouds like a goddess emerging from the heavens. In the rain, the white stone is slick, shining, and the rainbow of coloured umbrellas that float around her still couldn't draw your attention from the domed turrets. How many women through time must have gazed upon her and begged for some divine intervention?

With my skirts clutched in my hands, I sprint through the rain, dodging tourists as I flee down the boardwalk steps, retreat from the White Tower's glower, under the archways of the haunted Bloody Tower, past Traitors' Gate, and beyond, until I stumble back into one of the tents. My shoes drip, my hair clings to my neck and face, and I tear the dress over my body – or attempt to. The fabric clings to me, as though enchanted to never leave me, to always trap me in its lace and frills. Right now, this dress embodies him. And I need to get rid of it.

After wrestling for a few moments, I am finally freed. Exhausted from the battle, I sit for a moment in my underwear, listening again to the slowing patter of tiny drops on the canvas of the tent, trying to soothe my racing mind, my erratic body.

Before long, the sounds of voices replace the rain and disturb my equilibrium once again. Rushing to dress myself, I join the group that have returned to the camp, though this time in the comfort of my own clothes.

'Where did you rush off to? I was just about to compliment yourself and Mr . . . Sir . . . Theodore on your work. Fabulous display from the both of you.' Westley finds me out almost immediately. The thought of him witnessing us, of anyone seeing the spectacle of me embarrassing myself in the company of a viscount, makes my stomach drop.

Fearful of being caught skiving once again, and afraid of losing the job that I have consistently proven myself to be terrible at, I formulate a lie. 'I, er, needed the toilet. Dickie tummy.' I whisper the last part, for added sympathy and my boss thankfully enquires no further.

'I hope you kept that pretty dress clean.' Teddy's voice fills the gap that Westley has just left. The stalking royal has evidently been earwigging and is now in the know about my non-existent tummy troubles. Great.

My mind rushes with thoughts of him, the feeling of his breath ghosting down my neck returns though he's feet away from me now, yet I can't think of a single word to say. With the rain stopped, and the sun finally emerging from behind the blanket of cloud, I grow hot under its glare.

Why did it have to be me? Why did I have to be chosen to deal with him? Why did I allow him to worm his way into my head?

Teddy opens his mouth to speak again, but I am grateful when a new voice interrupts his next bothersome speech. 'Is that little Lord Fairfax I see? I've heard rumours of the trouble you've been stirring in my territory.' Both Teddy and I turn to the source of the voice. A tall figure smiles his way towards us, though his smile seems out of place against the scarlet uniform on his breast. Teddy chuckles at the sight of the King's Guard as he approaches. His tall bearskin hat is replaced by a formal cap, and the unmoving stern expression they usually wear is replaced with full animation at the sight of what seems to be an old friend.

'What is it I call you now? Captain Freddie Guildford is it?' Teddy outstretches his hand, which the guard clutches in a familiar embrace.

'Just Guardsman Guildford, these days, old chap.' The viscount gives the tall guardsman a perplexed eye, to which he is prompted to continue, 'Long story.' He says brightly, 'In fact, here said story comes now.' The guardsman gestures to a shock of red hair that makes its way through the crowd of tourists that has gathered in the wake of the great British summer downpour. Once clear of other bodies, a young woman emerges from behind the mane, her flushed face stretched into a smile so wide upon seeing the guard that it's hard not to catch its contagion. Freddie Guildford is infected so badly I think he has almost forgotten the original task at hand as he watches her take each stumbled step until she reaches us.

She leans up to give him a wobbly kiss on the cheek before offering a friendly 'Hiya.' First to me, and then to Teddy.

'This is Maggie. Maggie, this is an old friend and boarding school pal of mine, Theo Fairfax, and am I right in thinking this is Tom?' He looks at me with a cheeky grin, not too dissimilar to the one Teddy displays when he's in one of his more annoying moods.

'Tom?' Teddy voices the question on both of our lips with a confused smile.

'Caught this one peeping on the blokes in the guardroom this week.' Freddie winks playfully, and Teddy eyes me with an arched brow, and freshly reloaded ammunition with which to tease me again. As usual, my cheeks invent a brand-new shade of red.

'I was looking for a friend,' I mumble as the two men laugh.

'Ignore him.' The redhead nudges her boyfriend with a well-aimed jab to his ribs and rolls her eyes lightly. 'You two should come over to our place for tea sometime. I need all of the embarrassing stories of this one at school.'

'Oh, we're not, no—' I laugh awkwardly '—we aren't toget—'

'It would be our pleasure,' Teddy interrupts and sends Maggie a blinding smile, not before sending an inconspicuous wink my way, an act that renders me too defenceless to try and contradict him.

'Well, that's settled then,' Guardsman Guildford adds merrily, wrapping a long arm across the shoulders of his beloved. 'Now I had better get back to guarding those Crown Jewels, especially if they're letting just any old rogue through those gates these days.' He claps Teddy on the shoulder and they share a public schoolboy chuckle. The couple retreat back along the way they came and once they are suitably out of earshot, I turn back to the viscount with narrowed eyes.

'What?' he asks, feigning innocence. 'She was being nice, and Guildford's a good man. Plus, he will know that there is no chance that I would, or could, date someone like you, so he will know that the acceptance of the invitation was purely face-saving for his girlfriend.' Teddy says it so casually that the blow feels all the more lethal.

'Someone like me?' I can't help but pick him up on his language. That's a trait of the wealthy, talking of us normal people like we are 'others', talking about us as a whole detached species. It bothers me very little that he wishes to remind me how out of my league he is – he could be penniless and he still wouldn't look at me twice. Boys like Teddy Fairfax fancy supermodels, and I'd have an easier time convincing everyone I am a magical elf than one of those.

By law, of course he is above me, by divine right too, supposedly. But he is human before he is a royal, and I am human before I am common.

'You know what I mean.' The viscount shifts in his boots as he tries to smile it off.

'Do I?' I taunt him. Visibly, he grows hot in his costume and heat rises from his collar.

'Yes, you know, because you're, well you're not . . . I didn't mean . . .' This is the first time I've seen him stumble on his words. Mr Confident crumbles before me, and I admit I am enjoying watching him squirm, just a little.

'Oh yes, I do understand, quite well. You think you're better than me, so the thought of being with a peasant such as myself is revolting. Oh and God forbid anyone believes that you would ever find "someone like me" romantically interesting.' The words fire from my tongue like bullets from a gun. His face crumples on impact and it feels as if my attack had ricocheted from him and found its landing in my gut.

'No, of course not, Daisy, come on—'

'Permission to be excused from your presence, my lord?' I don't wait for his response, nor do I listen to him say my name, his tone racked with frustration.

I had hoped that that fighting off his insult with venom would make it hurt less when I don't even know why it hurts so much in the first place. But as I walk away, I can't bring myself to celebrate the victory, to rejoice in the way my words sting him like his burn me. All I'm left with is pain.

Chapter 22

'We're all heading off to the pub tonight, just for a post-work pint, and I was wondering if you fancied it?' Erin approaches me almost out of nowhere as I finish hanging the last of the costumes that our tiny knights have thrown at me before rushing home.

'Me?' I am the only one here. It's clear she's talking to me – though with my track record, I'm sure the ghosts are more likely to be invited out for a drink.

'Yes, you.' She laughs without a grin, and I smile cautiously, awaiting the deliverance of the fine print. Not long ago she rejected my attempts at friendship. Why would she ask me now? A change of heart perhaps? I haven't made her job harder for a couple of days or left her to fight off a rebellion of nine-year-olds. That could only help my cause I suppose.

When the 'ifs' and 'buts' don't come, I hesitantly accept. 'I'll just finish this up, and I'll join you.'

Another of the girls pops her head over Erin's shoulder. A cheeky grin dons her tanned face. 'Have you asked?'

'Yes, Daisy is going to join us once she's finished up here,' Erin replies.

'No, I mean did you ask about . . .' The second girl widens her eyes and twitches her head in what has to be a very uncomfortable way to convey something she doesn't want to ask aloud. Here's that fine print.

Erin shakes her head in the negative and grows increasingly agitated, shifting her friend's chin from her shoulder.

'Ask me about what?' I don't particularly wish to hear the conditions that are set out for me joining. Clearly there is some ulterior motive beyond being friendly enough to invite a colleague out, but I may as well hear what people want me for.

The girls look at each other. Erin shakes her head again but her friend proceeds tentatively anyway. 'Well, you are friends with Lord Fairfax, aren't you?'

Teddy, what a surprise. Even when he's not lurking in shadowy corners, I can't escape him. 'No, not really,' is the kindest answer I can proceed with.

'Well, you're closest with him out of all of us.' When I don't respond (mostly because I'm trying my best not to let my impulsive eyeroll materialise, and it's proving exceptionally difficult) she continues, 'We were just wondering if you'd ask him if he would like to come too? We think if it came from you, he'd actually think about it. He doesn't look twice at the rest of us.' She blushes as she finishes.

'Why would you want to socialise with someone who has only ever been rude to you?' I can't help myself. She flushes even deeper.

'He's not rude . . . he's just royal.' She whispers the final word as though spilling a dark secret. I look to Erin, a little part of me hoping that she will surprise me, assure me that my company is desired too, but she avoids my eye and busies herself looking around the tent.

I can't allow my own opinion of Teddy to get in the way of my opportunity to make more friends. This is my chance, so, reluctantly I agree. Erin's friend lets out a little squeak that takes us all, particularly her, by surprise and she rushes away giddily.

'You really don't have to,' Erin mumbles once she's out of earshot. 'If you don't want to.' I can't tell if she means to say I'm welcome to come without him, or that I don't have to join them at all. But something about this whole thing would make the latter most likely.

With this kind of communication my hamartia, and my chest aching a little with the reminder of my loneliness, I can only smile, nod, and say a quiet: 'It's okay.'

I find Teddy in his usual spot, sat at Westley's broad kingly desk in one of the few tents that most people are forbidden from entering. Most evenings he waits behind for a little while, awaiting a sleek car to escort him across the city back to one of his palaces. Ordinarily, this is where he retreats to glare at his phone with such a sternness that I worry the thing will shatter just from his gaze alone, but tonight, he sits, quite placidly, with his face buried in a book.

'I didn't know you could read,' is my awkwardly teasing attempt at drawing his attention. It works, Teddy smirks as he holds up a finger. His eyes furiously scan to the end of the page before he lifts his notice to me.

'There's a lot you don't know about me, Petal.' Teddy relaxes back into his chair to observe me in the entryway.

'I'm happy to keep it that way.'

'What can I do for you? Or are you just here to question my intellect?' Standing up, he moves around the wide desk, before perching himself on the front. Teddy crosses his arms across his broad chest and fills my eyeline with bicep.

'I have been invited to the pub.'

'Congratulations.'

'I have been invited to the pub, but under the pretence that I can also encourage you to attend. Apparently in all of the energy you exert in annoying me, you have no time for any of the others, so they're too scared to ask you themselves.'

'You know, if you wanted to ask me out, you didn't have to come up with this elaborate excuse, you could just ask.'

I scoff, '*Someone like me* wouldn't even think about it.' My own reminder of his words from just hours ago renews that feeling of coldness that has been prickling in my chest all afternoon. 'They want you there, and they only want me there because they think that would make you want to come. So, if I want any friends, I have to ask you.'

He contemplates that for a moment, stroking his chin.

'Look, are you coming or not?'

Growing increasingly impatient, I prepare to simply leave and tell the rest of the group that I tried my best. That's until Teddy grabs his blazer from the coat stand and strides out. Unable to process the last few seconds, I remain stapled to the floor.

'Are you coming then, or not?' Teddy pokes his face back

through the tent flaps and, in spite of all of my reservations, I follow him.

'What's the king like? Can you just talk to him like a normal person?' Teddy sits at the head of the table like the lord he is and the others have spent the last fifteen minutes firing questions down it. Surprisingly, he takes them all with little reluctance and plenty of poise, most likely acquired from a lifetime of media training. He safely deflects most of them that could quite easily become tomorrow's headline.

'He's an interesting man, incredibly competitive. No one in the last ten years has been able to beat him at charades at Christmas.' This satisfies that rabble as their faces turn to one another with each of his vague answers as if they have just been handed a government official document detailing the existence of the Loch Ness monster.

No one has said a word to me. Perched on the last chair, the furthest away from the viscount, I have not been of interest since my usefulness of acquiring a more noteworthy subject for the party. Though I can hardly complain. I haven't attempted to speak to anyone either, and in all honesty, I have no idea why I even wanted to subject myself to even more socialisation when it's my least favourite hobby.

Erin's friend, who I've since learnt is named Mei after she just about screeched it in Teddy's face when he asked, asks another question regarding the viscount's access to the Crown Jewels. I take that as my cue to remove myself to the bar for another drink. No one will be surprised to know that I have not often frequented public houses. I have, however, spent a couple of evenings in taverns where the tankards are filled with a mysterious ale, and the bar staff are all varying degrees of hybrid animal-human creations. But that may or may not have been a few low-budget scenes of improvised LARP.

This pub would fit right into the medieval backdrop. The wooden floors slope so the low ceilings get even lower the further you move into it. Much like at home, the walls bulge with decoration and the whole stretch from the table to the bar is covered with a breadcrumb trail of the pub's own history; black and white photos and antiquated portraits break up the frames of text. I have to rush quickly past Morton who sits alone at a table, an untouched pint in front of him as though that was going to make him look inconspicuous when the black-suited bulldog has been threatening every patron with his eyes since we stepped in. By the time I reach the slightly slanted bar, I have already been beaten there.

'Your round is it, Petal?' Teddy stands stiffly at the bar, speaking to me quietly.

'You're the one with the vault of jewels, are you not?' The landlady has yet to notice us, so I match my volume to his to allow him to go undetected for a few more moments.

'Ah, well, someone wasn't listening to our good companion's question, were we? I am afraid I am not allowed to simply carry the Black Prince's Ruby around in my pocket to exchange for a few pints and a packet of pork scratchings.'

'There is no way in hell that you, or anyone in your family, have ever eaten a pork scratching.' I can't help but laugh at the absurdity of his uncle, the king, cracking his teeth on an oddly hairy, crunchy bit of pig skin.

Teddy shares my look of amusement. 'I should introduce you to my cousins – you'd be surprised.' He chuckles, and I think the heat growing in my cheeks makes him realise exactly what he's said. His bashful expression quickly turns back to stoic seriousness as the barmaid finally approaches.

'What can I get for yous?' Clearly when you work in a pub once frequented by Dickens, the presence of a royal is nothing special as, thankfully, the middle-aged woman with worn features makes no special notice of Teddy.

'Can I have three pints of your IPA, one cider, an orange juice please. And, Daisy?' Teddy turns to me expectantly and I blurt out the only alcoholic beverage I can think of.

'A mead? Please?' Mead? Who the hell has enjoyed a casual tipple of mead this side of the Middle Ages?

With a slight smile, Teddy repeats my order to the barmaid and pays – with a bank card, no emeralds in sight.

With a tray of drinks in tow, we return to the table together. The viscount makes each individual at the table bumble excitedly as he delivers all of their drinks personally.

'Your mead, mistress.' He sniggers as he sets the small glass on the table before me and I thank him with narrowed eyes. Only the glass of orange juice remains on the tray, and he takes that one for himself before plonking down in the spare seat beside me. Now all of the attention shifts towards us, and I slightly regret my former complaints at having not had a conversation – their eyes remind me exactly why I am an introvert in the first place.

'Daisy, I feel like we know nothing about you!' I almost jump out of my seat at Erin's proclamation. 'You're always so quiet, you've come out of nowhere and you manage to kick everyone's arses with a sword. What's your story?'

'Er, well . . .' I have never been the best at introducing myself. I could never bring myself to accept job interviews with the threat of a team-building exercise, so I am highly unprepared for such a question. Particularly when it's coming from Erin, and every time I have tried to extend my friendship to her, she has shot it down with little to no explanation. Now, being on the spot, I have no chance to plan an answer that she might like, that might actually win her over. How do you politely, and interestingly, convey that your brain kept you from doing anything of worth for years and it has resulted in you being the most boring and inexperienced twenty-something?

'I come from a village, in Lincolnshire. Very small and quiet place. I still live at home with my parents, and my dad owns this really brilliant hobby shop, the nerd haven, we call it.' My confidence grows as my attention shifts to my family. They are the most interesting thing about me after all. 'It's full to the brim of anything a little bit geeky: fantasy maps, mini figurines, potions, dragon eggs – not real of course. I used to work with him, but it wasn't much work. It's quite a niche so we were never too busy. I have a twin—'

'There's two of you?' Teddy butts in. And this time it's

his turn to grow a little colour in his cheeks, as the group titter at his outburst.

'*His* name is Samwise. I have a sister too, younger. She's far cooler than I am.' I chuckle; no one else follows. I attempt a sip at my drink.

'But what about *you*? Come on, we want your juicy details. Boyfriend? Girlfriend? Cats?' Mei chimes in and I splutter on my mead – though I'm unsure if that is entirely caused by her question, or something also to do with the fiery alcoholic contents of my glass. Stumbling over myself for a moment, I can only vocalise some abstraction of a few vowels.

In my moment of need, I look to the man beside me, to Teddy, for some semblance of help and regret it almost instantly – he could take advantage of this weakness, tell everyone what I had told him during our dance, embarrass me to the point of having to leave. But he doesn't. 'No, what I really want to know, is how and why you know how to carve a man to pieces with a plastic sword,' he asks with a tone that sounds almost like awe and I could kiss him – but definitely do not tell him that.

A curious murmur follows his words, and with a deep breath and my special interest at hand, my tongue unwinds. 'Most of the best ones are actually foam and carbon fibre, bloody solid, break a few fingers, but won't snap like plastic. My whole family, we, er, do LARPing.'

'LARPing?' George chimes in. Teddy sits in my periphery with a smile wedged onto his face, and taking another shaking breath, I answer.

'Live Action Role Play. Basically what we do at the school,

except my family and a few others from the village dress up as different characters and battle in the Village Hall playing field. There are different plots and storylines behind it, and we train and things. It's not just hitting your next-door neighbour with a stick, it's actually quite proper – rules and stuff. There's a big community of people that do it all over the world.' My voice diminuendos, and for a moment, I panic that they are each internally laughing at me – it wouldn't be the first time.

'That sounds absolutely insane.' Robin speaks up, shaking his head with a smile. I falter as his words rip the confidence from me. My eyes begin to grow glassy before he quickly rushes out, 'In the best possible way. So, you dress up as elves and shit and just fight each other?'

A smile twitches at the corner of my mouth – they are actually asking more! They haven't laughed me out!

'Sort of. Sam and I are elves, my mum plays an orc, Dad is her squire, my elderly neighbour is a wizard.' This time, my colleagues chuckle with me. 'We are training for this big tournament in September. Most LARP groups from around the country come for this fantasy festival and we have the Great Battle. That's when it gets serious.' Looking nervously at Teddy, fully prepared to meet his bemused and judgemental stare, I find him watching me with a peculiar glint in his eye. It's the kind of look you have when you're gazing upon something you're proud of, like when you've finished icing a homemade cake, or finished polishing your armour and have restored it to its noble beauty. I'm grateful when the conversation around us continues and I have an excuse to escape from his grip on me.

'So that's why none of us have ever stood a chance against you?' Erin smiles down the table at me, a proper smile as she shakes her head softly.

'I'm sorry for kicking all of your arses.' I tentatively attempt a joke and am relieved when it's met with friendly laughter.

'It's funny because I spent all last year struggling to swing a rapier so you coming in and carving me up like a pumpkin on Halloween made me think I'd wasted my time. I had even been training in my garden over winter as well!' She laughs, a bit too hard, and I think for the first time I understand her just a little.

'You should come LARPing!' I'm excited as I speak. 'You all should. Erin, I've never seen someone fend off so many little goblins as well as you, and George, you're brilliant with that war hammer. You could start your own group!' Teddy's eyes still haven't left me. As I meet his gaze, a full beaming smile lights up his face, and I find myself returning it in earnest.

After a couple more questions, I am fully enthused, completely carried away and in intense danger of talking so much that we may be here until midnight. So before I get too adrenalised and start inviting everyone home for Christmas, I excuse myself to the bathroom.

Washing my hands slowly in the sink, I take in my appearance. My cheeks are flushed, not in the perpetually embarrassed state they usually are, but I am glowing. Again, probably the fault of the alcohol, but I have this weird fullness in me as though my heart is taking up even more space in the cavity of my chest. My hair wisps around my head, my eyes seem brighter, the dark green of my irises ripple with life. I look and feel alive. Best of all, in this moment, I am Daisy. Right now, I don't need Lady A's intervention, I don't need to force myself to get involved, to speak, to smile. Needing no one – not my parents, not Sam, not the voice in my head – I feel in control. I am completely and utterly myself and for once in my life, I actually don't mind it. This is who I am, who I want to be.

When I re-emerge, Teddy is pacing the little hallway outside, raking a jittering hand through his dark hair. At the creak of the door, he stops dead still, his eyes locking onto me like through the scope of a sniper rifle. He takes two meaningful strides towards me.

'You like waiting for girls outside of bathrooms now do—' He grips my jaw in both of his hands tenderly and before the rest of the words can fall from my lips, they are arrested by his.

Theodore Fairfax is kissing me.

Theodore Fairfax is kissing *me*. The real me. Not the woman I wish to be, nor the person I pretend to me, just me. Like a sword in its scabbard, our lips slide together as though that is their only purpose.

Chapter 23

I'm not quite sure how I made it home. All I remember is being stuck, stupefied, where he left me and have since been zombified where I lie on top of my duvet just running the moment over and over in my head, trying to make sense of any of it. I think I would have better luck making sense of the enigma codes than whatever *that* was.

He kissed me. *He* kissed *me*. And it was him who ran away, as though disgusted with even the thought of it. Not a single word followed it. Pulling away, it was only the wide eyes of a deer in headlights that screamed to me that whatever happens next, we are both royally screwed. Why didn't I follow him? Why didn't I yell at him, berate him for stealing my first kiss? Why did I let him do it?

Because it made your heartbeat quicken, and because if he hadn't done it first, a small part of you would have done it for him, the little voice in my head reminds me. I have always hated the sound of that voice, but today, I utterly despise it for its embarrassing truth.

The worst of all? From the moment his lips melted against mine, I was prepared to slay a dragon for just one more taste of him, for one more chapter in his tale.

Now I creep towards the Tower like a woman condemned. Lady Jane Grey, Margaret Pole, Anne Boleyn, Jane Boleyn, Catherine Howard, all women cursed in these walls, ruined by the men around them. I picture the Beefeaters waiting for me at the gates, partisans crossed, ready to escort me to my cell, for the king himself to meet me, to convict me for being a harlot, or even better, being a witch and seducing the viscount with dark magic. It wouldn't be the first time they'd blamed the woman for the mistakes of a man in power.

Most afraid of seeing *his* face again, I stalk through the Tower, scanning each shadowed corner, my heart throbbing in my throat at the sight of each passing face. Upon reaching the moat, the front line, his face doesn't appear there either, aside from my anxious imagination assigning his features to each male frame that joins us.

Teddy doesn't make another appearance until the hottest day of the year, two days later, the very last day of my probation. After two days of carrying around a stomach of lava, I woke this morning with the relieving thought that he may have sped up his plans of exile and I will never have to face him again. But there he stands, flanked so closely by Morton that it almost seems as if he has the viscount on a leash. Thus far, he hasn't noticed me as I cower in the archway of the Middle Tower. Gripping the walls for balance, I cool my palms on the corroding stone, deliberating whether to just integrate myself into the French language guided tour that flows behind me and hope that I can convince them to drive me back to Paris with them.

I'm in enough trouble. If I miss another day, if I mess up once more, I will lose the only thing I have to show for myself. I have no choice but to suck it up and hope that, if there is a God on my side, Teddy will simply ignore me.

Sweat pools in every one of my orifices. The heat of London in summer is oppressive, the shard fires red-hot beams across the river. It bounces from the curve of the walkie-talkie, and blinds anyone who dares to look at the surface of the Thames – summer in London is what I think it must feel like when a child first discovers their sociopathic tendencies and takes a magnifying glass to their ant farm, and I am one of the unlucky insects.

'Who are you hiding from?' Ellis's voice startles me as it sounds from beside me. As I'd been focusing on no one but Teddy and my sweaty underarms, his approach had gone entirely undetected. His face is so close to mine that when I jump, my damp cheek pushes against his and I am just inches from sharing my second unexpected kiss in a week. Ellis laughs as he steadies me. 'Sorry, I couldn't help myself. What are we looking at?'

Even more ruffled than before, my tongue knots itself in my head. I can't tell him the truth; I will have to take the truth to the grave but the longer we stand together, him looking at me with his wide St Bernard eyes expecting a reply, the more I panic about what else I can tell him. 'Er, just planning out the shadiest route . . .' Ellis wears a perplexed expression '. . . so I don't get sunburnt.'

He smirks. 'Get sunburnt? In the hundred and twenty yards to that gazebo over there?'

I nod, the sweat flooding my forehead.

'Wait there.' He chuckles again and disappears into the Middle Tower before quickly returning, this time with an umbrella in hand. 'My lady.' He fakes a posh English accent as he extends the brolly and offers himself as my shade escort. There really is no backing out now.

Of course, if there is one way to draw attention to yourself, it's to wander through a moat ushered by a handsome American carrying an umbrella on the driest month. Everyone notices me but it's not until I am almost upon him that Teddy looks up for the first time. The contours of his face seem sharper, angrier, lined with severity. It's unclear if he sees me at all in the way he stares through me, unflinchingly. I can't bring myself to look away. He holds me from afar in his gaze alone. My entire body throbs with the threat of him, the danger that he poses to everything I am, all that I thought I was; but still, I advance into battle.

'Ma'am . . .' Leaning this time into his American roots, Ellis delivers me to the camp with the thickest Southern accent known to man and an exaggerated bow. 'Are you suitably shaded now?' His dimples are so deep, I wonder if he ever ends up with a tan line in them.

Thanking him nervously, a small part of me hopes that he will need to get back to work now. As much as I do like him, this big public display, the fear of the speculation of everyone else as they gaze upon us curiously, is quite possibly my worst nightmare. What I wouldn't give to just disappear into another of his cold ancient rooms to listen to him talk of its history. My heart races, though not in a good way, not like it did that night, not like it did with *him*.

'Daisy, I was wondering . . .' Ellis trails off, and he searches my face for encouragement – I can only nod. 'Would you like to grab that drink or something tonight?' I can't help but look around the room at his words. Erin, Mei, Robin, and Alice all try and hide the fact they are watching and listening, but Mei's cheeky grin that she is desperately trying to hide behind her hand gives it away. Growing itchy with the attention, I try my hardest to keep it together, to save face, but I'm crumbling. I don't want to hurt or embarrass Ellis, nor do I want to cause a scene and flee, particularly when I'm already trying to cling to my reputation in hopes of making it past today. So, I compromise my comfort for him, for them.

Placing my hand on the top of his arm so lightly I can barely feel him, I try and manoeuvre us both a little further away. Uneasy of my silence he speaks again: 'Or I could show you the chapel in the Upper Wakefield Tower? Where King Henry VI was murdered whilst in prayer?'

Looking past his shoulder, unable to hold his eyes, it's Teddy's that I am met with. Teddy stares with such intensity it sucks the breath straight from my lungs and a gasp escapes me before I can control it. Quickly averting my eyes back to the man before me, a man who has only shown me kindness, I mutter my reply. 'I'd like that.' With one last glance at Teddy, I assure myself that this is the safer path.

Satisfied with my answer, Ellis retreats with the promise of seeing me later and just as my colleagues move closer, their grins loaded with a selection of words guaranteed to embarrass me, Westley's prompt beginning to the lesson saves me again.

'This here beast is what one calls a *trebuchet*.' He leans against its wooden beams, petting it like a living creature at his command. 'Now can anyone tell me what one of these was used for?'

'Flinging heads over the castle walls.' Barley, the timid boy who produced the unfortunate snake drawing, shouts across the field. The sound of his own voice seems to take him by surprise and, mortified, he cowers behind another student.

'You are correct, young sir! This here is a kind of catapult used to fire a great many things at the enemy. From great huge stones to break down fortifications, to dead carcasses of animals and enemy soldiers to try and spread both fear and disease into the castle they were attacking.'

It always makes me laugh how kids revel in the disgusting. This job has only reinforced the idea that the more revolting or creepy something is, the more children will listen to it. You can talk of handsome knights and pretty balls, but what really makes their ears prick up is poo, bodies, and all things gross. They all watch Westley now with such curiosity, such excitement at the prospect that I am slightly worried that a few of them think we are actually firing real heads into the Tower of London and letting them rain down on unsuspecting tourists.

Westley reaches into a bucket laid at his feet and, to my horror, picks up something rather wet, and rather head-shaped. After a small shriek from one of the less macabre children, Westley lifts it up so we can all get a better look. A water balloon sloshes around in his palms. 'Today, our ammunition will be much less terrifying, and much less smelly. As it is so warm, we will be using our trebuchet to water the flowers.' He grins, happy with himself.

As my boss and his tiny assistants prepare for a demonstration of his medieval, and theatrical, way of hydrating the garden, I take the moment to retreat under one of the gazebos to try and reclaim some of my composure lost to Ellis and Teddy's surprise appearances.

Just as my breathing settles back into its regular rhythm, Teddy strides towards me, disrupting it once again. Usually, he creeps like a rogue through the night, a sneaking assassin that always lurks in the shadow behind me, but this time, he wastes no time in furtiveness, in games. He is locked on to his target and is willing to collide head on. The anticipation of his approach twists my gut. His gaze is a fist in my stomach, one I can't pull away from.

His eyes dart around for any sign of eavesdroppers. To his relief, everyone has long forgotten the country bumpkin and the viscount as they watch the long arm of the trebuchet fire its ammo across the moat. 'Have you told anyone?' He speaks lowly, the tenor of his voice growling through the small space between us. Intensity radiates from him and I have to take a step back so as to not be bowled over by the closeness of his figure. Grasping me softly by the arm, he pulls me closer again, his passionate gaze interrupted for a moment of concern in his sloping brow. 'Tell me, have you told anyone about it?'

Dragging myself out of his grip, I step back again.

Though my legs tremble, I hold firm. I rely again on Alenthaea. 'About what?' I bluff and he runs a hand roughly over his face with frustration.

Teddy lowers his face so his cheek presses against mine as he speaks into my ear. 'About us.' He grunts. A hot wind of breath rushes across my lobe.

'Us?' I watch his expression as he leans back, the panic in his eyes. 'Oh, you mean when you kissed me?' Though there are metres of empty space between us and any other living person, Teddy scans around erratically, the fear of anyone overhearing me, hearing what has passed between us, enough to make him wild. 'When you kissed me only to run away?' I snap again. 'You made me question all I have ever thought, ever felt, only to leave me there, without a word. And now you have the gall to come over, all guns blazing, demanding to know if I have told anyone?'

'Daisy . . .' He's agitated, but only now, when I see him like this, filled with such regret, do I realise I'm angry. I hate that he is talking about kissing me as some filthy secret – as if to kiss me is to be disgusted with yourself afterwards.

'You're afraid of being caught with someone like me? A pleb like me couldn't possibly be any good for your image. Or is that the whole point? An exciting challenge for you to steal my first kiss, and the shame and embarrassment of it all is a sure-fire way to get yourself disowned.'

'Daisy . . .' he grunts again, but I move from him. Walking back towards the crowd, my fingertips tremble at the confrontation.

'I don't want to play your games, Teddy.' I stop to face

him, my shoulders curving in surrender. My anger is burnt up. Only grief fizzles in the embers now. Grieving for that little glimmer of hope that I had allowed myself, as it dies a little more with every one of his words and panicked glances.

'Have you told anyone or not?' His voice rises as I turn from him again, and I can't control myself. The words reach me just as I pass one of the tables; a jug of water sits in its centre, so still, so tranquil.

So, I take that pretty little jug of water, and throw its contents straight into the viscount's face.

No longer serene, the water drips around his wide eyes, his opened mouth, and I bend close to him so only he can hear. 'You can keep your crown on. I haven't told a soul, nor do I plan on it. I may have very little pride, but why on earth would I admit to anyone that I allowed *someone like you* to use me so despicably? You are *my* dirty secret, as much as I am yours.'

Freeing myself from his proximity, I meet the conspiring grin of Tristan Huntsford as he takes note of Teddy's soaked and pathetic face. The pocketful of chaos raises one nightmarish brow, and whilst still holding eye contact with me, creeps towards the bucket of water balloons. Tristan seizes one, raises it above his head, and with a shrill battle cry of 'WATER FIGHT!' smashes it over the skull of an unsuspecting peer.

Oh shit.

Chapter 24

'I'm sorry, Daisy, I have no choice but to terminate your contract after your probation. As this was the last day of your four weeks anyway, I'm afraid that you need to collect your things and take them with you tonight. You understand, don't you?' Westley drips into a puddle at his feet. His hair has escaped his ponytail and clings to the back of his neck. Even in its deluge, I can see the disappointment etched across his face.

Barely able to hear the sounds he's emitting, I nod. There's no point fighting it. I messed up; it's my fault. I am a failure. I should have controlled myself, been the bigger person and walked away, but in soaking the viscount, I triggered what could only be described as the Somme of all water fights. No person, mobile phone, or item of clothing was safe after Tristan began the warpath. A third strike on my final day of probation was never going to go down well so here I stand, soaked to the bone, facing the consequences.

Everyone expected more of me; *I* expected more of me. Sent off like a hero on a mission to slay the monster, only to return empty-handed and wounded – not by the beast, but by my own sword.

I have only myself to blame.

Once Westley departs with one final sigh, I waste no more time. Stripping myself of my armour, my costume, I dress quickly so as to not see any more of myself than required. Folding the borrowed garments neatly, I leave them on the table and make my last trip out of the tent, out of the moat.

Passing through the crowd, I see that each face is as drenched as the last. Some of the teachers stand, wringing out their tunics; others try and explain to disgruntled parents why their children are sopping in the middle of summer. Teddy fled the scene the moment it turned to pandemonium. Neither he nor anyone else is around to wave me off, and I leave as lonely as I came.

There is just one stop I have to make before I go. Walking slowly through the Tower, its walls seem to shrink around me. The stone is oppressive as it grows closer and closer until the harsh sun seems to retreat behind it too. Calmly, I climb the stairs to the Medieval Palace, a fusty-smelling room above Traitors' Gate filled with replicas of medieval furniture. It's a room that, despite all of its excess, feels empty, and I can almost picture its resident lying awake in the four-poster bed, wondering why the ceilings seem so high, why it feels so cold in spite of the wide fireplace just beside it.

Tracing along the corridor, I finally reach my target.

The king's private chapel is tucked away in the Wakefield Tower, enclosed behind dark emerald partitions. Arches embellished with red and gold are carved into the top half and through them the sun diffuses beams of colour as she glows through the stained-glass centrepiece.

Ellis stands at the altar, admiring the window from close up. The archivist is so engrossed in the kaleidoscope of fractured glass that he doesn't hear my approach.

I realise as I come closer that the coloured shards don't match up to make a scene; they are just fragments soldered together in a mosaic that seems to tell no story aside from the rainbow it spreads about the room. 'What happened to it?' I ask quietly. Ellis turns to me with his familiar smile on his face. The sight of it and the divinity of such a room brings me a fleeting moment of comfort.

'Many of the stained-glass windows in churches and chapels across London were bombed out during the Blitz – including this one. Instead of just replicating what was there before, they collected the shrapnel and created this.' He stares back at it as I meet him at the altar.

'They didn't try and hide the scars of war. They turned a tragedy into something beautiful,' I murmur.

'Exactly. Those shards of glass have seen things we can only imagine. I wonder what that window would tell us if it could talk.' Ellis gives a breathy chuckle. 'A weird thought, I know.'

'No, I agree. Perhaps if we could listen to the walls, we wouldn't make so many of the same mistakes.' We're both silent for a moment. 'I'm leaving London.' I speak more to the window, but Ellis shifts his full body to face mine.

'What?'

I can't look at him. 'I'm probably not even meant to be here right now.' My stomach stirs at the thought of being carried out of the Tower like a criminal. 'I didn't pass my probation period. I'm sorry, but I can't stay. And I can't have that drink with you anymore.' There would be no point. A successful man like him wouldn't want someone who can't even keep a summer job. I have nothing to offer someone like Ellis; I don't deserve him.

'There must be some mistake? I bet it's something to do with him – Theodore Fairfax. He's had it in for you since day one. Surely there's something you can do?' The sound of his name spat so harshly from his lips makes me flinch.

'I am plenty big and old enough to make my own mistakes. I messed up and these are the consequences. I really am sorry, Ellis.' I leave him at the altar, on the spot where King Henry VI was slain in his moment of vulnerability, stabbed in the back as he knelt to his God. I feel only numb.

The tears won't fall. I don't cry as I leave the Tower, nor do I cry when I tell my housemate of my lot, or cry when she does. Packing my things in complete silence, I move like a monster, built only of limbs, unencumbered by emotion.

'Can't you stay? Just find a new job? The café on Finchley Road is looking for staff – you could work there! It's only five minutes away.' Bobble stands in the doorway with the look of a bereaved woman. The cogs are visibly turning across her features, but it's no use. I moved away from home for this job, and this job only. The thought of having to start again, somewhere else, surrounded by new people, doing a job I don't know, would only send me spiralling. This was my big push, my attempt at turning everything around, and it has only served as a reminder as to why I never tried before.

After an hour of attempting to find some semblance of a solution to get me to stay, including a threat to overthrow the monarchy, Bobble makes her way into the room and sinks down into the mattress at the end of my bed. She is sensible enough to know that nothing she can say will make any difference. But just like my dreams, I push her away too. If you tell yourself for long enough that you don't deserve happiness, a good job, a best friend, it's easier to cope with the emptiness of losing them all at once.

The tears only fall when I climb into bed. My new life is packed in boxes around me. A single rogue tear starts it all – it sails across my face in the dark before abandoning ship at the tip of my nose. As soon as the traitorous drop soaks through the fibres of my pillowcase, the rest follow suit until they have invaded my bedclothes and I fall asleep in the dampness.

It's Teddy who stalks through my dreams, so lucid that when the sun begins to stream through my open window, I'm unsure if I've slept at all. My body is heavy as though I have to fight against the pull of hell below just to lift a finger. My neck still feels warm from the ghost of his breath, but it's coldness that sloshes around in my stomach and makes me shiver as I rise from my pit. Every emotion I have for him seems to contradict the next. The grief of leaving London had distracted me from the confusion of him for a short while, but he haunts me. I hate him; I bleed for him.

I'll never see him again. That thought can only be a relief. So why does it make me feel so homesick?

Before I have time to ruminate, the door to my bedroom is thrust open and bangs against the wall with a boom. Flailing in my duvet at the shock of such an entrance, I don't catch sight of the intruder until they're stood over the bed, looking down at me clutching the aluminium decorative dagger that usually rests on my bedside table.

'What are you going to do with that? Pick the food out of my teeth?' Samwise stands over me, an amused eyebrow raised. Tossing the stupid thing across the room, I scramble out of bed to hug him. He stiffens with the contact, but soon wraps two loving arms around me. 'Bloody hell, things really must be terrible if they've turned you into a hugger.'

Releasing him from my crushing grip, I take in his features for a moment. His hair has grown longer and curls around his ears, one of his lobes hangs with a new hoop earring, and everything about him screams 'home'.

'How did you . . . Who . . . How?' I breathe at the sight of him. I hadn't told anyone from home yet, I didn't know how, or where to even begin. Having Sam here now, I feel a fool for not telling him first. My twin is the only person in this dimension who could bring me any semblance of happiness right now. Nothing feels so hard when I'm around him. An asteroid could be heading for earth with the promise of ending the human race, and if I were with him, I think I could be erased from the universe with a smile on my face.

'Bobble called me last night; said you'd gone almost entirely mute. She told me what happened at work. I knew you'd feel better if you didn't have to ask me, so I'm here to help you. And take you home.' His words wrap around me like the soft fibres of a blanket. The thing I love most about him is his ability to understand my brain, when even I fail to make sense of it.

'And you're not disappointed? Not going to try and make me stay?' I ask nervously, though I already know the answer.

'Don't be stupid.' I'm not sure if it's some twin telepathy thing, or the fact we have spent so long in each other's company, but he sees me; he doesn't try and get me to change to fit into the standard box. My brother just acknowledges who I am, and holds my hand for the journey.

'Did you tell Mum and Dad?' The embarrassment moulds into anxiety as I await his response.

My brother shakes his head softly. 'I thought it would be best for you to do it, when you're ready.'

I nod; as much as I wish he had shouldered that painful burden for me, he's right. It has to come from me. There's just so much I can't tell them, that I can't even tell Sam.

Bobble peeks her head around the doorframe with a softly whispered, 'Knock, knock.' I invite her in and she tiptoes across to us. 'You will come to visit, won't you?' she asks timidly.

I'm not sure I can bring myself to promise her. Not because of her – her kindness and her friendship have been a whole love story in itself, one I don't think I shall ever get again. But this place, London, in leaving it I am failing, and in returning I am only reminded that I have achieved nothing. That really, when it all comes down to it, I am heading right back to the beginning, back to the isolation, to the anxiety, to insignificance. I have run head first into the future, without realising I am bound to my life of nothingness by a bungee rope that as soon as I have pulled it taut enough, gotten close enough to reach something, anything else, I spring right back again. Bobble wouldn't want to be friends with village nobody Daisy.

'You'll have to come to us too, Bob.' Sam speaks up as I lose myself in the depths of my own mind. 'We will have to introduce you to the Fellowship.'

My housemate clasps her hands together. 'I'd love that. I'd come with you right now if I didn't have a furry bra due in at uni on Monday morning.' She giggles and, despite having a twin sister and very much living in a matriarchal household, my brother flushes scarlet like a teenage boy in Tesco's tampon aisle.

A mournful silence falls over all of us as the time to get going finally comes. Packing the car without a word, I can't help but feel like I'm packing up all my progress of the last four weeks. In hardly a month, I have been more than I have ever been. I was so close, so close to being everything I had missed and now I am going right back to the start again.

The last bag is loaded into Sam's car and none of us really know what to say. All standing around the boot, looking at each other, no one making any attempt to move lip or limb. I manage to find my voice again for the first time in hours: 'I would rather say goodbye to the city and all its millions of inhabitants a thousand times than have to say farewell even once to you, Bobble.'

My housemate tries to hide her tears, but one gets past her and slides down her cheek. Quickly swiping it away, she clutches my hands in hers. 'Then you never shall. I shan't let you, nor will I let you forget any of this.'

I squeeze her hands tightly. 'Thank you, for everything.'

'You thank me as if being mates with you was some great act of altruism. Daisy, opening my house to you was the most selfish thing I have ever done.' She laughs at my perplexed face.

'You have given me something far more valuable, something I never knew I needed: a proper family. So you had better make room for me next to you at Christmas dinner because your dad has already invited me.' She continues to laugh through her tears, and even I manage a smile.

With another teary hug, Sam and I clamber into the car and leave London behind.

Chapter 25

Each day of the following week is torturously long, yet they all seem to disappear into the ether as though none of them happened at all. All of my things remain packed in boxes around my room, and as the days pass on, more of Marigold's belongings disappear into cases too.

She has just weeks until she leaves for uni and she only grows more excited as the hours pass. I watch my sister across the dining table, wondering why she got to be her, and I am stuck with myself. Why her narrow shoulders give way to handsome collarbones, why her rich dark hair frames her soft features so elegantly, why her brain can allow her to walk into a group of people and be the most charming one in the circle without so much as a sweat, why she is perfect at everything she turns her hand to, why I ruin everything I touch. The guilt of resenting someone you love so deeply is overpowering. How can I be jealous of someone I only wish the best for?

The only thing that has kept me going, that has drawn

me from the foreign familiarity of my childhood bedroom is, as sad as it sounds, the Friskney Fellowship. Yes, the only thing that has forced me from my depression pit is the sight of Richard in a wizard robe and tights. The Battle of Helm's Geek is just days away, and I am living every day waiting for it.

'Right, Hazel, Terry.' Stood in the Sunday morning sun on the village green, I address the two most likely to have some sort of medieval sex dungeon in their little village cottage. 'You're both going to guard Richard. We need to get him as far into the forest as we can so he is able to unleash a few of his spells before the other teams even realise he's gone. Your job is to get him there in one piece, and cut down anyone who gets in his way.' Today is our final meeting before the battle. Some of the characters before me may never return, may be forced to fight harder than they've ever known, and I find myself getting just a little carried away riling my troops. The couple accept their orders with a nod, although the urgency isn't quite there as they remain stood, with a handful of each other, stuck together like the two-headed serpents of ancient Greece.

Moving swiftly on before I get an eyeful of one of them, I wander over to Callum, the bard. 'Cal, make the use of that lute, my friend. We want a soundtrack, yes of course, but don't be afraid to use it as a weapon too.' The teenager strums a chord with a grin and I clap him on the back in appreciation.

'Where do you need me, Dais?' Dad asks eagerly. His squire's tunic is perfectly ironed and he gazes upon the orcish face of my mother, excited to be told to spend even more time in her monstrous presence.

'Mother shall give you orders. You exist to serve her. You must be at her side at every turn, ready to sacrifice yourself to save her if needs must.' My devoted father looks more than happy with his instructions. It's not much different to how he spends most of his life anyways so it will all come naturally to him.

After giving my orders to the O'Neill family, and not bothering to tell Richard to do anything, knowing he will only do the opposite, I come lastly to Sam and Marigold. 'Now, for the Battle of Helm's Geek, we elves must work together. The feuds of the Fellowship are on hold until we destroy the Ladybank LARPers, okay?' My siblings nod, and the excitement rushes over me.

'I have a tactic we could run.' Samwise's excitement is also evident as he rocks back and forth on his heels as he speaks. I push him to go on. 'The reverse arrowhead. Us three are each of the points of the arrow, but Daisy hangs back in the middle as we advance to the enemy. Mari and I push on, take down the weak human shield they offer us, and just as they think they have observed us, tired us, Daisy fires through the middle, takes them by surprise, and we take their heads.' My twin grins. 'What do you think, Mari?'

My little sister blushes at his address, refusing to look at either of us. 'I have actually been meaning to say . . .' She tails off and watches a hare bounce across the field for a moment. 'I'm not coming this year.' She rushes the words so quickly she is out of breath by the time she reaches the end.

'What?' My tone makes her flinch.

'I-I'm not coming, to Helm's Geek.'

'Why not? You don't like your character? We could always change it. You could be a druid? Ooo or a barbarian?' Samwise fusses as I stare at our sister with contempt.

'I just don't think playing with swords and pretending I'm an elf is going to help me at uni,' she mumbles. Sam falls back, silent.

'But . . . it's what we do together, as a family. It's the only thing you . . .' I tail off, unsure of really what I'm trying to say. LARP has been the one thing that has kept us close with her, the one thing I could talk to her about, could show her the ropes, care for her like a big sister should. With every passing day, she strays further from me, and I'm not sure if I know her at all.

'I don't understand?' My brother says softly, 'You were so excited. It's all we've spoken about over dinner for weeks.'

'It's all *you've* spoken about.' She still can't raise her voice above a murmur, but her words visibly crush him. 'It's always been *your* thing, you guys, Mum and Dad. I just don't want to pretend to be someone else. I don't want to be the person you want me to be, you tell me I am.' She looks to me as she finishes her sentence, a glimmer of remorse in her eye though she remains strong enough to not so much as stutter as she speaks.

'Mari . . .' Her words slice through me. 'The whole point is that you can be anyone, anything. I just, I thought, I *wanted* to . . . help.' I want to cry. To tell her that this was my way of being able to love her within the realms of what holds me back in the real world, but she could and would never understand.

'I think I just quite like being me.' She gives a sad smile with a shrug. Though she doesn't move at all, it feels like she's being pulled away from me, and no matter how hard I try to reach out and grab her, I could never reach.

'Do as you wish, Marigold,' I say as she waits for me to speak again. My tone is cold, though my blood runs hot and thick, and it's clear from her face that it hurts her just as much as it hurts me.

A knock at the door stirs us from packing the last of our bags. In just a few hours we will be making our journey down south to prepare for the Battle of Helm's Geek. Any interruption like this is always unwelcome when the preparation for the battle is so key.

Not only that but no one ever knocks on our door. One of the perks of living in the middle of nowhere is the fact cold callers simply cannot be arsed to cold-call us and anyone who knows us well enough usually just wanders in. The sound is foreign, almost ominous, so of course each member of the household emerges from their rooms and we congregate on the landing to share a look of suspicion and wordlessly plan our defence.

Mum takes the lead down the stairs; Dad, Sam, and I follow her, creeping as quietly as the creaking floorboards will allow. The leader of our pack grabs her decorative claymore from the umbrella stand and stalks towards the door. That's when we all see it, a silhouette in the frosted glass.

'What the fu— uh . . .' Sam catches himself as mum fires a stinging glare his way '. . . frig is that?' he whispers loudly, his face wearing all of the emotions that are currently coursing through my body.

Well over six foot, and built even wider than the glass can account for, it's the head that stirs the terror in us all. Ram horns. The beast has ram horns. The devil has found its way to Lincolnshire, and he's knocking on our front door.

Turning the key slowly, Mum opens the door, her claymore hidden behind it, ready to strike if needs be.

'All right, duck, can I help you?' Only a Lincolnshire mam can answer the door to the bloody devil and still call him *duck*. She doesn't flinch, nor does he attack, so we watch on, sweating. The door is only just ajar and not quite open enough for us to see the face on the other side. It's impossible to hear them too. 'Sorry. darling, you'll have to speak up. I didn't quite catch that.'

Sam catches my eye from across the hall. I ask him with just my expression if he can gather any more information from that side of the house but he only shrugs.

'Sorry, ma'am. I was just, well, I am looking for, wondering if this is the home of one Daisy Hastings.' The floorboards beneath me finally give way and explode into sawdust at my feet, or it feels as though they do as the sensation of falling envelopes my body until I grow nauseous. It's impossible. That voice has followed me everywhere, tracked me through my dreams, lingers in my moments of weakness, echoes in my failures. It cannot be here now. The voice doesn't belong to the devil, it belongs to someone far, far worse.

Mum looks to me for a moment. I am too frozen to say

a word, to run down the hallway and slam the door in his face. 'Oh my gosh.' She suddenly flurries at the sight of my flushed face. 'You must be . . . oh wow, you are a handsome chap. I can't believe she didn't tell us about you.' I can't bring myself to figure out which conclusion she has managed to leap to, but she winks at me dramatically before stepping aside and opening the door. 'You gave us all a little bit of a fright there, my dear. Not used to many visitors in these parts.'

And through the threshold of my family home steps Viscount Fairfax. With his presence, all of the heat is sucked out of the room and thrust at me like a flaming ball of feeling. My heartbeat rattles so hard that I feel it pounding in my toes. He is dressed in his knight costume, the black tunic with red accents, the very same ram-horned helmet I tried to get him to wear in the first few days of knowing him tucked under his arm as if he had never refused the request.

Weirdest of all, the royal rogue slots so seamlessly into the chaos of our cottage as if his black eyes had never once gazed upon the white walls of a palace. Now, they look to me like a lost and weary traveller pleading for warmth, fearful of rejection. The urge to scream in his face, to throw him out, to berate him with every bit of energy I have bubbles through me. Yet the desire to reach out, to brush his hair from his face, to kiss his soft cheek burns so hard that it cancels it all out until all I can do is watch him, frozen.

'Simon, this is one of Daisy's *friends* from London.' Mum winks at me again on the word, practically vibrating with the excitement of her true meaning. 'What was your name again, lovie?'

Teddy stretches his arm forward to shake Dad's hand; his nervous gait from when he approached is transformed almost instantly into a confident stride and pleasant grin as he speaks in a soft timbre. 'I'm Theodore, but I've taken to being called "Teddy" recently.' I retreat further into the shadowed corners of the hallway, desperately wishing to fall into one of Mum's many framed landscapes and run off across some Highland hills.

It's the face of my twin that really solidifies my humiliation. At the sound of Teddy's name, it has evidently clicked for him. Sam still watches me from across the hall, though this time his eyes are wide, his mouth stretched, both in shock but also in perhaps the widest grin I have ever seen him pull. It's the face of a sibling who is so incredibly bemused by the complete and utter torment of his sister, the face of a sibling that absolutely cannot wait to take the piss at the very next opportune moment.

Swanning out from his hiding spot, Samwise approaches the viscount for a shake of his hand. 'Ah Teddy, it's great to finally meet you. I have heard so much.' Sam keeps hold of his hand but his eyes flick back to me with such a glitter of excitement that he will be getting a swift gauntlet to the face as soon as we head back to the village playing field. 'I'm Samwise, but just Sam is fine.'

A sheepish smile fills Teddy's face and it's beginning to feel like everyone is having a brilliant time except for me. Have they planned this? Some awful way of pranking me? Or punishing me? *God, look, I know I called you a twat when I was twelve after I found that dead bird in the bottom of the garden, but come on, what did I do to deserve this?*

'Daisy, come and say hello to your friend. He's come all of this way just for you.' Sam doesn't drop his grin, and I have to grit my teeth to grimace back at him – though my eyes burn into him screaming many violent threats in his direction. 'She's terribly rude.'

'Teddy.' I speak through my jaw that's so tightly strung together that it almost hurts to say his name. 'What an unexpected surprise.' An understatement if ever there was one. The guilty expression returns to his usually confident face. 'To what do we owe this pleasure?' I'm grateful for the innocence of my parents, who don't quite grasp the sarcasm in my tone. They both fuss around him, patiently awaiting his reply.

Teddy looks at them both as they inch closer and closer. Clearing his throat, he says quietly, 'I had to see you.'

Mum steps behind the broad back of our unexpected visitor and claps her hands together with such excitement that for a moment I wonder if she managed to mishear his words as a proposal of marriage.

'Come in, come in. What are we like making you stand here in the draughty hallway, eh?' Mum takes his helmet out of his grip softly and sets it down on top of the piles of letters that she has stacked on the sideboard and escorts him into the living room.

Dad looks at his watch. 'We might just be able to catch *Bargain Hunt*.' I think Dad knows just about as much as I do in terms of what is currently unfolding before him. It wouldn't surprise me if he were speaking for the sake of it as he watches his wife flap around the guest as if he's the king. If either of them watched the news or read the papers, they would perhaps be a little more mortified by now. But into the living room we go, to watch *Bargain Hunt* with a man in line to the British throne, the same man who lost me my job just a week ago.

'Cuppa?' Mum asks as the viscount sinks down into one of the old sofas, almost swallowed by the soft cushions. His broad shoulders fold in on him. There's a look of boyish innocence on his face as he gazes up at my mother from beneath his thick black lashes whilst she fusses to take care of him like a lost babe found on her doorstep. Teddy accepts her offer and Mum scurries off to the kitchen to do what us Brits do best: panic that you've made it too weak/strong and argue with yourself as to whether 'two sugars' means two heaped teaspoons, or levelled ones.

Placing myself on the armchair furthest from Teddy, I keep my eyes firmly locked on him, the wise words of the code of chivalry swirling about my mind: *never turn thy back on thine enemy*. I have made that mistake already too many times, and I won't be caught slacking now in my own home.

Teddy's eyes track across the room, taking in the hoards of photos, the random collection of ornaments, and general tat. None of us speak. Dad, Sam, Teddy, and I all sit in separate corners, just looking at one another with no idea how to quash the awkward tension. Just as our visitor turns to me, taking a deep breath as he prepares to speak, Mum returns and delivers him a mug that she had made herself almost a decade ago. Despite its deformities, she looks proud as she hands it over.

'Thank you, Mrs Hastings.' Teddy takes it with a smile.

'Please, call me Iris.' Mum blushes, and I can't help but roll my eyes. She gets one singular attractive stranger through the door and she's all flustered. What happened to the Queen of the Orcs?

'So, Teddy,' Sam begins and I groan internally at the sound of his smarmy voice piping up, 'what was it like working with my sister?'

Teddy clutches his mug, still drooping further into the couch, but he wrestles against the fabric to straighten up a little to answer the question. 'She taught me a lot.' He says with a cough, 'She certainly knows her way around a sword, which is both brilliant and terrifying.' He chuckles, and so do the rest of the room – except me.

'That stuff's child's play. You should see her bossing us about in the Fellowship,' my brother continues as I glow like a fireplace across the room. My brother proceeds to list a highlight reel of my escapades as Alenthaea, to which Teddy listens with great interest.

'How long did you want to stay, my dear?' Mum vibrates in the corner, concocting a plan. Stay? They hardly know him – he could be a murderer for God's sake.

'I'll be heading back to London tonight. I just stopped by to see Daisy. I, well, I didn't get to say goodbye.' He blushes. Teddy Fairfax sits in my living room, blushing.

'You can't be going back tonight. I haven't even given you your dinner yet. You must stay the night. We insist – don't we, Simon?' Dad's staring analysis of Teddy is interrupted as Mum addresses him.

'Oh, yes, erm, indeed. More than welcome,' he mumbles, avoiding both their gazes now.

'Mum.' The words that have been swirling around in my head for the last half an hour finally grow enough strength to leave my body. 'Aren't you forgetting something?' She looks at me, confused. 'Helm's Geek?'

'Oh yes, of course! How could I forget?' She turns back to Teddy, hopefully to revoke her offer. 'How rude of me. We're actually meant to be heading down south for a, erm . . . role-playing festival – we've been training for ages so I'm afraid we won't be home. You caught us in the middle of packing up the car, and with the excitement of your visit it must have slipped my mind.' The weight on my chest lifts. I can breathe full breaths again. 'But, lucky for you, my youngest daughter isn't coming this year, so there's a spare seat in the car. You can put all of Daisy's training to good use. It's just for the weekend. We've booked a couple of tents and things. What do you think? You're already dressed for it and I'm sure Sam has a few other bits you could borrow.'

Teddy, who has been looking back and forth between myself and my mother this whole time, shuffles against his seat and places his mug on the coffee table. Although I threaten him with my eyes, he only smirks back in my direction before turning back to my mum and declaring: 'I'd be honoured.'

Chapter 26

'Has your head finally gotten so big that you have lost your tiny mind entirely?'

Once the family had given Teddy the entire history of the Battle of Helm's Geek and my mother had provided him with a meal that could feed a whole group of adventurers and their horses, he was finally allowed to breathe again. That is until I dragged him into the underbelly of our garden, shielded us both from prying eyes by shrubs and trees, and suffocated him again with my long-awaited confrontation.

'I—' Teddy attempts to speak, and the contented glow that had settled across his cheeks as he had made himself comfortable with my family dims.

'You can't just turn up at someone's house, expecting them to forget everything. You're the reason I'm here, remember? So why follow me? Come to ruin something else that I love? Or do you need me to sign an NDA so you can sue me if I talk about our . . .' I choke '. . . kiss? You should have saved all of our time and sent a letter

– how did you even get my address? Have you been stalking me on the MI5 database?' My chest heaves as, for once, my mouth moves quicker than my mind.

'Is this what you want? For me to be your enemy?' A sadness washes over Teddy's face as he speaks, as though he doesn't mean to be so blunt, but he can no longer keep it in. 'I never meant to hurt you in all of this. I panicked and I really, *really* messed up – I know that – but you have this fairy-tale binary in your head. There is only good and evil; people can only fit into the archetype that you have allocated to them. If you actually start thinking of other people as people, and not just characters in your quest, you'll realise that we're all just trying.' He rubs his hand over his face in frustration as he stuns me into silence. 'Daisy, I came to fix this. Please just give me the chance.'

He's the second person this week to tell me that I am guilty of assigning them a character they neither want nor see themselves as. Perhaps I have spent so long trying my hardest to reconstruct myself, to be someone I thought was the perfect version of myself, that I have got caught up in this story that only ever existed in my head. 'Why would you even want to? Fix it all, I mean.'

'Because I am trying my very hardest not to kiss you right now,' is the sentence that finally pierces my armour. As the words leave his lips, they hit me with such a force that I flinch, and have to face the stars to escape his scrutiny. The pinprick of Venus in the darkening sky catches me as the corners of my mouth twitch upwards. I try and suppress it, but I am almost certain that I see her wink. Bitch. 'And I could only do that again once I knew that I wasn't in any danger of losing my head, or anything worse . . .' His eyes flick down so quickly you could hardly tell he moved at all, but the shudder that follows it has never been clearer.

'Well, I'm glad you have some sense, at least,' I finally say after I have composed myself, and reminded myself that no matter how good he looks in his knight costume, he is still a dick. 'What do you actually want from me?'

'I've already told you.' His eyes won't settle and they flick back and forth across my face. 'I'm here to apologise, beg for your forgiveness. But most of all, I needed to see you, desperately. I don't know what is going on. I tried so hard to suppress my feelings, I tried to keep my distance. I can hardly make sense of my thoughts; I barely know how I got here. But all I know is that you have infected me.'

'Well, I haven't got anything, so it can't be me.' He laughs at my taking offence. A full-belly laugh, the kind I never thought I'd hear from someone like him. 'What?' I ask, trying to fight off the contagion of the sound.

'Nothing.' His chuckling slows until he simply gazes at me with soft eyes. 'I mean, I can't stop thinking about you, about how much I regret how it's turned out, about how much I have . . . missed you.' I can't tell if I'm breathing or not. The smothering weight of his words washes over me and I struggle to keep a grip on my senses.

'You don't even know me.' My voice comes out in a whisper.

'Then let me.' He steps forward; I step back.

'But you . . . you . . .' I should have something to say, some way to put distance between us, a way to fight against his words, but my mind fails me.

'If you tell me to leave, I'll go. But, please, at least allow me to apologise. After that, if you want to punch me, I'll give you a free shot.'

'Tempting,' I say under my breath, but it's clear that he hears me from the smile that appears on his face.

'I have been a complete and utter fool,' he begins, and with no pockets in his tunic, he runs his hands up and down his thighs.

'That's a bit of an understatement.' I can't help myself. It's childish, I know.

'All right then, I've been a right royal cu—'

'Okay, okay!' I cut him off quickly. 'Twat will suffice.'

'Fine, I've been a right royal twat.' His proper accent makes the word sound foreign, as if his tongue had not the ability to be so coarse. 'You challenged me in every possible way. You drive me mad, but everything about you excites me. I have spent the last twenty-seven years of my life being arrogant, never being confronted, allowed to live my life without a care for the consequences for those around me. I was so caught up in defying my family that I lost sight of my humanity. I desperately wanted to end my life as I knew it; I didn't stop to care about all of the others caught in the crossfire. Daisy, I know you could never forgive me, and I know all of this is my fault, and I am sorry. There is just something in you that makes me . . .' he pauses to chuckle '. . . you push every single one of my buttons, but I find myself waking up in the morning excited to hear you talk to me as if I am just . . . me.' Instinctively, I move towards him.

Before he can go on, our attention is stolen by the sound of Sam clearing his throat just on the other side of the lavender. By now, the sun has almost disappeared into the horizon. The lost light of dusk had concealed him until this point and I dread to think for exactly how long he has been there, and just how much he has heard.

'We're all packed up. Time to get going,' my brother says, unable to take his eyes off of the tomato plants in the corner of the garden.

'We were just coming,' I say, my burning cheeks thankfully shadowed in the twilight. I'm almost grateful for the interruption. The more Teddy speaks the more I feel myself losing my grip on sanity – the more he speaks the more I can feel myself falling for him, and with my armour cracked, there's nothing to protect me. It's easy to blame Teddy for everything, but it has always been my choice to retaliate, to poke the beast as much as he poked me.

The prospect of spending this weekend with him is beginning to feel slightly less torturous.

We follow Sam back out of the garden and find Mum and Dad at the car attempting to force the last bag into the boot. They're in the midst of trying a rather questionable technique of Mum slamming the door down whilst Dad tries to not lose his arm as he holds the obstinate bag into the car for as long as possible. The two of them grin at the sight of us, Mum's eyes lingering a little longer on Teddy before giving me her full beam of a smile. Just as she put her arms out to us, no doubt overcome with her misplaced emotions and desperate to draw us into a crushing group hug, the boot pops open and the contents spill out onto the driveway.

'Oh f— frogs spawn!' Mum cries. 'Can't you do without the bloody crossbow just this once, Simon?' Dad looks at her sheepishly as she holds up the offending weapon. He takes it from her and places it with an affectionate pat on the porch.

Teddy leaves my side and bends down to help Mum to load the car for the twelfth and final time – his new-found role of gentleman is really doing nothing to stop her imagination from leaping to marriage and grandchildren. It's written all over her smug face. With Teddy, Sam, and I all squashed into the back, I have no choice but to press myself so close to Teddy that I may as well be sat on his knee. After a few awkward wandering hands, we are finally on our way, and there is absolutely no chance of me relaxing for the entirety of this drive.

'Daisy. Daisy. We're here.' A soft voice stirs me from my slumber. Finally mustering the energy to pry open my eyes, I remember where I am. Night has flooded the car. I don't need my eyes to know that my tired head rests against the tall shoulder of none other than The Viscount Fairfax. Springing from him as quickly as my fatigued form will allow, I can only stare at him with widened eyes.

'Jesus, Daisy, you look like I've kidnapped you. I'm the one who's been trapped under you dribbling on my shoulder for the past two and a half hours.' The soft voice that woke me has returned to its most recognisable state. It's only Teddy and I left in the car now, and I try my hardest to wet my uncomfortably dry mouth.

'I don't dribble,' I mumble weakly, knowing full well my mouth now feels like it's full of cotton wool because I've been catching flies.

'You're lucky this thing has shoulder pads—' he points to his costume '—otherwise I'd be soaked through.' A familiar grin crosses his face, though a glimmer of hesitation follows. It's only when I finally allow myself to smile that he really relaxes into his.

'Teddy?' I ask after a brief moment of quiet. He seems surprised to be addressed, but urges me to go on nonetheless. 'Won't you get in trouble for being here? Isn't it . . . dangerous?' The absence of the ogre of a security guard who usually lives in his shadow hasn't gone unnoticed.

'You let me worry about that.'

'I wasn't worried,' I lie.

'Of course you weren't,' he says with a grin before clambering out of the car and, with a bow, offers me his hand. I take it, and when I am once again beside him, he gives my fingers a gentle squeeze and disappears to find the rest of my family.

Only now that I don't have Teddy clouding my senses can I immerse myself in the bustling of camp. The sound of merry chattering and wooden wheels trundling through the grass get louder as they pass me on the dug-out road. The darkness is lit by a string of tiny lanterns that border the edges of the single dirt track path between row upon row of round canvas tents. Flags of all colours – flown proudly over each camp – are still in the tranquillity of the night. The lanterns are hung far off into the distance so that the very furthest ones look like garlands of tiny fireflies lighting the way as weary travellers, in their capes and their livery, ferry their belongings in wooden carts across the trodden turf. A child scuttles past me, a crown of flowers adorning the dark curls of her hair. The friend's hand she clutches is covered with fur that carries on up the other child's arms until it ends up tucked inside a rather terrifying owl mask.

The soft strumming of a guitar accompanies a chorus of voices, men and women, elders and children, far off at the end of the track, where a great fire glows in the distance. I feel each one of my thumping heartbeats, as though until now my heart had been holding back, never reaching its full capacity. It throbs with the bittersweet feeling of this all being pretend – why is it that my real life doesn't take place in a wild community where goblins and kings walk hand in hand, and I can control my fate by parchment, pen, and a strike of my sword?

Sam and Teddy wander together down the road, bags thrown over their shoulders, and filter in amongst the rest of the outcasts. Before I can worry about what they might be conspiring together, Mum shuffles over and bumps me with her shoulder. Her whole face is lit up by the grin that has still not waned since we discovered that the devil at the door was actually just a handsome bachelor.

'Mum,' I half-whisper whilst I finally have the chance to correct her, 'you have really, *really* misunderstood this situation.' Her brows furrow; the smile slips for a second.

'Come on, Daisy, I know he's your first, but there's no need to be coy about it.' She puts down her bag of arrows to pat me on the arm bashfully.

'Mum, he's not my boyfriend, and he never could be.'

'Don't put yourself down like that, dear; looks aren't everything.'

'No, it's just that he's . . . hang on a second.' Taking a moment to process what she just said, I shake my head to try and forget it and return back to the urgent task. 'Mum, look, he is pretty much the entire reason I got fired. He's hardly a friend, let alone a boyfriend. Can you just cool it, maybe? Just chill out a bit and stop with the Cheshire cat smile, would you?' She agrees reluctantly and bends down to pick up her bag, but straightens again quickly as though suddenly shocked by the contact. 'You okay? What have you done? Are you hurt?'

'We may have a slight problem . . .' She looks to me with gritted teeth, and chuckles nervously. 'I thought it would be fine, since I thought it would either be normal for you, or force you to take that final leap to being a couple.' She rambles her way through, her eyes scanning across the tents. Sam and Teddy's long strides make light work of the distance and their faces come back into view just metres away.

'What, what is it?' I panic.

She gives me another guilty look. 'Well . . .' She hesitates.

'What!'

'Well, you know how you normally share your tent with your sister?' She fiddles with her thumbs, only stealing glances at my face. 'Well since she wasn't coming, I thought it would all be fine if . . .' she risks a look at the boys '. . . youaandTeddysharethetentmeantforyouandyoursister.' In her fretfulness, she speaks so quickly that I understand her just as much as if she had just spoken Dwarfish.

'Mum.' I hold her by the shoulders and force her to breathe with me. 'Again, but slowly.'

She takes another deep breath. 'There is only one tent. You and Teddy are going to have to share.' I release her. She has to be joking. Just some funny little attempt at turning this silly little situation into one of her all too predictable fairy tales. But the remorseful look on her face confirms it all.

'Surely I can just share with Sam. Doesn't he have room in his?'

'He's already sharing with Callum.' Mum's look of pity is starting to grow more annoying than her suspicious grin. 'I'm sorry, Daisy, I-I thought it would be okay. Since I thought you were . . . But I'm afraid there's nothing we can do now. It's nearing midnight. Most people will already be down for the night. Is there any way you can just do this one night? I'll try my best to sort it in the morning.' She looks genuinely worried, and I regret being so harsh on her, especially since she has been in such high spirits all evening. With Teddy and Sam almost upon us, I agree.

I must spend the night with him and if the novels I have read are anything to go by, this can only end in one way.

Chapter 27

I am certainly not the first woman in history condemned
to spend the night with a royal against their will so I
suppose, above anything else, I should just be grateful that
I won't be forced to marry him on the morrow. But as the
seconds tick away, and my legs carry me closer to my fateful
destination, the turmoil grows in my stomach, as though
beyond the canvas of that tent, my own execution awaits.

'You need to let me swap tents with you.' I stop dead
and face my smirking brother.

'And let you pass up the opportunity to spend the night
with the guy who's quite clearly in love with you? No
chance.'

'He's . . . He isn't . . .' I'm speaking but it's only Sam's
words that I hear repeated over and over in my head. Only
when the nervous tingling in my fingers blurs the line
between pleasure and pain do I snap out of it and react
in the only way I know how; by punching my twin on the
arm. 'You aren't funny, you know that right?'

He clutches the attacked shoulder, still grinning. 'Who said I was joking?'

'So, you're all of a sudden an expert on love then, are you?' I say, narrowing my eyes as he continues to mock me with his bemused expression.

'That man has worn every single one of his emotions on his face since he arrived. You don't have to be an expert to see it. Plus, only us idiots who love you are willing to let you boss us about for a whole weekend. So, either he's completely smitten, or has no idea what he's got himself into.' He shrugs, as though it's the most obvious thing in the world.

'Definitely the latter.' I murmur, unable to bring myself to look at his smarmy face any longer.

'Either way, this is the most exciting thing that's happened to me in . . . well forever.'

'Well, I am so very glad *you're* having great time.' Every inch of my body is slick with sweat and I worry if I say another word, before I finish the last syllable it will be vomit in my mouth.

'Hey.' He sets aside his teasing for a moment of seriousness. 'You'll be fine: it's sharing a tent, not a bed. It's hardly proper camping where you have to huddle together for warmth in a two-man tent; these ones are practically mansions. Don't you remember that one year where Richard's tent leaked and he had to bunk in the family tent with us and Mum and Dad?'

'Don't remind me.' A shiver racks through me at the memory.

'Either way, this doesn't have to be any different. Just,

for your sake, I hope he doesn't snore as bad as the old man.' Sam pauses for a moment and looks across the camp as though he's had a compelling epiphany: 'You know Daisy, he really is nothing like you described, I quite like him. Maybe you should just give him a chance.'

'All right, no need to kiss his arse. If you want to do that, you can share a tent with him.'

Sam holds his hands up in surrender. 'This is you.' He points to the softly glowing tent we have arrived at. 'Goodnight. And good luck.' He winks before floating off into the night like some sadistic fairy godmother.

Teddy's shadow is projected against the pale walls and I watch the lean silhouette for a moment as he paces back and forth. When he crosses the middle of the tent, his torso stretches taller, and taller, until he passes again and shrinks down to size.

Theodore Fairfax comes from a different world. A world where kings and queens aren't enthroned with plastic crowns on muddy fields, where his duties to give his life to the monarchy aren't completed by slaying mythical beasts in made-up lands. Theodore Fairfax comes from a world far more real, with far more consequences. His world terrifies me, and if I step into this tent now, there is no way I can avoid the pain of what comes with him. If I allow myself to be alone with him, I'm scared that I'll no longer be able walk away unscathed.

The wraith-like figure still paces, growing, shrinking, hypnotising. Led by my chest, I follow that shadow inside. I am well and truly under his spell.

Teddy freezes upon my entry and struggles to settle on

an expression. 'Daisy, believe me, this was never once my intention.' He steps aside and just one lone bed lies behind him. Clearly set up to mimic a royal command tent, tapestry blankets swallow the linen, and furs are draped over the width, barely lit by the dimming oil lamp on the bedside table.

Swallowing hard, I wrestle against my body and against my instincts. I could panic, I could take the easy way out and be rude, callous – the way I have been towards him every time he made me feel an emotion so foreign it has terrified me. Instead, I take a step towards him, my shaking breath exposing the hurricane of anxiety that fights constantly within me, like an unrelenting villain.

'Is that the great Viscount Fairfax flustered over the fact he has to share a bed with a girl?' My voice trembles as I try my hardest to cling to my composure. Teddy's splinters right before my eyes.

'Y-you're okay with this?' he asks. Absolutely not, not in the slightest.

'Aren't you?'

His eyes dart around the wide canvas of the bell tent until they rest on a chaise longue on the other side.

'I'll sleep over there. These tents are huge and it's as far away as I can possibly get. I swear I'll be gone before you even wake up in the morning.' Striding over to it, he moves the luggage that had been perched on top and sits down with a bounce. A flutter of something like disappointment tickles in my gut and my minute spark of confidence dies at the hands of my fears of rejection.

Afraid my legs won't hold me up for much longer, I take

a seat on the bed. Sinking further into it, and myself, I lie down against the furs, hoping they might hide me away for a few precious moments. If I close my eyes, unable to see his expression or analyse each twitch and blink, I can speak more freely, and pretend I'm speaking only to myself. 'If I'm going to be forced to spend a night with you, I think it's only fair that I know who you are.'

'You've worked with me almost every day for the last month, I'm hardly a stranger.' His faceless voice reaches me.

'But I don't know *you*. The real you. I want to know the things that I can't just find on Wikipedia.' The rustling sounds of fabric implies he too has lain down.

'I'd say you already know me better than most.'

'If that's true, then I pity you.' My voice is quiet, but I can tell by his silence that he heard it.

'Well.' I hear him take a deep breath. It audibly trembles just like my own. 'I have a younger brother. We were both mostly raised by our grandmother until we went to boarding school to be ignored by our mother and father. I played rugby for a long while. They wanted me to play cricket but I always found it horrendously boring. I didn't get to carry on many of my hobbies once I started work except in the comfort of my own home.' There's another pause as he thinks of something else to say. 'I am a very keen baker.'

'A baker? Like cakes and biscuits kind of baker?' The thought of Teddy Fairfax covered in icing sugar trying to perfect fairy cakes warms me as much as I am in disbelief at the thought.

'Is there any other kind?' He chuckles. 'My grandmother taught me,' he adds before falling silent. 'Go on then, what about you?'

'What about me?' I hear him shift from across the tent and I grow nervous with the attention.

'I know just as much of you as you do me, except I can't fill in the blanks on your life story with articles in newspapers.' His words only serve to prove my brother wrong. How can a man love me, if he doesn't even know me?

'Okay then, what would you like to know?'

'Why are you so afraid of the real world?'

I splutter against the weight of the question. 'And here I was thinking it was going to be something easy like "what's your favourite colour?"' The nausea starts growing in me again.

'But that one I already know, it's green and gold. Except you still only wear silver jewellery.' I sit bolt upright, but he hasn't moved. For the first time, I see how he's lying so uncomfortably with a body too long for the furniture and yet looks so serene, his eyes closed, a smile pinching at his cheeks.

'How could you possibly know that?'

Teddy opens one sly eye to look at me, before closing it again to speak.

'Whenever you had to pick a coloured pen at work, you'd always pick green. And every time you had to select your costume you'd always be drawn first to the green ones. Like your hand would just instinctively go towards those on the rack even though you'd seen all of them before and knew they weren't your size.'

He's confident, declarative, and he's absolutely spot on. It's as if every day that I have spent picking faults in him, he's been observing me, noticing the little things, as if he's wanted to know all about me. He has been *seeing* me.

'What about the gold then? And the silver jewellery?' I ask, bewildered. My voice is small, barely audible. I worry that if I say too much, if I move at all, I might break, might flee, or worst of all scare him away.

'You're like a dragon. You always pick up anything gold to have a closer look at it. Plus, it goes well with green, so of course you'd like it.'

Not discouraged by my continued silence, he continues, 'The only jewellery you wear is that silver chain that you keep hidden around your neck. It confused me at first – you didn't strike me as the type to wear those sorts of things, but you're sentimental, so I'm guessing it was a gift? From someone in your family most likely.'

Teddy sneaks another peek at me, proud of himself and his scarily accurate observations.

The satisfied grin he aims in my direction soothes me, silences the screaming in my mind. So, I dare to tease him, if only to encourage more words to fall from those lips. 'Impressive, Mr Holmes. Where did you learn to be so nosy?' I clap lightly and a jolt of warmth ricochets through me as his soft laughter sounds.

'There are many secrets in palace walls. No one will willingly tell you anything, even about yourself.' Swinging his long legs back to face me, he sits up with an expectant expression. 'So, who gave you that necklace?'

My fingers instinctively grasp it. A slightly tarnished tree of life hangs between my collarbones and has done for so many years even I barely notice it there anymore. 'My sister gave it to me, for my birthday when I was about thirteen. We've never been close, mostly because of the age gap, but she had gone out when she was only eight, saved up all of her pocket money, from birthdays and things, and chosen it for me herself. I don't know, I suppose I'm just a little attached to it. I wouldn't be surprised if my body had just grown around it by now, like the trunk of a tree growing around a bicycle that had been chained to it for decades. It's as much a part of my body as my blood and brain.'

Teddy gets to his feet, crosses the slight gap between us, and stands over me. 'May I?' He offers his wide palm towards me. I nod. The bed dips with his weight as he sits down so close that his thigh presses against mine and he takes the pendant softly in his hand to study it. My breaths are shallow, almost gasping, and each tiny inhalation is filled with him. The smell of fresh linen mixed with a hint of dew-soaked earth wraps around me, concocting a new high to intoxicate me.

As softly as he took it, he places the silver back against my sternum, his cold fingers sending a defibrillating shock through my chest as they ghost against the newly exposed skin. His soft thumb runs away from him and traces the contours of my clavicle as though never before had the feeling of flesh and bone been welcomed by those curious hands. Like the stinging touch of a nettle, his trailing fingers leave behind a path of tiny bumps that spread and multiply down my body until I let out an uncontrollable shiver.

Dropping his hand into his lap, Teddy shuffles against the bedcovers – my sudden movement clearly snapping him back to reality.

'Teddy?' He can't speak, only a 'mhmm' croaks from him in reply. 'Is *anything* in the papers true?' The question burns across my body. I know I'm glowing red. Teddy doesn't look at me.

'What do you think?' he says gruffly, the softness of just seconds ago frozen over.

'I-I hope not.' My knee bounces erratically. I watch it hypnotically as I feel his gaze burning through me.

'Everything that I am is in front of you right now. I came here with just the clothes on my back and this is all I want to be, all I have ever tried to be.' Right now, in this tent, in this field, he has that chance to be anything, and so do I. When we leave this made-up place, our lives may never converge again, and if magic can exist for such a weekend, I can let a royal take my heart for just those few days. Or hours? Minutes?

Perhaps it's Alenthaea thriving in this world that she was created for, or it is the puzzlement of the complete one-eighty my life has taken in the space of weeks, but I still my trembling limbs, ignore the alarm bells ringing through my mind, and I hold his face in my hands. I see myself reflected in the dark eyes of a deer in headlights as Teddy is motionless in my touch except for a strained gulp. Before my sense has time to be restored, I press my lips to his with a passionate ache that pulses through me like nothing I have ever felt before. When he finally recovers enough to kiss me back, it's as if his lips are the missing component in my emotional circuit that, until now, I had assumed to be broken forever.

Snaking a hesitant hand up the side of my jaw, he slides it into my hair and presses us even closer together. My heartbeat rings in my ears and throbs so hard through my body I am sure you must be able to see me pulsing from the outside. Teddy tastes of temptation in its purest form and I no longer want to fight against it. I am the heroine, sacrificing her piety, all she believes in, her quest, her destiny, to fall in love with the villain she set out to destroy. But how could this ever be wrong, when the world has never felt so whole, when peace dances on the surface of his tongue, when he makes me finally understand why all of those protagonists would move heaven and earth for the chance of living happily ever after?

There is only one thing I know for certain: my body was made to fit Teddy Fairfax's, and his to fit mine.

Chapter 28

The grinding sound of metal on whetstone stirs me from a deep dreamless sleep. Even from behind my closed eyes, I can see the morning sunshine as it glows through the canvas roof that traps its heat in a bubble around me. A slick trail of dampness begins to grow over my face and I reach up to wipe it away with my arm. The clothes I had worn the night before still cling to my body, and when I find the strength to pry open my eyes to the burning light, I realise that the duvet is still tucked under the mattress and I never even made it into the bed.

Looking about the room, all is undisturbed. Not a thread seems out of place, aside from the crumpled blankets around me. It looks as though no other body had ever passed the threshold.

I am alone. Teddy has left without a trace.

The only reminder that he was ever here at all and not just some lucid dream is the ghost of his lips that still lingers down my neck – a feeling impossible to replicate with just imagination alone. For a moment, I sit replaying the images of last night in my mind. Did I do something wrong? I don't remember falling asleep, or even attempting to. I had thought it would be impossible to even shut my eyes with such an overdose of adrenaline coursing through me. Yet I feel more rested than I have in weeks. What would be the use in dreaming those same dreams of Teddy Fairfax that have kept my mind up working overtime, when he had his arms wrapped around me? He definitely did, I'm sure of it.

Too confused about where reality begins and my imagination ends, I quickly change my clothes and dash out of the tent in search of him. Forgetting my shoes, my bare feet hit the soft earth. Long blades of grass reach up and tickle between my toes.

'Good morrow, young lady.' A stranger, already dressed in his day's costume and very much already in character, bows to me as I pass. A little distracted scanning faces for a certain viscount, I return the bow and mumble a greeting before weaving my way through the camp.

'Good morrow!'

'Tension stirs in the air. Battle is almost upon us.'

'Fine morning for battle, is it not?'

Greetings and premonitions are thrown in every direction as I gain speed through the gathering hordes. Fighters add the finishing touches to their weapons, squires deliver breakfasts to their families, and mages practise their spell-casting against the leftovers. Though I pass at least four blacksmiths, and two headless men, Teddy is still nowhere to be seen.

'Fair, brave Alenthaea, come again to lose?' I tense at the voice. It's spoken almost entirely through the nose of the utterer and there is only one person annoying enough to have a voice to match so perfectly.

'Rufus,' I say, turning to acknowledge him. Rufus Hogg: leader of the Ladybank LARPers, and our greatest enemy. When the Fellowship were just a hair away from winning last year, it was Rufus and his cronies who swooped in last minute to steal the crown. If there is one thing that Rufus Hogg hides, not very well, beneath his scraggly black moustache, it's pride. No older than me and Sam, his wispy face furniture is twisted up at the corners and hangs so heavy with wax that I wouldn't be surprised to see a bee land on the end wishing to claim it as its own.

'Are you sure that you're brave enough to face me without your pack of barbarians to hold your hand?' I ask. 'If I remember rightly, didn't they have to wash the piss out of your pants after you had a little dance with my partisan last year?'

The weasel of a man makes a strained noise, as though drowning on a mouthful of water. Rufus makes half an attempt to laugh, but it is lost to the spluttering. 'It's the Red Ranger to you.'

I don't even try to hide the eyeroll.

'You do realise that the basic requirement to be a lone-ranging, savage, monster-hunting ranger, is . . . well, actually having a set of metaphorical balls?'

'And you know full well that elven high-borns are famed for their beauty, but you're happy to overlook that one. Aren't you?' he snipes back, looking me up and down. The more he speaks, the more I cannot wait to hand him his arse in battle this afternoon. 'Speaking of rare beauties . . . Where's your sister this year? I haven't seen her and I've heard she's just turned eighteen . . .'

If he calls himself the Red Ranger, then I am a raging bull. I will trash-talk a man into battle and happily buy him a pint afterwards, but as soon as my family join the equation, the urge to plough through him like a rampant beast overtakes me before he can even finish his sentence.

Lunging toward him, I snare his collar with one hand. The brave Red Ranger trembles at my touch, eyes wide and pleading. I wouldn't hurt him; as violent as my imagination is, the only time I would ever think to act on it is in the middle of battle, armed with a carbon-fibre sword that couldn't so much as pop a balloon. But the little whimper that escapes him pleases me greatly.

Just as I lean forward to give him Alenthaea's best leg-trembling monologue I feel a soft tap on my shoulder. Whipping around to face the new threat, I finally remember my original objective.

Teddy stands, fully costumed, his arms crossed and eyebrows raised. 'As much as I am glad it is not me staring down the pointy end of your wrath for once, and I have no doubt that he deserves it, but do you maybe want to let go before he wets himself?' I release him at once, and Rufus runs back through the tents like a wounded deer. I hiss at him, 'See you on the battlefield, Red Ranger.'

He doesn't look back but there's no mistaking that he heard me by the way he mutters 'crazy' as he flees.

A little disappointed I didn't get my movie monologue

moment, I turn back to Teddy, whose expression is still stuck in the same look of intrigue. 'Ladybank LARPers,' I offer him as an explanation, but his confusion only deepens. 'Our greatest nemeses. Beat us last year, but never play fair. Hogg over there is their leader, and despite the fact he couldn't fight his way out of a wet paper bag, he doesn't have any issues making pervy comments about people's younger sisters.'

Though looking amused only seconds before, Teddy's expression turns dark and he scans the camp for signs of the pest.

'It's fine. I'll deal with him when the time is right.' I place a hand on Teddy's shoulder and he relaxes.

'I've been looking for you,' he says softly, brushing a soft thumb over the creases in my forehead. His tender touch releases the tension that pulled at my brow. Forgetting Rufus almost instantly, thoughts of Teddy and last night wash back over me with a shiver.

'Me too,' I say quietly. 'I thought you'd left.' The heat rises to my face as I speak. 'I thought, maybe, you'd changed your mind? Or I scared you off?'

'I did think about it when the snoring started . . .' A cheeky grin returns to its regular spot on his swollen lips. I shove him lightly on the shoulder, and he holds his hands up in surrender. 'Okay, okay, you don't snore.' He laughs. 'But you must have been dreaming about me because all I could hear through the night was you mumbling my name.' I chase after him as he begins an impression that would make even a grown orc blush. But not Teddy – he happily skips over guide ropes until I catch him and softly clamp my hand over his mouth in an attempt to silence him. Sharing one another's giggling breaths, we stay for a moment in this closeness.

'Why did you leave, really?' I ask softly when the adrenaline dies down.

'I had a few things to sort out. Turns out, if you disappear from your private security, they send a whole team out looking for you.' He chuckles, though the tremor in my stomach doesn't find it so funny. Evidently sensing my anxiety, he rubs his hands down my arms soothingly. 'Nothing to worry about – it's all dealt with now.' His words assure me, but the faltering grin not so much. Visions of spies in dark glasses lurking in the treeline, watching our every move, occupy my imagination. Stepping back, I force more distance between us, just in case.

'I often forget that you're a man of global importance.'

'That's why I like you.' Wrapping an arm around my waist, he pulls me back to within striking distance of his lips.

Trying to struggle through the nerves, I resort to what I know best: teasing him. 'I had always assumed that important men were meant to be a little less, how can I put it? Annoying.'

Teddy feigns being shot through the heart and falls to one knee dramatically.

'And that,' he begins as he gets back up to his full height, 'is why you like me.' Speaking with such confidence, he proves my point by being so infuriatingly right.

Once Teddy is suitably silenced from embarrassing me, we head back into the camp. The viscount leads me to my family who all sit about the rekindled bonfire handing out bacon rolls to the others in the Fellowship. Richard has managed to find himself with one in each hand, brown sauce on one, ketchup on the other. Hazel and Terry both offer a smile, their cheeks bulging with their breakfast, and the O'Neills – vegetarians, of course – each wave softly with their greetings, their breakfast of grapefruits and yogurt very much befitting their pristine morning appearances. Flora glows in the daybreak dew, Sam has noticed, as he always does, and they sit side by side, completely unaware of our presence.

They don't seem to notice Teddy until Mum offers him a roll, to which he assures her that he is full enough already – although I have a sneaky feeling that it's his upbringing making a rare appearance, and a bacon sarnie cooked in the middle of a field, and served on a paper plate, is perhaps just a little too out of his comfort zone. I wonder if he's ever been introduced to a chip butty . . .

Clearing my throat, I interrupt their silently intense decoding of Teddy's aura before one of them voices their thoughts. 'Everyone,' I begin awkwardly, 'this is Teddy. I worked with him down in London—'

'What did I say about bloody southerners, eh?' Richard grumbles to himself.

'And . . .' I say a little louder to be heard over the old wizard's musings, 'he has come to fill in for Marigold. I've taught him all he knows, which isn't as much as I would have liked when I've already had Rufus of the Ladybank LARPers acting the knave this morning—'

'Bobolyne! Cumberworld! Prick!' Richard shouts out again like a heckler in Shakespeare's Globe.

'We need as many swords on the field as we can if we want to stand a chance of beating them, so for this weekend, please accept Teddy as one of us. After that we can see if he is worthy of joining the Fellowship officially.' I wink at him as he stands behind me, hands folded in front of him as he fidgets like the new kid at school being introduced to his class.

'Please be nice . . .' This last bit is mostly aimed at Richard, whose drone of grumbles continues. Terry comes over to clap the viscount on the shoulder, and Hazel places a soft hand on his forearm, both of them glancing at the other. Before they can hatch a plan of inviting a man in line to the British throne home for a threesome, I rescue him from their grip and offer him a seat.

The only seat left, however, is the one beside Richard, for obvious reasons. As the viscount sits beside him, the old man looks him up and down once again, brows furrowed. 'You look familiar, son,' he muses, mostly to himself. 'Your mam doesn't work at the Big Tesco's in Skegness, does she?'

I cover my mouth to hide my laughter, but Teddy just smiles politely and shakes his head, not bothering to explain that his mother, the princess royal, does not often frequent a 'big Tesco's' and certainly not one in Skegness. He doesn't need to anyway; he has already become a victim of one of my neighbour's rants where any contribution from the other interlocutor is highly discouraged.

Sam takes that as his cue to creep his way over, the foxy grin he wears suggesting that he means only to taunt me. 'How was your night with the prince? Did he find the pea I put under his mattress?'

'No, because he is not a prince. Excuse me, I need to get my ears on.'

'Dais.' Sam stops me as I begin my retreat. 'Is it going to be safe? You know with him being . . .' My brother twitches his head towards Teddy, who is still squashed in beside Richard, smiling and nodding.

'Stuck with our slightly insane, geriatric neighbour?' I laugh.

'You know what I mean. We're not going to get in trouble? Kidnapping a royal? Throwing a royal into a sword fight? What if he gets hurt? Have you thought any of this through?' That image of spies in the bushes returns to my mind again.

'I thought I was supposed to be the worrier.' I chuckle, but I am worried, I very much am. The niggling nausea has barely left me since he arrived, yet I have so selfishly allowed the loud pounding of my heart to drown out any other, more sensible, thoughts. Watching Teddy now, it only beats louder. I feel it in my ears, down my throat, creeping through my body until it hits my toes only to scale me once again. Those dark eyes meet mine for a moment, and at the contact, a disarming, beguiling smile spreads across his face.

Teddy Fairfax has bewitched me. For the first time in my life, I don't care about the consequences, for that smile transports me to a fantasy, a whole new universe, where falling in love with him is as natural as the blood I bleed at the touch of a blade.

'I can handle it. I promise.'

Mum is reflected behind me in the mirror, her fingers twisting my hair softly into plaits at the back of my head.

My face has been transformed into something of an ethereal being. My cheekbones have been sharpened by the shadow of soft makeup, my lips are drawn up into high peaks, and the hair braided around my ears reveals the seamless way that they have grown into points. Finally, I look like the woman that I keep on the inside, and I hardly recognise myself.

'You seem different. Only slightly, but in a good way,' Mum says softly as she places the last pin against my scalp with a kiss.

Manoeuvring myself to get a better look at her in the flesh, I let out a breathy laugh. 'You think so?' I can't hide my confusion. The only thing that has really changed is that, this year, I have been responsible for the disappearance of a member of the royal family. When we get back home, it will be like nothing changed at all. I still have no job, any friends I had I left behind, and any attachments I have formed can only exist in this fantasy. When we return to the real world, I will once again have nothing to offer.

Mum only smiles. I've always liked the way her teeth ever so slightly overlap each other as if they're holding hands. One of her incisors has a chip in it, a reminder of the time she and all of her friends had rushed off up to Edinburgh to dance about a field to 'Wuthering Heights' dressed as Kate Bush and she got an accidental improv hand to the face from another Kate Bush. She still came home giggling, showing off her battle scars, laughing every now and again that a 'Wuthering Heights' flash mob should be considered an extreme sport.

Her stunning smile looks just ever so slightly out of

place now that she has assumed the form of her rotting orc.

'You're more confident. I don't see much difference between the real Daisy and this version anymore.' She chuckles as she pinches the latex of my elf ears gently between her fingers and gives them a wiggle. 'I think a certain someone might have been a good influence.' She can't raise her eyebrows in the usual teasing manner due to the amount of Pritt stick she has used gluing them down, so instead she moves her entire forehead up and down like a Botox job gone wrong. I don't reply. She knows me well enough not to expect one. 'Anyway, what did you say Teddy's background was? Molly – you know the alchemist from the LARPing Loonies – seems to think he looks like some famous fella that she's seen in the paper.'

Chuckling awkwardly, I scramble for an excuse. Do I just tell her? I haven't intentionally kept it from her. It isn't like she can't be trusted with the secret; I just know she would be intimidated. Selfishly, I want Teddy to feel just like me, so for one weekend I can feel like I am enough for him. 'Well . . .' I begin, but Mum seems preoccupied with having the conversation with herself.

'I didn't think it could be true. She said that famous boy is always getting himself into trouble. I told her that couldn't be our Teddy; he's a lovely young man.' For a moment she seems to give me a knowing smile, as if deep down she knows there's truth in Molly's gossip, but she keeps talking in spite of it. 'He's been helping me and your dad all morning, and won't stop thanking us for bringing him, bless his soul. Oh and my my how he did talk about you. You've made an impression on him – that's for sure.'

She grins to herself as she talks and, although she pays little mind to me, I grow hotter and hotter in my costume. My stomach leaps to hear the details, to have her sit down and recount every one of his words verbatim, just to hear the words he hasn't yet told me, but my mouth stays quiet and I let her move on to telling me the latest camp gossip.

Halfway through explaining in great detail how one of the goblins from the Duct Tape Dragons had an affair with one of the mages from the Bournemouth University Role Players Society last year, the fanfare sounds outside, summoning us to battle. After shoving in her fangs with a slurp, Mum helps me to lift my armour over my shoulders and tightens the leather buckles until the leather feels like a second skin. With one last grim smile and a nod, her demeanour changes and we both stride from the tent, meaning business.

Chapter 29

'Ladies and gentlemen, younglings and elders, nobles and peasants, heroes and monsters, welcome to our fifteenth annual Battle of Helm's Geek!' The game master's voice booms through the field. An eruption of cheering, mixed with the orchestra of wizards banging their staffs, orcs growling, and goblins cackling sings out in reply with a monstrous echo.

Mum and I squeeze our way through the jubilant hordes until we find the Friskney Fellowship congregated at the very front. Without a second thought, Dad wraps his arms around Mum's shoulders and kisses her bald head as though the whole monstrous get-up doesn't exist and he finds her as attractive as every other day he has kissed her in the same way.

The viscount, my Black Knight, stands beside Sam, his ram-horned helmet tucked under his arm, so immersed in the moment he doesn't notice me. Teddy looks across the crowd with a wide grin, cheering at everything they cheer at. It's my turn to sneak up on him.

As I prop my chin on his shoulder, he instinctively rests his head on mine without even looking. 'Enjoying yourself, my lord?' His shoulders shift with a soft laugh as he replies in the affirmative. 'Who'd have thought, the Rogue Royal, the Party Prince, the Vicious Viscount, is actually one huge nerd.'

'And who would have thought the great headstrong enigma of Daisy Hastings would have her arms around my waist in public?' He looks at me from the corner of his eye and I realise that my impulses have betrayed me and I am indeed cuddling him in front of hundreds of eyes (thousands if you're including the giant spider hanging in the Fabled Forest).

Pulling away from him in shame, I can only take one step before I am arrested in Teddy's grip and it's his turn to embrace me. Without either of us saying a word, and without me objecting, we watch the game master as he lays out the rules for the great battle. With the feeling of his body against mine overwhelming every one of my senses, I don't hear much of anything. Even the joyous crowds are muted against the soft thumping of his heart.

'. . . you will battle beasts, black magic and, scariest of all, your fellow man all for the glory of holding the mighty fortress of Helm's Geek (and a £150 voucher for any Brewers Fayre of your choice).' I finally tune back in to chorus of ooo's that falls across the mob at the thought of a free microwaved meal in a rather basic pub chain. Unsurprisingly, the look on Teddy's face would suggest that the royals have never had the treat of a steak and ale pie from the Hammer & Anvil in Lincoln.

'Once you've made it through the bog, survived the Fabled Forest, and fought off your determined competitors, you must take on the reigning champions, the Ladybank LARPers, before you may raise your flag over the battlements. At least two of your team must remain alive to capture the fortress. Healing potions may only be used once and only by a designated healer. If you step onto this field, you must be prepared to lose your life.'

Another cheer ripples through the crowd.

'Wow, serious stuff.' Teddy speaks close to my ear. 'Perhaps I should have written to my great love and told her not to wait for me to return.' Wiggling out of his grip, I can't hide my alarmed expression. Teddy is unperturbed, however. 'She would probably just tear it up; she can't read it anyway.'

'And who might this great love be?'

'My cat . . .' He smiles shyly at the confession and I shake my head, a similar grin falling on my face before I turn back towards the stage to hide it.

'Just one last word from health and safety . . .' the game master drops his over-pronounced medieval accent for a moment and returns to his usual Brummie '. . . they just ask if you have any magical powders, ninja stars, or smoke flares, please use suitable eye protection. We don't want any repeats of last year, do we, Andy?' He points at a man on the front row sporting an eye-patch who points back at him with a finger to his nose.

Teddy pales. 'Did he say ninja stars?' he asks me softly with an audible gulp.

'What were you expecting? Foam and Sellotape?' Seeing

him so nervous makes me chuckle. He wouldn't be the first to underestimate just how seriously these things are taken, and he certainly won't be the last. 'Don't worry – they're all blunt. Andy didn't lose his eye in battle; he got too drunk last year and ran naked through the camp with a flare. It was some nasty infection he got from the smoke and probably something to do with him falling asleep face down in the woods.'

Teddy's expression can't seem to settle on either awe or fear so it falls somewhere between the two. Back in character now, the game master gives one final call: 'Challengers, take your marks. And remember . . . "Cowards die many times before their deaths . . ."'

The crowd finish the words of Shakespeare's Caesar as they disperse across the field. '"The valiant never taste of death but once!"'

With a roaring cheer, I lead the Friskney Fellowship across the mauled earth until we huddle in the treeline of the Fabled Forest. As I stand before my team, every pair of eyes follow me intensely, awaiting my orders, ready to trust me blindly with their lives. Choking with the pressure, my commands stick in my throat. Their expectant gazes grow more impatient the more I stammer. Warm pressure spreads over my hand as Teddy takes it in his. Squeezing it gently, he presses me on with a careful nod.

With a deep breath, I deliver my battle plan to the horde like the king on his white horse, with Teddy's hand now clasped in my damp palm.

'Richard,' I address the old wizard directly, who, despite refusing to let go of his unbothered façade, listens carefully.

'We need your skills in the Fabled Forest. I need leg-binding enchantments, flashbangs, and as much fog as you can muster.'

Richard pats the pouches tied about his waist with a coy smile, excited at the prospect of finally getting to use his props after being banned by the Village Hall caretaker when he accidentally dyed the lino jet black.

'Mum, Dad, keep him alive.'

'I suppose we could try,' Mum teases, giving Richard a grin, which comes out rather a lot more sinister than I think she intended thanks to the whole orc thing.

'Er, sorry to interrupt . . .' Teddy's voice comes out meek as he speaks. 'Is there a particular place you wanted me? Anything I can do? Carry any weapons?'

'Teddy, you're with us. But are you willing to give your life to make sure we succeed?'

He looks around sheepishly again. 'Y-yes? I suppose I am,' he says with a shrug and draws his sword, a little too excited and just a little too close to the huddled team.

Grasping him softly by the wrist, I push down his weapon until it is at a safe distance from the tip of Hazel's nose as she watches it nervously, cross-eyed.

'Just make sure you know where you're swinging that thing, lad.' Dad chuckles. 'You'll want all of your fingers during the battle.'

Teddy sheathes it with a cough as each of the team breaks character to giggle at the novice.

'Just stick with me.' I speak softly to him, though unable to hide the amusement in my voice. 'I can protect you from everyone but yourself, so just don't go rogue.'

He nods, the tint to his cheeks not quite dulling the excitable expression on his face.

'Weapons in,' Sam demands from the circle, outstretching his sword. Mum adds her mace, Hazel her whip, Richard his staff, until each of us touch in the middle. 'THE FRISKNEY FELLOWSHIP!' my brother roars, and the rest of us follow, the viscount included.

'Never surrender!'

'NEVER SURRENDER!'

With the sound of the horn reverberating across the bog, all in my mind falls silent but the pounding of my heart and echo of my own breath. The terrain underfoot tremors with the weight of the thundering boots that race across it. Open-mouthed attackers call to their enemies, teeth bared, weapons raised.

Half of our Fellowship, as commanded, race off into the forest, leaving behind those brave enough to defend our escape. It's the barbed wire of my panic that keeps me rooted in the ground below. Though I have waited all year for this moment, everything around me seems to slow down, and all I can do is watch it unfold, watch the bodies that race towards me with murderous intent. The smell of the earth is strong in the air as each rumbling step stirs its peaceful slumber.

Teddy stays beside me, sword drawn, smile so broad that his eyes can hardly keep open. 'As much as this is utterly exhilarating, I think we should get going. I am pretty sure that troll-looking thing right there is sizing my head up to his war hammer . . .' Noticing that I am in need of a little encouragement before I can snap into

Alenthaea, he grasps my hand with an excited jitter and pulls us both into the Fabled Forest. It's a simple gesture, but his ability to notice, to understand without so much as a word, helps me to find the strength to hold my nerve.

Though the midday sun drew the sweat from my brow only moments ago, beyond the treeline the light has departed and it grows cold in the shade of the great oaks. Beasts are hidden within the branches, under the foliage. Thankfully they are the kind that have been lifted from someone's Halloween collection, but that doesn't stop Teddy from taking swipes at a twenty-foot stuffed python.

Though the danger of being 'disembowelled' lurks only around the corner, I take a moment to watch him. He throws himself into character, doesn't try to control the boyish grin, or push away that lock of hair that bounces against his forehead. Teddy is unbound, unrestrained, and utterly beautiful.

'Could you consider this our first date?' Teddy asks as I skulk through the grove, scouting for rogue goblins in the trees.

Trying not to let slip how my stern façade splinters into a smile, or how the feeling of being struck by lightning bounces through my body, I pretend to remain immersed, unable to tear my eyes from the enemy for a moment to look at him. 'I thought a gentleman was supposed to ask the lady first?'

In that very moment, a knight of the Duct Tape Dragons comes flying out of the treeline towards us. With the ease of slicing a jam sandwich in half, I cut down the wretch with one hard slam to his back plates and he crumples like a house of cards at our feet.

'I believe that, since I am evidently the damsel in distress in this relationship, you should be the one to ask me.' He glances between myself and the body he steps over with a chuckle.

'And who is to say that I even want to ask you?'

Teddy's face falls into a childish frown that only makes me smile harder.

Unable to torture him any further, I cross the clearing to meet him eye to eye. 'Fine, fine, this can be our first date.'

'Really?' His eyes are wide, bright as he rushes his words. 'I mean . . .' he coughs, lowering his voice to the gravelly timbre I'm used to '. . . very well.'

'What usually happens on a first date?' I ask. My only experience of dates has consisted of religious idolatry in the dusty back room of a castle, so I can't say I have much to go off.

'Well usually, there aren't loads of people interrupting to try to kill us both. But I would start off by saying something about how beautiful you look.' Teddy's dark eyes scan me up and down and I can't help but let out a little giggle at the absurdity of standing in a muddy forest, pretending to be an elf, and him somehow having to find a compliment for me. 'And just like that, you will blush and turn your face from me as you think of the words to tell me how handsome I am.'

'Mmm,' I murmur as he continues.

'Then I will ask you something safe, like "what's your favourite food?" and you'd say?' He waits for my reply.

'Hmm, spaghetti hoops.' I eye him suspiciously, nervous of where this is going.

'Spaghetti hoops? Really?' He gives me a disgusted glance. 'No one's favourite food is spaghetti hoops.' I can only shrug before he continues, 'Then you'd ask me in return, and I'd tell you that mine is a lemon meringue pie. You'd agree that I have impeccable taste. Then I'd ask a terrifying question that you choke on like, "have you ever been in love?"'

I'm almost grateful when the strangled screams of battle echo about the place, reminding us where we are, and interrupting his expectant stare. The sharp snap of a twig has me spinning my head like an owl scouting for prey. In the middle of the footpath, we are surrounded, as four knights and a goblin creep up on us, their sinister smiles a sickening sight.

Breathing deeply, I look to Teddy, and notice as his Adam's apple shifts with a nervous gulp. Just as I prepare myself to take all of them alone, a small black orb drops at my feet. The sight of it makes my heart leap, and I look around for the source of our saviour. I find Richard, the pensioner who insists on hiring a mobility scooter in the supermarket, halfway up one of the trees, safety goggles on, giggling to himself at his great aim.

My attackers grow closer and closer and just as they reach the point that I can see the whites of their eyes, I kick the ball hard towards them. On impact it explodes into a thick black curtain of smoke, giving me ample cover to grasp Teddy's sleeve and slip off into the treeline. We pass Richard as he continues fire with a box of bang snaps, the harmless toys that burst and sound like bullet fire as they hit the ground. The knights gawk about the woods frantically; the goblin scuttles off in terror.

I find the orc, her squire, the healers and my twin huddled just a few trees away from our wizard. All my Black Knight can seem to do is shake his head in an amused disbelief, chuckling softly to himself.

'There you are,' Dad pants. 'We thought we'd already lost you.'

'Sorry, we got a little caught up.' Sam sniggers and I have to stop myself from wasting one of my throwing knives on him. 'The enemy are gaining. Richard won't be able to hold them for long. You must go and aid him,' I order my parents, who rush off into the action, their rubber swords dully clashing with those of the enemy.

'Let's go,' I say to the remaining team and we push on through the trees. Stumbling upon a pack of barbarians, Sam and I take the lead but it's Teddy who delivers the style points. After manoeuvring himself around his assailant, Teddy plants his sword in his back; well, pokes the player gently in the spine where he proceeds to howl in pain and writhe on the ground. As the gurgling continues, Teddy draws his dagger and slides it into the barbarian's throat until his legs fall still.

'Nice one, posh boy.' Sam claps him on the back as all of the slain bodies surround us on the ground.

One of the corpses stirs to offer his praise. 'Yeah, great finish, real theatrics.'

'Wouldn't think he's a newbie, would you Jono?' my brother replies.

'Well, you're always welcome in the LARPing Loonies, if you ever fancy switching sides, lad,' another cadaver says from the ground, not shifting his dead position. A murmur of agreement sounds from around the circle of death.

'Thank you.' Teddy's confidence slips as he grows bashful with the compliments.

Clapping him on the shoulder, I push us on. 'Come on, Golden Boy, we'd better get going before the archers catch up with us.'

'See you later, lads!' Sam says to his latest kills, and a chorus of polite goodbyes follow him.

'You did good,' I admit to Teddy as we draw further out of the forest.

'What was that?' Teddy says with a smile, retrieving his phone and opening it up to record.

'You heard me.' I place my palm over his camera and he returns it to his pocket with a laugh.

'I'm glad you came,' I say as quietly as possible as I scout our route, sword still drawn. A rogue elf runs wildly from behind a bush, yelling in attack, arms windmilling. With barely a blink, and ever so annoyed to be interrupted when talking about my feelings, I plant my blade in their stomach.

The elf falls to the ground. 'Oh, come on,' he moans, evidently annoyed that his attack was extinguished so quickly and with little effort.

Teddy and I walk away as though there isn't a grown man wearing pointy ears pretending to bleed out just metres behind us. 'You're actually not bad considering the whole diamond-encrusted silver-spoon-up-arse thing.'

'You really have a way with words, don't you?' Teddy chuckles. 'Is this your attempt at flirting?'

One of the elf's paladin pals emerges on the path before us, and Teddy neutralises the target, eyes never leaving my reddening face.

'Me? Flirting?' I scoff. 'Get lost.' I hide my embarrassment by sinking my longsword into a player crouched, seemingly out of sight, beside the path ready to pounce. 'So have you?' My voice is quiet, nervous, as I think back to the conversation interrupted at least six dead bodies ago.

'What? Had a silver spoon in my—'

'No.' Cutting him off quickly, I elaborate nervously, 'I mean, have you ever been in love?'

He takes a second to absorb the question, busying his eyes with the foliage about us. 'For many years I had believed that falling in love was impossible.' I don't think either of us know what to say next, so it is almost a relief when an oncoming attacker bursts from the bushes for Teddy to take swipe at. The orc takes three blows before Teddy finally defuses him into a heap.

'Orcs.' I whisper, 'We're getting close.' Looking back at Sam and Flora, I give my twin the signal and he replies with a curt nod.

'You never answered my question last night.' Whispering now, Teddy draws up close beside me.

'What question?'

'Why are you so afraid of the real world?'

I muse on it for a moment. I look through the eyes of my younger self, the eyes of a little girl who only ever wanted to be loved and was mocked for being herself.

Always having to prove to girls at school, or men who thought they owned the hobbies she loved, that she was enough; she was worthy of acceptance.

'The real world never had space for me. In fantasy, I have control. I make my own space. In the real world, I am stuck as Daisy Hastings whether I like it or not.' Deciding not to cower from my candour, I hold Teddy's gaze as he strokes a thumb across my cheek. I shiver against his touch.

'Well, for what it's worth, I rather like Daisy Hastings, and I believe she is far more of the brave Alenthaea than you give her credit for. I've heard the way you rally the Fellowship. That isn't Alenthaea, that is Daisy, a woman who wants to empower those who would otherwise filter into the background.'

I grasp him by the face and press my lips to his with such intensity, as if the only way I can take another breath is if I steal it from him.

I realise for the first time today that I haven't been pretending. This has been me, all me. Yes, today I might actually look more like Alenthaea and I have been pretending to kill people, but at every turn, every word, I didn't need her help. I have trusted myself.

'Oi, lovebirds!' Sam's voice comes through, loud, urgent. 'LadyWank LARPers in the clearing. Save the spit swapping for when we throw that squealing Hogg from the parapet.'

I turn to Teddy. 'Ready?'

'Ready.'

Chapter 30

The fortress of Helm's Geek stands proud before us as we scout it from our hidden positions in the treeline. It is an old ruined tower that has been left to crumble in the English countryside as with so many castles and manors only miles away, such a small spectacle is only worthy of a tiny placard explaining its history as an old lookout point from the fourteenth century. The LARP community have essentially claimed it as our own, and it has been dressed with banners and plastic heads on spikes.

'Four barbarians,' Sam murmurs as he returns from his brief flank of the guards. 'Potentially a fifth inside. I doubt little Hogg will be cowering in there alone.'

'Definitely not. He'll be too afraid that it's haunted.'

'What's your plan, Lady A?'

Lady A may well want to plan it all out, strategise her moves, relish each moment of death. But I say, 'We just go for it. I'm confident that the three of us can take them, and Flora still has her healing powers. If we go in with brute force, we can slay the Red Ranger before he has a chance to call for his mummy.' I imagine him pacing behind the walls, and it fills me with glee to imagine his face as I drain the life from him with my twin and my . . . Teddy, at my sides.

'After you . . . Daisy.' Sam gestures and we race into combat like animals on the hunt. With the surprise, it's easy to cut down the first, leaving one each. Our swords clash with theirs until the sweat breaks on my forehead and I am panting into every swipe and jab.

My own assailant wears a fake beard and, despite the way it flaps away from his hairless cheek with the slightest breeze, I've heard him in camp swear that he grew it himself. 'You fight like a girl.' His voice cuts through the noise of the fight as he continues to dodge my weapon.

Failing to land any fatal blows thus far, I change tack. Hooking the tip of my blade in whatever poor animal he has stuck to his chin, I rip it clean off. As he dances around, grasping at his cold, bare jaw in shock, I take my moment to take his head clean off – well, I tap him on the side of the neck and watch as he falls like a sack of spuds at my feet.

'Thank you very much.' I take his compliment with pride and leave him to roll his eyes and rub at his likely stinging chin.

The other two still live, and fight mercilessly, unrelentingly, and I notice Teddy beginning to tire. Do I save him? Or shall I let him win his own fight? As I watch for a moment, my toes curl in my boots, my heart leaps at every near miss his opponent makes. Edging forward, I have to stop myself from calling out as Teddy is thrown onto his back, his sword flung across the grass as the knight looms over him, a grim smile on his face.

'Come on, Teddy. Come on,' I whisper to myself as the Black Knight grasps through the dirt for his weapon. Only when his attacker straddles him, sword raised, do I make my move. Dashing across the grass, I let out a bloodcurdling yell. The knight looks up to me, smile still etched across his face. I run faster, harder, but I'm too late.

Teddy, gripping his sgian-dubh, which he still has pressed against the throat of the man on top of him, rolls the dead man off of his chest.

'You took your time.' He chuckles breathlessly. Outstretching my hand, I pull him to his feet, and he walks beside me, limping for a few steps.

'A limp?' I ask, amused.

'I took a stray swipe to the thigh – nothing terrible.'

'Wow, you're really getting into this aren't you?' My chest feels full. Pride spills from me as I throb with affection for him.

'Well yes, and being sat on by that lump may have given me a little bit of a dead leg.' He looks back at the knight lying dead in the grass with a tickled expression.

'I can hear you, you know,' the dead man grumbles into the soil. I grasp Teddy's hands as I try to make my shaking laughter as silent as possible. His amusement overtakes him equally and we stand clutching each other, vibrating with laughter. For once my heart doesn't beat erratically because I am afraid; my heart beats this madly because I am falling in love.

Then it all stops. I hardly see it happen it's so fast.

Teddy is struck in the chest.

Hearing only the dull thud against his tunic, we don't see the arrow as it soars through the open space, slicing the air in its path, until it falls at our feet, the little orange sucker on the end not quite getting enough momentum to stick to him indefinitely. Staring at each other wide-eyed, I can barely comprehend what is going on until another flies past, missing me only by a hair. Taking one of the knives from my pocket, I fire it at the archer in the clearing, striking her dead before she can load another arrow.

Teddy clutches at his heart, his face reddening as he crumples to his knees. I hold him until the both of us are lying across the earth, him across my lap as the life drains from him.

'Flora!' I shout across the battlefield. She doesn't come. I search desperately for sight of her until there I find her, crouched over my twin, her healing hands reviving him from his own near death that I had failed to even notice. 'No,' I whisper to myself, holding Teddy's face in my hands.

''Tis but a scratch.' The Black Knight chuckles weakly.

'How long have you been waiting to say that?'

He breaks character for a moment to give me a cheeky grin before throwing his head back against my arm and resuming his emotional death.

'This is it, isn't it?' he asks me softly, a boyish look of fear crossing his features. I can only nod, clutching him harder. 'Well, my Lady Alenthaea, it has been a pleasure to fight and die by your side. I would take a thousand deaths if it meant I would be held by you in my final moments each time.'

'You can't die – I need you.'

Teddy raises a mud-caked hand and holds my cheek softly.

'All you need is a belief in yourself. I have devoted my faith to you like a god and my piety has never failed me. Be your own god; take your fate into your own hands.' He drops his palm back to his side and a final strangled breath escapes his lips until all the life has drained from him. Planting one final kiss to his forehead, I rest him back against the soft loam before clambering to my feet and sending a prayer for his safe deliverance.

Flora aids a weak Sam across the battlefield and we meet in the middle. 'Teddy?' my twin asks when he reaches me. I can only shake my head.

Sam turns to Flora, whose brow is furrowed in concern as her gaze fails to waver from her patient. 'You must return through the Fabled Forest, look for surviving members of the Fellowship. If there are any, send them to us. Tell them we are just a breath away from glory, but we need all of the swords we can gather.'

Flora nods her head attentively.

'And Flora.' Sam takes her by the face, staring into the depths of her hazel eyes. 'Take care. Stay alive.' And with that she rushes off back into the forest where only luck may help her now.

'Ready to kick some ugly, moustachioed arse?' My brother addresses me this time.

'I want nothing more.'

'Psst, Daisy,' a small voice interrupts us. Looking around the battlefield, only when it speaks again do we realise it comes from Teddy's corpse. 'What do I do now? Do I just lie here until you win?' He still doesn't move his lifeless body, only side-eyes us expectantly.

'No.' I chuckle. 'They've got tea and a hog roast back in the camp. You can hang out there. We won't be long.'

Teddy clambers to his feet, and though he is head to toe in mud, brushes off his breeches with his hands. 'Excellent. Good luck,' he half whispers before awkwardly jogging back through the forest.

Time to end this thing.

Sam leads us through the door, and down the passageway of the fortress. Light streams through cracks in the brickwork and illuminates the rubble-filled floor. Braziers sit either side of a doorless entryway at the end of the path, and we creep towards them as silent as death.

The Red Ranger stands, staring through the glassless window at the foot of a spiral staircase that no longer reaches the first floor. He has no escape.

'Oh silly, silly elves,' he says, his back still towards us. 'Surely you haven't forgot one important rule?'

'What rule?' I grunt. My voice echoes in the empty space.

'You must have two of your team alive to take my crown.' Turning to me now, he grins through his moustache.

'I knew you were stupid, but I thought you could at least count to tw—' Sam can't finish his sentence as the Red Ranger grips him by the shoulder and plunges a hidden blade into his gut with such stealth that neither me nor my twin have time to react.

'Sam!' I breathe as my brother crumples to the floor.

'Hmm, that's a little disappointing. I was hoping I'd get to play with you first, really drag it out until you're both begging me to end it. Oh well, never mind.' He struts along the length of the room, the tip of my blade tracking him with every footstep.

'So, what happens now? You kill me slowly? Or just get it over with?'

'Whether you die or not you have lost. What would hurt Lady Alcnthaea's pride more? Dying at my hand? Or is it pain enough to have watched your great new love die in your arms? To outlive your family and be quite alone in the world?' Rufus paces back and forth, flicking his dagger in his hand. As he crosses the window, I notice a flash of something familiar in the treeline before a cloaked figure dashes across the clearing towards us.

'Wow, well played. What did you do all of this time? Sit in your high walls and let everyone else do you dirty work? Sounds terribly boring to me,' I taunt him, biding my time.

'The powerful don't need to get their hands dirty. What is so boring about triumph?'

'There is no glory in cowardice.'

'No, I suppose not. But there is a Brewer's Fayre voucher. Do you think your sister would like to come and spend it with me?'

Before Sam can defy the God of Death and leap across the room to finish him, a silhouette appears in the corridor behind him.

'I'd rather die.' Marigold's voice makes Rufus turn so quickly towards her in shock that he drops his blade. 'Better yet, I'd rather see you die.' Her usually quiet voice is strong, and actually a little terrifying as she takes her curved dagger and plunges it into the Red Ranger's stomach.

He crumples to the floor with a quiet: 'Bitch.'

But my younger sister isn't quite finished yet. 'What was that?'

'You, *bitch*.'

She drops a handful of bang snaps beside his head and with the pops, he actually does squeal like a stuck hog. Leaving him with the shame of such a display, and my twin's laughter too hysterical for him to move from his position on the floor, my little sister and I re-emerge from the tower, my heart swollen.

'You, you are bloody brilliant!' I yell. As soon as the air is fresh again, I embrace her for the first time in years. She laughs uncomfortably, but hugs me back nonetheless. 'But, what? How? Aren't we going to be disqualified?'

'I made it just in time. I had arrived just as you all took your places, and I registered before the horn. I spent most of my time helping Hazel and Terry in the bog. Half dead, I had only just survived by the time Flora found me. She met her fateful end at the hands of a vagrant orc. The rest are gone.' For the first time in years, I see my sister animated, passionate. I see her as herself, finally.

'What about preferring to be yourself? Not wanting to be the person I told you to be?'

'I'd say that being someone who's there for their family

when they're in need is exactly who I want to be.' She smiles weakly, and I draw her in again to hold her.

'I've missed you.' She tightens her arms around my waist, 'Who'd have thought that my little sister is a maverick, eh? I've taught you well.'

'You should have seen her! Just a flash of a cape, and there she was, looming like the Reaper in shadows. My gods, I wish I could have filmed little Hoggy's face. I thought he was going to cry. What was it you said? "I'd rather die. Better yet—"'

'"—I'd rather see you die."' My little sister shyly finishes my sentence for the group for the fourth time since we returned victorious. The Friskney Fellowship all sit around the fire, mostly drunk, celebrating the victory. Every now and again a passing member of another team offers their congratulations, and Richard, freckled with the multicoloured powders of his smoke bombs, accepts them all with pride before launching into a mostly exaggerated story about how he was the main reason we secured the win. Marigold, as is her nature, sits blushingly in the shadow, growing more and more bashful with every congratulatory clap she receives to the shoulder.

Dad hasn't stopped his random bursts of crying since we announced our victory, and just keeps on muttering about how proud he is that all of his children are such skilled killers. I'm pretty sure I also caught Mum shedding a little tear, filled with the reflection of the fire as it carved a streak into her white face paint.

Tucked away in shadows, both of my siblings are fully

engrossed in conversation. Sam sits beside Flora, making her laugh with every second word. He seems so sure of himself, so fulfilled to be appreciated by someone he has long admired. The hand that Flora lays on his arm to steady herself as she throws her head back with laughter is a friendly one, but I think even that is enough for my brother. The glory of his smile is contagious and I find myself watching him, feeling the closest we will ever come to identical twins.

Marigold sits nervously folding her hands over and over as Callum strums his guitar beside her. Every now and again she shifts her gaze from her shoes to catch a glimpse of him through her eyelashes. When the bard shifts slightly closer to her and begins to teach her a series of chords, I am half expecting her to shoot off into the heavens and glow so brightly she outshines all of the other stars in the sky.

The night is clear; the sky is wide open and filled with pockets of starlight. Tracing constellations with my gaze, I lose myself in the map they lay out across the darkness.

'It could make you believe anything is possible, couldn't it?' Teddy's voice draws up close beside me.

Not taking my eyes from the stars, I agree. 'I always thought that the fate written for me in the stars was to be like those faint ones at the back, so far away, so dull that you'd hardly notice if they fell out of the sky. Now I'm not so sure.'

Stealing a glance at Teddy, I am caught in his gaze. He glows with the heat of the fire, the flames reflected in his dark eyes. He watches me just as I watch the stars. Teddy leans closer, the smell of the smoke thick on his clothes, and he places a tender kiss on my lips.

'You did pretty good for your first try, Black Knight.' I rest my head against his chest and we both stare into the glowing embers.

'I suppose you could say I had a good mentor. Harsh, but not bad.' I try to squirm from his grip to offer up my own teasing reply, but he only hugs me harder to his chest. I concede almost instantly and stay in the warmth of his embrace. 'I have never spent a day surrounded by such happiness. Who would have thought that the best day of my life would be spent lying in a muddy English field pretending to kill grown men wearing capes?' The soft vibration of his titter tickles at my ear.

And who would have thought that the best day of my life ends with me wrapped in the arms of Teddy, Viscount Fairfax, both of us smelling like freshly dug produce – for once not afraid of the feeling of falling in love.

Teddy slides his hand across my jaw and embeds his fingers into my hair. Drawing me up towards him, he plants another tender kiss on my lips. Before he pulls away, he rubs the pointed tips of my ears between his thumb and finger. 'And who'd have thought that I'd be kissing an elf and wishing that this is how every day begins and ends from now on?' he says against my lips before kissing me again with such passion that there is no doubt every utterance is truth in its purest form.

When he draws away, I watch him. I see the way his face lights up with his smile, the way he can't help but look at the group with an expression of pride I have never seen before. For the first time, I really see him. Not a single part of him seems caged. It's like he's unafraid of showing all that he is. Right now, Richard could turn himself into a Pegasus and fly away, and I wouldn't notice. Teddy has me entirely.

'What kind of person would you like to be, if you could be anything?' I ask shyly. I realise I've never actually asked him.

Teddy muses for a moment. 'Now, I was thinking I'd like to try my hand at being a wizard, but I have a feeling that wasn't your question.' He looks down at me with a soft smile as I shake my head. 'I would be *this* person. Every day.' As he tightens his arms around me, I squeeze him in return. 'There is so much love to be found in this life. Growing up, I'm not sure I ever saw it, not in my parents towards each other, or towards me and my brother. Everything was so clinical, so pristine, so perfect. But none of it ever felt right. It's only now I see you, your parents, Sam, Marigold, even Richard for goodness' sake, that I realise what real perfection is.'

Following his eyeline to my family, my adopted extended family, I see what he means. Love is emitted in every conversation, every smile, every eyeroll. 'I suppose it is pretty amazing.' I can only mumble as the image before me grows blurred, deluged. 'Though I'm not sure you'll ever find Mum admitting that she loves Richard.'

'I think I would be content with being loved so completely by a family, like that.' Teddy's voice strains in a whisper. Without our proximity it would be impossible to hear him.

The urge to tell him, to scream at him, to stand upon the nearest log and declare to the entire world simmers through my bloodstream like an enchantment. But I'm not sure I am ready to admit it even to myself. So instead, I rest my hand against his cheek and he presses his face further into my palm, and plants a kiss against my thumb.

Chapter 31

M any sore heads, and sore feet, clamber reluctantly into the car the next morning. With the fantasy packed away into the boot for another year, we return home, return to the monotony of the real world. For the journey, at least, the haze of make-believe still sticks as Teddy's fingers spend the hours softly stroking back and forth across my hand in such a hypnotic motion, I can't quite figure out what is really real anymore. So, when we pull up to our higgledy-piggledy house in the middle of nowhere and a sleek black Rolls-Royce with tinted windows is parked on the drive, I hardly notice it at all.

Teddy notices, and only when I feel his body turn to stone under me do I finally slip from my bubble of blissful ignorance, and feel the whole thing pop around me.

'Is that . . . the *Men in Black*?' Dad stammers from the front seat as two suited men emerge from the car. One I recognise as Morton leans against the bonnet in his black sunglasses; the other walks towards our vehicle with purpose.

'Daisy, you haven't been posting online about all of the men you've beheaded again, have you?' Mum asks cautiously.

'What? No? At least I don't think so?' I pull my phone out to double-check.

'I reckon they're probably here for the prince,' Sam mumbles beside me. Teddy stays stiff and silent.

'Prince? What prince? Who's a prince?' Dad grows increasingly anxious as we all make a wordless pact to stay sat in the stationary car, trying not to look at the scary spy-looking guy peering in the driver's window.

'No one is a prince.' I jab Sam with my elbow and he gives an exaggerated yelp. 'But Teddy may or may not be a . . . viscount . . .' I finally confess and Dad turns rapidly in his seat to face us in the back.

'You mean in the game, right?' Dad looks back and forth between me and Teddy. 'You just mean he's got a royal title in the game, don't you? Ha ha, very funny.' When even Mum stays silent the sweat begins to roll down his forehead in fat droplets. 'Iris? You knew?'

'The boy's face is on half the billboards in London.' Mum looks sheepishly at Teddy. 'I just thought it would be nice if he could have a weekend away from all of that business.' She fires an apologetic glance at me, then her husband.

Her words fail to calm him. 'Oh my God, we've kidnapped a royal. We're going to jail. I won't survive in jail.'

I look to Teddy, waiting for him to say something, but he only stares bitterly at the car. After a few more moments of Dad slowly losing his mind, the suited man finally decides to knock on the window. My father, a man terrified of authority, rolls down the manual window only far enough for the strange man on our driveway to remove his sunglasses and peer into our car.

'Fairfax, time to go. HM gave a direct order to deliver you to Windsor without delay.'

'E-Excuse me. Wh-what is the meaning of you t-trespassing on my property and ordering around my g-guests?' Dad struggles through his anxiety to give a warbled confrontation. Still, he steps out of the car, and meets the intruder at his full height.

'With respect, sir, just be glad that I am not having you all arrested for kidnap and attempted murder along with a whole other host of crimes that come with harbouring a royal.'

Dad finally chokes on his false confidence and is silent under the stare of the guard.

'I'd thank you to not make threats to civilians, Dawkins.' Teddy steps out of the car coolly, his tone so icy it sends a shiver through me. Both Dawkins and Morton offer him a slight bow.

'Sir,' Dawkins replies with a submissive nod like that of a scolded dog.

'Now tell me the meaning of such an intrusion,' the viscount demands. His whole demeanour has shifted. The Teddy of the weekend is long gone, left behind in my mother's oil-leaking car.

Dawkins looks at me as I watch on, horrified, trying my hardest to keep a clutch on my nerve. 'There has been another . . . worrying headline, sir,' he says sheepishly, his eyes still glancing between me and his boss.

Teddy's expression darkens until I hardly recognise him at all. Like a machine reprogrammed, he seems to shut down for a moment, only to reboot as a stranger. 'Headline?' He speaks through his teeth, moving himself and his guard across the drive to escape from us.

'Yes, sir. This morning's paper.' Dawkins speaks in a low tone as Morton hands Teddy a folded newspaper.

After scanning over its front page, the viscount tosses it to the ground in a fit of rage I never thought him capable of creating. Theodore leans close to Dawkins, and says something inaudible through gritted teeth.

'Come on, kids. Let's give them some privacy.' Mum looks at me with an anxious smile as she begins her sheepish retreat into the house. Sam and Dad follow her in but my intrigue gets the better of me. I take a peek at the newspaper he had thrown in rage. I see the headline that stirred such a craze in him.

'*Prince given up on love, now just kissing frogs?*' it reads alongside two photos that fill most of the sheet. One of Teddy and I, lips pressed together in that gentle moment of intimacy last night beside the campfire. The other is of me, smiling widely at the Fellowship, smothered in muck, genuinely overjoyed at getting to live my life. I can only bring myself to read the first line before something in me breaks. '*Theodore Fairfax abandons supermodels in last-ditch experiment to discover whether there truly is beauty under the beast.*'

I feel everything and nothing all at once. Pain floods

each of my cells until the desire to tear the flesh from my bones erupts through me.

Storming into the house, I ignore everyone and don't stop until I reach the back garden. Retching into the compost bin, I feel like I'm still in the car and we're hurtling down the motorway, no brakes, no control, just awaiting the fatal crash.

'Now, sir. Let us not be hasty.' Dawkins's heavy voice rips through the fence and though I am mostly concealed from their view, I can hear every breath. 'His Majesty has asked that you bring this woman to him so he may deal with her demands.'

'There is no need, Dawkins. Does she look like the sort of person for His Majesty to have to bother himself about? You only have to read that headline to know that she and her family are inconsequential.' I hear every word. Unable to tear myself away, I submit myself to the torture.

'His Majesty was particularly insistent to see the girl, sir.' Morton speaks surprisingly softly and I have to muffle a sob as it rips through me like a blunt knife.

'She is no threat, there is no wild love affair that he must extinguish, I assure you. I wouldn't wish the king to waste his time on such people.'

Only last night, Teddy held me as he spoke of his affection for my family. He kissed me so tenderly that even my cynical mind fooled me into believing that maybe he could love me.

I had trusted my heart, I trusted myself, and I had been so, so wrong.

'He will still insist that you meet with him. He will require your reassurance, in person, sir.'

'Then let's go.' Taking long strides to the car, Theodore looks up one last time, and as though by instinct, his black eyes find mine through the chipped white paint of the fence. Sucking in a painful breath, the wind is knocked out of me with just the split second of contact, like the final blow of the executing bullet.

With a look that crushes me more than a pathetic headline ever could, he averts his gaze and retreats behind the blacked-out windows. Just like a dream, he disappears out of our lives as if he was never real to begin with.

Paralysed, I watch the space that the car disappeared into for what feels like days, the pain so visceral that my body would rather shut down than acknowledge it.

I only come back to my senses when my family emerge onto the patio. Mum looks at me, brows sloped and those eyes filled with such intense sympathy that I feel pathetic to be the object of such a gaze. 'Daisy . . .' she begins, and I notice the discarded newspaper clutched in Dad's hand.

'Don't you dare,' I warn them and their pity. 'Just don't. I don't . . . I'm fine.'

Before she can say another word, I rush down the garden. I push my way through the back gate and into the wide-open fields behind the house. Harvested for the year, for miles and miles the flat land is littered with broken and dying roots. With their fruits and flowers plucked from them, all they can do now is die before they are replaced again. Dry stalks cut through my clothes as I storm across the acreage and don't stop until I fall exhausted under the lonely tree that can only muster enough strength to grow leaves on one single branch as the others grow cold and hard.

My tears water the cracked earth. Out here, no one can stop me as I sob with such animalistic ferocity that my whole body cries with me. Only the soil can hear me scream.

It's not the article, or the way he left, or his coldness, the thing that feels like every breath I take carves another stinging chunk from my body is the fact I allowed myself to wonder. So caught up in wondering about what could be possible, whether this could really work, I forgot that none of this is real, and it never could be. I thought I could just swap out Alenthaea and start living this life as me, no longer pretending. But it was all just a weekend fantasy. Arrows in this world don't have suckers; they don't just bounce off with no consequence. Here they're set alight, take your life before you even notice them strike, and burn everything around you in collateral.

My body can't settle on a feeling. It hops between all of them; it rips my heart so savagely from my chest until I am too exhausted to feel anything at all.

At some point, I must have fallen asleep. It's the soft voice of my sister that finally stirs me. 'Mind if I join?' I have no energy to protest, so she sits down beside me. 'You have always surprised me, but I have to say, falling for a prince definitely takes the biscuit on this one.'

'He's not a prince,' I muster the strength to mumble, unable to look her in the eye.

'You know, I've always wanted to be you.' She looks at me, her sparkly eyes glassy, her soft cheeks pink. She reaches up to touch my face. Slick snot is smeared up the sides of my cheeks, my eyes feel swollen, and my hands are caked thick with topsoil. How could such a perfect creature ever wish to be me, when even I wish I was anything but?

'Don't patronise me.' My words all slur together and my sister takes a tissue from her pocket and wipes my face for me.

'Everyone in this world is just trying to fit into a mould that was made for none of us. I was never strong like you. Every day I would wake up and wish I had the gall to get out of bed and be exactly who I was, unapologetically. I tried so hard to fit in, to find a place I belonged in this world, when really, I should have made a world to fit around me. Daisy, I have watched you for years, hoping I could be a fraction of what you are.'

'But I am nothing. I have achieved nothing. My greatest accomplishment is having some national newspaper discussing how beastly I am.'

'If there is one thing I know, it's that Daisy Hastings doesn't give one single shit about what people think of the way she looks. And she certainly doesn't believe the words of a tabloid newspaper only good for starting fires.' She laughs softly. 'Daisy, you've always assigned your strength to a fictional you, to Lady A. You give this fantasy all of the credit when really, it's just you; it's always been you. This will pass, and you will survive and one day, both you and Lady A will get your happy ending.'

'I love you.'

We sit in silence, hand in hand, until night falls when Marigold clambers to her feet and pulls me with her. 'Come on. If we don't wax our swords, we're going to have to completely remake them before next year.'

Wandering back through the moonlight, I let my little sister guide me home. She steers me like an empty vessel for the rest of the night, washing my face, helping me change my clothes, tucking me into bed before crawling in beside me like she used to as a child.

Marigold holds me tight against her through the night, and every night for the next few days. Every time I open my eyes, my head pounds with the weight of Sunday and I can't bring myself to see anyone but her. Today, I wake up with my body feeling just that little bit lighter. Snaking myself out of Marigold's grip, I push the soft hairs from her face to kiss her on the forehead and leave her sleeping soundly.

The dread of seeing anyone else freezes me on the staircase. The grief I feel around the whole situation shifts into embarrassment. I still can't face my family. Slinking down against the banister, my bare feet grow cold on the wooden steps but still I sit, staring at the front door, afraid of seeing a silhouette in the window again.

My long-forgotten phone chimes in the pocket of my dressing gown and without thinking, I answer it.

'Oh my gosh, hello? Daisy? Oh my, I have been trying to call you all week!' Bobble's frantic voice comes through the speaker and I can almost see her pacing her room, swinging her latest sewing creation around in a frenzy.

'Hey, Bob.' My voice is strained, gruff.

'I saw the papers.' I haven't spoken to her since I left London. I haven't spoken to anyone I knew, though Bobble has been the only one to try. The guilt of leaving her behind catches up with me and the familiar sickness overtakes me. I love her. She has been my greatest friend, yet the failure of my job, the failure of leaving behind the thing I had begun to adore meant all I could do was tear myself clean away from all of it or risk grieving what could have been forever. If I pushed Bobble away, it wouldn't hurt so much to have been so close only to lose it all.

'Look, Bobble, I'm so sorr—'

She cuts me off. 'Are you okay?' She really is just a sunbeam of a woman. After all I have done, all she has to be angry at me for, for all of the reasons she should call me a terrible friend, her priority is still seeing how I am.

Bursting into tears on the stairs, I realise the extent of my foolishness for the first time. 'Hey, hey, hey,' she says softly, 'it's okay. It's okay.'

'I'm sorry I haven't called.' I speak through my tears.

'Oh shush, never mind that now. Do you think you could get me up to speed?' I start from the beginning, telling her all of the things I had kept to myself about Teddy, and all that has happened since his sudden appearance. For a while she stays unusually quiet, listening, digesting. 'Now that is a real pickle,' she says calmly. 'And he just left without saying anything to you?'

'He was like I'd never seen him; he was just . . . empty.'

'Perhaps it's for the best,' she says softly, and I know her whole face will be clouded in sorrow. Bobble likes her happy endings. Every evening when I would come home from work, I'd find her scrolling down the Wikipedia page of whichever film she had decided on, trying to work out if the ending was a happy one. On more than one occasion, usually involving a film with a loveable dog, I have seen her switch it off entirely after learning of the characters' fates to rewatch *The Princess Diaries* one and two back-to-back instead. For her to accept this as my tragic end proves there really is no going back now.

No knight in shining armour is going to turn up on a white horse and canter us off into the sunset. This world is not a fairy tale, Teddy is not my Prince Charming, and I am no princess.

Chapter 32

Bobble calls every day for the next week and a half. She's not the only one. My phone is set alight by hundreds of calls from unknown numbers, mainly journalists asking me to sell my story to them for thousands, or Teddy's disgruntled fans reiterating the sentiments of the first article and informing me that they would be better suited for such a handsome man. After the third or fourth, I stopped answering.

Teddy himself has simply faded back into that place where royals live, suspended between fiction and reality, kept close enough to see their influence, but just far enough away that it would be futile to try and reach out and touch them. Though I wake each day hardly able to push through the weight of my duvet, feeling that the lumps of my mattress are holding me tightly against them, warning me that there is danger beyond its confines, the thought that Teddy will finally get what he wanted all along brings me some relief. With such a scandal, his banishment will be imminent, he will be afforded the peace he has always craved – perhaps that was his plan all along, and yet I can't bring myself to be angry.

I find myself longing again for London. For the thousands of unknown faces, my own equally anonymous, with the world carrying on so quickly around me that I hardly have time to sit with the thoughts in my head. My heart pines for the city as much as it does for *him*. My job, my independence, Bobble, even Erin and Tristan – all of the things that I was proud of, all the things I cultivated, constructed only for myself. I grieve for all of it, for the person I almost became.

Only the incessant vibration of my phone ejects me from such a stupor. With the hope that it could be Bobble, calling to tell me of her latest project, or how she has befriended one of the neighbourhood foxes, I check it anyway.

The very last name that I had expected crosses the screen. I watch it ring for a moment, unsure if my lucid imaginings are fooling me again. What could he want to say to me after a month? Growing hot, then cold, I shudder, unsure whether to answer it at all. With just seconds to spare, I hit answer.

'Westley?' My rasping addresses him after a short while of silence.

'Ah, Sir Daisy, ye answer to your carrier apple at last.' His cheery tone is a relief, though it stirs up my heartache over losing such a job with such a boss when, until now, it was planted far down on the pile of things for me to grieve. 'How've ye been?'

'Well, I've been well, thank you.' I choke out, 'How is all with you?'

'Yes, well, all well. That Tristan Huntsford, ha, that boy certainly keeps us busy.' Westley chuckles to himself nervously, evidently lost in his own memories of whatever the tiny menace has been up to this time.

'Is there anything I can do for you?' I enquire before he can stray too far from his original purpose.

'Ah yes, my apologies. I'd like you to come back to work as soon as possible,' he says with such conviction that it is hard to doubt his sincerity.

'W-what? Why?' With my brain in overdrive, all I can do is question.

'I, er, have had a change of heart. You were a great asset to the team and I have just recently, um, had my eyes opened to that fact. I understand if you do not wish to return, but it would be . . . sublime to have you back.'

A change of heart? Eyes opened? The inside of my skull feels like it has been melted and is just sloshing about in the space, trying to make sense of everything. 'Really?'

'Of course. There isn't too long left of the summer, but we'd love to see you return to the team.' Both of us sit in an almost silence for a moment. I listen to his anxious breaths on the other end. 'How are you fixed?'

This time, I don't even have to hesitate before giving him an answer. 'I'll be there tomorrow.'

Rushing through the house, I collect all of my necessities, and a few spare daggers and scale mail, and pack them into my case with more energy than I've had for weeks.

'You running away?' Sam appears in my doorway, and watches me whilst he grazes on a Pot Noodle.

'I,' I begin with a smile, 'am going back to London.'

'You're finally going to chase down your prince and make him pay for abandoning you to the press?' he says with a slurp.

'Jesus Christ, when will everyone learn that he's a viscount, not a flaming prince? It's not the same thing!' Hurling another jumper into my bag, I can't hide my frustration. 'And no. I got my old job back.'

'Slightly more boring, but cool. You needing a lift?' God bless brothers.

'Please.'

Sam shrugs and ambles away muttering something about putting some shoes on.

With a quick phone call to Bobble, just to double-check that she hasn't already rented my bed out to anyone else, or overtaken it as a wardrobe for her new designs that practically have a life of their own, we set off. As always, Mum and Dad wave from the porch, still ever so slightly confused but as supportive as ever (probably mostly of the fact I actually managed a shower for the first time in a week). We drive into the night before we reach the titan skyline of London.

Before we can even knock, the door swings open and without even stopping to check if we might be cold callers, Bobble binds both me and my brother in a crushing hug. 'I am so, SO happy you're home.' Once she finally decides to release us, she snatches my suitcase from my hand and we follow her into the flat. 'Tea anyone?'

'We're good thanks, Bob.' Sam gets his reply in quickly before my housemate launches into her menu of exotic teas. 'I should be heading off soon anyway.'

'You are not driving back right now. You must take the sofa.' Sam gives her a look that would suggest he is about to protest, but motherly Bobble gets there first. 'I absolutely insist.' Unable to argue with her rare sternness, my brother agrees.

'Thank you, Bobble. For letting me come back.' I speak quietly and she softens into her usual self.

'I have been waiting for that call since you left. I hope you don't mind but I look the liberty of making your bed up. It's all ready for you. Well, it's been ready for weeks – I thought I'd keep it ready for whenever you were going to come and visit.' Her bejewelled teeth are all on display as she smiles so widely, I think she might pop.

'I really have no idea what I did to deserve a friend like you,' I say sincerely and she grows shy, giving me a soft squeeze on the shoulder before scuttling off to the kitchen.

The night disappears in a haze of teas and chatter, and before I really have any time to catch up on my life, I am back on the familiar Tube journey that ends at Tower Hill station. Though barely weeks, it feels like a lifetime since I climbed these stairs, bustled through the rush of tourists and stood looking over the barriers at the great monument before me. I suppose the best thing about a fortress that has stood for almost a millennium is that now we have less need for thirty-foot walls, murder holes, and cesspit moats, it's the one thing that stays the same in a landscape that is constantly growing up and out. When another glass monolith of a building shoots up, colonising more of the sky, it stays right as it is, holding its own as the others begin to block out the sun.

As always, I watch it for a while. Picturing children throughout the centuries kicking balls against the walls, or guards of old and new bored at their posts and carving their initials into the stone, or delivery drivers, once sent to deliver parchments, or royal jewels, now Chinese food and Amazon packages, feeling the same sense of awe of carrying out their job against such a magnificent backdrop – not quite believing it to be true.

'Did you know that despite having a reputation for torture and beheadings, in the whole thousand years of the Tower, only forty-eight people were officially tortured here and only six people were officially beheaded behind those walls?' A familiar voice catches my attention and I look around for it with a smile as it continues, 'Of course, that doesn't include the *unofficial* ones.'

Ellis gives an excitable smile as I find him in the very place that I met him for the first time, with a different woman now at his side. I hang back, waiting for my opportunity for a reunion.

'How do you know all of this stuff?' the young brunette asks him, eyes wide, intrigued by his intelligence.

'I work here. I'm an archivist.'

'That's crazy, me too. Gift shop.'

Ellis leans in closer. 'Really? I haven't seen you here before, and I'd definitely remember a face like yours.' The girl giggles and hides her toothy grin behind her hand.

'It's actually my first day.' The conversation continues

in a familiar fashion, until it ends with Ellis, ever the gentleman, escorting her to her first appointment and promising to meet her once her day is done.

Perhaps if my heart hadn't already been accessorised by the spear lodged into my right ventricle, it would hurt more. I never fell for Ellis in the way I did for Teddy, but knowing my first real attention from a man that I truly thought enjoyed my company is just an older guy's way of seducing every new girl under the age of twenty-five does not feel great. It is a feeling that reminds me why I locked my heart in a gibbet for twenty-three years and refused to allow anyone near it. Perhaps I should have had it removed completely and fed to the Thames seagulls – it sure would have made the last two months far easier.

Refusing to allow today to be dampened, I push on, plastering a smile on my face. The moat is quiet, with no one else yet arrived. I beeline straight for Westley's tent. Knocking against the opening, I make the sound with my voice, and he invites me in. Spread across his desk are piles and piles of paperwork, and his glasses hang low on his nose as I interrupt his perusal of a smaller stack on his lap. Upon seeing me, he beams.

'Daisy, Daisy, what a lovely sight. And my word, you travelled all the way down to London and you still beat the rest of my protégées in.' He chuckles, removing his glasses and setting aside the papers. 'How are you?'

'I would be lying if I didn't say my brain is struggling to keep up with everything as it is right now.' I surprise myself with my honesty.

'All is understandable, child.' He gives me a sorrowful

glance, a glance that tells me that his carrier pigeons also deliver tabloid news to him.

'I'm glad to be back.'

'I have to say, it hasn't been the same without you. I should probably just run a few things by you, HR things, I'm afraid.' For once, I'm happy to listen. He finishes his warnings, mostly of *'don't start water fights or ride any horses'*, just as the others begin to filter in.

With my muscle memory kicking into play, I get to work paying little mind to anything else. On my way to costume, I politely greet my colleagues though, strangely, they only stare in return. No one expects to see a fired colleague return to work weeks later as if nothing has happened. I suppose it's like seeing someone return from the dead and just carrying on as if they aren't half decomposed. Thinking little of it, I head straight for the racks and filter through all of them until I find one that suits me today.

'. . . *you'd always be drawn first to the green ones. Like your hand would just instinctively go towards those on the rack even though you'd seen all of them before and knew they weren't your size.'* Teddy's voice comes through so loud in my mind that I look about the tent expecting to find him. Lowering my hand from the forest green tunic that I know full well is a child's size six to seven, I decide to stick safely with Alenthaea. Taking my own costume from my bag, I throw it on, almost wishing for that irritating voice to speak over the curtain and call me a 'nerd' or say something to push my buttons. Only the muffled voices outside accompany the silence.

When I re-emerge, the sense that something is missing

is overwhelming. The camp is full, bustling, a chorus of laughter and conversation, yet it feels empty. How is it that the one thing I thought ruined my dream job, is now what makes it such a dream?

'Do we call you lady now? Or princess?' Alice slinks up to me, her voice so sickly sweet. She's the kind of person where you can never quite tell whether she's being nice or it's just her two-faced way of laughing at you.

'Well technically since I am the leader of our group and we won the crown, I'm actually queen,' I reply, a little confused at how she knows anything about the Battle of Helm's Geek.

Her thick brows furrow, and her face twists into a series of expressions until she bursts out in a cackle of false laughter. 'Hilarious. How did *you* manage to pull it off?' She's serious again, as this starts to feel like an interrogation.

'Well, my sister killed the king. He was a real arsehole so it was perhaps the most satisfying thing I have witnessed.' I smile as I replay the moment in my head.

'What is wrong with you?' Alice looks at me with disgust.

'Oh shit, you don't know Rufus, do you?' That could explain why she is so interested in the battle, but again that confused grimace returns.

'Ugh!' she grunts in frustration, her pretty face reddening. 'Just tell me how the hell someone like you managed to pull Theodore Fairfax!'

'What?' The sound of his name out loud makes me flinch. 'You weren't talking about Helm's Geek?'

'What? What even is— No! I want to know how on earth you made a viscount fall in love with you.' Alice trembles with vexation. 'See! How does she manage it? She's a freak.' She speaks to herself, laughing, more in bemusement than hilarity.

'Oh! Fairfax! I actually hexed him. I can give you the spell if you'd like?'

She turns on her heel and marches away with a grunt. Laughing to myself, I return my attention to Westley who begins another morning speech by discussing the ways to order a meal as a knight visiting a tavern. Very few others listen as they spend much of the speech turning to look at me, the amount of whispering so intense that the hushed voices begin to drown out Westley altogether.

Growing hot under the scrutiny, I feel my chest tighten until I have to remind myself to breathe, and I take small gasping breaths. Tapping my fingers compulsively against my thigh, I attempt to regulate myself to little avail. When a colleague I have only spoken to once to ask him to pass a glue stick turns around and loudly exclaims to the class, 'It was her?' I finally cave into my rebelling body and rush into the nearest tent to escape.

'Just ignore them. They're only jealous.' I have spent weeks trying to have a conversation with Erin, a proper one, and now it is her voice that finds me pacing the tent, chest heaving hard with every straining breath, each one threatening to bring up my breakfast with it. 'It's a story that half of the girls here have dreamt about since they were six years old. And it's made the other half look at their own boyfriends and wonder where it all went wrong.' She laughs softly.

'They're welcome to it; they're welcome to *all* of it,' I

say sadly. Where is the fairy tale in a trashy newspaper printing awful photos of you to discuss all of the things you already hate about yourself? Only to be left with even less than you had before this whole nightmare began?' Though the frustration is pouring out in my words, I'm grateful that she's here, that I have someone willing to listen to my side. This is what I wanted: a friend at work, someone to talk to who's not Teddy, but he's ruined that too. Erin glances about the room, looking as if she is fighting with herself.

'It's not about the article, not really, anyway,' she begins but stops herself. 'We're not meant to say anything. He made us swear.'

'What? Who? Say what?' The threat of a meltdown has subsided but the anxiety very much still persists and all I want to do is scream. Why does everyone seem to know everything about my life when I hardly know how I've ended up here at all?

'Lord Fairfax.' Erin draws a deep breath. 'He was here, a day or so after that article was printed. Said something about it being his duty to be here but it seemed like this duty was to get you back. Every day he would sit in meetings with HR telling them that it was all his fault with the pictures, the horses, the water, you know. He said to me, if he was fired, they'd be short-staffed, so they'd have to bring you back. They weren't having any of it. We all said that his family must have made some serious threats because they wouldn't budge, even when he made up stories about him breaking into the White Tower and wearing Henry VIII's armour.'

She pauses to laugh, but upon noticing my serious concentration on her story, coughs and resumes. 'After the third day, he changed his approach. In these meetings he would spend an hour talking about your brilliance, how much you've helped the kids. He'd take on extra hours, be here well into the night to be the perfect employee, something about appeasing his family so he could use their influence. The more he behaved, the more he could ask them to loosen their grip on the Tower and allow you back. That must have been what happened. He left yesterday, and you're back today.'

None of this makes any sense. I heard every word he spoke; I felt the malice he spoke them with. *Inconsequential* is the word that has swum about my subconscious for weeks. To him, I mean nothing; I have never meant anything. Erin must be mistaken. Perhaps she's just trying to make me feel better? Why on earth would he purposefully give up his chance at breaking free and being himself for *someone like that?*

'But this was his ticket out of it all. He's undone all of that for me to work two more weeks of a summer school?' My pacing resumes as I speak mostly to myself. If what she says is true, then Teddy has given up on his emancipation, only to return me to my job. All he had worked for, all he had done to escape the binds of an institution and a press who all want to make him a puppet – gone. He worked off his punishment, proved himself to his family, to return him to his cycle of isolation and misery. For me?

'You managed to straighten out the royal rogue. I reckon you'll be getting your knighthood in the post any day now.'

Chapter 33

After a few anxious retches into a spare helmet and Erin trying her best to comfort me whilst being entirely ignorant of the weight of what she had just revealed, I return to work. Considering a viscount has just passed up his shot at freedom to allow me to be here, the least I can do is not get re-fired on my first day.

'Just stick with me. I'll cover for you if you need a break,' Erin reassures me with a friendly smile, a relieving sight right now. I had tried so hard to win her friendship, doing everything I could to prove myself as a worthy friend, and it feels odd now to know that the pressure I had put on myself was unneeded. Some people just need a little more time to warm up; I realise that now.

With me only overhearing the odd comment here and there, the day passes relatively uneventfully after the initial interest plateaus. Just as Erin and I put the final bench away, a flaming blob of red fur comes flailing into the moat.

'Is that . . . Elmo?' Erin asks, no hint of jest or sarcasm in her tone.

'Nope, just my housemate.'

Bobble comes flying across the grass. The sight of her puzzles me, not because she is wrapped in another of her 'skinning your favourite childhood characters collection', but this surely can't be good news that she brings. That, and I can't quite believe that the security for the most secure fortress in the world has just allowed a furry fashion student in without questioning.

Scratch that, behind her follows a string of King's Guards in their combat uniforms chasing her down. By the time she reaches us, she is panting so hard that she can't seem to cling on to enough air to speak. Once I have managed to explain to the guards that Bobble is my best friend, and not actually a terrorist or international jewel thief, they march away, greatly inconvenienced.

As the seconds pass, Bobble has finally sweated enough to be able to talk again. 'Ooo this is nice,' she says casually, looking about the moat with great interest.

'You ran all of this way, chased by royal guards, just to tell me that my workplace is nice?' I can't help but laugh.

'No, oh shit, where is your TV?' She switches suddenly back to her mania.

'A TV? We're stood in a moat of a one-thousand-year-old castle? Why do you need a TV?'

'Did he . . . did Teddy ever mention anything about going to the press?' she asks cautiously.

'The press? Why would he? He's never given an interview in his life.' Teddy Fairfax has articles written about him

352

on the daily, but never once has he given them a direct quote, or shared his opinion on the whole affair, always making his opinion on those whose only objective is to villainise him to the world very, very clear (to me at least). I can't imagine he'd ever go to them willingly. He just takes it all in silence, accepting what they say, unable to defend his own honour.

'Well . . .' Each moment she hesitates, I grow more restless.

'What is it?' I demand, my nerves mounting.

'It's just I've seen something about "setting the record straight" himself . . . about you.'

'What does that mean?'

'It means he's giving a live interview, in . . .' she looks down at her watch '. . . four minutes.'

He's lost his mind. He has gone completely insane.

'I know where there's one.' Erin speaks up quietly. 'A TV, I mean.' She looks nervously at Bobble who notices her for the first time.

'Yes, yes, yes!' is all Bobble can say. Thankfully Erin translates that as *please may you take us to the aforementioned television set?* and we follow her with haste.

'Bobble, I don't understand.' I stop her mid run and clutch her by her furry arms. 'Why would he do any of this? Why would he sabotage everything he's worked for?'

'Why? Because he loves you, of course!' she says, as if it is the most obvious thing in the world.

'But I told you what he said, when he left, without a word. How could he love me and say any of that?'

'Teddy lives a life neither of us could ever understand.

Don't get me wrong, if I see him again, I will be having words with him.' A threatening aura overtakes her for a moment until she softens again. 'But you said it yourself: they were demanding to send you before the king for goodness' sake. Why would Teddy want you dragged into a life you never chose, the same life that was thrust upon him, and that he has always resented?' She pauses for a moment to squeeze my hands. 'Daisy, he was protecting you in a way that no one has ever done for him. I'd bet every single one of my hats on it.'

'I'm . . . I can't . . . I'm not worth any of that. What if you're right, but it's just a passing crush, and six months from now, he regrets it all?' Bobble holds me by the face, and I don't fight out of her grip.

'Has your little world in here never seen a happy ending?' She taps on my temple. 'Love is the one thing we will never fully understand, but the one thing we would risk everything for. Maybe you're right, maybe in a year it could all be over and he's just another memory, but that is his choice to make. But the feeling of falling, the feeling of being *in* love, and the feeling of losing it all is the most alive a person can feel. The pleasure, the peace, the pain, is all so human that, royal or not, it binds us all together. Even if a happy ending isn't guaranteed, you should never be afraid to feel.' She doesn't let me answer, only drags me forward, my body not able to function alone as it tries to keep up with my racing mind.

Erin waits for us at the door to the Byward Tower. As we reach her, she knocks urgently but pushes it open before anyone has the chance to permit us. A Beefeater, dressed in his scarlet Watchman's coat, sits at the desk at the centre of the round room, the fireplace barren behind him, watching a rerun of an episode of *EastEnders* from so long ago that Phil Mitchell still has hair. Each wall of the stone chamber is covered with a slate of names, listed in beautiful calligraphy, and for just a moment I remember one of my first conversations with Ellis: the missing Beefeater.

'So sorry to interrupt your work, sir.' Erin looks between the Beefeater and the television. Annoyed at the interruption, he strokes his red beard. The jolly Father Christmas demeanour has shifted into that of a hungry dog guarding his kibble from a thief. 'I was just wondering if we could, perhaps, potentially, borrow your TV for a sec?'

'No,' the Beefeater grunts and returns his attention to the screen. 'This post has been manned continuously since 1280, the longest manned military post anywhere in the world. You must not disturb me whilst I protect that tradition.'

'Okay, I'm sorry. I should have said . . .' Erin begins, giving Bobble and I a sneaky wink. 'I have a friend who works as a baker in the New Armouries Café. If I promised to bring you a cake on your post each day, may we borrow it just this once?'

The Beefeater thinks about this offer for a moment, tapping on his chin as if he hadn't made up his mind as soon as she mentioned cake.

'Fine, deal. But be quick, *Tipping Point* will be on in a minute.'

'Thank you, thank you, sir,' I rush out, as Bobble scrambles for the remote.

'—you may know him as the king's problem nephew, may have seen him in the papers again and again causing headaches for the royals but tonight, The Viscount Fairfax will become the first royal in recent years to sit down with the BBC for a tell-all interview. After recent news broke in the press of his latest relationship, he approached the BBC directly to finally tell his side of the story. In a world exclusive, His Lordship is coming to us live from his home in Windsor. Good evening, Lord Fairfax, thank you for speaking with us tonight.'

Teddy's face flashes on the screen. Where his hair had been growing out over the last few weeks and tickling at his ears, it's now perfectly trimmed so not a single strand falls out of place. He's buttoned into a tightly ironed suit. A tie is knotted so tightly at his neck that he attempts to pull at his collar discreetly, but a deep red mark begins to appear down his jugular. Shaved smooth, styled, manicured, he looks in every way perfect, yet is nothing like the man I knew. Perhaps I never knew this man at all.

'Good evening.' His deep voice comes through the speakers and I have to steady myself against the Beefeater's table.

'Now, I think it would be fair to say that you haven't been a stranger to the press all of these years, but you have never given an interview until now. What prompted you to take this interview? Why wait until now to tell your side?' The journalist tries to balance his instinct to interrogate him with the clear orders he has been given to treat the royal with respect, but it's impossible to miss the aggression in his tone.

I can't feel my heart beat in the time it takes Teddy to answer. His expression is strict, controlled. 'I have always understood that as long as my family represent this country, my life belongs to the nation. The nation can own my image, can push the stories onto me that they wish, because that is my duty. My family are the nation, and I am thus a product with which the nation can do as they please.' Though his expression remains firm, it's his blackening eyes that tell the true story.

No one in the room says a word, but Bobble and Erin watch me closely as Teddy continues, 'What I failed to realise is that in associating myself with anyone else, I was offering them up for the press to do with them what they have done to me for my entire life. Watching those closest to you be picked apart and insulted on a global scale is a pain like no other and I don't believe I can sit by and allow false narratives to persist about people who deserve the love of the world.'

'It's widely known that all of your relationships have been highly publicised. Why do you only feel the need to defend now?'

'Because every single one before now has been a lie.' Erin can't hide her gasp, and I am grateful that her loud exclamation distracts everyone from seeing how I have to steady myself by clutching the back of a nearby chair. My knuckles turn white, along with the rest of my complexion, as Teddy continues, 'All of those women you have seen with me on front pages have been friends, or they have been someone searching for a headline, for the status they can achieve by making the front pages.' Somewhere along the way I stop breathing.

'All of your relationships have been just publicity stunts?' The interviewer wears a triumphant expression as he looks around at his peers hiding just off screen. Everyone will be gaining a tasty bonus after such an exclusive.

'If you can call them relationships, then yes.'

'And this . . .' the interviewer looks at his notes '. . . "Daisy Hastings", what makes her different? Why is this seemingly normal girl so special to the man who could have whatever and whomever he wants?'

'Because the most valuable people in life are those who make you feel like you did as a child. When each day you could wake up and choose to be anything in the world: an astronaut, a firefighter, a prince, a knight. The people who make you feel like you can be anyone, do anything, are the ones who make a dull life so utterly beautiful. Daisy Hastings is the kind of woman who makes you believe in magic.' Teddy smiles briefly, as though forgetting where he is.

'So, it's safe to say you are in love with her?'

'Unequivocally so.'

'Still think it's just a crush?' Bobble calls across the room, a smug grin etched on her face. All I can do is laugh. It starts off a nervous chuckle, until I am bent double and trembling.

Teddy Fairfax loves *me*.

The only thing I can fully comprehend right now, stood in this room, with Bobble's fiery fur occupying my periphery on one side, and a Beefeater filling the other, is that I love him back. I *love* Teddy Fairfax. And though I feel myself losing my grip on reality as I have known it until now, *that* is the one thing I'm sure of.

358

'What are your family's thoughts on falling for commoners? Can we expect a royal meeting for the both of you in the near future?' The journalist seems to relax into his work, excited by such emotional rawness from a family that are known for their impenetrable façades.

'Well . . .' Teddy tugs at his collar, his moment of happiness quickly replaced with discomfort '. . . as my devotion is to the nation, I must focus on my royal duties. To give myself to anyone else would only distract me from my loyalty to the United Kingdom and the Commonwealth.' He is robotic, speaking as though he is reading from a script. 'And days from now, I shall be relocating abroad to continue my duties with renewed enthusiasm and to prove my loyalty and piety to our great Kingdom and Commonwealth. My intention with this interview was not to announce my relationship, but rather request that the British and global presses respect the privacy of those who never intended to live this lifestyle. My heart belongs to the nation, and I vow to serve in the Commonwealth with as much affection as I have for home soil.'

Chapter 34

'He's leaving?' Erin's voice snaps me from my trance. 'He can't just leave!' Bobble reiterates. 'Daisy, you need to do something!'

'What can I do? He's made up his mind.' My body is numb, yet my heart is aflame. Burning brighter, hotter, than ever before.

'Has he made up his mind, or has he had it made for him?' My housemate struggles to hold in her anger. We all know the answer.

'It's too late,' I whisper, watching him speak on the screen, though hearing none of it.

The sound of sniffling distracts all of us for a moment. The bearded Beefeater sweeps a tear from his cheek before blowing his nose noisily into his handkerchief. 'You are not going to let that kind of love get away, young lady,' he says between sniffs.

'What am I meant to do? I don't know what to do.' I run my hands over my face, trying to think of any kind of solution and ending up with nothing.

'Rescue your princess.' The Beefeater blows his nose again, but looks at me with such seriousness. It's clear that he isn't joking.

'Yes! That's it!' Bobble exclaims. 'Go to him. You can be his knight in shining armour.' I would laugh at her, at all of this, had my emotions not gone through such extremes in such a short space of time and left me feeling like my whole body is shutting down.

'Is this really happening?' Erin looks between the crying Beefeater and Bobble as she clutches me tightly. She is the only one who looks half sane in this moment.

Just weeks ago, Teddy confessed that he had never felt love, thought it impossible to fall in love at all, and now he has surrendered to his greatest enemies, to tell the whole nation that he loves *me*. For a girl he has known for a matter of months, he is willing to give up everything just to protect me. But who does he have to protect him? Who is loving him?

'I-I think it is,' I say, hardly knowing myself, but letting my body do all of the thinking for once. Teddy may have been raised being taught the divine right of kings, but the divine right of all mankind is to find someone to love, and to be loved. The only thing truly divine in this world is the way another person can make us feel. And I can't let him move halfway across the world, never knowing that his love is requited.

As soon as I step out of the room, I wait for Lady Alenthaea to spring into action. But she doesn't. Nerves tremble through me, tickling at my fingertips, churning in my stomach. Still, I am Daisy, feeling every synapse pulse in my body. I need her. Where is she?

That's when my sister's words reach me: '*you give this fantasy all of the credit when really, it's just you; it's always been you.*' I was always Lady A. She has always been me. It was my body charging head-first into battles against all the things that terrify me, it was my lips that fought back against those who mistreated me, it was my heart that would beat rapidly in my chest to remind me that through it all, I can survive. I don't need to wait for Lady Alenthaea; all I need is myself.

Storming back to the moat, I dress for action. In black from head to toe, I strap myself into a scale-mail corset, add my pauldrons, armouring myself from neck to fingertip.

'I think you should probably leave those here . . .' Bobble says, pointing at the sword I had grabbed from the table. 'Don't want them thinking you've come on an assassination attempt or anything.' She hums nervously.

Throwing down my rapier, my sabre, dagger, and three ninja stars, I look to my housemate for approval. 'That all of them?' she asks, eyebrow raised in suspicion. With a huff, I take out the pointed dagger from my boot and toss it with the rest on the table. 'Excellent. Now, time to save your love.'

Windsor is much further from central London than films would have you believe. Since this knight has been banned from horses and wouldn't dare get on one anyway, she is lumbered with public transport. So, all whilst I'm dressed like a sexy King Arthur, we have to take two Tubes and an entire bus route, gathering all of the stares expected with such a spectacle, until Bobble and I find ourselves walking through the eerily quiet Windsor streets like two lone mercenaries strolling into battle.

The Long Walk to Windsor Castle is exactly that. The castle lies at the end of the straight path but we never seem to get closer to it despite each passing step. With the destination closer than it's ever been, I can't help but feel like I'm only getting further away. What if he's not here? What if he is?

What would I say to him?

How on earth am I meant to tell Viscount Teddy Fairfax that hating him, disliking him, tolerating him, liking him, loving him, is the greatest adventure I never meant to have?

'We aren't going to get in trouble, right?' Bobble suddenly turns to me about halfway down. 'This royal thing is serious stuff.'

Until now, I had trusted every step I have taken. This is what I want, and I shall stop at nothing to achieve it. But her panic is infectious and I too begin to flap. 'How am I meant to know? This was your idea!' Perhaps I should have at least consulted my head before my heart got so carried away. But it's far too late for that now.

'You definitely didn't bring any weapons? Even the decorative ones?'

'No, I don't think so.'

'You don't think so? This is a matter of life and death! You really need to know so.' She paces, running her hands through her hair. Frisking myself quickly for any missed blades or arrows, I reassure her that I'm clean. 'Okay, okay.' She breathes heavily. 'I suppose we're really just calling on a friend. Should be fine, right?'

Unsure myself, I can't assure her, but we continue walking anyway. When we reach the castle doors, I freeze. 'No, you know what, he will like going abroad. The vitamin D will do him good. It's for the best. He'll meet another girl out there. They'll have a beautiful family. He'll be fine.'

Bobble catches me as I turn to walk away and gives me such a stern stare that I am actually more terrified of her than what's on the other side of that door, so I knock.

I wait with bated breath for minutes that pass like years, but no one answers. Bobble takes my place on the step to knock again, but still, the door stays stuck. We both knock frantically until we fall against the step in defeat, staring silently back down the Long Walk.

'At least you tried,' Bobble mumbles as I rest my head on her shoulder.

'It was a stupid idea anyway.'

The crunching of gravel stirs us from our miserable stupor. 'Oi!' a deep voice calls across the gardens. A trio of security guards pound their boots across the gravel towards us, and for some reason, they don't look like they want to invite us in for afternoon tea.

'Shit. Time to go.' I pull Bobble by her wrist as she sits and stares at the guards, wide-eyed.

Trying to find cover amongst the trees and bushes, we run over the grass and lose ourselves in the gardens, the three very large, angry-looking men gaining rapidly. Scale mail was the wrong choice. Not only does it add an extra few kilograms to my load, but with every pounding step, it chimes together, making me jingle like a Morris dancer getting down and dirty – hardly an outfit suited to hiding.

'Stop where you are!' they call as we leap over flower beds. 'You are trespassing on His Majesty's property.'

'Oh testicles, oh balls, oh bollocks,' Bobble rants to herself, growing increasingly breathless and increasingly terrified.

Seeing an opening in a hedge we duck through it quickly, stumbling into a clearing with a cottage in the middle of it. Stopping for breath, we take a fleeting moment to look around. The all-white building has high gables, fringed with intricate eaves, and looks more like a miniature castle than a modest country cottage. Though, unlike a castle, there is a homeliness to it. You can see the marks of an inhabitant. The garden is evidently professionally tended, but there's a small allotment at the side that bears the signs of an amateur keeper. A tall black bicycle is propped up under the porch, and a little garden gnome is just tucked away in one of the planters.

'We're so fucked,' I whisper to Bobble as the loud pounding of security guard boots grows closer.

'I don't want to go to prison.' She looks at me like a kicked puppy, so sad, so innocent.

Just as I am ready to give myself up, a figure strides out from the side of the house. His dark hair falls onto his forehead. A book is clutched in his hand. The sight of him is like English rain. You never asked for it, but you never knew just how much you wanted it, needed it when it cools the muggy summer air and you wake up in the morning to see the world renewed. At ease, blissfully ignorant to his being watched, I see Teddy Fairfax as he is. Every point of tension within me seems to ease, as though merely the sight of him is the remedy to any pain, and the armour against anything that could ever hurt me.

Best of all, he is real, so very real.

'Daisy?' Teddy's voice is soft but it still comes to me clearly across the garden. He looks at me like I'm a mirage, like something he thought he had lost forever. Stepping cautiously towards me, he moves as though afraid any sudden movements may scare me away.

Wanting to waste no more time, I run towards him, ready to finally leap into his arms. Ready to finally tell him of my love. His smile grows closer and closer until . . . a great force smacks me from behind. Teddy's face shifts to horror, and soon my vision is overcome with a very, very close-up look at the grass. The guards, finally having caught us up, tackle me to the ground and I am imprisoned against the earth by a pair of large thighs clamping over my back.

The world beneath me pounds as Teddy closes the distance between us. As soon as I see his face, contorted in shock, still unsure if all of this is real, I can't hold it in any longer.

'I love you, too,' I say through my mouthful of grass. 'Unequivocally.'

Epilogue

Six Months Later

'Close your eyes.' It's almost impossible to hide my grin as I speak. 'Don't open them until I tell you.' Parking at the entrance to the Village Hall, I jump out of the car and open the passenger-side door with a shudder of excitement. 'Right okay, you're going to step out of the car now. Keeping your eyes closed. Good, now take my arm and I'll guide you.'

Bobble lets out a muted squeal as she disembarks. I'm not sure she'd be able to open her eyes if she wanted to. They have disappeared completely into her smile and that doesn't look like it's going anywhere anytime soon. With both of us dressed head to toe in her new line of furry armour, there is a slightly limited range of movement but she manages to thread her arm through mine and hands me her complete trust.

Today marks twenty-four years of this earth being made

all the more colourful: the day Bobble was born. Since she has never known the joy of a Village Hall birthday party, it's only right that after almost a year of dealing with all of the things that have come with being my friend, including being arrested for trespassing on royal property, she gets the party she deserves. And since I told Mum and Dad that Bobble never had the joy of throwing up jelly and ice cream on a bouncy castle, or witnessing musical bumps turn into a physical fight, they have made it their mission to change that.

'Daisy.' Bobble suddenly turns to me though her eyes remain screwed shut. 'Please just promise me that we're not going to another one of Terry and Hazel's art classes. I still haven't quite recovered from seeing Richard as their semi-nude life-drawing model.' That's another thing I still have to make up for. Granted, none of us knew that a seemingly unassuming and innocent art class involved any nudity, let alone that of my elderly neighbour, but it was always risky bringing Bobble to meet the Friskney Fellowship for the first time. Thankfully it didn't put her off too much as every fortnight since, she has come to stay for the weekend, taking up her new role in the Fellowship as tailor and mage. We not only have considerably more fur in all of our costumes now, but we have a new member of the family.

Laughing, I reassure her that what lies beyond her closed eyes will hopefully not give her any more nightmares.

Sharing my jittering look of anticipation, Sam greets us silently at the door. 'Ready?' I mouth to him and he nods, pushing open the door to a chorus of 'happy birthdays'.

Snapping open her eyes, Bobble takes in the sight before her. A buffet table of triangle sandwiches, sausage rolls, trifles, and anything else that you can find in your freezer, runs in an L-shape along the wall. Dad and his dated DJ decks are set up playing the same playlist of songs I'm sure he had at my ninth birthday. Two rotating disco balls flank him, the electrics just that little bit too worn so that their lights only reach to the edge of the table and no further. The music itself is accompanied by the continual drone of the bouncy castle pump that sits just outside the side door. A small collection of tables seat most of the Fellowship and give way to a wide space designated as the dance floor, with Terry and Hazel already making the most of it and somehow managing to make every song by S Club 7 sensual.

It doesn't look like much – it's all tired, tacky – but that doesn't seem to bother Bobble. She vibrates beside me before turning to arrest me in a crushing hug and squealing her way to the dance floor.

All is as it should be: Mum and Richard are arguing over whether the buffet is open yet; Flora watches Erin carefully as the latter teaches her some of the skills she has picked up at Knight School as the former returns the favour of offering some first-aid tips for clumsy children; the O'Neills join Terry, Hazel, and Bobble on the dance floor, relaxing their usual decorum for something a little more carefree. Even my sister made the journey home from uni, bringing a couple of her friends to share in all of what we are without shame, or embarrassment. They sit together discussing something far too intellectual for me to even bother eavesdropping on, and Marigold looks upon the room with such intense pride, it makes every moment up to now worthwhile.

Best of all, every single one of the people in this room wears something designed and sewn by the birthday girl.

I never thought I'd say it, but this scene right now is as close to perfect as I ever thought life could be. Only, there's one thing missing.

Viscount Fairfax left to take up an unspecified post in the days that followed Bobble and I being arrested. Apparently, he has found his calling in his new role, settled down, and has no plans of returning anytime soon.

At least, that's what the press were told.

'Daisy, I think you might need to rescue your poor boyfriend.' Mum bundles over, unable to suppress the amusement in her concern. 'I may have just heard your great-auntie Carole swearing at him for overwhipping the buttercream for the fairy cakes.'

After sharing a snigger, I weave my way around the conga line and make for the kitchen.

'I don't care if you've baked for the king, lad, you're in Lincolnshire now and we do things proper up here. I've seen my brownies make better cupcakes and they're seven years old.' My great-aunt's voice flows out of the serving hatch and I manage to catch a glimpse of Teddy's sheepish face as he looks about the Village Hall kitchen that hasn't been updated since it was put in in the 1970s.

'Auntie Carole, Mum is asking if you had those cocktail sticks for the cheese and pineapple,' I interrupt and Teddy's relief is evident on his face. The stern old woman lets out a huff and mumbles to herself about going out to the car, and as soon as she is out of earshot, Teddy throws himself into my arms with a sigh.

'Thank you.' He gives me a breathless kiss on the forehead.

'Forever the damsel in distress, you, eh?'

'Well, I'm just lucky that I have my very own knight in . . .' he looks me up and down and finishes off with a laugh '. . . furry armour.'

Teddy's interview set off a whole new kind of media storm and I certainly didn't help matters when the papers caught wind of my attempts at heroism that resulted in an overnight stay in the police station. Everything seemed worse to begin with, but something about his honesty, the rawness of such a public confession gained far more favour than a perfectly planned and executed PR move could have ever achieved.

Once he'd bailed us out, Teddy never went home. Instead, he came back with me. I think the royal family were confident in the fact that no one was going hunting for a runaway nobleman in Lincolnshire. And even more certain that they wouldn't think to look in the flat above a hobby shop. So, with the promise to keep as far from the limelight as possible (it would have actually been harder to have remained in said limelight from here), they let him go.

Teddy wraps his arms around my waist, resting his chin on my shoulder as we both sway along to the music that flows through the serving hatch. Bobble has managed to get Richard up for a dance, well a slow two-step, and he almost cracks a smile.

'It's been six months,' I murmur softly as Teddy's hair tickles at my cheek and neck, the long strands no longer confined by protocol of formality. 'You haven't changed your mind?'

Standing back up to his full height, Teddy grabs me by the hips and manoeuvres me to face him. 'Changed my mind?' Concern flashes across his face before he cups my cheeks in both his wide palms, brushing a thumb over the freckles that are just beginning to emerge with the new spring.

'I always worried that this was just some passing fancy, your rebellion. I thought you'd tire of me by this time.' I can't look at him as I speak but I notice a wide smile spread across his face from the corner of my eye.

'Daisy.' He gives a breathy laugh, though I know it's not meant to mock me. He presses his lips to my forehead again, and I feel him smile against my skin. 'In every conceivable way, you are the greatest thing that has ever happened to me. Now, I'm not just saying that because I'm living in your dad's shop and need somewhere to stay; I mean it. I never fell in love with you to defy my parents, or to find my escape route. I fell in love with you because you showed me what it was to choose: choose who you want to be. You taught me that a person is more than one defining feature, more than what everyone wants or expects from you. Daisy, you are strong, powerful, yet you're unafraid to be vulnerable, to allow emotion to take you. You adapt parts of yourself to survive each moment life throws at you. You may think that you are wearing a mask, hiding the real you, but I think it's *all* you. It isn't a mask, it's an armoury. Before I met you, I was wandering through no man's land, unarmed, unprotected, and waiting for the day the cavalry ended it all. You showed me that I can fight, that I can choose my fate, so I chose you.'

Burying my head into his neck, I hold him tightly, afraid that all of this is just some dream, some story that I've taken too far, and that if I let go, he will disappear into a page of my notebook. Truth is, it's the challenge of Teddy Fairfax that made me realise all of those things. Perhaps they've been there all along, but it is his provocation, him testing every part of me that made me realise that Alenthaea and I aren't much different after all.

'Although, if I knew this all would end in the Village Hall being subject to Scout Leader Hell's Kitchen, maybe I would have thought twice . . .' he teases, swiping away the tears that had gathered for a battle with my freckles without me realising. Completely unafraid of who's watching, even if Auntie Carole will complain of the lack of hygiene, I kiss him in this 1970s kitchen, in this children's party for a twenty-four-year-old, surrounded by my gallimaufry of a family.

'Who'd have thought that the story of the rogue royal and the knight would actually end up with a happy ending, eh?' I smile up at him, my whole body at peace.

'It's an ending Bobble can be proud of.'

'The only one she would accept.' We laugh together. The sound of it, the vibration of his chest against mine, the sight of his eyes crinkled at the corners like loved parchment, completes me.

'Oh, I almost forgot to tell you, we have four new recruits

joining tomorrow evening's Knight Academy. Would you be able to bring the new costumes and swords from the shop when you come over?' I didn't give everything up for a man, just to return to the same monotony that had made me miserable before. When we arrived home, I set up the Knight Academy, where kids after school, adults of all walks of life, and young people looking for entertainment outside the walls of the same village pub they've drunk in since they were teens, can come and see what it is to be a knight. Using all I had learnt from Westley, and now unhindered by an arrogant viscount hellbent on sabotaging everything, I have established a space for anyone and everyone to come and explore who they are, and who they want to be. This time, the Black Knight is my ally.

'Come on, you two, we're going to have a game of musical chairs.' My brother sticks his head through the hatch, the same grinning face of a schoolboy who's had too many e-numbers. 'Don't worry, I have confiscated all of Richard's weapons, and already told Terry and Hazel that they cannot share the same chair.' He buzzes off as quickly as he came, leaving Teddy to turn to me, eyebrows raised in disbelief.

'You should know by now what you're getting yourself into.' I chuckle, grabbing his hand and dragging him towards the dance floor.

We all know that Teddy will never truly be free, not really. But for now, he doesn't have to pretend. Outside of this hall, we are all different people. We have to be accountants, shopkeepers, nurses, viscounts, but in here, we are a motley crew of people who get to pick and choose what and who they wish to be. None of us fit in, but we all fit together.

Acknowledgements

Writing this book was nothing short of a quest.

First of all, it was a quest for treasure. 'Treasure' here being a successful story. A story that won't disappoint the readers who have continued to support me. A story that would silence that voice in my head telling me it was just a fluke the first time around. A story that my family can be proud of (and continue to post about on Facebook all hours of the day). So first of all, thank *you* for reading this book, for getting this far. If it made you feel, if it transported you from reality for even a moment, then this quest is complete.

Then, it was a quest to slay a monster. I have never been more excited by a narrative before; *Love at First Knight* was a wonderful excuse to live out all of my nerdy fantasies. But as many writers and publishing friends told me, book two is a whole different beast. You know what you're going to face, you spend hours upon hours figuring out what to do differently, what you did well the first time, and sending yourself into a frenzy trying to please everyone and worrying that you've pleased no one. I would never have finished this book without the constant support and reassurance from my fantastic agent Florence Rees, and my wonderfully understanding editor, Amy Mae Baxter. Molly Walker-Sharp, I wouldn't be a writer without you, so I thank you, for this book, for the last book, and the rest to come. Rebecca Ritchie, thank you for being a brilliant agent and working with Florence to get this book off the ground. The whole team at Avon and Harper Collins are nothing short of miracle workers, this book wouldn't exist without the incredible work of every single one of you. Thank you, Raphaella Demetris, Emily Chan, Maddie Dunne Kirby, Ella Young, Samantha Luton, Katie Buckley, Emily Gerbner, and Vasiliki Machaira. Thank you to the immense talent that is Sarah Foster for her work on the cover, and to Helena Newton and Rachel Rowlands for their sharp eyes. It really does take a village to slay such a beast.

Last of all, this book was a quest for self-discovery. Half way through writing, I moved out of the Tower of London, back to my hometown, and into my childhood bedroom. All of a sudden, I felt like I had lost everything I had created for myself, I had lost my family at the Tower, and I had to figure out who I was outside of being the "Tower of London Girl". This book became by bridge back home, it became my way of reminding myself that in spite of all that held me back, I can carry on, I can continue to make something of my life. I have to thank Debbie Pries. She is the first professional that listened to me, understood me, and in her noticing my neurodivergence, made my own book make sense to me. I will always have to thank my friends in the Tower, I miss you all (Gary B, I miss your laugh most of all). Gary and Tamika, you will always be my family, and I love you both. To my whole family, who will always remind me who I am, and support me every step of the way, thank you for your unconditional love. George, thank you for reawakening the geek in me and encouraging every one of my whims and obsessions.

I have to say a special thank you to Jon Gaish at Warhammer, Boston. Thank you for answering all of my LARP questions, and for planting the seed of this book. Most of all, thank you for creating a safe and welcoming space in our community. Anyone in your shop is free to be who they want to be, you offer people a place to belong, whether that's for five minutes or a whole day. You talk to every single person that walks past your threshold like you would an old friend. The value of such kindness along with a friendly smile can never be understated, you are truly an inspiration (even if my boyfriend does spend far too much money in your shop!)

If this book has taught me anything, it's that quests can be perilous, but you don't have to slay the dragon alone – and, hey, with the right people, it can actually be quite fun.

Don't miss this royally good rom-com . . .

Despite living in an actual castle, happily ever after is evading Margaret 'Maggie' Moore.

From her bedroom in the Tower of London, twenty-six-year-old Maggie has always dreamed of her own fairy-tale ending.

Yet this is twenty-first century London, so instead of knights on white horses, she has catfish on Tinder. And with her last relationship ending in spectacular fashion, she swears off men for good.

And then a chance encounter with Royal Guard Freddie forces Maggie to admit that she isn't ready to give up on love just yet . . . But how do you catch the attention of someone who is trained to ignore all distractions?

Can she snare that true love's first kiss . . . or is she royally screwed?